SURRENDER

Mariah lifted her face to Thorne's, and this time he instigated the kiss. His mouth covered hers and Mariah was afraid to breathe, afraid he would stop the wonderful sensation that sizzled through her body. She thought she'd been kissed before, but the pecks of her former suitors were nothing like the full-blown glory of a man's passion. He dropped his hands to her bottom and tugged her against his body. Never had she dreamed that merely kissing a man could be such a glorious experience.

Just when she thought she couldn't take any more of the exquisite torture, Thorne broke off the kiss. His breathing was harsh, as if he'd run a great distance. "Irish, we have to stop."

"No," she moaned against his throat. The pulse was pounding like the beat of a bass drum. Although she wasn't sure what to expect, she needed more, wanted more of him. Quite simply, she wanted to make love with this man who'd turned her heart and life upside down. "Don't you want me?"

He buried his face in the crook between her shoulder and neck. "More than I've ever wanted anything. Are you sure you know what you're asking?"

Mariah threw all caution to the wind. On that high mountain, with a fortune of gold at their feet, she wanted nothing more than to become one with this man who had stolen her heart when she wasn't looking. "Make love with me," she whispered. "Make me your woman. . . ."

Books by Jean Wilson

SWEET DREAMS

MY MARIAH

Published by Zebra Books

MY MARIAH

Jean Wilson

Zebra Books
Kensington Publishing Corp.

http://www.zebrabooks.com

For Jeanne, Carl, Karissa, and Kyle—
with all my love.

ZEBRA BOOKS are published by

Kensington Publishing Corp.
850 Third Avenue
New York, NY 10022

Zebra and the Z logo Reg. U.S. Pat. & TM Off.

First Printing: November, 1998
10 9 8 7 6 5 4 3 2 1

Printed in the United States of America

Prologue

Philadelphia, Pennsylvania, 1873

"Ye can not go, Rosie. And that's the end of it." Sean O'Reilly slammed down his mug, sloshing beer on his wife's time-scarred oak dining table. The Irish police sergeant's face turned crimson as he glared at his oldest daughter.

Mariah Rose mopped up the foamy liquid while she struggled against a temper as volatile as her father's. She lifted her gaze over Sean's shoulder and sought help from her mother.

"Yer da is right. It is too dangerous for an innocent young woman to travel all the way to Mexico by herself. And a foreign country at that." Kathleen touched a finger to her forehead, her chest, and each shoulder in turn. Then she kissed the crucifix that hung from a silver chain around her neck.

"*New* Mexico, Mum. It's in the West. A territory of the United States of America." Exasperated, Mariah dropped the damp rag.

Kathleen shivered. "I read there's nothing but outlaws and Indians in the West. Look at what happened to your brother. And he's a man."

Inwardly Mariah groaned. No help there, either. "Francis fell from a horse. It could have happened anywhere."

The brother one year her junior shifted his broken leg on the chair and took a swig from his mug. With his red hair, he looked and acted so much like their father he should have been named Sean. "Maybe Mum and Da are right, Rosie. I'll put one of the men on the case."

"Oh, no, you won't, Francis. I've been in on this assignment from the beginning. I know all the details, and I know I can complete the job." She softened her tone. "Besides, Mrs. Thornton doesn't want word of this search spread around. And we don't want Pinkerton's men to get that fine bonus."

"Bonus or not, Rosie. I forbid ye to go." Her father stood and locked gazes with Mariah. The beefy Irishman jabbed a finger toward her.

She planted her fists on her hips and stared into blue eyes the exact color as hers. "I happen to be twenty-five years old. I'm a grown woman, and I can do as I please."

"Ye should have married Danny Malloy when he asked ye instead of hanging around the detective agency. I knew no good would come of it."

Mariah gritted her teeth. Although she loved her parents and eight siblings, she had no intention of following in her mother's footsteps. "I don't love Danny, but I do love working at the agency."

Sean snorted. "He's a fine boy, and he makes a good living as an officer. He'll be promoted to sergeant soon. Lots of girls will be after him."

"Danny isn't good enough for Rosie." Seventeen-year-old Jenny tossed her long fiery red hair over her shoulder. "Rosie has grand ideas. She wants a man who'll give her a fine house and fancy clothes."

Little did they understand that Mariah didn't want any man, especially a wealthy one. She'd seen firsthand how Irish women were treated. Her encounter with a well-to-do, so-called gentleman had left a bitter pill in her mouth. He'd wanted her, sure, outside the bonds of matrimony. When she'd insisted on marriage first, he'd laughed in her face and called her an Irish slut. She'd kept her secret, certain that if her father knew, there would be hell to pay—for the man. Nobody dallied with Sean O'Reilly's girls.

Mariah planned to be independent and self-sufficient. "What's wrong with wanting better? I hate buying clothes at the secondhand shop, and wearing other women's hand-me-downs. Someday that will all change. I don't intend to marry at all."

Sean shook his head. "She goes to too many of those suffragette meetings. Next thing ye know, she'll be wearing those bloomers like that Amelia woman."

"I wear what I please," she said.

The ten-year-old twins chose that moment to play chase around the kitchen. "Rosie's wearing bloomers, Rosie's wearing bloomers!" they sang in unison. For twins, the boys didn't look anything alike. Joseph was stocky and redheaded like their father, while the taller Andrew had the same black hair as Mariah and their mother.

"Be off, the pair of you." Kathleen swatted at her youngest children with a dish rag.

"A good Irish daughter doesn't talk back to her poor old mum and da," Sean returned.

Since she wasn't getting anywhere arguing, she switched tactics. "Ye're not old, Da. Why, you're in the prime of life. And Ma is the prettiest woman in the neighborhood, or in the whole of Philadelphia. Don't you think so?"

A hint of pink tinged her mother's plump cheeks. "After nine children, I'd hardly be considered pretty."

Sean planted a quick kiss on her lips. "Aye, Mary Kathleen, you're as beautiful today as you were twenty-five years ago when we boarded that ship and left Ireland to come to America."

Mariah took heart in her father's softening voice. "Da, it isn't just for me. Mrs. Thornton is paying a good fee to locate her grandson. Francis will be able to hire another operative and the agency can expand.'' She didn't mention that her brother had promised her a full partnership in the Erin Investigators and Detective firm if she succeeded in the assignment he'd failed to complete. ''And Mum can have that grand new stove she's been eyeing at Rosenberg's Emporium.''

''The old one is good enough,'' her mother said, the gleam in her green eyes belying her words.

''Ye deserve a new one.'' Mariah slipped into the brogue she'd worked so hard to lose. ''And Da needs new boots, and the twins have outgrown all their clothes for school. Not to mention something special for Jenny, Maggie, and Maureen.''

Sean's weathered face softened as he took another draft from his mug. '' 'Tis still too dangerous for a woman.''

''It won't be dangerous at all. All I have to do is take a stagecoach to a little town in New Mexico and deliver a message. If I can convince Michael Harrison to return to Philadelphia with me, we'll get an extra *five thousand dollars* when he returns home. With that much money, we'll be able to buy our own house and move out of this crowded brownstone.''

At the mention of the bonus and a home of his own, a tiny smile curved the Irishman's lips. ''That old Mrs. Thornton has more money than good sense. But I can't blame her for wanting to find her missing grandson. I'd tear up heaven and hell to find one of my boys. But what makes you think he's still alive? He's been missing since the war.''

''She'd just about given him up for dead when she received a letter from him, saying he was in New Mexico. For some reason, she doesn't want anybody to know he's still alive. Francis traced him as far as Los Amigos before he fell off that horse and had to come back home.''

''I should have been more careful,'' Francis groaned.

''What do you think, Mother? Should we let our Rosie go?''

Kathleen shrugged. ''Aye, I doubt we can keep her home. She's just as headstrong as her da, and that's the truth.''

"Her da?" Sean sat and pulled his wife onto his lap. " 'Tis her ma who rules the roost, I'd say."

Mariah grinned. The battle was all but over. "I'll be careful. Da taught me how to use a gun, and, with four brothers, I learned to fight."

Francis frowned at her. "Mariah, are you sure you want to go west alone? Wait a month or so until I'm better, and we can go together."

She shook her head. "For all we know, Michael Harrison could be long gone in another month. We've got to strike out now, while the trail is still warm."

"Ye'll be careful, won't you, Rosie?" Kathleen asked.

"Ma, I'll stay off horses, and in my nun's disguise, I'll be as safe as a baby in his mother's arms."

"Saints preserve us, and my stubborn daughter."

Chapter 1

New Mexico Territory, three weeks later

"Thorne, come quick."

Running Deer skidded to a stop in front of the cabin. Thorne looked up from the Journal of the New England Medical Society he'd received last week. Although it was a year old, he devoured every work like a wolf after a fresh kill. He only wished . . . Wishes were for children. Like the pair who were gesturing excitedly to get his attention.

He eyed the youngsters, wondering what new mischief they'd gotten into. Juan followed at the girl's heels and stared up at Thorne with frightened dark eyes. "What is it this time?" He knelt to face the children at their level.

"A bird, a giant black bird. It fell from the sky. A ugly black bird." The little Indian girl's words ran together. "It tried to smash us like pumpkins." She clapped her hands together for emphasis.

At her side, Juan remained silent, but he gestured with his arms open wide. In the year and a half since Thorne had found the boy, he hadn't uttered a word. Running Deer's chatter more than made up for the boy's silence.

Thorne tugged at his beard. He couldn't remember when he'd last shaved, not that it mattered up here. The only people he ever saw were the two children, and Sung Lo, the ancient Chinese man who did the cooking and wash for the unusual family. And, of course, Father Callahan when he went into Los Amigos for supplies.

Running Deer tugged at his hand. "Come. It tried to attack us."

Sung Lo appeared in the doorway, his ever-present cleaver in his hand. "Bring back bird. You kill. I cook. We eat."

Of habit and necessity, Thorne picked up his rifle and followed behind the children. The pair knew paths and trails that a seasoned tracker couldn't find. After they'd gone about a half mile, they stopped and pointed toward a small clearing. Thorne gestured them to silence, and signaled them to stay put. He eased forward, then stopped beside a scraggy oak. A cracked branch hung almost to the ground.

"It was here," Running Deer said. "I thought it was dead."

Thorne knelt and examined the ground. Something had been there. Something big—bigger than any bird he'd ever seen. He spotted a piece of torn black cloth snagged on a juniper bush. He rubbed the fabric between his fingers. Their bird walked on two legs—human legs. A man.

And any man on his mountain meant danger to him and his makeshift family.

"Go back to Sung Lo," he whispered.

"We want find bird," Running Deer protested.

He shot the girl a stern glance. "Go."

After he was certain they'd obeyed his orders, Thorne followed the footsteps left in the dust. The man wasn't trying to hide his tracks. That made him even more cautious. And it made the prey more dangerous. A footprint here, a broken twig there, crushed wildflowers, it was as if he wanted to be followed.

Alert for an ambush, Thorne ran on silent feet. His moccasins left no prints for another to trail. He heard the crack of broken branches and the rustle of dry pine needles. His quarry was only a few dozen yards ahead in the shadows of a thick stand of aspens.

He slipped behind a tree, and watched the figure struggle through the fallen branches that littered the ground. In black from head to toe, he understood why the children mistook it for a bird. The man wore some kind of cloak, or robe, much like the priest at the mission. He wasn't very large, Thorne guessed not much over five and a half feet. But he was a tough hombre. Thorne hoped the man would keep going, so he wouldn't have to make physical contact with the stranger. The fewer people who knew about him and his mountain, the safer they all were.

Whoever the stranger was, he had no business anywhere in those parts. Thorne had bought the mountain and the surrounding hundred thousand acres from a man named Lucien Maxwell, and he didn't welcome strangers.

A couple of months back, he'd heard about an easterner asking questions in Los Amigos. Then the man had fallen from a horse and gone back East. He didn't like strangers, and he sure wasn't up to answering any questions. If it weren't for the children, he'd have moved further into the mountains, deeper into the wilderness. As soon as Father Callahan located good parents for them, and a place for Sung Lo, he'd be on his way. When men started climbing his mountain, it was time for Thorne to move on.

He studied the man's sluggish movements. In the blink of an eye, the figure disappeared from sight. A loud shriek followed, and the clatter of fallen rocks. Thorne dashed forward. The black-clad figure lay unmoving at the bottom of a small ravine.

Rifle in hand, he jumped down the ten or so feet and landed at the stranger's side. The black garment lay spread out like a raven's wings, and a small foot and slender leg protruded from the bottom along with lacy petticoats.

It wasn't a man. It was a woman.

And no ordinary woman—a nun.

He'd found the great black bird.

For the second time that day, Mariah had fallen and knocked the wind out of herself. She lay on her stomach, not sure if she was dead or alive. Every inch of her body ached. Maybe, just maybe, if she pretended to be dead, the outlaws who'd been trailing her would go away and leave her to suffer in peace.

What if she'd broken her leg as her brother had? Would she just be left here for the buzzards to pick her bones clean? That thought made her shudder.

"So you're still alive." A gruff voice came from close to her face. A gentle hand touched her jaw.

"I'm not sure." She turned her head, her cheek scraped and raw from the rocky ground. "I hurt like the devil."

The man stayed her movements with a hand to the middle of her back. "Don't move until we find out if anything is broken."

She obeyed without question. His voice sounded different, not at all like the outlaws who'd robbed the stagecoach and killed the other passenger. Maybe God had sent an angel to rescue her. Not that she deserved an angel. A sinful woman dressed in a nun's habit must surely be committing a mortal sin, and breaking one of His commandments.

His touch was quick and efficient as he probed her arms and legs, much like a doctor would examine a patient. "Can you roll over?" he asked.

"I suppose, if I have to." Gingerly, she shoved to her side. The black habit caught under her hips and pulled up at the hem. Modesty was of little concern out in the wilderness while being hunted by outlaws. No telling who or what this man was.

He helped her roll to her back. Mariah shoved back the veil that had slipped from her hair into her eyes. The bright sunshine and blue sky momentarily blinded her. She blinked, and gazed into eyes the color of cold, hard steel. Not a hint of warmth glittered behind his thick, pale brows. He sported a full beard, and silver-streaked brown hair touched his wide shoulders.

Then, in the blink of an eye, he pulled a knife from the sheath at his waist. He lifted his hand and Mariah knew she was gone. She'd escaped stagecoach robbers, a tumble from a tree, and a fall down a hillside, only to be murdered by the man she'd thought her rescuer. Too shocked and hurt to move, she closed her eyes and prayed for deliverance.

As she recited the rosary, she heard the shaking of rattles, the whoosh of the knife in the air, and a thud as it stuck its target.

Her eyes flew open in time to see the man reach for her. She shifted her gaze and spotted the knife in the head of a large snake. The horrible creature was only inches from where she lay helpless on the ground.

In one quick movement, the man tugged her arm and flipped her neatly over his shoulder. She screamed as her stomach banged into his hard flesh. Her head hung clear to his waist, and she viewed the world upside-down.

"Rattlers, Sister. They didn't like the way you disturbed their nest."

Mariah shivered. In the past twenty-four hours she'd come near to death more times than in her entire twenty-five years. The man took off at a trot, jiggling her insides so she could hardly breathe.

Moments later, he deposited her on the ground in a careless heap. The veil slipped over her face, and she ached all over. She bit her lip to keep from crying.

"Thorne kill great bird."

Mariah cleared her eyes and gazed into the fresh faces of two small children.

"I'm not a bird," she said while struggling to sit up.

"It's a woman—*señorita, Hermana*." The man hunkered down and stared at her.

She stared back. Brown buckskin trousers clung to muscular thighs, and a worn blue shirt was unbuttoned to his waist. A mat of thick brown hair curled over the muscles in his chest. She shivered at the power and strength of the man. Lifting her gaze, she caught the deep frown on his mouth nearly hidden by the shaggy beard.

"How do you feel?"

"I'm fine," she lied. She slipped into the Irish brogue and stern voice of the nuns who'd taught her at St. Bridgit's in Philadelphia. "If you'll be so kind to help me up, sir, I'll be on my way."

"Where're you headed, Sister?" His soft voice had just a touch of a southern drawl.

"West."

"And how do you happen to be here? On my mountain?"

Something about the man put her at ease. Instinct told her he didn't mean her any harm. Especially with the children watching. "I was on the stagecoach to Los Amigos when we were waylaid by notorious bandits." She picked up the crucifix from around her neck and touched it to her lips exactly as Sister Mary Louise had done every day in the classroom. "They killed the driver, and the other passenger."

Nausea rose in her throat at the memory of the dead men lying around her. And she'd told her father she wasn't in any danger. "They were debating whether to kill me or not when I ran away. I hid until dark, and I made my way up this mountain. When I heard someone coming, I climbed a tree. The branch broke, and I tumbled to the ground. When I heard somebody again following me, I tried to find a place to hide. Next thing I knew, I was rolling down that hillside. That's when you found me."

"Who are you?"

She dropped her gaze to the rifle clutched in his right hand. Better to keep up the charade—surely he wouldn't kill a nun. "Sister Mariah Rose. And you are?" she asked in her best imitation of Sister Mary Louise.

The little bronze-skinned girl in trousers and long pigtails peeked from around his shoulder. "He Thorne. I Running Deer.

I Cheyenne. He Juan." She gestured to a boy about the same size as herself dressed in identical trousers and shirt. "He Mexican. And Sung Lo is old Chinaman."

Thorne's scowl deepened and his gray eyes turned stormy. The children didn't seem to notice his anger, or they didn't care. Mariah shifted her gaze from one to the other. What a strange trio. She guessed their ages to be about six or seven, not much older. Neither child resembled the man in the least. The little girl hadn't called him her father. Simply Thorne.

"You can call me Sister Rose."

Running Deer giggled and covered her mouth with her hand. The boy remained silent and stared at her with beautiful, expressive brown eyes. So much pain and need was reflected in the child's gaze, her heart ached for him.

"We'd better head back to the cabin. Can you stand?" Thorne stretched to his feet and reached out a hand to Mariah.

She clasped his fingers. He tugged, and Mariah stumbled forward. Pain shot up her leg, and she clung to Thorne for support. He wrapped one arm around her waist to steady her, and pulled her hard into the solid wall of his chest. His heart beat strong and warm against her palm. With his body crushed to hers, awareness of him as a man sizzled through her. Not just a man, but a strong, virile male.

Mariah had been held by men before, she'd danced with them, she'd even been kissed, but none had ever made her feel so wholly feminine or excited her as this gruff mountain man. His gaze met hers, and something sparked between them— like a flash of lightning in the face of a storm. Just as quickly, it disappeared. The chill returned to his gaze.

She shoved against his chest and tried to put her weight on her left foot. Only his grip on her arm kept her from tumbling to the ground. "It's my ankle. I must have sprained it during the fall."

Thorne tossed his rifle to the boy. "Carry my rifle, Juan. And be careful." The boy nodded and slung the weapon over his shoulder like a soldier off to war. "I'll carry you, then we'll see about that ankle."

"You can't—" Her protest was broken off when he scooped her up in his arms. One arm under her knees, and the other behind her back, he cradled her as easily as holding a baby. "I'm too heavy." She twisted to see which way they were headed.

"Quit wiggling, Sister, or I'll drop you over the cliff. Next time I won't go after you."

"Yes, sir," she said, annoyed at his threat. She wrapped her arms around his neck for balance and prayed she could keep up her act as a nun. No nun should feel the excitement of being held this close to a man. And no nun she'd ever met would let a man get this close to her. Sister Mary Louise would have chosen to crawl ten miles with a broken leg rather than let a man carry her in such an intimate manner.

Thorne was strong, and his body as solid as an oak. He walked at a fast clip, following a narrow path in and out of the shadows of tall pines. The boy led the way while Running Deer trotted at his side.

The girl chatted constantly, pointing out a squirrel that scurried across their path, a jay that squawked in a treetop.

Mariah tried to study her surroundings. But the trees all looked alike, and the rocks blended together into one huge heap. How these people ever found their way was beyond her. Give her the streets and roads of civilized Pennsylvania any day.

But she was here in the wilderness of the Sangre de Cristo Mountains to do a job. She glanced up into Thorne's face and caught him unawares. Recognition clicked in her brain. Something about him was so familiar, she just had to reach out and grab it. Those eyes. Soft gray eyes. The eyes she'd seen on a young man in the portrait in Mrs. Thornton's parlor. And in the small photograph in the packet hidden in her habit.

Michael Thornton Harrison. It all made sense. He called himself Thorne.

She'd found her man.

Chapter 2

Who was this woman?

Thorne lengthened his strides, eager to free himself of his burden. Not that her weight bothered him. Far from it. He'd lugged heavier burdens for longer distances. The problem was simple: she was female. His fingers dug into the soft flesh under her breast, and his arm felt the pressure of long, slender legs. The side of her full bosom pressed against his chest and her fingers clung to his shoulders for balance. Feelings he hadn't experienced in a long time vibrated through him. She might claim to be a nun, but she was all woman.

Something about her didn't sit right. Good instincts had kept him alive for too long not to trust them now. His gut feeling told him that she wasn't telling him the whole truth—if she was telling any.

He ignored Running Deer's constant chatter, and tried not to think about his burden as a woman. She was an unwanted intruder, a stranger. Trouble. He wondered what part of her story to believe. It was just too much of a coincidence that she'd wound up on this mountain. Her story about a stagecoach robbery and running from bandits didn't sound plausible. Most women he'd known in his distant past would have fainted dead away at the first shot. Yet, according to her, she'd outsmarted the robbers and managed to end up in the safety of his arms.

Thorne dropped his gaze and caught a glimpse of her face. She was dirty, her cheeks skinned from the fall, but she was none the worse for wear. With her hair covered by the black drape, he couldn't tell much else about her.

As if she felt him staring, she lifted sparkling blue eyes and boldly met his gaze. This Sister Rose was anything but a shy, retiring novice. "If I'm too heavy, I'm sure I can hobble along," she said.

He pulled his gaze away and concentrated on the rocky path. "No. I'll manage. We're almost there."

"Where are we going?" Her soft Irish brogue was tinged with a hint of fear.

"To my cabin."

"I hope it isn't too much trouble, sir."

"No trouble," he lied. Any woman on his mountain spelled trouble with a capital T. He needed to find out who she was and what she wanted. Besides, it wasn't in his nature to leave any human or animal injured and alone.

Running Deer raced ahead announcing their arrival. Even before he reached the clearing where Sung Lo had his garden, he heard the girl reciting the story about how they'd found *Hermana*. He doubted Sung Lo understood much.

As expected, the old Chinese was there to greet them with the children at his side. Juan set down the rifle, and Sung Lo held his cleaver at ready. Running Deer danced excitedly.

"Where bird?" the Chinaman asked. Thorne knew almost no Chinese, and Sung Lo spoke little English. Yet, they managed to communicate and make their wishes known.

Sister Rose cringed, and tightened her grip on his neck. "Is he going to butcher me?"

Thorne resisted a laugh. "No, I reckon you're a mite too tough."

Her ribs jiggled with suppressed chuckles. "I suppose I am."

Gently he set her on a tree stump. "Sung Lo, this is Sister Rose."

The old man shuffled forward and bowed from the waist. "Sissy Losie." He studied her for a moment and lifted his gaze. "No bird for cook?"

Her gentle laughter rang out. "No bird. I'm very glad to meet you."

Sung Lo grinned from ear to ear. The man reached the middle of Thorne's chest and couldn't weigh much over a hundred pounds. Thorne didn't know how he would manage without the man. He gathered around Sister Rose with the children. All three were curious about the woman. Not that he could blame them. Since he'd found each of them, they rarely saw strangers, and never a woman.

Thorne hunkered down in front of her. As gently as possible, he lifted her foot. She pulled back slightly. "Does it hurt?" he asked.

"Some." She lifted the hem of the heavy black skirt. A bit of white lace peeked out. Another thing he found odd. Since when did nuns wear lace? He'd expected plain muslin or home-spun petticoats, not lace.

"Let me get this boot off, and I'll see what kind of damage you've done."

"It wouldn't have happened if you hadn't frightened me. I thought those bandits had found me. I was running away when I slipped and fell."

"What happened to your brogue?"

She covered her mouth with her hand. "I've been in America long enough to lose it. Sometimes it just slips out."

He ignored the explanation that didn't sound true. He would bet his gold mine that she'd never set foot in Ireland. Even her boots didn't look like what he'd expect of a nun. They were of soft leather, and fairly new. He loosed the buttons and slipped it from her foot. She moaned slightly. He pressed gently through the black cotton stocking. "It's swollen, but I don't think it's broken."

"Are you a doctor?"

"No." The answer came harsher than he'd intended. Thanks to a war and a situation beyond his control, that dream had passed him by. "I know a thing or two about getting along without one." In one quick movement, he sprang to his feet. "Take off that stocking while I get a bandage and a salve for your cuts and scrapes."

"Sir!" she gasped as if he'd asked her to strip naked. "I can't . . ."

"You will or I'll cut it off, Sister." He turned on his heel and strode into the cabin. Once inside, he took a minute to catch his breath. A woman—a nun—was the last thing he needed on his mountain. How was he going to get rid of her without rousing suspicion?

Moments later, he returned with strips of cotton cloth and a smelly concoction. To his surprise, she'd complied with his orders and had propped her foot on a stump.

Running Deer ventured closer, and placed her small hand on the nun's shoulder. "Thorne not hurt you. He make you better."

Sister Rose smiled at the girl. "Thank you, Running Deer."

Juan simply patted her arm.

"You, too, Juan," she added. The boy graced her with a tiny smile.

Even Sung Lo, who was afraid of his own shadow, remained at her side. "I fix food. Sissy hungry?"

She glanced up at the man and grinned. "I'm starved."

Sung Lo took off at a shuffling run. "Cook good for Sissy."

Thorne didn't understand what had happened in the few minutes he'd been gone. Were they all so lonely they accepted the first female who smiled at them? A woman who had fallen from the sky into their lives.

He sank to the ground and folded his long legs Indian-style. Without explanation, he lifted the foot into his lap. As he'd done hundreds of times during the war, he wrapped the bandages around the swollen ankle. "Stay off it, and by tomorrow, the swelling will be down. You'll be able to walk on your own.'' *Right back down this mountain and out of our lives.*

Next he opened the small pouch of salve he'd mixed from herbs, roots, moldy bread, and bear grease. She flinched and pulled away.

''What's that? It smells like something died in there.''

Running Deer giggled, and Juan squeezed her shoulder.

''You don't want to know what it is. But it will help those scrapes and abrasions heal.''

She wrinkled her nose when he smoothed the salve on her cheek. Her skin was smooth and white as porcelain. Tingles raced up his arm at the contact. It had been so long since he'd touched a woman, he couldn't even remember when or where. That thought brought him up short. He jerked his hand away and forced his voice to remain normal. ''What about your hands and arms?''

''Thanks to my gloves and these long sleeves, only my face was exposed.'' Carefully, she worked the gloves from one hand, then the other. Women's fashions had changed in the last ten years, but he recognized good quality leather when he saw it. This nun definitely liked nice things.

She stretched out her fingers and flexed them. He caught her left hand in his. ''Where's your ring?''

''Ring?''

He stroked a rough finger along her smooth one. ''Don't all nuns wear wedding bands as a symbol of being wed to Christ?''

Crimson sneaked up her cheeks under the brown salve. ''Oh, that. I took it off before I left the convent.'' She let out a deep sigh. ''I didn't want some savage cutting off my finger for the bit of gold.''

''Bad men not hurt Sissy Rosie.'' Running Deer draped an arm across her shoulder. ''Thorne take care of you, too.''

She lifted questioning eyes to him. ''Who else is here? Do you have a wife?''

''No.'' Without offering further information, he jerked to his feet. ''I'll see what kind of mess that old Chinaman is whipping up." He fairly ran into the cabin to get away from the woman. He couldn't understand the strange sensations he felt when he touched her. And her a nun. Or so she said.

Mariah studied the man who stalked away as if the devil was hot on his heels. He was an enigma, this reclusive Thorne who lived on a mountain with two children and an old Chinese. Mariah determined to solve this mystery. She was almost certain he was the elusive Michael Harrison.

The pair of children remained at her side. They were beautiful, sweet, and hungry for affection. She doubted the gruff man had much time or attention to give the youngsters. With a smile, she wrapped an arm around each, eager to gain their confidence. Although Juan hadn't spoken, Running Deer was a fount of information.

"Is Thorne your father?" she asked.

Running Deer cocked her head and gazed at Mariah with confused brown eyes. "Fa-ter?"

"Papa? *Padre?* Understand?"

"*Padre* Callahan live in village. I have no pa-pa. Juan has no pa-pa. Sung Lo has no pa-pa. Thorne has no pa-pa."

"Do you have a mama?"

The child shook her head. "No ma-ma."

Mariah's heart swelled at the loneliness in the child's face. Both she and Juan needed a woman's touch. Some feminine part deep inside told her that Thorne also needed help.

"Sung Lo says to clean up and go in to eat." Thorne's voice startled her. She hadn't heard him approach. "I'll help Sister to the table."

The children scurried off, as the dinner was far more important than any guest. When they were out of earshot, he hunkered down beside Mariah. "Sister Rose, I won't have you interrogating the children. If you want to know anything, ask me."

She nodded. "I was simply curious about them. Neither looks like you, and I wondered about your relationship. Perhaps

I can help you, as a servant of the Lord, I mean." Remembering her disguise, she lapsed back into the brogue.

He shook his head. "We're doing just fine. And no, I'm not their father. Running Deer was the sole survivor when her tribe was massacred by the Army. Juan had been left for dead when renegades raided his family's small homestead. Sung Lo was left behind by the railroad in Wyoming. He was too old to keep up with them."

Warmth settled in her chest. This big, rough man had taken in strays and provided for them as his own. "So you're taking care of them."

"It's temporary. Only until Father Callahan finds decent homes for them."

"Oh, I see."

"No, I don't think you do, Sister. I'm not some do-gooder who goes around looking for strays. All I want is to be left alone."

She didn't believe a word of it. Hadn't he tended her wounds and taken her into his care? "Juan does not speak English?"

"Juan does not speak." He stood and stretched out a hand. "Careful, Sister. Don't put any weight on the leg. Lean on me."

Obeying his instructions, she balanced on one foot. She'd helped Francis get around with his broken leg, and she knew she wouldn't make it unless she stretched her arm around his waist. When they took the first step, she stumbled on a stone, and would have fallen had he not grabbed her in time.

"Oh, hell," he muttered. "Sorry, Sister." In one fell swoop, he scooped her into his arms and carried her into the cabin. He dropped her onto a hard, wooden bench.

She adjusted her veil, which had again slipped down toward her eyes. Mariah wished she could shed the hot habit and confining veil. But she had to keep up the charade. Besides, a change of clothing was in her carpetbag somewhere near the stagecoach, unless the robbers had stolen it, too.

The children sat quietly on either side of her, while Thorne settled at the head of the large, planked table. There wasn't a touch of decor in the cabin—not a curtain, tablecloth, or scarf. She'd never seen anything so austere and plain.

Her home in Philadelphia was cluttered with so many personal treasures, they could hardly move about.

Sung Lo bustled about the large stone fireplace that filled nearly one entire wall. Across the room sat four small cots, each with a drab blanket folded at the foot. The Chinese filled five bowls and set them on the table.

"It smells heavenly," she said, although she didn't recognize either the aroma or the ingredients.

Thorne dug into his bowl with a spoon. "Don't ask what it is. I just let him cook whatever he wants. He hasn't poisoned any of us yet."

Mariah caught herself before she stuck the spoon into the bowl. A nun wouldn't dare touch a bite of food until she prayed. From years in the convent school, she could emulate the sisters to perfection. More than a few times, her mockery had earned her a rap on the knuckles. After a brief prayer, she studied the mixture in the bowl.

Hunger overrode the questions in her mind. Like the children, she dug her spoon into the strange greenish stew. After the first bite, she decided that the blend of unusual spices and vegetables couldn't hurt her. After all, the Chinese people had been eating this for thousands of years, and they were still going strong. It was surprisingly good. Sung Lo grinned when he noticed her empty bowl, and refilled it immediately, along with Thorne's. The old man devoured the same amount of food using chopsticks. How he managed was beyond her.

No one spoke, and even Mariah remained silent. The quiet dinner was quite a contrast to the noisy O'Reilly household. A tear burned at the back of her eyes. Her parents were so dear and precious. She couldn't begin to understand the sacrifices they'd made for their nine children. Sean had endured prejudice against the Irish and had fought his way up the ranks in the police department. More than anything, they deserved their own house. With the bonus from Mrs. Thornton, she would buy them a house large enough for the entire family. That meant learning all about this man, and discovering his true identity.

The meal over, Thorne and Sung Lo shoved back their chairs. Mariah did the same. When she began to stack the bowls as she'd always done at home, Thorne stopped her with a touch of his hand.

"The children will clean the dishes. It's their chore. You can stay in here and keep them company, if you wish."

"Yes. But I would like to help."

He shook his head. "I'll be outdoors when they finish." Sung Lo retrieved two long, curved pipes from the mantel. He and Thorne retreated to the clearing in front of the cabin. Mariah watched through the open door as they puffed on the pipes and blew smoke rings into the air.

The boy and girl made short work of the dishes. They were clearly being taught to be self-sufficient. It was a good lesson in life. Thorne might not be their father, but he was teaching them discipline and responsibility. When they finished, they returned to Mariah. "What fine workers you are. Thorne must be very proud of you."

Running Deer's cheeks turned pink, and Juan looked down at his moccasins. The orphaned children stole her heart. She prayed that Thorne would find a good home for them before she convinced him to return to Philadelphia with her.

"Sissy Rosie, you stay with us?" Running Deer rested her cheek on Mariah's shoulder.

"For a little while." Until her ankle healed and she could make sense of her mission.

"We show Sister Rosie many things—rabbits, squirrels, a bear and her cub. We know secret places that Thorne not know."

Juan pointed to the girl's chest. She giggled. "Juan says he show you deer and the fawn."

Mariah smiled. How easily the boy made himself understood without words.

A shadow fell across the doorway, darkening the interior of the cabin. Thorne took one step onto the hard-packed dirt floor. "Sister, come out here. I want to show you something."

He caught her elbow in one big hand and helped her to her feet. Funny, the ankle didn't hurt nearly as much as earlier. Gingerly, she touched a toe to the ground, and hobbled along beside him. "What is it, Mr. Thorne?"

"Drop the formality. Just Thorne."

They moved a little past the clearing, to a space between the thick growth of pine and firs. The sun had dropped low behind the mountains, and the sky was streaked with a resplendent display of color. Red, purple, pink, and blue lit the evening with nature's glory. She caught her breath at the display. As far as she could see were mountains and mesas dropping off to deep green valleys. The canyon walls glowed as if an artist had painted a rainbow across their surfaces.

"It's magnificent," she said. "I've never seen a sunset like this one."

"You won't see it anywhere else, either."

She shivered. "We're so far from civilization, don't you get lonely?"

"No. I like my privacy."

"I take it you don't like strangers."

"That's why I chose to live on this mountain."

It sounded very much as if he were trying to get rid of her. Well, it wasn't going to be quite so easy. She dug in her heels. "Oh, my ankle. I believe it's beginning to swell again. Are you sure it isn't broken?"

"I'm positive. You just need to rest. It's almost bedtime anyway. You can take my cot. I'll sleep outdoors."

"Sir, I can't do that."

"Don't argue, Sister. I want to set out at dawn to locate that stagecoach you said you were on. If the men are dead, they need to be buried. I'll go into Los Amigos and report the robbery, if it hasn't already been found.''

He sounded almost as if he doubted her story. That part at least was very true. ''Please look for my carpetbag. It holds all my meager belongings.'' Except for the packet of important papers, a pouch containing her expense money, and the letter her fellow passenger had given to her before he was killed. In her rush, she hadn't bothered to open it. Now she was becoming curious as to its contents. Tomorrow, when Thorne was gone, she would learn what was so important that a man had lost his life.

''I'll do that.''

Chapter 3

Mariah woke up the next morning stiff and aching. If only she could have removed the heavy gabardine garment that covered her from the top of her head to the tips of her toes and from her chin to her wrists. Since the night on the mountain was cold, she welcomed the warmth. Not only did the lack of privacy prevent her undressing, but no God-fearing nun would remove her clothing except in the privacy of her little room. Sister Mary Louise was so strict, she supposed the woman even bathed in her habit and veil. At times she smelled of it, too.

Which reminded Mariah that if she didn't wash soon, she'd be as ripe as a nanny goat in summer. During her stops at small hotels, she'd only taken time to wipe the dust from her arms and face.

She opened her eyes and studied her surroundings. She'd slept little, aware of every rustle of wind in the trees, every animal that howled or hooted, and every creak of the cabin. Although only the palest light of dawn glowed through the single window, she noticed she was alone. She swung her legs to the floor. How had Sung Lo and the children managed to leave without her hearing?

Taking advantage of the few minutes of privacy, she tugged the veil from her head and rubbed her temples. No wonder her teachers were always so cross with the students. Any woman forced to wear the heavy habit day in and day out had a right to be out of sorts.

Her hair was matted and greasy and black tendrils poked from the thick braid. The nasty salve coated her face, and the habit was dusty and splashed with mud. But Mariah had no reason to complain. She was safe and on her way to successfully fulfilling the mission.

A childish giggle drew her gaze to the doorway. Three heads, all in a row, poked around the opening. Sung Lo was on top, with Juan next, and Running Deer at the bottom.

"Sissy wake?" the old man asked.

"Yes. I didn't realize everybody else was up." The trio stepped into the cabin. "Is Thorne out there?"

Running Deer sat beside Mariah and fingered the long black gown. "Thorne go to village. He find bad men who hurt Sissy."

Maybe he did believe her. "When will he be back?"

"When sun goes down."

Good. That gave her time to gain the children's confidence and learn something about the mysterious man. Sung Lo bustled into the cabin and rushed to the fireplace. He spooned something into a bowl and carried it to Mariah.

"Sissy eat," he said, shoving the bowl into her hand.

She stared at the things swimming in the clear broth. It didn't smell bad, and if she thought about the chicken soup her mother served when she was sick, she might be able to get it down. Mariah dug her spoon into the soup and took a sip. Like the concoction the night before, it was very good. In a few minutes, she finished what she was certain passed for breakfast.

"Thank you, Sung Lo," she said, although she doubted the man understood her words. "Now I must go outdoors."

"Juan and me help," said Running Deer.

The children on either side of her, Mariah hobbled from the cabin. On the previous night, Thorne had shown her the facilities. She paused to splash water on her face from the bucket, then proceeded to tend to her personal needs.

Without the veil, she felt more relaxed. Of course, she would have to put it back on before Thorne returned. It wouldn't do to promote any more suspicions.

Later that afternoon, the children showed Mariah a mountain stream where hot water bubbled from the earth and formed a small pool. She smiled with delight. A real spa, like the ones for which the resorts in Europe were so famous. Sung Lo generously supplied soap and toweling for her much-needed bath. As if afraid they would be required to bathe, the children scurried away.

Surrounded by a thick growth of shrubs, large boulders, and willow trees, the pool offered as private a bath as her own room. Nobody would bother her here, especially Thorne, who wasn't expected back until dark. The fresh-smelling water bubbled and churned. From the shore she could see clear to the stones at the bottom of the stream.

Eager to step into the water, Mariah stripped from the foul-smelling habit. It really should have been thrown away, considering the caked-on mud from her adventures since the stage-coach robbery. Until she found other clothing, she decided to try her best to wash it. Stripped down to her chemise and drawers, she opened the hidden pockets in the gown and retrieved her valuables.

The leather wallet held a letter from Mrs. Thornton to her grandson and a photograph of the young man. Mariah pulled out the picture, hoping she could recognize him. In a streak of sunlight through the canopy of overhanging branches, she studied the hand-tinted picture. The subject was photographed wearing the blue uniform of a Union officer. With his hat in his hand, she was able to get a clear look into his somber gray eyes and brown hair. Of course the colors had faded over the past twelve years since the picture had been made. The man was quite handsome, and instead of holding a rifle, a leather bag—much like the one doctors carried—sat on the floor at his feet.

She wrinkled her brow. Mrs. Thornton hadn't mentioned that Michael was a doctor. She'd revealed little about the man's personal life. Was this another piece of the puzzle that she had to fit together? Hadn't Thorne nursed her ankle and tended her wounds with his own salve. His touch had been soft and gentle, healing and nurturing.

Her fingers brushed at the unsmiling face. It was hard to tell if Michael was indeed Thorne. The mountain man wore a thick, gray-streaked beard, and his hair hung to his wide shoulders. Since he was seated, she couldn't tell the man's exact height, but Thorne was definitely tall, well over six feet, and built like a lumberjack.

Tingles raced up her arm. She yearned to touch this man, to learn all his secrets. Mariah laughed. She'd spent so much time studying the photograph of Michael Harrison, she imagined herself halfway in love with him. She snorted in an unladylike manner at the very thought. Thorne certainly hadn't inspired any romantic notions in her. The man was brusque, hard, and unrefined. Michael Harrison was a product of Philadelphia society and Virginia aristocrats. He'd had every advantage that an Irish immigrant's daughter would never know. Yet, she couldn't help comparing Michael to Thorne. Even the name fit. His middle name was Thornton. She would just have to wait and see if he revealed his identity. Carefully, she returned the letter and photograph to the wallet.

Hidden in another pocket was a drawstring bag containing her traveling money. Mrs. Thornton had provided a very generous expense allowance. As she shook out the habit, she heard the rustle of paper. She'd nearly forgotten about the envelope handed her by the passenger who'd been killed in the robbery. He'd asked her to hold it for him, and when he was killed, she'd slipped it into the folds of the habit.

Curious, she opened the envelope to see what was so important. Expecting money, or something valuable, she frowned to find only two torn pieces of paper. Each showed strange markings, almost like a map, but with no indication where it was, or what the "X" stood for. She couldn't make a lick of sense out of it. Intuition told her that it was important. Her heart raced. Could it be a map for a gold mine, or hidden treasure? Everybody had heard stories about Cibola, and other lost riches. Perhaps this was the reason the robbers had searched the man's body and bag. Had a man died for these scraps of paper?

Mariah returned the maps to the envelope and placed it along with the wallet and her money under a rock along with her rosary. Her gun she carried with her. No telling what kind of animal, four legged or two, she was likely to encounter in the wilderness.

At the edge of the swift-flowing stream, she dunked the gown, veil, and her petticoats into the water. She rubbed on the soap, and did her best to get them clean. Her mother would be shocked to see Mariah beating her clothes on a stone in a stream. Mariah hated washday, and tried her best to get out of the chore whenever possible.

Satisfied that the garments were as clean as she was likely to get them, she stretched the black habit and her muslin petticoats on the bushes to dry. In the high altitude and hot sun, they should be ready by the time she finished her bath.

Carrying the soap in her hand, Mariah stepped gingerly across the slippery stones to the pool where the hot water met the cold mountain stream. Sheltered by the boulders and the trees, Mariah sank up to her chin in the mineral bath. She stretched out her legs as she'd never been able to do in the washtub at home and sighed with pleasure. The water bubbled and tickled her skin. For modesty's sake, she left on her unmentionables, but she wished she'd had the nerve to strip naked.

The peaceful gurgle of the stream relaxed Mariah. Overhead the birds chirped and sang, ignoring the human who'd dared invade their kingdom. Wind whistled through the branches, lulling her to sleep. As her eyes drifted shut, she saw Thorne's face. His icy gray eyes melted and his beard was replaced by a smooth jaw and wide smile. A smile meant for her. She imagined his muscular, sun-bronzed body beside her in the pool.

In her dream, he drew her into his arms and gently caressed her body. His mouth covered hers with a kiss that left her breathless. Excitement turned her body to liquid, and she smiled at the delightful sensations.

Thorne parted the bushes that surrounded his private bathing spot. The children had pointed in this direction when he'd asked the whereabouts of Sister Rose. He stared down at the woman immersed in the water. For long moments he studied her. The only part of her visible was her head. But that was enough to get his pulse pounding. Her body was obscured by the bubbly mineral stream, but if she moved a little, nothing would be hidden under the clear, clean water.

Long midnight-black hair floated on the surface, swirling and moving in the current with a life of its own. Except for the scrapes on her face, her skin was flawless. She was asleep, and an enigmatic smile curved her lips. He wondered what had brought that contented look to her face. Probably a plan to dupe some other poor soul, he thought.

The woman was a rare beauty. He frowned. So was Suzanna. Thorne stepped back and let the brush snap back into place. He hadn't thought about his former fiancée in years. Anger surged through him at the reminder of Suzanna's deceit. When he'd most needed her support and love, she'd rejected him and married his brother.

Now this woman had invaded his mountain hideaway and his life. He hadn't been able to stop thinking about her since he'd rescued her from that fall down the mountain yesterday.

This so-called nun was a mystery. He didn't believe a thing she'd told him, and he didn't trust her any more than he would trust his brother who'd tried to kill him during the war.

One thing was true, though. The stagecoach had been held up and the driver and passenger killed. He'd buried the bodies, and retrieved a woman's valise and clothing from where the robbers had strewn them. Again, the lacy underthings, flower-trimmed blouses, and sheer stockings weren't what he expected of a nun.

He dropped her valise to the ground and spotted something glinting in the sunshine. Bending, he saw it was her silver crucifix beside a stone. Something else was under the stone. He moved it aside and retrieved a leather portfolio, a drawstring pouch heavy with coin, and an envelope.

Although Thorne normally wasn't a curious man, he needed to learn more about the woman who could spell danger for him and his wards. He opened the packet and started to withdraw the contents when he stopped cold. The hairs on the back of his neck prickled. He recognized the distinctive click of the hammer of a pistol. Instinctively, he reached for his rifle.

"Don't!" a female voice ordered. "I know how to shoot."

As he raised his hands over his head, his heart began to beat again. "Is this how you repay hospitality, Sister?" Slowly, he turned to face the woman.

"Do you always ransack your guest's belongings?" With one hand, she clutched a large piece of toweling to her chest; the other pointed a gun at his head.

"I seldom have guests. I apologize for my lack of proper manners." His gaze drifted slowly over her. Her long, unbound hair dripped on the towel, making it nearly transparent with the dampness. Her breasts made round wet spots on the front of the cloth, and drops of water gleamed like diamonds on her milky white shoulders. The short length of material stopped at her knees, revealing the edges of her pantalets and shapely legs. Barefoot, she shifted from one foot to the other.

He gripped the leather wallet and cursed the heat that settled in his gut.

"If you're done staring at me, please return my belongings

and allow me privacy to dress.'' The pink in her cheeks belied the chill in her tone.

''Certainly. If you can imitate a nun, I can impersonate a gentleman.'' He dropped his hands and tossed the packet to her, much harder than necessary. It hit her in the arm, causing her to drop her aim.

Instantly, Thorne was on her. He twisted the gun from her grip and shoved it into his belt. She reached out with her free hand. ''Give it back.''

He laughed, a cool mirthless sound. ''So you can shoot me? Not on your life, *Sister*. I value my worthless hide too much to trust a woman with a gun. Sit down. It's time we had a little talk.''

She tightened her grip on the towel. ''Sir, this is highly improper. Please allow me to don my apparel and make myself decent.''

His gaze drifted from her fiery blue eyes to her pink toes. In between was enough to tempt a hermit out of hiding. ''No, I like you just fine as you are.'' If he had an ounce of horse sense, he'd allow her to dress in the heavy habit and cover every inch of that tempting body. Looking at her brought images of forbidden desires. He fought his needs, wanting the advantage of having her uncomfortable and at his mercy.

''I prefer to stand.'' She tossed her hair, and it flowed around her like a lace mantilla.

''Have your own way, but I'm tired. I hurried back from Los Amigos so I could see you.'' He settled on a large stone. ''Aren't you curious about what I found?''

Her gaze dropped to her valise. ''I see you found my valise. Now do you believe me?''

''Less than ever, though you were right about the stage robbery. I buried the dead, then I reported it to Father Callahan so he could notify the officials.''

She shifted from foot to foot, covering the toes of one foot with the other. ''In Los Amigos?''

''Yes. Now, tell me: Who are you?'' He stared hard at her

as if staring would bring out the truth. All it did was increase the heat in his blood.

"I told you. I'm Sister Mariah Rose and I'm headed for a mission in Santa Fe."

He snorted. "Lady, you're as much a nun as I am King of England."

"There is no king in England. Queen Victoria is the regent."

"Exactly my point. The padre said he didn't know anything about a nun traveling this way. And this is quite a distance from Santa Fe."

"I wanted to see some of the country." The towel slipped on one side, revealing more of her white camisole. She gripped it tighter, struggling to keep it from revealing too much.

Thorne curled his hands into fists to keep from reaching out and snatching the towel away. "He did say that two men were asking about a nun just yesterday. He thought it rather odd."

Her face paled. "Two men? They must have been the pair that held up the stagecoach."

"I guessed as much. Why are they looking for you?"

"I don't know. Unless . ." She bent and snatched the envelope from the ground where he'd dropped it. "The passenger who was killed gave this to me for safekeeping."

He took it from her fingers, careful not to touch her. "Looks like scraps of paper." Turning the pieces of paper around, he didn't see anything worth dying for. "Did he tell you anything?"

"No. Only to keep it for him. I think it's a map of some kind." Clutching the material to her chest, she leaned over him. He lifted his gaze and was greeted by the swell of full white breasts above lace and pink ribbon. He swallowed hard. She smelled fresh and clean, with a hint of lye soap. Thorne feared he'd been celibate too long. His body hadn't betrayed him like this since he'd been the untried youth his father had taken to a sporting house in Richmond.

He returned his gaze to the paper. "Looks like a map. But part of it is missing."

"Do you think it's a treasure map?" Her eager voice was filled with excitement.

"No." He shoved the scraps back into the envelope and reached for the leather wallet. "Let's see what else you're hiding."

Their hands collided on the portfolio, and she gripped it hard. "It's mine."

"What's in here you don't want me to see?" He refused to loosen his hold.

She yanked hard, and caught him off balance. Together they tumbled to the soft grass, neither willing to release the wallet. In the melee, her towel fell away. The sight of her shapely body in sheer unmentionables stunned him for a moment. Her breasts strained at the wet camisole, the tips dark against the material. Her waist was slender, and her legs long and shapely.

She lifted on all fours to gain her footing. He grabbed her by the waist and rolled her onto her back. She was soft and warm, and his reaction was immediate and hard. He straddled her middle, and cuffed both her wrists in one large hand. With the other, he snatched the wallet from her fingers.

"Let me go." She bucked her middle in an effort to dislodge herself. She only succeeded in arousing him further. There was only so much a man could take.

Her legs twisted around his like a lover's. Black hair spread on the ground and her eyes blazed with passion. Their gazes locked and her movements stilled. For long moments they stared into each other's eyes. Her pink tongue snaked out and moistened her lips. The strap of her camisole had slipped, her breasts were nearly bare. His breath caught in his throat, and he thought he would explode with need. And her a nun, of all things!

Thorne had to get away from her while he could still walk and before he did something sinful and wicked. As he snatched the wallet from her hand, it opened, and several items flew out—a letter and a photograph.

He froze, his gaze locked on the picture. He remembered

when he'd posed for the picture. He'd been proud to wear Union blue, even if his father and brother wore Confederate gray. He'd joined the Army as a medic, unwilling to be a party to death.

Immediately, he released her and sprang to his feet. He stared at his own face. Had he ever been that young and naive? To believe the war would end shortly, that his father would forgive him or that Suzanna would wait for him? "Where did you get this?" he demanded.

She struggled to her feet, and again wrapped the toweling around her body. "It was given to me by your grandmother. Haven't you been hiding long enough, Michael Harrison?"

Her words doused him like a dunking in hard-packed snow Thorne felt an old familiar panic bubble up from his stomach. His first instinct was to run as far away as his legs would carry him. Instead, he stood his ground and faced her without even blinking. "I don't know what you're talking about. I don't have a grandmother, and I sure as hell haven't heard of any Harrison."

Chapter 4

The man was lying through his teeth. Mariah tightened the grip on the towel and faced him boldly. Given another few seconds with his hard, masculine body pressed to hers, she would have begged him to kiss her, and there was no telling where that would lead. Good thing he'd jumped up when he had. For some reason, she felt strangely adrift, as if they'd started something that needed to be finished before either could have real peace.

Her face heated and flushed at the reminder of what had happened between them. Here she was showing herself shamelessly to a man, and about to make love with him. She shifted her gaze from his stormy gray eyes to the photograph clutched between his fingers.

"You know very well what I mean. What are you hiding from?"

He shoved the contents back into the wallet. "I'm not hiding from anything. I'm just a man who likes his privacy—a hermit who wants to be alone."

"Alone? With two children and a Chinese?"

He'd opened his mouth to speak when his protests were cut off by a child's frantic shouts. "Thorne, where are you?"

Both turned and spotted Running Deer and Juan shoving aside bushes and racing toward them. They grabbed Thorne's legs, gasping for breath. "Hold on," he said, his voice gentle. "What happened? A bear after you?"

Juan shook his head. The little girl gestured toward the cabin. "We see two men on horses. Come up path. Sung Lo say tell you."

"I'll take care of it." He shoved her packet and envelope into his shirt. "Take Sister Rose back to the cabin, and wait for me there."

They nodded. Thorne swung his gaze to Mariah. "Get dressed and drop the nun routine. Put on something different and hide that black rag."

"Why? Who are the men?" In her confusion, she'd loosened her hold on the towel, and both children stared at her as if they'd never seen a woman before. At least they'd never seen a nearly naked woman.

"I don't know." He pulled her gun from his belt and passed it to her.

The gun felt good back in her hands. "Why don't we ask them what they want?"

"I'll tend to them in my own way. I told you about the men asking for a nun. They may have come up here looking for you. Do you want me to just hand you over to two murderers?"

She shivered. "No. What do you want me to do?"

"Get dressed and go back to the cabin with the children. You'll be safe there."

"What are you going to do?"

"Anything I must to get rid of strangers."

"Let me help. I'm a crack shot."

His gaze dropped to her exposed body. "You can help by going along with whatever I say. If anyone asks, you're my woman and you don't know anything about a nun." Snatching up his rifle, he took off at a trot down the concealed path.

Mariah reached for her valise, and pulled out a blouse and skirt. By the urgency in his voice, she knew time was at a premium. She tugged on the garments, without bothering with petticoats, stockings, or buttons. After she gathered up her still-damp garments, she shoved her feet into her boots. Juan and Running Deer watched with wide-eyed amazement.

"You Thorne's woman?" the little girl asked.

Her question brought Mariah up short. She hated to lie to the children, but what was one more lie piled on the stack she'd already told? When she finally reached a priest, her confession would be a killer, and she hated to think about her penance.

"Yes. Now let's hurry to the cabin. The men are probably just lost and looking for directions. There's nothing to be afraid of."

She picked up her valise and bag of money. Thorne had taken the map and the packet from Mrs. Thornton.

The children darted through the undergrowth on a path so narrow, only a rabbit would find it. Mariah followed at a slower pace. Thorne's words echoed in her mind. "My woman." A shiver raced over her. What would it be like to be his woman? To be held in those strong arms, to have those full lips claim hers? Of course, the beard would have to go. Her imaginings made her heart flutter. She couldn't deny the heat that sizzled between them when they'd rolled together on the grass, or whenever he touched her. But to live in a one-room cabin in the middle of the wilderness did not fit her plans for the future. No matter that she wouldn't mind having him as a lover—a thought that shocked her maiden sensibilities. But as a husband, he was totally unsuitable. And if he really was Michael Harrison, that was an even more improbable dream.

As the cabin came into view, the sound of a gunshot echoed across the mountain. Fear gripped her heart. What if Thorne had been killed or wounded? He'd gone alone after men who could be murderers.

"Sung Lo." She shoved the black habit into his arms. "Hide this and protect the children. I'm going to help Thorne."

The old man waved his cleaver. "I care children."

Mariah took off at a run, the gun in her hand. She followed another narrow path that led down the mountain. Bushes tore at her skirt, and tree branches brushed her arms.

"Who are you? What do you want?" Thorne's voice carried over the trees.

She continued in the direction of the sound. A voice farther away answered, "We're from Los Amigos."

That voice. The harsh, angry sound was all too familiar. She stopped and skid to a halt. A twig snapped under her foot. Below her, Thorne swung the rifle at her.

"Woman," he whispered, "what are you doing here? You nearly got your head blown off."

She dropped beside him behind a large boulder. "I came to help."

Thorne cursed under his breath. "Never did meet a woman who could follow orders. Get your head down before *they* blow it off."

Through the gaps between the tall trees, she spotted two men on horseback, about a hundred yards away. They rode single-file on the narrow ledge that formed a path. With their hats pulled down on their eyes, Mariah couldn't be sure of their identification. She prayed they meant no harm.

"What do you want on my mountain?" Thorne called down to them.

"Can't we come up and talk? Our horses are thirsty, and we could use a drink." The man first in line glanced around, as if trying to pinpoint Thorne's location.

"You can talk from there. I don't allow strangers on my property."

"The priest sent us to look for a nun."

"A nun? What are you talking about?" Thorne lowered his voice to Mariah. "Stay here and wait for my signal. When I raise my hand, fire a shot in their direction. Try not to hit me."

He crawled away, and dropped behind a large boulder about twenty feet away.

"She was supposed to meet the priest in Los Amigos, but she never showed up. He sent us to look for her."

In spite of the warm sunshine, Mariah's skin chilled. Nobody knew anything about a nun except Thorne and the outlaws who'd robbed the stagecoach. These had to be the men who'd committed murder with no remorse.

"I don't know anything about a nun." Again Thorne changed positions farther away.

The men below shifted their gazes to the sound of his voice. "A woman, then. Maybe she wasn't a nun."

"You're the only strangers on my mountain. Get off while you're still upright in the saddle."

They strained toward Thorne's new location. "Come out and talk to us."

"Get off my land."

Thorne moved again. Mariah followed his every movement. He lifted his hand and dropped it. She took careful aim, and her shot fell short, kicking up the dust at the horse's feet. Darn. She could do better than that. The man in the lead lifted his rifle and fired in her direction. She dropped back behind the rock. The bullet shattered tiny pellets into the air. At the same instant, two more shots blasted. Thorne's shots took them by surprise. Mariah lifted her head in time to see the rifle fly from the man's hand, and the hat from his head.

The second man spun his horse around and headed back down the path. His hatless companion followed at his heels.

Thorne ran back to Mariah. "Go back to the cabin. I'll be along as soon as I make sure they keep going. Don't want them sneaking up on us after dark." He took two steps, and turned back to her with a grin. "By the way, nice shot—for a woman."

She stood and returned his smile. "Thanks. That's quite a compliment—from a man."

* * *

This time, Mariah followed orders and returned to the cabin. Sung Lo stood guard at the door ready to do battle with his cleaver and a large knife.

"Everything's all right, Sung Lo. Thorne will return after a bit." He stepped aside and let her enter.

"Thorne chase away bad men?"

"Yes. How are the children?"

"Children eat. Sissy hungry? Eat?"

"I'll wait for Thorne." The sun was setting, and soon it would be dark. After all the excitement of the day, food was the last thing on her mind. She wanted Thorne to return to make sure he was safe.

"Sissy Rosie!" Running Deer called. Both children wrapped their arms around her waist. She patted their heads, and bent to give each a kiss. Their suntanned faces flushed with joy and love. Her heart tightened for the lonely orphan children. She prayed Thorne would find good homes for them—a mother and father to love and to be loved in return. Parents like her own, a couple who poured out love and affection on their nine children and one grandchild. Six-year-olds like Juan and Running Deer deserved just as much.

Running Deer lifted a lock of Mariah's long unbound hair, snarled and knotted. "Sissy have hair like me and Juan."

She touched each dark head. "I surely do. We're the same."

The youngsters grinned from ear to ear. "We same," the little girl repeated proudly.

For once, Mariah was glad she hadn't given in to her rebellious streak and cut off her hair. Whenever she'd mentioned the nuisance of long hair, her mother had a fit, quoting Bible scriptures about long hair. Now her long black hair gave her a resemblance to the children.

"Mine is all snarled." She took her brush from the valise and worked out the snares. Neither child took an eye off her as she twisted the hair into a single braid down her back and finished off the end with a length of black ribbon.

Running Deer fingered the satin ribbon, then studied the string that tied off her plaits. "Would you like me to fix your hair like mine?" Mariah asked.

The girl nodded and sat very still while Mariah performed the chore she'd done every morning for her younger sisters. Mariah brushed the patient child's hair into a single braid, then added a length of red ribbon. Running Deer flipped the braid over her shoulder and studied the bright red scrap of cloth. Mariah had never seen a happier child.

At their side, Juan fingered the ribbon, and frowned. Without words, he said he felt neglected. Mariah took her brush and gently smoothed out the boy's shorter hair. "Boys don't wear ribbons in their hair," she said. An idea hit her. "But they do wear ties around their necks." She pulled out a dark blue strip, looped it under his collar and tied it into a bow at his throat. Sitting back on her heels, she studied the children. "What a beautiful young lady, and what a handsome young man. Don't you think so, Sung Lo?"

The old man studied the trio. "Pretty."

Juan twisted out of her grip, and pulled a chair to the window. He climbed up and studied his reflection in a cracked mirror. The young boy's smile would warm a house on a chilly Philadelphia winter morning. He raced back and flung his arms around Mariah's neck.

Outside the cabin, the sun was rapidly setting behind the mountains. Sung Lo scuffled around, lighting kerosene lamps. "Children go bed," he said.

Both frowned, not ready to end their day. "We want wait for Thorne."

"Why don't you sit with me while I eat?" She smiled at Sung Lo, who filled a bowl with a delicious-smelling stew. Again, she didn't dare ask the ingredients, but finished every bite. The children were nodding off, but neither wanted to go to bed. "I'll read to you, then you can go to sleep," she said.

Each raced to their cots, and waited while Mariah searched for something suitable for children. Thorne had shelves full of books—everything from Shakespeare, to Homer, to Dickens. All worn from handling and reading. He also had a stack of medical journals and ledgers full of notes and handwritten entries. The man was an enigma, a recluse who read the classics and medical books. More and more, she was certain he was the man she was seeking.

Mariah picked up a volume and sat down to read aloud as she'd done so many times for her siblings. The story of Romeo and Juliet, star-crossed lovers, never ceased to intrigue her, although she didn't like the ending at all. If she were Mr. Shakespeare, she'd have had the couple tell their families off and let them live happily ever after. By the time she was only a quarter through the play, both youngsters were sound asleep.

Thorne stood in the doorway, his rifle clutched in his fist. His gaze was locked on the figures seated on a cot. Rose—he had trouble thinking of the woman as "Sister"—was reading aloud to the children, her voice lifted and dropped with emotion as she added her own version of Romeo's dialogue and Juliet's response.

Dressed in normal clothes, she was even lovelier. Her eyes were soft and loving, and she looked young and vulnerable. How had this woman gotten involved in the fog of lies that surrounded her?

She looked up and her smile widened. "They're sleeping," she whispered.

In a few long strides, he was at her side. He lifted each child in turn and placed them into their respective beds. The woman returned the book to the shelf, then gently tucked a blanket over each child and planted a kiss on their cheeks. His heart twisted at the sight. She was giving them the love and attention they deserved, something only a woman could offer.

Sung Lo called him to the table. Rose followed and sat while he ate. "Have the men gone?" she asked.

He looked at her over the kerosene lamp. Her cheeks were smooth, and her lips full and pink. The scrapes had almost disappeared, thanks to his salve. "Yes. I followed them to the road that leads to Los Amigos."

"Do you think they'll be back?"

"Not tonight. I think we convinced them that we don't know anything about a nun. Were they the men who'd robbed the stage?"

"I'm almost positive. It was all so confusing, I can't quite remember everything that happened. Why else would they be looking for me?"

"You tell me."

"Unless it had something to do with that map. I'd never seen them before."

It was time to learn the truth about this woman. He shoved his empty bowl aside. "Let's go outside to talk. I don't want to disturb the children."

Stopping only to pick up the rifle, he gestured to the clearing that overlooked the mountains. The moon was high in the sky, and stars twinkled from a field of black velvet.

"Are you going to shoot me?" she asked, coming to a stop at the edge of the clearing.

"Not yet. All I want are some straight answers."

She sighed and sank to a stump. "Fire away."

"Who are you? What do you want out here?"

"I told you I left the convent to take up a position at a mission in California."

"A while ago you told me you were headed to Santa Fe. Which is it, *Sister?*"

Even in the darkness, he noted the high color on her cheeks. The woman wasn't much of a liar. "I made a mistake because you confused me. I'm going to California, that's why the priest in Los Amigos didn't know anything about my arrival."

"That's a lot of crap. How'd you come by that picture? And

why are you interested in Michael Harrison?'' He hunkered
down in front of her.

Mariah shifted her gaze over his shoulder. He'd caught her as
neatly as a fly on a spider web. "I told a woman in Philadelphia I
was headed west. She asked me if I could find her grandson
for her.'' Part of the truth was better than all. He was too
elusive to come right out and confess his identity.

"Why didn't she hire detectives? Pinkerton? Why send a
woman to do a man's job?''

"She did. He traced Harrison to Los Amigos. Then the
operative broke his leg and had to return to Philadelphia. She
asked me to try to contact the man.'' She didn't dare reveal
that she, too, was a detective, and she stood to reap a generous
reward upon his return.

He gazed at her through cold, hard eyes. "Why does she
want to locate this man?''

"Mrs. Thornton is getting old, and she wants to see her
grandson before she dies.''

His lips thinned, and emotion sparkled in his eyes. She'd
touched something in the man. It was time to scrape the bottom
of the pot. "Who are you really, Thorne? Why are you hiding
on this mountain?''

He let out a bark of humorless laughter. "I'm a hermit. A
mountain man who just wants to be left alone.''

"If you want to be alone, why are you raising two children,
and caring for an ancient Chinese?''

His gaze shifted to the dark, shadowed mountains in the
distance. "I don't rightly know that myself.'' He tugged at his
shaggy beard. "But as a nun, you should understand. What
would you do if you found a lost little girl crying because her
mother had been shot by soldiers? The child may even have
watched her mother being raped.''

Mariah swallowed the bile that rose in her throat. The pain
and violence the child had suffered was unthinkable. "Was she
. . .'' She couldn't spit out the words around the lump in her
chest.

"Thank God, no. At least, there was no evidence. I came along shortly after the raid. Her mother was dying, and she begged me to take care of her child." Again, his eyes grew cold and hard. "I left her for a time with a family in Colorado, but they moved on to California. So I took her with me."

Tears burned at the backs of Mariah's eyes. "What about Juan and Sung Lo?"

"Sung Lo was injured while building the railroad through the mountains. He insisted that they leave him to an honorable death. I found him nearly there. Against his wishes, I nursed him back to health. I brought him here, and he took care of Running Deer when I had to leave."

The kindness in this gruff mountain man tore at her heart. He had so much love to offer, yet he seemed afraid to give it, even to those in his care. "And Juan?"

"He's been with us for about a year and a half. He was wandering in the desert after his village had been raided by renegades. Sung Lo fed him, and I tended his injuries. He seems fine, except that he's never spoken a word."

"Juan can hear, can't he?"

"Yes, too well. He can whistle like the birds, and mock any animal he hears. But he refuses to, or he can't, speak."

"Perhaps if you take him to a doctor in the East. Philadelphia has some fine hospitals and institutions."

He leaped to his feet. "I'm not taking him anywhere. As soon as Father Callahan finds families for all of them, I'm going deeper into the mountains and live out my life in peace."

"Good. These children need parents to love and care for them. They deserve it." She shivered and wrapped her arms about herself.

"The mountains are always cold at night. Go on in. I'm staying out here." Abruptly, he turned away, and stacked wood into a fire.

"We'll talk again in the morning." Then maybe she would get some real facts from the man.

* * *

Mariah took off her boots and stretched out fully clothed on the cot. Beside her cot, the children and Sung Lo were sleeping with the peace of angels. Her mother always said babies and old people could sleep through an earthquake because they had clear consciences. That was something Mariah lacked. She'd told so many lies and half-truths, it would take more prayers than the entire church could offer to get her out of purgatory. If only Thorne would be truthful and agree to return to Philadelphia with her. He could take Juan to a special doctor, and she could return to a normal life. This wilderness wasn't for her. She was a city girl, and Fairmount Park was rural enough.

She wondered if Thorne was comfortable outdoors sleeping on the cold, hard ground. Draping her blanket across her shoulders, she moved to the single window and looked out. Thorne was seated in front of the fire studying something on the ground. He'd taken the letter, the photograph, and the map. Could he be thinking about them? About his grandmother? About going home?

Barefoot, Mariah crossed to the door, and slipped into the shadows of the cabin. He glanced up as she approached his fire.

"Couldn't sleep, either?" she asked. "My mother always said that the reason for insomnia is a guilty conscience."

"Speak for yourself, Sister Rose. If that's your name."

Mariah threw back her head and stared into the heavens. The stars twinkled, as if mocking her. "My name is Mariah Rose O'Reilly. And yours?"

"Thorne."

She let it pass. No use resurrecting that argument. "Is that the map the man gave me?"

He shuffled the two pieces, turning them this way and that. "Yes. It looks as if a sheet was torn into four sections. Two pieces are missing. You wouldn't happen to have them, would you?" Even the darkness couldn't hide his suspicion.

"No, that was all he gave me." She settled at his side on the same log. Her legs brushed his. As if hit with a hot poker, he jerked away. "Do you think those men wanted this badly enough to kill for it?"

"Unless that man gave you something else, that's my guess."

"Maybe they have the rest, and they need this to find the treasure."

He shot her a hard glance. "What treasure? This could lead anywhere. It could just be a map to somebody's homestead."

She shook her head, more convinced than ever that the map was important. "Would they kill to get directions? I don't think so. It must lead to something worth dying for, or else the man would have handed it over to them when they stopped the stage."

"That makes sense." He picked up the map and inspected it closely. "Some of the landmarks look familiar. These could be twin peaks, and a smoke hole." His finger traced the lines and symbols. "This looks like a road, and this mark could represent a fort."

"And the big X marks the spot. Can we find where the treasure is hidden?"

"It would be like looking for a needle in a haystack."

She leaned closer, pressing her shoulder to his. His warmth spread to her through the blanket. "What could it be? Are there any lost mines in the area? I read in school that Coronado had been searching for the lost cities of gold. Surely nobody's found it."

"That was a legend. There are always stories of lost mines and treasures that everybody looks for and nobody finds. Adam's lost mine, Cibola, some prospector's dream. There was even a report of a shipment of Union gold stolen during the war. None of it was ever recovered."

The thought of lost gold sparked her interest. "Do you think we could find it?"

"There probably never was any gold. It's just a story." He

stood and shoved the map back into the envelope. "Go back to bed. I'm going to check my traps."

"We'll look at it again tomorrow, Thorne. Maybe you'll recognize the landmarks."

"Don't bet on it."

Chapter 5

The first pink glow of dawn found Thorne in the same position he'd been in all night. After he'd sent Sister Rose away, he'd gone off to be alone. He'd checked the traps, skinned a couple of rabbits, and sat down to think.

He clutched the leather wallet in his fingers, afraid to open it, scared of what he'd find. Most of all, he was afraid of his own reaction. As much as he hated to think about it, he must come to a decision. If the detective had traced him this far, and this women had found him, others would follow. Unless he hid deeper in the mountains, his days of peace and solitude were gone.

If he didn't have two children and an old man to care for, things would be much simpler. A soft gray fog dipped into the valley, hiding any trace of life beyond his mountain. He didn't regret taking the orphans and old man under his care and protection. They'd more than rewarded him with their love and joy of life. He'd gained a whole new outlook on living as a result of knowing them. They'd given much more than he'd given them.

After he'd found Juan and realized he was as lost as the little

boy, he'd written to tell his grandmother he was alive. He felt
as if she needed to know the truth.

He shouldn't have been surprised that she'd sent somebody
to hunt him down. After all, he was her only living kin, the
son of her only daughter. Grandmother had loved him dearly,
and had been the one member of the family to support his
decision to join the Union Army as a medic.

Opening the wallet, he pulled out the letter addressed to
Michael Harrison, a name he'd dropped years ago. The few
people he encountered knew him simply as Thorne. His hand
trembling, he tore open the end and slipped out the letter. By
this action alone, the woman would know his true identity.
Curiosity overrode common sense. By the pale morning light,
he studied his grandmother's shaky handwriting.

Emotion flooded his heart. When she'd last written, her hand
was bold and steady. This was the penmanship of an old woman.

> *My dearest grandson Michael,*
> *How I thank God for your letter. Although all the*
> *evidence said differently, my heart told me you lived. I*
> *am old, and not as strong as I once was. I would move*
> *heaven and earth to see you again. Whatever problem*
> *sent you into hiding can be solved. The Army quit looking*
> *for you years ago. I am in contact with President Grant*
> *for a full pardon. The person who delivers this letter*
> *speaks for me. Please come home so I can see you one*
> *last time.*
>
> *Your loving grandmother,*
> *Amelia Thornton*

Thorne dropped his head. How he loved this woman. Pain
tore at his chest. Over the years, he'd tried not to think about
her. To him, she was invincible. Now he realized that she had
few years left on the earth. Time was running out for him to
see her.

He had decisions to make, but first he had to get rid of the woman.

Picking up the skinned rabbits that Sung Lo would cook for their dinner, he headed back to the cabin. Getting rid of Sister Rose wasn't going to be easy, but he had to try. That, too, weighed heavily on his chest. If he dumped her in Los Amigos, the outlaws would find her, and no telling what they would do to a lone woman. Thorne didn't know what it was about him that attracted strays, but he now had four under his care.

Only Sung Lo greeted him when he entered the cabin. In his limited vocabulary, the old man told him that "Sissy" had gone off with the children. He drank coffee and ate breakfast, then took a sheet of paper from the shelf. Pulling out the pieces of map, he laid them on the table. The more he studied the landmarks, the more familiar they became. Yet, with so much missing, he couldn't be sure of anything.

Thorne lay the torn scraps on the sheet of paper, changing positions until the pieces matched. He added a few marks of his own, putting a road here, a mountain there, doing his best to reconstruct the map. While he was wandering northern New Mexico territory looking for his own hideaway, he'd made notes and maps of his own. It was too easy to get lost without having some point of orientation. He studied the partial map, wondering what it all meant.

"Looking for that needle?" Sister Rose leaned over his shoulder.

His heart leaped. Since this woman had fallen into his life, he'd been in a constant state of turmoil. Now, it was the flowery scent of the blossoms braided into her hair that fired his senses.

He shrugged, not daring a glance at her. "It's useless. I know this country, but nothing makes sense."

She snuggled next to him and bent her head to the paper. "What does this mean?" Her fingers brushed his.

"I'm guessing twin peaks. There are a lot of those out here. And smoke holes." He touched another marking.

"Surely the way they go together must mean something."

She took his pencil and added a few directions. "I studied a map of New Mexico before I left home. 'FU.' Could this be Fort Union? And 'Rio,' a river? North?"

Her knowledge surprised him. There were few maps of the territory available. "Possibly. This could be Turkey Mountain, but it's still like looking for a needle in a haystack." He stared at her. The woman was lovely. Her black hair shone and her blue eyes glittered with excitement.

"What if that needle is a treasure? A lost mine? That gold shipment? We could be rich."

He'd seen gold fever before. Heck, he'd had it himself. Her enthusiasm nearly infected him. "I don't want to be rich." He crumpled the paper.

"Well, I do." She snatched the sheet and straightened the wrinkles.

"Don't nuns take a vow of poverty? Why are you so interested in treasure?"

Her face flushed, and she visibly flinched. He'd caught her this time. "I'm not sure I'm cut out for this kind of life."

Thorne didn't try to hide his amusement. "That's the first thing you've said that I believe."

"Thorne, it's important to me. Not just for me. But for my family. My parents were Irish immigrants who left Ireland during the potato famine. They settled in Philadelphia where my father is a police officer." She glanced at the row of cots lined against the wall. "I have four brothers and four sisters. My parents could use the money. They need a house of their own, a place large enough for all of us."

"What about the Church?"

"They will get a nice share."

"Suppose we do find the treasure, and it turns out to be Yankee gold, you'd be obliged to return it."

She frowned, but met his gaze. "But I'll bet there's a big reward for its return." Her voice rang with the enthusiasm of a child at a party. "Have you made up your mind to help me?"

Thorne shoved away from the table, his arm brushing her

soft breast with the movement. Heat sizzled through him. He shouldn't have these kinds of feeling for a nun. "You're determined to do this, aren't you?"

"Yes. With or without your help." She folded the papers and shoved them into her pocket. "I'll go into Los Amigos and hire guides."

"Like the pair who're already looking for you and the map?"

"Well, I'll be careful."

He shook his head at her utter naiveté. "You'll only succeed in getting yourself killed. As soon as word of gold gets out, it's like a fever. You saw for yourself how easily those men killed the stagecoach driver and that passenger."

Her fingers gripped his shirtsleeve. "Then you go with me. Be my guide. You said you know this country. Help me find the treasure."

His gaze dropped to the pleading look in her eyes. "We could be way off in our guesses. It may just be a wild-goose chase."

"I'm willing to take the chance."

"What makes you think you can trust me?"

She stroked his sleeve, sending prickles up his arm. The woman was either a complete innocent or a practiced coquette. Either way, she had worked her wiles on him and had his gut twisted into a knot.

"You've had more than one chance to get rid of me, yet you've helped me at every hand."

He stepped out of her reach, and felt strangely at a loss. "I'm seriously considering taking you to Los Amigos and dumping you on Father Callahan."

"I'll just come back. Or somebody else will come. Either after the treasure or looking for you."

Under his shirt, the packet he'd taken from her burned his skin like fire. "Why would anybody be looking for me? I'm nothing but a mountain man, a recluse."

Mariah studied the man. His face was without expression, and his eyes blank. He could play a great hand of poker. "I know who you are, and if I found you, others will also. It's only a matter of time before somebody comes after you.''

''I can move so fast and so far back into the mountains even a mountain goat won't find me.''

''Then why haven't you? I believe you want to be found. Or else why would you have written to your grandmother?''

He clasped her upper arms and shook her. ''Who are you? Don't give me that bull about being on a mission for God.''

His fingers dug into the flesh on her arms. His anger was as evident as the shaggy beard on his face. The man could break her in two with his bare hands. ''Sit down,'' she said. ''I'll tell you everything.'' He released her with a shove toward the table. ''May I have a drink of water, please?''

He snorted and dipped a gourd into a bucket. ''Here. You can start by telling me your name.''

She took one sip to loosen her tight throat. Being so close to him, having him touch her, had her heart pounding and her throat dry. ''I told you the truth. I'm Mariah Rose O'Reilly from Philadelphia.''

''Are you a nun?''

''No.'' She touched the crucifix that hung around her neck. ''But I'm a good Irish Catholic girl.''

He laughed, again without humor. ''Good? That's debatable. Why are you here?''

''To find you . . . or Michael Harrison.''

''Why you?''

''I'm an operative with Erin Investigators. Mrs. Amelia Thornton hired us to locate her grandson. My brother started the investigation and he traced Harrison as far as Los Amigos. Then he broke his leg and had to return East. I took his place.''

''You're no better than a low-down bounty hunter.''

She cringed at the term. If he only knew all of it. ''I'm doing a job.''

''You're going to get your man dead or alive?''

''He's no value to us dead. His grandmother wants to know he's well and happy. She wants him to return home to her.''

He braced his fists on the table and leaned over her. His face was inches from hers. "You can just go back to Philadelphia and tell this woman you failed. I'm not Harrison, and I've never heard of the man."

"You took the wallet. Read the letter. Look at the photograph. I believe you're one and the same."

"Lady, you don't know what you're talking about." He snatched up his rifle and stalked to the door.

"Where are you going?"

"Hunting."

"You can't hide. You'll have to come back." He was already out the door when she stood and followed him. "The children need you. Sung Lo needs you." He reached the edge of the clearing. "I need you," she whispered, painfully aware of the truth of her words.

For the next three days, Mariah worried and watched. Thorne had been so angry when he left, she wondered if he would return at all. Surely, he wouldn't leave Sung Lo and the children to fend for themselves. Thorne was a man of honor, a man who'd accepted the responsibility of these strays and who wouldn't desert them now.

He was a special man. One a woman could easily love. She scoffed at the thought. Some woman, maybe, not Mariah Rose O'Reilly. His reclusive life wasn't for her. Already, she was lonely for noise and society. Mariah liked people, and was rarely alone. In school she'd gotten her knuckles rapped many a time for talking out of turn.

Having been raised in a boisterous household with Irish parents and lots of friends, this isolation was wearing on her nerves. To relax, she'd taken to teaching the children Irish songs and jigs. Although Juan didn't speak, he danced and did hand gestures to the songs. Sung Lo, too, joined in the activities she'd devised to occupy the children. He was thrilled to learn how to make Irish stew and fluffy biscuits. "For Thorne," he said.

At midmorning the fourth day, Mariah returned from the thermal baths and found Thorne seated on a stump outside the cabin as if he'd never left. Running Deer and Juan sat on his knees, and Sung Lo hovered over him with a plate of biscuits he'd proudly baked.

Thorne glanced up when she approached. Mariah couldn't stop the twinge that settled in her heart and dropped to her stomach. She resisted the urge to run into his arms and welcome him back. A slight smile curved his lips when she approached.

She flipped her long braid over her shoulder. "Well, the prodigal has returned. What did you catch, or is it shoot?"

"A nice ten point buck. I skinned him out and put the venison in the cellar house." He looked her over from head to toe. Her body grew warm under his glance. His eyes turned a deep turbulent gray. "You children run along with Sung Lo," he said. "I have to talk to . . . Sister."

"Call me Mariah," she said with a smile.

The little boy and girl followed Sung Lo into the cabin, always ready to find something to eat. When they were alone, Mariah found a seat on a fallen log. She wondered what decision he'd come to. Would he help her or throw her to the wolves?

"I've been thinking. About the possibility of gold, or a mine, or whatever that map means."

Excitement bubbled up in her. The idea of riches beyond her wildest dreams had kept her awake at night. "Do you mean you'll help me?"

He took a stick and made scratches in the dirt. "I'll make a deal with you."

"What kind of deal?"

"I'll help you on this quest for treasure, and you'll forget you ever saw me."

Mariah chewed the end of her thumbnail and studied the recluse. He'd made his decision not to return to his grandmother. Even the old woman's pleas didn't sway him. The man was

far more cold-hearted than she'd supposed. What reason could
he have to remain in the wilds of New Mexico Territory at the
expense of his family? If she didn't bring him back, she stood
to lose the reward. Not that it mattered. If they located the
treasure, she wouldn't need Mrs. Thornton's money. Mariah
O'Reilly would be wealthy in her own right. Only her reputation
would be tarnished if she failed the mission. She could live
with that.

"Okay, you have a deal. Help me find the treasure, and I'll
return east and say I couldn't locate Michael Harrison." She
leaped to her feet. "When do we get started?"

"Do you ride?"

"No. But I can learn."

"I'll go into Los Amigos tomorrow for supplies. I have a
wagon and horses in a corral at the base of the mountain. We'll
leave the next day."

She grabbed both his hands in hers. Her fingers were swallowed up in his large hands. "Thank you, Thorne."

"Don't thank me yet. We may not find a thing. And don't
forget this won't be any carriage ride in the park. This is wild
country, and the trip won't be easy."

"I know. Nothing's been easy since I left Philadelphia."
She stood on tiptoes and pressed a light kiss on his beard-
covered jaw. "Let me know what I have to do."

"Obey orders. I don't want to wire those Irish parents and
eight siblings that you were killed through your own carelessness."

She stepped back and touched her forehead in a salute. "Yes,
sir. I'll do anything you say." *Within reason,* she added under
her breath.

As Thorne returned to the mountain late the next evening
with the wagon of supplies for their trip, he again questioned
his sanity. How was he going to survive days, maybe weeks,
alone with Mariah?

Every time he touched his jaw, he remembered the pressure of her lips against his skin. Even the thick beard didn't cover the feelings of her warm mouth or what he would like to do with her. He cursed the needs she'd aroused in him. When he thought her a nun, he could use that as an excuse to keep his distance. Now that he knew for sure she was an ordinary—no, extraordinary—woman, he would have to work hard to maintain a strict code of honor with her around. It wouldn't do either of them good to let down his guard and do something foolish with the woman.

He drew the team to a stop near the stable low on the mountain. After purchasing the supplies at the small trading post, he made sure the store owner knew he was going on a journey. He was careful not to reveal where he was going, or how long he would be gone, only that one other person was going with him. Word spread faster than a bullet in the small town, and by now the pair who'd come looking for Mariah had learned about his upcoming trip.

By letting word get out, he was taking a chance on being followed. That was exactly what he wanted. Thorne suspected the pair had half of the map, and they'd killed to get the other half.

After unhitching the horses, he loaded part of the goods on his back for the remainder of the trip up the trail too narrow and dangerous for a horse. Sung Lo had asked for another sack of flour to make the biscuits as Mariah had taught him. The woman certainly had won the old man's heart.

Mariah greeted him at the cabin, the children at her side. It seemed she couldn't take a step without them. Running Deer wore a red ribbon at the end of a single plait, and Juan proudly displayed his growing collection of neckties.

"Did you get what we need?" she asked, the color high in her cheeks. In the few days she'd been with them, her white skin had tanned pale gold and a row of freckles bridged her nose. His heart fluttered every time he looked at her.

"Yes. We can leave at daybreak. I brought shells for that revolver of yours, and more for my rifle."

"Are you expecting trouble?"

"I like being prepared."

Running Deer looked up at Mariah. "Do Sissy go away?" Any fool could see the pain on the child's face.

She dropped to her knees and took both children in her embrace. "For a little while. Thorne and I have to go on a journey. We promise to come back. We'll bring you back a surprise if you obey Sung Lo while we're gone."

Thorne's pulse quickened at the sight of the woman and two homeless orphans. With her large family, she knew all about children and how to care for them. He was at a loss most of the time. It had been years—twelve to be exact—since he'd been in any kind of normal home.

"Let's get ready for bed. I want to get an early start."

Mariah stepped out of the cabin before the first light of dawn. She was dressed in a simple black skirt and a white blouse with a black shawl draped over her shoulders. A remnant of her nun's habit, he supposed. In her hand she carried a small bundle of clothes. He'd already stashed away a change for himself in the wagon. Sung Lo followed at her heels with a tin cup of coffee and biscuits for him.

"Thanks," he muttered, hoping he was doing the right thing. Where this woman was concerned, he was never sure of anything.

"I've already eaten, and Sung Lo wrapped up some biscuits for us to eat on the road."

"Road? Irish, I told you there are no roads where we're going. It's mostly uncharted territory."

"Whatever. I'm ready. I can't wait to find the treasure." She hugged her shawl against the chill morning air.

"Don't get your hopes up. We could come up empty-handed."

"I've got my fingers crossed, and I said a special rosary that we succeed."

"Then we might as well get going." He hunkered down when Running Deer and Juan exited the cabin. Both ran into his arms and hugged him tight. "We'll be back soon. I promise."

"We be good. Bring Sissy back."

He glanced up at Mariah. "I promise I'll come back with Thorne," she said.

Thorne gritted his teeth. Whether their mission was a success or failure, he planned to put Mariah on the first stagecoach headed east. He'd decided to give her a letter for his grandmother, but there was no way she could convince him to return to Philadelphia with her.

At the wagon, he checked and double checked the trail. When they started on their way, he propped his rifle against the seat between them and his shotgun under his feet. They reached the base of the mountain and headed east in the long narrow valley.

Mariah unfolded the map they'd reconstructed. "Thorne, I thought we would be headed north." Her expression was puzzled. "Are you sure you're going the right way?"

He glanced behind them. There was no sign of human life. "I'm going the right way. I spoke to Father Callahan when I was in Los Amigos. He knew a little more about that gold shipment than I did. It seems that there were at least four men responsible. The Army suspected they'd caught two of them, but they denied any knowledge of the shipment. There were other charges against them, so they spent eight years in prison. One of the bandits was killed in prison, and the other was released a few months ago. I think that was the man on the stagecoach."

"The one who gave me the map?"

Nodding, he again glanced to the rear. "I think the killers have the other half and they were looking to get the other part from you."

She shivered and hugged the shawl tighter. By then, the sun

had broken through the shadows in the valley. "Are they still looking for me?"

"For both of us by now. I think they followed me yesterday, and that they'll be following us today. That's why we're going in the wrong direction. I want to make sure they don't catch up with us until I've got a trap ready to spring."

"Isn't this dangerous? Won't they just ride up and shoot us?" Her voice quivered. Thorne knew he was making the biggest mistake of his life in letting this woman involve him in her schemes. It was dangerous for her and foolish for him.

He snapped the reins, and the horses took off at a clip. "That's the reason we're in open range. I don't want to be ambushed in the mountains. I want to choose my own battlefield."

Chapter 6

They kept up a steady pace, not going too fast, nor slow enough to draw suspicion. By midafternoon, Mariah shed her shawl and thanked heaven that Thorne had brought a wide-brimmed straw hat for her from the village. The sun was increasingly hot, with not a hint of a cloud in the clear blue sky. An occasional buzzard circled in the air, and she spotted an assortment of small game. Not much grew in this country. No trees dotted the landscape, and only tumbleweed and sage grew in the hilly terrain. She wished they were back in the greenery of the mountains. When they reached an outcropping of boulders, Thorne pulled to a stop.

"We'll rest here in the shade and water the horses. Grab a bite to eat, and keep your pistol handy," he said to Mariah, then leaped down from the high wagon seat.

Grateful for the chance to stretch her legs, Mariah started to climb down when strong hands circled her waist. In one easy movement, Thorne lifted her to the ground. Her body brushed his, and tingles raced over her skin. His hands lingered for a moment on her waist, then, with a grunt, he released her.

"I'll be back in a few minutes." Abruptly, he spun on his heels and disappeared behind the boulder.

Stunned, Mariah wondered about his brusque behavior. The warmth of his touch lingered, and the flutters in her stomach made her angry with herself. Of all the men to make her feel so alive, so womanly, it had to be this impossibly hostile hermit. She stalked off into a secluded space and took care of her needs as quickly as possible. Then she returned to the shade of the boulder and munched on a biscuit and drank from her canteen.

Moments later, Thorne appeared in front of her. She hadn't heard a footstep, or even the snorts of the horses. "If I were one of the bandits, you'd be dead by now," he sneered. "Where's your gun?"

"Pointed at your belly, Mountain Man," she replied. Pulling her hand from her pocket, she aimed the barrel at him.

"Not fast enough. You didn't know it was me. Next time, quit daydreaming and keep on your toes."

"Should I have shot you to prove you're right?" She stood and shook out her skirt. "You should be thankful I waited to see who was coming up on me." Mariah didn't dare let him know he was right—that she was lost in her musings and didn't hear him approach.

"You'll have to keep alert. We're definitely being followed."

"Are you sure?"

"I climbed that rock and I could see for miles." He gestured with the long spyglass in his hand. "Two men and a packhorse. Could be the pair who came looking for you a couple of days ago."

"What are we going to do? We can't let them follow us to the treasure."

"We still don't know if there is a treasure. If there is one, they might have the other half of the map. We'll just have to convince them to give it to us." He took a shovel and dug at the base of the rock. A tiny pool of water appeared.

"How do you expect to do that?"

He led the team to the small watering hole. "I figured you

could talk them into giving it to you. After all, you convinced me to go on this wild-goose chase with you.''

She tugged on his arm and made him look at her. "Thorne, those men are dangerous. I watched them shoot two men in cold blood. They won't listen to me.''

"Then, Irish, we'll have to do it my way.'' He watched as the horses drank, completely ignoring Mariah.

"What's your way? Do you plan to kill them?'' In spite of the hot sunshine beating down on her, she shivered.

He looked into her eyes. "Only if I must to protect us. I don't like killing.''

"Is that why you were a medic in the war?''

"What makes you say that?''

"The picture, Mountain Man. You never gave it back to me.''

With a grunt, he tugged at the lines of the horses. "I reckon I forgot. Load up. I know a place where we can spend the night. I want to make camp before nightfall.''

Throughout the day, Mariah couldn't help but look over her shoulder. Thorne spoke little, only grunting in answer to her many questions about the landscape, the animals, plants, and other things she saw in the valley.

Somewhere behind them in this vast wilderness were men set upon robbing or possibly killing them. She kept the gun on her lap. Like Thorne, she didn't like killing. However, if it came to her life or theirs, hers would win every time.

With the sun dropping behind the mountains to the west, Thorne pulled the wagon to a small stream lined with several sturdy trees. "We'll camp here. The horses need water and rest, and we can wait for whoever is behind us to catch up.''

Mariah stared at him, her mouth agape. "You want them to catch us?''

"How else are we going to get them to help us find your gold?''

"I thought westerners believed in shooting first and asking questions later.''

''Try it my way this time. And if they start shooting, we'll defend ourselves.''

Mariah jumped down and took her small package to the stream. Quickly, she washed the day's dust and grime from her face and arms. A full bath would have to wait. Thorne loosed the horses and tethered them near the water. Then he made a campfire, and put on a pot of coffee.

''Won't that fire bring them right to us?'' she asked, still concerned about his so-called plan.

''That's right. Think we should ask them to join us for supper?'' He busied himself with a small skillet. ''Hope you like rabbit. I shot it this morning, so it's nice and fresh.''

Her stomach rumbled. ''Yes, I'm starved.''

By the time they sat opposite each other to eat, the sun had completed its journey and purple and gold streaked the sky. Since she'd been west, she'd seen more magnificent sunrises and sunsets than in her entire life in Pennsylvania. Her da often spoke of the blue skies and green hills of his beloved Ireland. Mariah didn't think it could be any more beautiful than the country surrounding her.

''How do you know this territory so well, Mountain Man?'' She took a bite of the roasted rabbit, every bit as good as what her mother made.

''I traveled quite a bit looking for a place of my own.'' He wiped his mouth on a handkerchief he'd pulled from his pocket. The men she'd met since leaving home would just as soon use their sleeves or the back of their hand. This was just another clue to Thorne's refined upbringing.

''Just think, when we recover the gold, and get the reward, you'll be able to buy some land of your own.''

He tossed aside the bones. ''I already own a hundred thousand acres, including my mountain. What would I do with more acreage?''

Mariah choked on a sip of coffee. Was she hearing right? ''You own what?''

''I bought a hundred thousand acres from a man named

Lucien Maxwell. He held the deed to over a million acres from a Spanish grant.''

"A hundred thousand acres. I didn't know anybody could own so much land. I dream about owning a little lot and a grand house, but I never imagined . . . How did you manage? Did you steal a gold shipment?''

His face blanched as if he'd been struck with a rock. "I sold an interest in my gold mine so I could buy the mountain and be alone.''

It all came out so casually, Mariah was dumbfounded. "Now you're telling me you own a gold mine?''

"The Colorado mine is mostly played out now.''

She sat and stared at him. No wonder he was reluctant to go after the treasure, or to return home to his wealthy relatives. He had lots of money of his own. "Next you're going to tell me you found gold or silver on that mountain.''

"And turquoise. I mine enough to buy supplies, but not enough to draw curious prospectors.''

"Is your name King Midas? It seems everything you touch turns to gold.''

"Not quite. Let's get ready for bed. Our visitors should be along shortly.'' Before she questioned him further, he held up his hands to quiet her. "No, we aren't going to sleep. I have a little surprise in mind for both of them.''

Mariah eyed him suspiciously. "What are you going to do?''

"Just trust me, Irish. In a few days, you'll have your gold and I'll have my peace.''

Thorne hoped it would work. Their lives depended on his ability to judge the situation. Mariah agreed that this was their best chance. She only balked when he put the torn pieces of map in his saddlebags in plain sight.

He climbed behind a rock to watch the trail. Mariah hid in the branches of a leafy willow where she could see the campsite and not be seen. He checked her gun to make sure it was loaded. She promised to await his signal before making a sound.

They didn't have long to wait. From his vantage point, he

watched the two riders and packhorse amble in their direction.
The moon gave enough light to recognize the pair as the ones
who'd been following them all day. Several hundred feet away,
they dismounted and drew their weapons. He'd been right not
to trust them. They were up to no good. Honest men would
call for permission to approach the fire.

The strangers glanced around, and moved slowly toward the
fire. When they got close to the bedrolls, they opened fire,
blasting into blankets and hats rolled up to look like bodies.

''That should take care of you and that nun!'' one of the
bandits shouted. ''Now let's look for that map.''

The pair rummaged through Mariah's bag, throwing her skirt
and blouse on the ground. Next they attacked Thorne's saddle-
bag.

''I've found it. Here it is.''

The other man shoved his gun back into his holster. ''We're
rich. In a few days, we'll have that Yankee gold and get out
of this stinking hellhole.''

Tossing another log on the campfire, they each pulled out a
scrap of paper from their pockets. ''I knew Hiram gave the
map to that nun. Now we don't have to share with nobody.''

''Except us.'' Thorne leveled his shotgun at the men. Both
jumped up and reached for their guns. ''Don't try it. I've got
enough buckshot to cut both of you in half. Hold one hand
over your heads and loosen the buckles of those gunbelts.''

They shifted their glances at the bedrolls, which were riddled
with bullets. Thorne doubted they had any cartridges left in their
revolvers, since they didn't reload after their initial rampage.

''Is that any way to treat innocent blankets?'' Mariah said
from the shadows of the trees.

''The nun. You ain't dead.''

She laughed.

Mariah was a rare woman to keep her composure under
pressure, Thorne realized.

''No thanks to you. Just do as the man says, and I won't be
tempted to treat you the way you treated our bedrolls.''

"You're a nun. You won't shoot us."

"I'll just go to confession and do penance. When I give the Church a share of the gold, I'll receive complete absolution." She cocked the hammer of the gun.

Thorne hid his grin. The lady had grit, that was for sure. "Drop them." The strangers obeyed. "Now the map. Put it down on that bedroll—all the pieces."

"It belongs to us," the taller man said.

"Not anymore." Thorne gestured with the shotgun. "You killed two men for that map, and you would have killed us."

"Look, fella, there's enough for all of us. That Yankee chest was full of gold bars. We can share."

Thorne kept his gaze locked on the pair. "Like you shared with Hiram? No, thanks. We'll just keep all of it for ourselves. Now put it down. I might inform you that the lady is a crack shot. She believes in shooting first and asking questions later."

"Never did trust a woman with a gun," the shorter man grunted.

"Sit right down," Thorne ordered. "Take off your boots."

"Our boots?"

"Don't argue. My trigger finger is getting mighty itchy." They sank to the ground and tugged off their boots. The sour odor nearly made him gag. "Sister, get that rope."

Moments later, he had both bandits thrust up like calves ready for the slaughter. "You can't do this to us. That gold shipment is ours."

Thorne hunkered in front of them. "Tell me about it. How many men did you kill to get it?"

"Nobody but a few no-good Yankees."

Fury rushed over Thorne. A stolen Yankee payroll had gotten him court-martialed and sent to a firing squad. It was only a freak turn of events that had saved his life. "What happened?"

"We almost got away, but another troop heard the gunshots and started to chase us. We didn't know the territory, but Mel did. He led us to a hidden canyon. After we hid the gold, we

made a map. Then we tore it into four pieces. We were supposed
to meet up when the coast was clear.''

''Why didn't any of you go back later and recover the gold?''
Mariah asked, her gun never wavering.

''After we left the canyon, we got caught in a storm and
split up. Hiram and Mel got caught, and went to jail. Mel was
the only one who knew the way. Me and Nick looked, but we
couldn't find the canyon without the rest of the map. Mel died
in jail and Hiram got his part. We had to wait till he got out
to put the map together.''

''Why did you kill him?''

''Why not?'' The outlaw twisted and pulled at his bonds.

The cold-blooded attitude chilled Thorne. ''Why shouldn't
we kill you?''

The shorter man wiggled and stared at Mariah. ''Sister, don't
let him kill us. I'm plumb sorry for what I did. If you let me
go, I promise I'll go to church every Sunday. I won't cuss or
chew. You're supposed to help people.''

She looked up from where she was piecing the map together.
''Oh, I won't watch while he shoots you. And I'll see that you
get a decent burial.''

Their faces blanched. ''You can't do that to us.''

''Okay. I won't kill you. I'll leave that to the rattlesnakes
and other varmints out here.'' Thorne tossed the bedrolls and
supplies into the bed of the wagon and added the outlaws'
goods. Mariah led the horses to the stream and let them drink.
Then he hitched up the team and tied the saddle horses and
pack animal to the rear.

''Where are you going?'' the man called Nick asked.

''Going to look for that gold,'' he answered. He'd already
stashed their guns and boots under the wagon seat.

''What about us? Aren't you going to untie us?''

''Thorne, wouldn't it be more humane to shoot them?''
Mariah climbed onto the high seat.

''Yes, but they deserve a fighting chance. You should be
able to get loose in a couple of hours. Then you have a choice.

You can wait here until I send the Army after you or you can start walking back to Los Amigos.''

"Without our boots?"

"Maybe it would be better to wait here. Sometimes a deer or rabbit comes to drink. You'll have lots of water and shade. You should be comfortable until the no-good Yankee soldiers find you."

Thorne climbed aboard the wagon and picked up the lines. A string of curses erupted from both men as they scooted on the ground. "That's no way to talk in front of the lady. And her a nun."

The horses took off at a gallop. He headed the team due west, away from the rising sun. "Don't tell me again, Irish. I know this isn't the right way. I'll head north when we're far enough away so they won't know where we're going."

She shoved the bullet-ridden hat onto her head. "Very clever, Mountain Man. I couldn't have done better myself."

He laughed. "That's quite a compliment coming from you."

"Don't let it go to your head."

"Believe me, I won't."

If Mariah thought her westbound stagecoach ride was uncomfortable, it was pure luxury compared to the wagon that bounced over every rock and rut on the prairie. By early afternoon, pure exhaustion from the ride and lack of sleep made her eyes heavy. She dozed off, and dropped her head on Thorne's wide shoulder. When she awoke, which seemed like only minutes later, he'd placed his arm around her and nestled her close to his side.

"I was afraid you would fall off and I'd run over you," he said, and casually removed his arm.

"I'm sorry. I shouldn't sleep when you can't." Strange, she felt mildly adrift without his touch.

"I'll sleep tonight. You can stay up and keep watch."

She swung around and studied the landscape behind them.

It looked exactly like the scenery in front of them—hills, rocks, boulders, brush. "Do you think we're still being followed?"

"No. I didn't see any signs. But there are still wandering Indians in the territory. I don't want to take any unnecessary chances."

"Indians? Are they hostile?" Her mother's warning echoed in her ears. A warning Mariah had curtly dismissed as silly.

"Some are, others are simply trying to live the only way they know."

"How far do you figure it is to where the gold is hidden?" The sooner they accomplished their mission, the sooner Mariah could return to Philadelphia. Her real problem was trying to convince Thorne to return with her. She'd set out to do a job, and she intended to see it through. A lonely grandmother was depending on her.

"I figure another day and a half, unless we have to take another detour." He snapped the reins, and the horses trotted a little faster. "I think I remember another watering hole up ahead. We'll spend the night there."

Thorne seemed to know every stream and resting place in the area. She didn't know how he managed to find water in the arid land. As far as she could tell, not much grew out here. Only knee-high gamma grass and an occasional cactus broke the monotony.

"Do you ever miss the green meadows, the tall spreading trees, and changing seasons of Pennsylvania?"

He shot a glance at her. "No. The seasons here change. It snows in the mountains, and in the fall the aspens change to bright yellow and orange."

"This land doesn't look as if it will grow anything. I haven't seen any animals and only a few birds all day."

"If you stood still and looked, you'd see a whole menagerie out here. There are foxes, snakes, prairie dogs, rabbits, and a whole assortment of birds. They're probably hiding from us. Not much will grow out here without water, but this is rich grazing land. Sheep and cattle thrive on the grasses. There are several huge ranches to the east of here. Others are starting up every day.''

''Is that what you plan to do with your hundred thousand acres? Build a ranch?'' She still couldn't believe anybody could own so much land.

''No. I plan to retire to my mountain and live in peace. Alone.''

By the finality in his voice, Mariah decided it was best to drop the subject. She still felt an obligation and loyalty to Mrs. Thornton to convince her grandson to return home. At the right time, she would try again.

That night, their camp wasn't along a stream, but in the shelter of a rock that trickled out water into a pool. Thorne made a fire and they ate canned beans and bacon. She was thankful for such a resourceful companion. Alone she wouldn't even know how to get the fire started, much less cook on it.

Mariah offered to take the first watch to allow him time to rest. He assured her it wasn't necessary. There wasn't a human within fifty miles. They would be safe, and the fire would keep away animals. As Thorne spread his bedroll beside the fire, she remembered her encounter with the nest of rattlesnakes when Thorne had found her. She cringed at the thought of another encounter.

''What about snakes?''

''The fire will keep them away, too.'' He stretched out on his blankets. ''But if you're afraid, Irish, come over here,'' he said, patting the ground between his bedroll and the fire.

Mariah didn't hesitate. She spread her blanket on the hard ground and settled with her back to him as close as decency allowed.

As the night grew cold, Mariah snuggled into the warmth beside her. On winter nights, she and Jenny often shared their blankets to ward off the chill Pennsylvania air.

''Jenny, don't hog all the blanket,'' she muttered. The body shifted away, taking its heat with it. ''Lay next to me. I'm cold.'' She rolled over and her arm struck her bedfellow. Strange, when had Jenny, or Maggie, who often crowded into her bed, gotten so large? An arm curled across her and a hand pressed against her stomach. Warm and secure, safe and comfortable, she fell into a sound sleep.

Long before she was ready to relinquish the delicious flutters in her stomach, something disturbed her dreams. Seldom did she dream about a lover. But on this cold night, she'd had the warmest, most delightful, and rather erotic feelings. Her dreams had been filled with images of a man—tall, muscular, and with light brown hair and smoldering gray eyes. He was handsome, and wore a blue Army uniform. The name Michael whispered across her mind.

Not wanting the dream to end, she rolled over and gripped what she supposed was the blanket. Her fingers reached out and touched something much harder and more solid than either of her sisters.

The dream ended, and her eyes slowly crept open. She struggled for a second to savor the delightful feelings. With a soft moan, she blinked against the shimmer of daylight that was slowly working its way across her bed. "It's too early," she groaned.

"Not if you want to locate that treasure."

Her eyes popped open, and she found herself staring into a man's unsmiling face, his gray eyes locked on hers. His arm lay like a heavy weight across her side, and his fingers were drawing tiny circles on her back.

"Thorne." Awareness hit her like a douse of cold water. "What are you doing?"

Thorne's hands stilled. A thousand curses erupted across his mind. What the heck was he thinking of? What was he doing holding this woman so intimately, not to mention the dreams he'd had about her? "Keeping you warm like you asked." Exerting more willpower awake than he'd had while sleeping, he rolled away from her. In one quick movement he was on his unsteady feet. He still reeled from the touch of her soft, feminine body next to his.

Her cheeks turned crimson. "I asked you to keep me warm?"

He took a step away, then glanced over his shoulder. "I surely hope Jenny doesn't look like me." Quickly he strode away, eager to put some distance between himself and the woman who'd invaded his life and now his dreams. They had better find that treasure quick if he was to retain an ounce of his sanity.

Chapter 7

That day, they started climbing higher and higher into the hills. Thorne loved the mountains, but he sensed that Mariah wasn't comfortable with the narrow paths, and ledges that dropped off into deep ravines. That morning, they'd spotted the twin peaks that pointed the way to the hidden canyon, and by afternoon, they'd identified the smoke hole, a long-dormant volcano. Mariah's excitement was contagious, and, by nightfall, Thorne was eagerly anticipating finding the entrance to the canyon. Still, he doubted they would find the gold. After all these years, it could have been recovered and carried away.

They were deep into the mountains, by the time Thorne made camp beside a small stream and again prepared the evening meal. Mariah, being a city girl, knew next to nothing about surviving in the wilds. She was as out of her element as he would be back in Philadelphia. The thought of Philadelphia and the rolling green hills of Pennsylvania brought a pang of homesickness to his chest. Only a truly heartless man could ignore the pleadings of his grandmother's letter. She loved him, and wanted him home. Thorne wished it was as simple as that. But too much stood in his way to enjoying a normal life.

As if she could read his thoughts, Mariah looked up from her plate of bacon and more beans. Personally, he was getting rather tired of their limited diet. He didn't realize he'd miss Sung Lo's cuisine so much.

"What are you going to do after we recover the gold?" she asked.

"Turn it over to the Army like we planned. Fort Union is the closest outpost, so we'll head there, *if* we find the gold."

She set the remains of her dinner aside. "I mean, after that. Have you thought about returning to civilization?"

Actually, he'd thought of little else. "There's nothing for me back there. My home is here."

"What about Mrs. Thornton?"

Heat surfaced to his face. "What about her?"

"She wants you home. When are you going to admit that you're Michael Harrison? You can't keep running forever."

"I can sure as heck try."

She reached out a hand and touched his arm. Her fingers curled around his wrist. "Thorne, come back to Philadelphia with me."

His heart pounded against his ribs. "Hell, Mariah, I can't." He shook off her hand and jumped to his feet. "Don't you think I would have returned to see my grandmother if it was at all possible? I love her. She's the only person in this world who understood when I rebelled against my father and joined the Union Army."

"Your father was a southerner?"

He raked his hands though his long, shaggy hair. "My mother was a Philadelphia debutante, my father an aristocratic Virginia planter. She died shortly after I was born, so I spent most of my childhood with my grandmother in Philadelphia. Of course, when my father remarried, he insisted I return to Rosehaven with him and his new family."

She sipped her coffee and stared at him. "Is that the family plantation?"

"Yes. We raised cotton and slaves. I hated the idea of slavery, but it was a way of life in the South. My brother, Gabriel, was more suited to the life of a planter. I wanted to be a doctor, so I entered medical college, much to my grandmother's delight. My father didn't really care, as long as he had one son to follow in his footsteps. Things were going well, before the war. Suzanna, my fiancée, didn't want me to be a doctor, but she didn't object too strenuously. We were to be married as soon as I finished my studies."

She stumbled on her words. "What happened to her?"

"Suzanna was a true southern belle. She loved the lifestyle that slavery supported. She didn't understand my decision to fight for the Union and not for Virginia. I hadn't been gone a month when she married my brother, Gabriel." He stared into the fire, trying to make sense of a situation he still didn't fully understand.

"Your father fought for the Confederacy?"

"He was a staunch secessionist, and he and Gabe fought for their glorious cause. I believed that the Union should be preserved, so I joined on the side of the North as a medic. I couldn't bring myself to raise arms against my fellow southerners."

"That happened in any number of families. Surely there can be forgiveness after all this time. Your grandmother needs you."

Thorne dropped back to the log he'd been using as a seat. "It isn't that easy." His gaze shifted to the woman watching intently on the other side of the fire. Sparks flew upward, and he felt as if they could singe his very soul. This was the first time he'd told his story, the first time he felt compelled to share his heartache and misery. Even his grandmother didn't know the full story of why he'd run away. The kindness in Mariah's blue eyes urged him to continue. "I'm a deserter—a fugitive."

He could see her struggle not to act shocked. "What happened?"

"I was serving under a doctor in northern Virginia. We were moving farther north, with a troop guarding a payroll wagon.

The Rebels ambushed us, outnumbering us two to one. I was tending a downed soldier, when I saw one of the Rebel officers darting toward me with his bayonet.'' He swallowed hard. Nobody would believe what happened next. Certainly, his commander hadn't. ''The lieutenant was my brother, Gabriel. I stood and stared at him, too shocked to react. I yelled his name, but there was fire in his eyes.'' How could he tell Mariah that what he'd truly seen was pure, unmitigated hatred? ''He didn't stop until he reached me. I had a gun at my side, but my hand refused to reach for it. Gabe didn't feel the same. He jabbed at me with the bayonet. I sidestepped, and it caught me in the shoulder.''

''He stabbed you?''

He nodded. ''He lunged at me again, and this time, I knew he was going to finish me off. I jabbed my good shoulder into his stomach, and caught him off balance. He tumbled to the ground. I heard a voice behind me order me to take out my pistol and shoot him. I couldn't. I couldn't kill my brother, my own flesh and blood. I think I must have been in shock. There was nothing but confusion all around. I turned and ran. Next thing I knew, Gabe had gotten away with the payroll, and I was under arrest for treason and cowardice in the face of battle.''

Mariah moved so quickly, he hadn't even noticed until she was standing directly behind him. Her hands rested lightly on his shoulders. ''They arrested you because you couldn't kill your own brother?''

''That's the military way. War is hell, Irish. It doesn't matter who you are or who the enemy is. It's either kill or be killed.''

Her touch was warm and comforting. The first bit of comfort he'd felt since that fateful day nearly ten years ago. ''Did you go to prison?''

He let out a bark of bitter laughter. ''Prison was too good for me, so they said. I was court-martialed and sentenced to the firing squad. They'd scheduled the execution for the next morning. Before they could carry out the sentence, the Rebels attacked again. In the confusion of battle, I managed to escape.

In spite of the wound in my shoulder, I started running. I didn't stop until I reached Philadelphia, where I secretly contacted my grandmother. She helped me escape, and gave me enough money to make my way west.''

"What happened to your father?"

"I heard he was killed at Shiloh, so I suppose that Gabe is running the plantation." He hated the hardness in his voice. Lord help him, but he'd never had the chance to reconcile with his father.

Her body pressed against his back. He hadn't been this close to a woman in years, at least not a decent woman. The whores he'd bought on occasion were a sorry comparison to a warm, respectable woman like Mariah. Her fingers tangled in the hair at his nape. "Surely, after all this time, it's forgotten. Or you can explain the reason you couldn't fight that day."

"The military has a long memory. As much as I want to see my grandmother, I can't take the chance of being arrested, or worse." He lifted his gaze to the heavens, where the stars glittered like diamonds on a sea of velvet. He gave thanks every time he looked up, thankful to be alive to enjoy the beauty of nature.

"I think I understand," she said, her voice as soft as the whisper of a shooting star. She brushed her fingers along his neck, and gently squeezed his shoulders. Without even considering his action, he tilted his head and placed a brief kiss on the top of her hand.

"If you understand, then go back to Philadelphia and forget you ever met a man named Thorne."

"I can't do that. I owe your grandmother the truth."

He sighed. Her touch was doing strange things to his body, putting unseemly thoughts into his head. Best to get away before he did something they would both regret. "And I owe her my life." Standing, he shook off Mariah's hands. She staggered backward for a moment, caught off balance. He reached out and grabbed her arms to steady her. She stumbled into his chest. Her face lifted to his.

In the pale moonlight, her eyes reflected the stars in the heavens. Deep blue, like the vast heights of the sky, her eyes invited a man to drown in their glory. Momentarily lost in her gaze, he bent his head to hers. Their lips touched in the briefest of kisses. Her breath came in short gasps, her fingers twisted in his shirt. He should stop before it went any further, before he started desiring her with all the pent-up passion of his soul. Passion that had lain dormant for far too many years.

"Thorne." She whispered his name against his lips. He breathed in the fragrance of woman. His body reacted in kind. Wild, riotous needs surged through him. His blood turned to fire.

She pressed her breasts into his chest, scorching his flesh where the hardened tips met the solid wall of muscle. She opened her mouth for his kiss. The woman was his for the taking, his for tonight. In the darkness her needs were as easy to read as his own. There was no doubt that she wanted him, and would offer no protest if he laid her down on the ground and they gained comfort in each other.

The temptation was there, as real as the desire in her eyes. As real as the tightening in his groin. He felt as if he'd reached the end of a precipice and had to make a choice. Take a step forward or back. Either way, he was doomed. To take her meant accepting responsibilities he didn't want or need. To deny both of them was like burning in a hell of his own making.

Hell won. Thorne exercised every bit of his hard-earned self-control and shoved her away. He spun on his heel, leaving her stunned in his wake. Before he lost his nerve, he picked up his rifle and headed into the darkness.

"Where are you going?" Her words were tight, as if whispered with great pain.

"Hunting."

"For what? You won't find anything out here."

"I have to find myself."

* * *

Mariah huddled in front of the fire, watching the wood slowly burn down to ashes. Her tears had long ago dried, leaving in their place plain old anger. She'd felt the softening in Thorne when he'd told his story. He was a man who would love deeply and passionately. That much was evident when he spoke of his grandmother. Her heart had melted at the pain in his voice. Then, when he'd held her in his arms, that same heart had fluttered with emotion more akin to love than sympathy.

"Love." She spit out the word as if it were a bug that had gotten into her mouth. How could she love a man who obviously didn't want to love or be loved? At least not by Mariah Rose O'Reilly, daughter of Irish immigrants. In spite of the way he dressed, or how he lived, Michael Harrison was from one of the finest, most aristocratic families on the East Coast.

Once before, she'd been taken in by such a man. When she'd finished school, she was employed as a maid in the household of a wealthy attorney. Mariah hated housework, but she took the only position available to an Irish girl to help her family.

The younger Mr. Willard Shepherd, Esquire, assumed that Mariah had been hired as his personal playmate. He'd courted her as if she were something special, going so far as giving her flowers and candy. Later, she learned he'd taken the gifts from his mother in order to curry Mariah's favors. They sneaked kisses under the staircase, and he promised her the moon. He told her she was beautiful, and that he couldn't live without her. Mariah was so young and naive, she believed his lies. His love disappeared when Mariah demanded marriage as a condition to sharing his bed. He laughed and sneered in her face. An Irish tart would never be a proper wife for a Philadelphia gentleman. In a single day, she'd lost her job and her reputation. And set her mind on never being taken for a fool again.

Now, here she was, moping over another man who could never love her. Thorne was no different. She didn't need his love or his kisses or his caresses. She wanted the gold. The treasure. The reward. And the bonus for bringing the impossible recluse back to Philadelphia.

At the sound in the brush behind her, she jumped. Her heart leaped, a stone settled in the pit of her stomach. She picked up her gun and pointed it in the direction of the noise. Since Thorne had stalked off into the night, she started at every flutter of the leaves, at every creak of the branches, at each distant coyote howl. The hair on the back of her neck prickled. Could there be somebody or something watching her from the shadows? Where was Thorne when she needed his reassurance? If it was he skulking in the shadows, he had no right to frighten her like this.

Without trying to draw attention to herself, Mariah tossed a thick piece of dry wood onto the fire. It caught immediately, and flared up, throwing eerie shadows on the trees and shrubs. In one quick movement, she stood and eased back into the shelter of the trees, hiding among the thick trunks. The fire would either draw the nocturnal visitor or chase it away. Mariah held the pistol at ready in either event.

The fire settled into a low blaze, warming the night and giving off light. Mariah continued her vigil. Moments later, she spotted her quarry. Something on four legs crept toward the fire. She readied to shoot. It was large, and looked like a wolf. As the figure crawled into the dim light, she held her breath preparing to fire. As she started to squeeze the trigger, she stopped. Cold sweat beaded on her forehead. It was no animal.

It was human.

Still on hands and knees, he stopped and glanced around. Then he reached out and snatched a chunk of bacon she'd discarded from her plate. Long black hair hung into dark eyes with the hungry glare of a hunted animal. The strip of meat disappeared, and he scooped up a handful of beans and shoved them into his mouth.

From her hiding place, she had a clear view of the figure,

more boy than man. When she heard no sound from beyond the clearing, she supposed he was alone—alone and starving. Without leaving her hiding place, she cocked the hammer of the gun. The click vibrated like the roar of thunder.

She deepened her voice to sound masculine. "Stay where you are. I have a gun and I know how to shoot."

His head popped up and he looked about to dart away. She fired one shot into the air. "I said, stop. I won't hurt you unless I have to."

Fear glittered in the dark eyes. He raised both dirty hands over his head in a sign of surrender.

"Who are you? What do you want?" she asked.

From his defiant stance, she wondered if he was going to answer. After several long, tense moments, he answered, "Food."

She slipped from her hiding place and faced him. He was Indian, young, about Maggie's fifteen years, and horribly thin, as if he'd been starved.

"Sit down," she ordered. "There're beans in the pot, and coffee if you want it."

He dropped to the ground and sat cross-legged. Again, he scooped out handfuls of beans into his mouth as if he couldn't get enough to eat or eat it fast enough. When the pot was empty, his hollow eyes lifted to Mariah. "You woman."

"Yes, I'm a woman. And my man is nearby, so don't try anything."

Careful to keep her eye on him, she reached into the sack of supplies they'd taken from the robbers. "Here." She tossed a chunk of sourdough to the young man.

He tore into the bread and seemed to swallow without chewing. His dark eyes never left Mariah's face, and her gaze never strayed from his.

"Who are you?" she asked when he finally paused for breath.

Resuming eating, he ignored her question.

"Answer." Thorne's harsh voice startled her so, she nearly dropped her gun. Intent on watching the Indian, she hadn't seen nor heard him approach. The big man moved into the circle of light, his rifle in hand.

"Tongo."

"Cheyenne?"

"Apache."

"You're a long way from your hunting grounds."

His eyes lit like fire—blazing with hatred. "Soldiers take hunting grounds. My people have no buffalo to hunt, no land."

Thorne nodded in understanding. Of a truth, she supposed he did. He, too, was a man without a home, without a country.

"Thorne, you scared the life out of me," she whispered when she was able to catch her breath. "Where were you?"

"Upstream. I heard gunfire and I came running. I was afraid something had happened to you." He shot a glance at her. Emotion glinted in his eyes.

"You were afraid for me?" she asked, her heartbeat picking up speed.

"I promised to protect you, Irish, and I aim to keep that promise."

Was that all she meant to him? An obligation, a burden he couldn't put down? "Well, I'm fine, just grand. What are we going to do with him?"

"Damn if I know." He hunkered down opposite Tongo near the fire. "Had enough to eat?"

The youth shrugged.

"Where's your tribe?" Thorne's voice lost its harshness.

"East. I look for game to feed women and children." A long bow and quiver of arrows hung down his back.

Mariah's heart twisted. If he was starving, she couldn't imagine the deprivation of his family. Too well she remembered the horror stories her parents had told about the potato famine in Ireland, how so many family and friends had died of starvation and disease.

"I spotted some game. Tomorrow I'll help you hunt. Then you can bring back meat to your tribe."

The youngster's eyes widened. "White man help Indian?"

"Man helps man."

She wanted to throw her arms around Thorne's neck and tell him how proud he'd made her. He truly was a man of conscience, a man of honor. A man worthy of love.

"Thorne, we have the supplies from the outlaws. It's more than we need. Can't we give some to him?"

Thorne nodded. "We'll share what we have."

Chapter 8

Mariah remained at camp while Thorne and the young Indian hunted game. They'd left before sunrise in order not to waste the day. Not fully trusting the stranger, Thorne had taken the precaution of tying him up so they could sleep securely. "No use tempting fate," he'd said as he stretched out beside the fire. When she'd hesitated with her blanket in her hands, he signaled her to lie beside him as she had the night before. "We don't want him to slit our throats and take all our supplies."

She agreed he was right. A desperate man would take desperate measures to provide for his own.

But wouldn't the twins think this was a grand adventure? She would be sure to tell them about the wild Indian who'd invaded their camp. In fact, she might decide to write her own dime novel about her trek through the wilderness—meeting a mountain man, running from outlaws. and capturing an Indian brave. And all this was before she located the hidden treasure. Wouldn't it make a glorious story?

According to Thorne's estimation, they were only a half day's ride from the entrance to the canyon. She hoped to locate the missing gold before nightfall.

Thorne had done the right thing in helping the young man find game for his people. He was pitifully thin, and she doubted he would survive the winter unless something was done to help him. She'd heard stories of how the government was trying to relocate the natives to reservations, and how many of them refused to leave their homelands. Some had deserted the reservations and become fugitives hunted by the soldiers.

Indignation lodged in her heart. She understood only too well their dilemma. Since childhood, she'd heard tell how the Irish were treated by the English—oppressed, mistreated, and forced from their homes by soldiers acting on behalf of absentee landlords. Her sympathies lay with the Indians.

From time to time, she heard the crack of the rifle echoing in the distance. Sound carried for miles in the clear, thin mountain air. She heated more of the canned beans, fried some bacon, and did her best to make coffee according to Thorne's instructions. The meal was ready for the hunters when they returned.

She took advantage of the time alone to wash in the stream. Not sure how safe she was, Mariah kept her gaze on the area, and managed to wash her extremities. Although the cool water invited a full bath, she dared not let down her guard. Still, she felt clean and refreshed, and even managed to rinse out her blouse and laid it out to dry in the sunshine.

Thorne and the Indian had taken the saddle horses and the packhorse. The previous night, he'd tethered the wagon team where they could reach the water and eat the grass. That left little for her to do. She climbed a boulder and studied the surrounding landscape. For miles, all she saw were mountain peaks, white with snow, deep valleys, and stand after stand of trees. Wildflowers danced in the meadow breezes, and she spotted an eagle soaring into the heavens.

What a glorious day. A grand day to find the gold.

The morning sun had crested the mountain when she heard the sounds of approaching riders. To be on the safe side, Mariah hid among the trees until she recognized Thorne's voice as he called out her name.

As she returned to the campsite, she was surprised at the amount of game they'd killed in such a short time. A litter trailed behind the packhorse filled with freshly cleaned meat. They'd fashioned two long poles, and slung deerskin between them as a carrier.

"Hope you figured how to fix something to eat," Thorne said as he dismounted. "All we had this morning were berries and roots."

Mariah gestured to the meal heating on the fire. "Beans, bacon, and biscuits aren't much better. I would surely enjoy one of Sung Lo's strange dishes about now."

Thorne glanced at the makeshift meal. "Reckon I would, too." He signaled the young Indian to the fire. "Come on, Tongo, there's plenty."

The young man didn't hesitate. He quickly devoured the food on his tin dish, then looked up as if asking permission for more. Mariah hurried to refill his plate.

"Looks like the hunting expedition was very successful," she said to break the silence as the pair ate.

Tongo looked up from his food. "Thorne mighty hunter. He find game in forest that Tongo not see."

"You're quite a shot with that bow." He turned to Mariah. "Tongo brought down a ten point buck. That's his hide we used to fashion the litter. I'll give him the packhorse and some of our supplies for his tribe."

"Good. We can get more when we reach the fort."

At the mention of the fort, Tongo jumped and scooted back. "You go tell soldiers."

"No," Thorne reassured him. "We go to the fort on business. We promise not to tell the military about you or your tribe. I understand that you don't want to live on the reservation. However, times are changing. The white man is killing the buffalo, and soon the Indian will have to adjust to changes."

The youth jumped to his feet, his hands clenched into fists.

"No. This our land. We fight. Geronimo run white man from our land. Tongo join fight."

Mariah's blood chilled. The anger in his eyes was justified, but she knew the Indian had little chance against the Army's guns and manpower. "You're sure to get yourself killed." Thorne spoke what was on Mariah's mind. "The white man is looking for land, and there's little you can do to stop him. I agree it's wrong, and I wish they would stay in the East. I'm afraid that isn't going to happen. New Mexico is already filling up with large cattle and sheep ranches."

"Apache need land, too. We hunt buffalo for food. White man kill for hides."

Thorne shrugged. "White man is greedy. I don't think you'll be able to stop him."

"We fight, or we die."

Mariah huddled in her shawl. Her heart went out to the young man. Her own parents had been forced to leave Ireland because of famine and disease. The Indian was being forced from his homeland by greed and seekers of wealth. Yet, she couldn't blame the settlers, either, many of whom moved west to provide a better life for themselves and their families—just as her parents had done. If only the two cultures could live together in peace and harmony. She shivered. Mariah knew only too well about prejudice and bigotry. She'd seen for herself the signs on some businesses: "Irish need not apply."

With a shake of his head, Thorne stood. "I wish we could all live together as brothers." He stretched out a hand to the young man. "Take the game to your people."

After a moment's hesitation, Tongo accepted the offered gesture of friendship. "Thorne good man." Then he glanced at Mariah. "Thorne's woman good cooker."

Her gaze locked with Thorne's. His woman? The words lingered and echoed between them. Heat sparked in his eyes for a brief instant before the usual chill returned.

"Thank you" was all she managed to say.

Thorne strolled to the wagon bed and filled a sack with cans and pouches of supplies. "Take this. It isn't much, but it will keep your people from starving."

The young man nodded. "I give to women and children." He slung the sack across the packhorse.

"Take care of yourself," she said as Tongo jumped on the horse's back.

"Wait," Thorne said. He dug into his pockets and pulled out a handful of gold coins. "Use these to buy supplies for your family. Go to the mission at Los Amigos and Father Callahan will help you. He's a good man, and he'll see that you aren't cheated."

Tongo looked at the coins for a long moment. "I not take white man's gold."

Thorne shoved the coins into the bag with the food. "You can buy blankets to keep your people warm, and food to fill their stomachs. Don't buy guns, they will only get you killed."

The young man didn't answer. He kicked his heels into the horse's withers and rode off. When he reached the edge of the clearing, he glanced over his shoulder and lifted a hand in good-bye. He rode into the trees, and disappeared from sight.

Mariah's heart went out to the youth. "Do you think he'll heed your advice?"

Moving closer to her side, Thorne's arm brushed hers. "I hope so. But I doubt he will. His people are angry at the way the government has treated them. I don't blame them for wanting to fight. I suppose I'd do the same thing if my home were threatened."

She slanted a glance at him. "Isn't that what the southerners thought at the outbreak of the War Between the States. What did they call it? The War of the Northern Invasion?"

Thorne jerked away from her as if she'd touched a sore spot. "That was different. We were one country, not like Ireland and England. The Union needed to be preserved. If we were split into two weak countries, we would have been ripe for European invasion. Americans would be no better off than your Irishmen are today."

"You're right." Not wanting to argue further, Mariah bent to scrape out the leavings of their meal into the fire.

He took the skillet from her fingers. "Are you ready to look for that gold?" The look in his eyes softened. "If we find it, Miss Mariah Rose O'Reilly will be one of the richest women in Philadelphia."

She flashed a smile his way. "Won't that be just grand? I could surely do with a few new gowns." She stuck out her foot with the dusty boot, scuffed and worn from travel. "Not to mention some fine dancing slippers."

"Do you like to dance, Irish?"

"We all dance and sing. Even Joseph who has two left feet tries to dance, and Francis who can't carry a tune in a bucket loves to sing."

"Are all your sisters Irish beauties?"

Smiling, she dunked the tin pans into a bucket of water. "Jenny has the most glorious red hair and green eyes. Maggie's smile will light up a cloudy day, and Annie looks exactly like our mother—the prettiest woman in all of Philadelphia, according to Da. Maureen is only twelve, but she'll surely be the most magnificent of us all."

"It's a good thing your father's a police officer to help keep the rowdy young men at bay." Thorne kicked dirt on the fire to put it out.

She laughed. "He's tried awfully hard. But Annie married Jamie Collins and they have a baby. Molly is the next generation of Irish beauties." She halted in scrubbing the plates and looked up. "If, I mean *when,* I get the reward for locating the gold, I'll give my sisters the finest weddings Philadelphia has ever seen."

Thorne stashed the skillet in the bed of the wagon. "What about you? Don't you want the finest wedding Philadelphia has ever seen for yourself?"

Mariah dried her hands on her skirt. Marriage held little appeal for her. "No. I'll be independently wealthy and I'll have my choice of suitors. I may decide to simply take on lovers and leave marriage to my sisters.''

He stared at her as if she'd grown two heads. ''What, a good Irish Catholic girl talking about love outside the banns of matrimony? Don't you want children?''

She lifted her skirt and strutted toward him. ''If I marry, my husband had better be wealthier than me, or else I'd think he was marrying me for my money. He'll have to give me a grand house, and, in return, I may be willing to give him a child. One child.''

''Before you spend all that money, we'd better see if we can locate that stolen gold.'' He offered her a hand up into the wagon. His touch was firm, his hand warm. ''We'll go as far as we can by wagon, then you might have to get a quick riding lesson.''

''I can do it. And I won't fall off like my clumsy brother.''

Thorne laughed, one of the few times since she'd met him. ''It's a good thing he did. If he'd have come snooping on my mountain, I might have been tempted to shoot him.''

Mariah punched his arm. ''Then I would have had to shoot you. And I would never be this close to—''

''Being an independently wealthy woman,'' he finished for her.

The deeper they went into the mountains, the rougher the terrain became. More and more, Thorne regretted becoming involved in Mariah's scheme. He doubted they would find the gold. Even with all of the map, it was still a wild-goose chase. For Mariah's sake, however, he hoped he was wrong. That they would recover the gold and she would get the reward. And maybe his conscience would be salved and he would feel a bit of redemption over the payroll Gabriel had stolen during the war.

He slanted a glance at Mariah. She clutched the map pieces

in her fingers, clinging to them as if they were a lifeline. To her, they were. To him, they just might be his destruction.

With a steep incline ahead, Thorne tugged the team to a halt. "This is as far as we can go with the wagon. From here on, it's either horseback or foot."

She looked around her, the wheels of the wagon perched close to the precipice. Her face turned pasty. "I suppose we'd better get off before this thing tumbles over the mountainside."

"I'd hoped to go farther. The closer we get with the wagon, the less we'll have to carry your gold, if we find it."

"You're an awful cynic. I firmly believe that this is the end of my rainbow and I'll find my pot of gold."

"You Irish are sure a superstitious lot." Thorne leaped down and gestured her to follow from the same side. She set her hands on his shoulders, and he caught her waist to lift her down. Her breasts brushed his chest and heat shot through him. He hesitated a second when her feet touched the ground. Her fingers clutched his shoulders. Their gazes met and held. One look into those blue eyes sent his senses swimming.

Mariah was everything a man would want in a woman. She was smart, clever, resourceful, and kind-hearted. And beautiful to boot. His heart raced every time she came near him, and his body reacted like a man starved too long. She was everything he'd missed in his self-imposed exile, and exactly what he didn't need to complicate his life. He shook his head to ward off the thoughts that could lead only to disaster. Abruptly, he set her away from him. He backed away as if being near her had scorched his soul.

"Thorne?" She stumbled and caught herself on the side of the wagon. "Is something wrong?"

"We'd best be going if we're going to find that hidden canyon before nightfall."

Cursing his own inability to deal with the woman, he caught the halter of the team and led them toward a small stream. "They'll have water and grass here. We shouldn't be gone more than a day." Another day in which he'd be alone with the woman who was rapidly getting under his skin. Or another day closer to the time she would be on her way back to Philadelphia. Alone.

He ignored the twinge in his heart at the thought of her leaving. Of her returning to a full, happy life. Of him being alone again. Kneeling at the edge of the water, he splashed cold water on his face. Alone—that was exactly the way he wanted it. As soon as he made arrangements for the children and Sung Lo, he would slip away so deep into the hills that even a mountain goat wouldn't find him. He would be alone to perform his experiments, to develop the medicines he'd been studying since coming to New Mexico.

Dry pine needles crunched under Mariah's footsteps as she approached his back. He didn't bother looking up. "That water looks tempting. I wish we had time to bathe."

His stomach clenched. Memories of the day when he'd found her soaking in the hot pool sprang to mind. Thinking she was a nun had cooled his ardor, but he remembered the way her breasts pressed against the damp camisole and the way she'd felt in his arms when they'd wrestled over the packet. In the past weeks, his resolve to stay away from her had slipped a little at a time. He doubted he could be strong enough not to join her in the water or make love to her. That would never happen. He dunked his head into the stream, then shook his hair and beard like a dog. It hadn't cooled him off a bit.

"I suppose I'll have to settle for a few drops. I am eager to locate our treasure." Mariah knelt beside him and dipped a handkerchief into the water.

His gaze followed her movement. She wrung out the cloth, then proceeded to wipe her face and neck. The top buttons of her blouse were open, and drops of water rolled down from her shoulders into the valley between those full, and much too tempting breasts. He bit back a groan to keep from lapping away the drops with his tongue.

Shocked at his errant musings, Thorne sprang to his feet and darted into the bushes. He dug his fingers into the bark of an

aspen and rested his head against his forearm to control his
runaway desires. Mariah trusted him to guide her, and to protect
her. She hadn't known she would need protection from him.

"Thorne?" she called.

"Meet me at the wagon." *As soon as I can trust myself
around you.*

He heard the sound of her tramping into the bushes in the
opposite direction. By the time he supposed she'd returned to
the wagon, he'd gotten his breathing under control and had
gained a bit of relief.

"Ready?" she asked, as he moved past the horses into her
line of vision.

"I'll fill the canteens, and pack some food, then we can be
on our way."

The sun was dropping rapidly in the sky by the time they
were ready to venture on horseback. "Are you sure you're up
to this?" he asked.

Mariah eyed the horses suspiciously, but she nodded her
assent. "Ready as I'll ever be."

"We can wait until morning, and get a fresh start."

"No. I want to find that gold as soon as possible." She
glanced over her shoulder. "You never know when we might
encounter more outlaws or Indians."

"Okay. The quicker we get this over, the sooner we can get
back home."

She paused for a moment with her hand on the horse's saddle.
"Where's home for you, Thorne? Have you decided to return
to your grandmother in Philadelphia?"

He gestured to the mountain. "This is my home, Irish. I
can't go back."

Disappointment crossed her face. "I wish you'd change your
mind. Mrs. Thornton needs her grandson."

Thorne tugged his battered hat lower on his eyes. "That man
died during the war. All that's left is a shell."

She clutched his arm with her fingers. "That isn't true.

You're a good man, Thorne. She would be proud of you. Of everything you've done to help others."

His gaze dropped to her hands, encased in the kid gloves now worn and dirty from the road. Lord, he wanted to believe her. To return home and resume a normal life without fear of reprisal. But that wasn't to be. Michael Harrison was a fugitive, and he always would be hunted by the Army for desertion.

"Are we going to stand around here gabbing all day? It will soon be dark. Do you want to locate that gold or not?"

"Can you give a hand up? This horse is awfully tall."

He leaned down and linked his fingers. "Put your left foot here and I'll give you a boost up. Then swing your other leg over the saddle."

She looked at him, then at the horse, as if trying to come to a decision. Just when he thought she was going to change her mind, she set her foot into his grip. In one easy shove, he lifted her high enough to mount the horse. Thorne chose to ignore the goodly amount of slender leg that showed as he adjusted the stirrups and slipped her feet into them.

"How's that?" he asked, not daring to look at her. Only minutes earlier he'd won the battle to get his lust under control. He could easily lose the war over a comely turn of ankle.

"It's awfully high. If I fall off, just bury me here. I couldn't bear to return home and have my brothers gloat over me."

"You won't fall off. Keep your feet in the stirrups and hold on to the reins." The horse shied, and Mariah clutched the pommel. Thorne caught the halter and brought the horse to a standstill. "Whoa, boy. Be good for the pretty lady." He handed her the reins, not sure he was doing the right thing. "Mariah, do you want to wait here for me? I can go faster alone, and if I find anything, I promise to bring it back to you."

"No. I've come this far and I won't stay behind. Besides, you might need my help in finding that canyon." By the set of her jaw, he knew it was useless to argue with her.

He mounted the other horse they'd taken from the outlaws.

"I'll lead the way. Stay close behind. Trust the horse to know his steps. If the going gets too bad, we can continue on foot."

Certain he was making the biggest mistake of his life, Thorne nudged his horse onto what was barely a goat path, and continued up the mountain.

Mariah wanted to close her eyes, but even that frightened her. With one hand she gripped the reins, and the other she clutched around the saddle horn. Within a few minutes, her legs felt stretched out of place, and her backside ached from bouncing on the swaying animal. Silently she prayed to every saint she'd ever heard of for a safe journey. If hell was anything like riding a horse, she hoped she wouldn't go there.

Thorne rode easily, clearly at home in the saddle. Of course he was; he'd probably ridden before he could walk. Weren't all southern gentlemen known for their horsemanship? And didn't the gentry in Philadelphia ride in the park just for pleasure? Women as well as men. Of course, the ladies rode side-saddle, not in this outrageous manner with their limbs exposed for all the world to see.

Still, she'd insisted on going on this jaunt. Thorne had warned her it was no picnic, that they would face danger and discomfort. She lifted off her bottom hoping for relief. All that did was make her legs ache and stretch even more. She bit her lip to keep from begging Thorne to stop. Never would Mariah Rose O'Reilly cry "uncle" or admit defeat.

"We'll ride a little farther then we'll have to walk. Think you're up to it?" Thorne shot a glance over his shoulder.

Mariah settled in the saddle, and smiled back at him. "I'm doing fine. I haven't come close to falling off." She didn't mention she'd been tempted to jump off and take her chances on foot.

A few minutes later, Thorne stopped. "This is as far as we can go. If we can't find the entrance to that hidden canyon by nightfall, we'll make camp here. Then look again in the morning.''

Disappointment flooded Mariah. ''I thought for sure we would find the gold today.''

He vaulted from his horse and stepped back to help her down. ''There's still a couple of hours of daylight left. Who knows, we might get lucky.'' He reached out his hands. ''Need help?''

''No, thank you,'' she said with more bravado than she felt. She kicked her foot free and tried to execute the same movement as Thorne. Only her leg refused to clear the back of the horse. And the horse refused to stay in one spot. He shifted from foot to foot, causing her to hold on for dear life. ''I think I'm stuck.''

Hidden behind his beard a small grin curved his lips. He grabbed the reins and steadied the horse. The animal stood statue still. ''Kick your feet free, and I'll get you off.'' Wrapping one arm around her waist, he easily plucked her from the saddle.

Thankful to be on solid ground, she stretched out her legs, only to find they refused to support her. Thorne caught her before she crumpled to the ground. ''I can't stand up,'' she moaned.

''You'll be okay in a few minutes.''

She splayed her hands against his chest for support. ''And they tell me people ride for pleasure.''

He laughed softly. ''Irish, you're a brave colleen. Not many women would take on this escapade. For your sake, I hope we find your treasure.''

Looking up into his eyes, she saw something new in the gray depths. Warmth replaced his usual steely expression. Respect, concern, and even a bit of affection glittered behind his bushy eyebrows. He lowered his head, and for a moment she thought he was going to kiss her. His arm had remained around her waist and his fingers tugged her closer. Heat from his gaze sizzled through her. Surprising herself, she reached on tiptoe to accept his offer. That never came.

"Think you can stand on your own?" he asked. Thorne set her away and caught her elbow in a polite, impersonal manner.

A chill of loneliness washed over Mariah. She'd been a fool to imagine he wanted to kiss her. All he really wanted was to locate the gold and get rid of her as soon as possible. She straightened her legs and strengthened her resolve to complete the job she'd been assigned. Like it or not, he was returning to Philadelphia with her.

"I think so." She pulled her pride around her like a cloak. No use letting girlish daydreams get in the way of reaching her goal. She took a couple of tentative steps and found she could really walk, although with some difficulty. Not wanting him to know how badly her backside and thighs ached, she reached for her canteen. "Let's not waste any more time. Let's find that gold."

Thorne again wore his mask of indifference. He took a shovel and sack of supplies from the back of his horse. "We'll set up camp for the night wherever we find water."

After he tethered the horses to a low bush where they could graze on the grass growing through the rocks, he filled his battered hat with water from his canteen and offered it to the animals.

Mariah looked up at the solid wall of the mountain in front of her. How anybody ever found their way in this country was beyond understanding. On all sides, she saw nothing but rocks and low scrub trees. The outlaws had made their way to this hiding place while being chased by a troop of soldiers. A mesa in the distance pointed the way to this spot. From there, she also noted the twin peaks from the map. Yet, to her, every other mountain looked the same. Every boulder looked exactly like the other. Thorne seemed confident that this was the right direction.

Once the animals were secure, Thorne joined her. Without speaking, he led the way along the sheer face of the mountain. Mariah followed in his path, the going not as rough as she'd expected.

The sun was dropping behind the hills, leaving them bathed in shadows. Mariah shivered at the loneliness and desolation of the place. Give her a big city any day. Thorne led her into several shallow caves formed by the overhanging cliffs. Nothing was there.

While Thorne checked out still another indent in the mountain wall, she shoved aside some bushes, needing a moment's privacy for nature's call. She slipped into a narrow crevice and took a few steps. She could barely see the sky above the slender opening. Expecting a dead end, she was shocked when she turned a corner and the opening grew wider. Taking a few more tentative steps, she found herself facing a narrow canyon. Below the craggy cliffs, a small stream twisted and curved like an angry snake.

She'd found their hidden canyon.

And her ticket to wealth and happiness.

Chapter 9

Thorne stepped from under the overhanging cliff and into what little daylight remained. They'd soon have to set up camp, and resume their search at first light. That is, if they were on the right mountain. By now he doubted the validity of the map. The outlaws had been on the run. No telling how accurately they'd given the directions to the hidden canyon.

Expecting to find Mariah waiting for him, he came to a halt when he didn't spot her. Panic gripped his heart. Didn't the woman have better sense than to wander off alone? He followed her footsteps into a thick stand of bushes.

"Mariah" he called. Her name echoed back at him until it faded into the distance. No answer. He shoved aside the bushes and faced a narrow slit between the walls of the mountain. "Irish!"

"Thorne . . ." Her voice came back to him from a distance.

"Where are you?" A rope wound tightly around his chest. In his mind's eye, he saw her at the base of a cliff, twisted and broken. He took off at a run, navigating through the narrow passage. He would never forgive himself if anything happened to her. In that moment, he realized that he cared far more than he dared.

"I'm here, Thorne. I found our canyon."

He shoved aside a large bush and found her standing at the edge of a precipice. Skidding to a stop, he didn't know whether to thrash her or kiss her. Instead, he merely glared at her. "Didn't I warn you about wandering off alone?"

She flashed a smile that would chase away the stormiest clouds or heat the coldest day. Or melt the hardest heart. "Don't you understand? I've found our canyon. The gold is hidden here. All we have to do is find it."

"Is that all? I'm sure they left arrows pointing the way. Where should we start?"

Her smile didn't waver. "Don't be so cynical. I know it's close by. I can feel it in my bones."

"What you feel is a chill, because the sun is going down. Soon we won't be able to see a thing. I don't want you falling off the edge." He caught her arm, and pulled her toward a small indentation in the wall. "We'll make camp here."

"I hear water splashing ahead. Sounds like a waterfall. Why don't we camp there?"

"The map didn't show a waterfall. Maybe we have the wrong canyon."

"This is the right one." She stamped her foot like a petulant child.

Thorne lifted his hands in surrender. "It's getting late, and I want to start a fire." He clutched her elbow and guided her toward the small waterfall that flowed from a crack in the wall. "Don't ever go off without me," he said between gritted teeth. "You have a habit of disturbing rattlers, if you remember?"

She twisted out of his grip. "I well remember. I won't try that trick again."

The waterfall splashed over rocks and filled a small pool before it tumbled down into the valley. It was the perfect spot to set up camp. A cave offered shelter, and they had ample fresh water. All in all, it was an ideal location from which to begin their search.

Thorne dropped his pack and started to gather dry twigs for a fire. "Don't wander off," he warned as Mariah made her way through the sparse bushes.

"I won't. I just need a moment alone. If you don't mind."

"Be quick. If you find some dry wood, bring it back for the fire."

"Yes, sir," she grumbled on her way out of his line of vision.

He hadn't meant to be cross with her, but when he couldn't locate her, he felt as if a knife had been jabbed into his chest. It wasn't a sensation he liked, and he surely didn't want to experience it again. Nor was he ready to examine its meaning. He struck a match to the kindling, and fanned it into a fire. Opening the pouch, he pulled out a slab of bacon and now-stale biscuits. He wondered if there was game in the canyon. With ample water, and grass, he supposed he could hunt a rabbit or squirrel for their dinner. He rejected that plan. There was no way he would leave Mariah alone. No telling what kind of trouble the woman would find.

He stood and glanced around. Little daylight remained, and long shadows made the canyon even darker. It seemed Mariah had been gone an awful long time. Damn! He had taken one step when rustling came from the bushes.

"Thorne!" Mariah ran into his arms, her face flushed and her eyes wide.

His heart sank. "What's wrong? What happened?"

"Come see. There's a cave behind the waterfall. It's hidden. That might be where they left the gold."

He fastened his hands on her arms and gave her a shake. "Didn't I warn you about wandering off alone? Any kind of critter could be lurking in the cave."

"I didn't go in. I just peeked behind the waterfall." She reached up and planted a brief kiss on his mouth. "Please, this could be where they hid the gold."

Momentarily stunned by her action, he stared into her face. Her cheeks were smudged with dust, her hair disheveled, and her travel clothes worn and dirty. In spite of it all, Mariah Rose O'Reilly was the most stunning woman he'd ever seen. Excitement glittered in her eyes. Thorne wondered how those eyes would look in the heat of passion. Spasms of desire nearly doubled him over. Before he had a chance to react, she spun away and grabbed his hand.

"Come with me."

Thorne paused only long enough to snatch up his rifle. The woman was going to be the ruination of him yet. He didn't know how long his tortured body could endure her allure without acting on its demands.

She lifted her skirt with her free hand and ducked behind the narrow stream of the waterfall. Releasing his hand, she shimmied along the wall, and stopped at an opening in the cliff. "This must be the place. It's perfect. Nobody would accidentally find the gold if the waterfall hid it."

As much as he hated to admit it, she was right. "They were being chased by soldiers, so they probably had to look for a quick place to stash the gold. Let me go first," Thorne said firmly. The roar of the waterfall dimmed as they entered the dark interior of the cave. "Wait here." Reaching for a dry twig, he struck a match and make a temporary torch. The torch gave off little light, but it was enough to guide the way.

He brushed aside a large cobweb and took a tentative step. He wasn't surprised to find Mariah inches behind him. "Let's hope this isn't the lair of some hungry mountain lion," she whispered.

"Didn't I tell you to wait outside?" The walls were damp and the cave smelled of animal droppings. "There may be bats in here."

"I'll not let you have the pleasure of finding our lost treasure. Not on your life, Mountain Man."

The cave roof grew lower, and Thorne had to bend at the waist to keep from tearing off the top of his head. Another dead end. He turned to Mariah, ready to retreat, when his foot struck something solid. It banged like a hammer hitting wood. The noise echoed through the cave, followed by the wild fluttering of wings. Grabbing Mariah, he shoved her to the cold, wet ground and covered her with his body.

"Thorne!" she yelled. "What are you doing?"

"Bats! Didn't I warn you? Stay down."

Disturbed from their slumber, the ugly rodents flew over their heads, their wings stirring the musty air.

Thorne remained on the ground, his body protecting hers. The torch died out, and plunged the cave into total darkness. Within minutes, the noise receded. "I think they're gone," he said. Helping her to her feet, he searched for the dry twig. His hands brushed her leg. She yelped and jerked away. "It's just me, Irish." He struck a match and relit their torch.

She crawled on all fours. "Something's here. Bring the torch."

He hunkered down beside her. She tore away a piece of canvas and brushed at the lid of a wooden box. Even in the dim light he had no trouble reading the stenciled letters: "Prop. of US Army."

The torch sputtered and went out. Mariah flung her arms around his neck. "We've found it. This is the missing gold. Just think of the reward we'll get."

All he could think about was getting his lust under control. "Hold on. Let me strike another match to be sure. It could be an empty box."

She released her hold freeing him to strike another match. He relit the twig, and handed it to Mariah. "Hold this."

"Please let it be the gold, please, Lord, St. Mary, St. Patrick. I promise to be good, and I'll give a huge donation to the Church," she mumbled under her breath.

"While you're praying, Irish, guide the way to the mouth of this cave. I'll drag the box. Then we'll find out if our treasure is nothing but bricks."

"Don't be so cynical, Mountain Man. I know it's our gold."

Unable to stand, he chose to drag the box rather than carry it. Mariah led the way, and by the time they reached the entrance to the cave, the torch again went out. Dusk had fallen, and it was nearly dark. Thorne heaved the box onto his shoulder and headed toward their campsite.

Mariah was fairly dancing as they skirted around the waterfall and shoved through the bushes. The fire had burned low, but he was too excited over their find to worry. He was as ecstatic as Mariah over the gold.

"Hand me that shovel, and I'll try to open the lid."

"Hurry!" she cried. "I can't wait."

Thorne hesitated for an instant. He wondered if he was opening a Pandora's Box. He hoped good would come out of the box—good for Mariah and her family. However, he suspected that it would bode ill for him. Taking one quick whack with the shovel, he broke off the lid.

Mariah bit her lip to keep from crying out. Thorne lifted the lid on the box, and shoved aside a layer of straw. Underneath, lined up in a row, were gold ingots—a king's ransom.

Her breath caught in her throat. As much as she'd hoped, as many rosaries as she'd prayed, seeing her dream come true stunned her into silence.

The reward on this much gold had to be enough to make Mariah a wealthy woman.

Thorne looked up at her and grinned. "Well, Irish, I reckon you were right. Now all your dreams can come true."

"Yes, yes, yes." She lifted her skirts and performed an impromptu jig. Grabbing Thorne by the hand, she tugged him to his feet and danced around him. "We're rich, rich, rich."

"Hold it a minute. We've still got a long way to go to get this back to Fort Union. Haven't you ever heard about not counting your chickens until they hatch?"

She threw her arms around his neck. "My chicks have hatched, thanks to you." Unable to curb her exuberance, she kissed him soundly on the mouth.

He threw back his head and let out a howl of genuine laughter.

"Irish, you started counting them the minute you found that map." His arms wrapped around her waist, holding her tight against him.

"This is a grand day, Mountain Man. I'll remember it always." She lifted her face to his, and this time he instigated the kiss. His mouth covered hers, and Mariah was afraid to breathe, afraid he would stop the wonderful sensation that sizzled through her body.

His beard scratched her chin, but she didn't care. All that mattered was the delicious way his tongue stroked her lips, the way he sought entry to her mouth. Wanting more of him, she parted her teeth and invited his entry. Her tongue tangled with his, in a battle in which both were winners.

The blood pounded in her ears, drowning out the roar of the waterfall. She'd thought she'd been kissed before, but the pecks of her former suitors were nothing like the full-blown glory of a man's passion. He dropped his hands to her bottom and tugged her against his body. The hard ridge of his manhood pressed into her stomach. She brushed her breasts against his chest in an effort to ease the tingling that had her squirming with need. Heat settled in her stomach and lower, in the secret place women only whispered about. Never had she dreamed that merely kissing a man could be such a glorious experience.

Just when she thought she couldn't take any more of the exquisite torture, Thorne broke off the kiss. His breathing was harsh, as if he'd run a great distance. "Irish, we have to stop."

"No," she moaned against his throat. The pulse was pounding like the beat of a bass drum. Although she wasn't quite sure what to expect, she needed more, wanted more of him. Quite simply, she wanted to make love with this man who'd turned her heart and life upside-down. "Don't you want me?"

He buried his face in the crook between her shoulder and neck. "More than I've ever wanted anything. Are you sure you know what you're asking?"

Mariah threw all caution to the wind. On that high mountain, with a fortune of gold at their feet, she wanted nothing more

than to become one with this man who had stolen her heart
when she wasn't looking. "Make love with me. Make me your
woman."

Thorne let out a long, painful groan. He cupped her face in
his big hands. With a shake of his head, and a look of surrender
in his eyes, he answered her needs with passion of his own.
The kiss started out as tenderly as if he were afraid to hurt her.
His tenderness only added fuel to the inferno blazing through
her blood. A small voice in the back of her mind warned
that, after tonight, she would never be the same again. Mariah
ignored the warning, and gave herself fully to the man she
loved.

He sank to the ground, carrying her with him to a bed of
grass and pine needles. His mouth never left hers, and his hands
tore at the clothes that separated them. Mariah worked the
buttons of his shirt free, and moved away only long enough to
slip it over his head. Her blouse followed, then her skirt. With
only her camisole and pantalets to cover her body, he shoved
her to her back and continued to work his magic on her body.
His mustache and beard tickled her sensitive skin, his lips
nipped and caressed, his hands stoked the fires in her body
until she cried and pleaded with him to grant her release from
the erotic torment.

"Are you sure?" he asked, his mouth against her breast. His
teeth found the tip and Mariah was certain she would go mad
with pleasure. Long before, she'd shed the barrier of her under-
clothing, eager to bind with him as one flesh.

"Yes, now."

At some point, he'd managed to remove his buckskin trousers, and now he met her in all the glory of his manhood. He
hovered over her for a moment, then he settled between her
thighs. His mouth covered hers, catching the moans that she
couldn't hold back.

The first thrust came as a surprise, and she stiffened. He
eased back, as if he were going to stop. She dug her fingers
into his back to keep him from leaving her. His tongue stroked

hers, and she relaxed, inviting him deeper into her body. Tenderly, carefully, he claimed her as his woman. He thrust slowly, then, as her body adjusted to his, he increased the tempo, until Mariah felt as if an entire brass band was playing in her body.

Just as she doubted she could stand any more, the crescendo broke, and she tumbled down from a place so wonderful, she didn't want the tremors to end. Thorne gave a final thrust, and followed her into a private world that was theirs alone.

Thorne cradled Mariah to his chest. Never had he felt such peace and contentment. Locked in her embrace, he'd found the man who had been missing for ten long years. She'd given him back his soul.

As he brushed a lock of dark hair from her forehead, he stared into her exhausted face. He'd seen the passion and fire in her gaze as she'd welcomed him into her body and into her heart. The second time, he'd slowed the pace, eager to give her the fullness of pleasure she'd given him. His own heart continued to pound madly. She'd offered a precious gift, the gift of her virginity, the gift of her trust. He pulled her skirt over them against the chill of the coming night.

He frowned. What did he have to offer her? Under normal circumstances, a man would offer marriage. A shiver not from the cool night air racked his body. Thorne had nothing to offer. Marriage was out of the question. She would never consent to living an isolated life on a mountain, and he would never ask her to make such a sacrifice.

Even their lovemaking fell short of what he wanted for Mariah. She deserved a fine feather bed, silk sheets, a warm quilt. Instead, he'd given nothing but the cold, hard ground in a canyon. In his rush to fill his own needs, he'd cheated the woman who'd given herself so willingly.

She shifted in his arms and lifted sleep-swollen eyes to him. The fire was a mere glow of embers, and he sensed more than saw her smile. "Am I hurting you?" he asked.

"No, but there's a stone in my back that's going to leave a grand bruise." She rolled on top of him, her breasts pressed to his chest, her legs tangled with his. "That's much better."

He laughed, and kissed her chin. "We had best get up and see to a meal. If you keep tormenting me like this, we may never leave this canyon."

"Just think how rich we are. All that gold, and it's ours alone. If we leave, we'll have to share it. Just for tonight, let's pretend that it belongs to us."

"Pretending won't fill our stomachs, or warm us when the night grows cold."

"Cold? I'm on fire." She kissed him briefly on the mouth. "Mountain Man, I wonder what it would be like to kiss you without that beard."

He stiffened. Already she was trying to change him, make him adjust to her life. A life in which he would never be satisfied. He forced a smile. "I've grown accustomed to it. Shaving can be a great nuisance."

She brushed her chin across his beard. "It tickles, and I suppose I like it."

With every breath she took, her breasts brushed over his chest. Thorne wasn't sure how much more he could take before his desire again rose to the breaking point. They'd already made love twice, and he didn't want to make her sore or wear her out. They both needed a dunking in cold water or neither would sleep or eat.

On a loud roar, he rolled her off him and sprang to his feet. She let out a surprised cry and stared at him in disbelief. Before she could protest, he scooped her up in his arms.

"What are you doing?" she asked, her arms clutching his shoulders.

He walked purposely toward the waterfall and stepped under the narrow flow. Her protests were cut short at the first blast of cold water on their bare skin. She sputtered and flailed her arms. He dropped her into the small pool that gathered in a basin. "We both need to cool off and get rid of some of the trail dirt."

She sat waist deep in the water and glared at him. "Are you trying to drown me, or freeze me to death?"

Sinking down beside her, he laughed and splashed her face. "Neither. You'll get used to the cold water. Here. I'll help you." At the first touch of his hands to her flesh, he realized he'd made a mistake. Once his fingers connected with her chilled body, he was lost.

The light from the full moon high in the sky found its way down the narrow passage. Droplets of water danced like diamonds on her skin. Gently, he rubbed his hands up her arms to ward off the chill. For himself, he welcomed the chill mountain stream that did little to cool his rising temperature.

"I wish I had some fine perfumed soap to smooth across your skin," he whispered, the words catching on the lump in his throat.

"Don't stop. I already feel the heat from your body." She brushed a kiss across the scar that slashed across his shoulder. "Is this what your brother did?"

The hate and pain of the years fell away at her touch. She was a miracle worker; she'd given so much and asked so little. "That was long ago. The pain is gone."

His mouth lowered to her throat, his tongue licking away the pearllike drops of fresh mountain water. He followed the path of the drops, and caught one particular bead that hovered at the hardened tip of her breast. She moaned, and tightened her grip on his head. "More." She wrapped her legs around his hips and pressed against the arousal. The splatter of the cascade roared around him, but all Thorne heard was Mariah's needy plea. Heedless of the chill stream, ignoring his own guilty conscience, he entered her and let the tide of sensation sweep them both into oblivion.

Their passion spent, Thorne carried Mariah to the fire, now a tiny flicker in the night. He wrapped her in the blanket he'd carried on his back and slipped into his buckskin britches and shirt. Again, he rubbed her flesh to dry and warm her. This time he was careful not to touch her skin. To do so would only get him started again.

As he built up the fire, his thoughts remained on Mariah and what had happened between them. It was a glorious mating of body and soul. Yet, he knew it would do them both no good to admit the truth. He had to make her understand that this could not happen again.

"Mountain Man, you're frowning as if something is terribly wrong. Didn't I do it right?" she asked, still wrapped in the blanket, her hair a tumble of black silk around her shoulders.

She was so lovely, so eager, so vulnerable, he nearly dropped the skillet into the fire. "I was just thinking about the gold. We have to get away from here at first light. I didn't want to frighten you, but I spotted moccasin prints in one of the caves outside the canyon. I don't believe they're fresh, but I don't want to take any chances on meeting up with a war party."

"Why didn't you tell me sooner? I'll get dressed and we can leave immediately." As she spoke, she snatched up her discarded clothing and struggled to dress under the protection of the blanket.

"If Indians are about, they won't do anything at night. Besides, it's too dangerous to try to make it back in the dark."

She settled on a small boulder and fastened her boots. "Won't the fire bring them?"

"No. We're pretty much hidden under an overhang of the cliff. Nobody can spot us here. Come get a bite to eat. You must be starved." His words came out rougher than he'd intended.

They ate in silence, as if struggling to understand this new alliance between them. When the fire died down, Thorne continued to stare into the embers.

Mariah spread their blanket on the ground. "Thorne, won't you come and lie with me?"

Her quietly spoken words socked him in the belly like the kick of a mule. More than anything he wanted to snuggle with her, to feel her soft body, to smell her womanly fragrance. To make love until he forgot his past, the present, and even the future.

"I don't think that's such a good idea."

"What do you mean? Didn't you like . . ." She let the words trail away into the night.

"Of course I did. But we were both caught up in the excitement of finding the gold. That's all it was."

"That's all?" Even the darkness couldn't hide the pain on her face.

"Mariah, we're a man and a woman alone. Those things happen. It was good, but it won't happen again."

"It's never happened to me."

He rubbed his forehead with his fingers. "I know. I'm sorry I took your virginity, it's something you were saving for your husband. It should not have happened."

"You're right, it should never have happened."

"An honorable man would offer marriage, but I can't. As soon as we deliver the gold to Fort Union, I'm going to ask for an escort to take you to the nearest railroad depot so you can return home to your family."

"Does that mean you aren't returning with me?"

He'd nearly forgotten about her quest to locate him. "No. I'll give you a letter for my grandmother. She'll understand why I can't go back."

"I see," she said as she snuggled down into the blanket. "I suppose I should get some sleep and dream about how I'm going to spend all that money from the reward."

"I'll wake you when it's time to leave."

"Thank you," she said, her voice strained. "Another thing, Mountain Man. I didn't ask for marriage. I'll never marry. As for your taking my virginity, don't give it a second thought. I lost it long ago."

Chapter 10

Mariah rolled to her side, her back to Thorne and the fire. She bit her lip until she tasted blood to keep from ranting at the man who'd stolen her heart, then thrown it back into her face as if it were nothing but garbage. The pain in her chest rose to choke her, sobs of despair lodged in her throat. But she didn't make a sound. Tears poured unwelcome from her eyes, tears wasted on a man who didn't want her. A man who'd used her to satisfy his lust, then tossed her away. He was no better than the lot of them.

She'd lied about her virginity. Mariah had saved herself for a man she could love forever. She'd turned down any number of suitors who'd tried to make love to her. It had taken twenty-five years to find the right man, and all he wanted was to get her out of his life as quickly as possible. It hurt clear down to her toes. Even her rejection by Willard hadn't hurt like this. She'd have thought she'd learned her lesson.

How could something so wonderful, so beautiful, something that meant so much to her, mean so little to him? He was a man. A recluse. A hermit who had chosen to live out his time alone. She hadn't asked for marriage. What she'd done had come from a heart of love. She understood his unwillingness to return to Philadelphia. But he didn't have to make light of what they'd shared.

She squeezed her eyes shut and thought about the reward for finding the gold. Let that stubborn mountain man rot on his mountain. She would find the handsomest, kindest, and richest man in Philadelphia. A man who wouldn't care about her background, a man who would love her for the woman she was. And Thorne could warm his bed wondering about the men who were warming hers. And a grand bed it would be—a four poster with a feather mattress and silk sheets. Who needed a husband when a woman was independently wealthy?

"Irish?"

His voice was soft, a husky whisper nearly drowned in the roar of the waterfall and the splashing on the rocks. Not ready to face him, she feigned sleep.

"I know you're awake. I think I should explain. Nothing I said came out right."

Under cover of the blanket, she dried her face as best she could. In the darkness her red eyes and nose wouldn't be seen.

"My name is Mariah. And I believe there's nothing more to be said." She snuggled deeper into the blanket, the stony ground a sorry excuse for a bed.

"I don't want you to think that our lovemaking meant nothing to me. It was wonderful, and I'll always remember you."

"Thanks for a small favor." The blanket muffled her words.

"I didn't intend for any of that to happen. Most of all, I didn't mean to hurt you." He was close, so close, his knees brushed her side.

"I'm not hurt," she muttered between her teeth. Never would he know how badly he'd shattered her emotions. "I'm angry."

He reached for a lock of hair and stroked it between his fingers. Mariah snatched it away and tucked her hair under the blanket. "I don't blame you. I'm angry with myself, too."

"Don't be. You only did what any man would do under the circumstances. I threw myself at you, and I'm responsible for

my own actions. We both enjoyed it. You weren't my first,
and you certainly won't be my last. Let it go at that. Now I'd
like to get some sleep.''

''Dream about your lovers and your money.'' With a growl,
he left her alone to wallow in her misery.

Mariah lay awake all night, alert to every noise and sound
that echoed off the canyon walls. She heard the coyote's howl
in the distance, the buzz of insects, and every time Thorne
tossed a log on the fire. Above it all, she heard the shattering
of her heart. Not that he would ever know. Let him believe
she was a flirt, a loose woman, a wanton. He had proof of her
impropriety.

Before the palest light of dawn crept into the canyon, she
roused herself from the blanket. Stretching her arms above her
head, she pretended that she had, indeed, gotten a full night's
sleep. The campsite was swept clean, and the fire out. Thorne
had packed their meager supplies, and had fashioned a sling
for the heavy box of gold. The only thing remaining was the
blanket where she'd spent the most miserable night of her life.

''Here, eat this.'' He tossed her a stale biscuit.

''Thanks,'' she grunted. Munching on the hard bread, she
slipped behind a bush for a moment's privacy. When she
returned, Thorne had rolled the blanket into a neat package,
and had swept the site with brush.

''We don't want any sign of our passing,'' he said, glancing
up at her. A spark of emotion glittered in the pale light of
dawn. ''No telling who else will come along either by accident
or looking for the gold.''

She caught the hint of anxiety in his voice. ''How long will
it take us to reach the fort?''

''By nightfall, if we don't encounter any delays.'' He heaved
the heavy box of gold onto his shoulders, having covered the
box with the blanket. ''Give me a hand, then I'll help you with
your pack.''

She brushed her fingers across his shoulders, straining from the weight of the gold. "Why don't you divide up the gold; that way I can carry my share."

He adjusted the straps he'd fashioned from rope and his leather belt. "No. I can manage. We don't have far to the horses, and I want you to carry the rest of the supplies and have a free hand for your pistol."

Until that moment, she'd given little thought to danger, or the necessity of needing her gun. She pulled it from the deep pocket of her skirt, and shoved it into the waistband.

"Ready?" he asked.

The canyon was dark with shadows; a glow of pale sky told the coming of morning. She understood the urgency to leave before they were trapped in the canyon. Thorne led the way, his burden slowing his progress along the narrow canyon ledge. With every step they took, Mariah imagined that they were being followed, or watched. She glanced up and down the canyon. There was no sign of life. Not even the animals stirred.

At the narrow hidden passage, Thorne stopped and rested on a boulder. He unfastened the straps of his burden and stretched his cramped muscles. When Mariah opened her mouth to question him, he signaled her to silence.

"Wait here, while I go ahead and make sure we aren't stepping into an ambush."

That thought hadn't occurred to her. "Be careful," she whispered. As badly as he'd hurt her, as many times as she'd wanted to shoot him, she didn't want him to come to harm. She slunk against the opening wall, and waited.

After what seemed an eternity, Thorne slid through the opening beside her. "All clear. Let's go."

Again, he picked up his burden, and led the way out of the canyon and onto the mountainside. The going was still rough. Mariah's foot slipped more than once, but she managed to keep her balance and not tumble down the slope. Although exhausted, thoughts of the gold kept her going. She sighed with relief when they reached the spot where they'd tethered the horses. Thorne dropped his burden, and sagged to the ground. He wiped the sweat from his forehead with his sleeve. By then, the glow of morning had crept up the mountain.

"Can't we divide up the gold now, so the horses can carry it?"

Thorne shook his head. "I want to leave it in the box as proof for the Army. There's a number to show where the gold came from. We don't want anybody to think we stole it."

"If we stole the gold, we certainly wouldn't be returning it back to the fort."

"I want to make sure it's recorded that the gold was returned so you can get your reward."

"Of course. We have to do everything by the book."

"By the book."

"Then how are we going to load it on the horses?"

"Simple. I'll tie the box to one saddle, then you and I can ride double on the other horse."

"Double? That's not decent."

He glared at her from under the brim of his hat. "After what we did last night, riding double is nothing."

Ignoring her show of indignation, he strapped the box to one horse, along with her backpack. Then he approached the other horse and reached out a hand to Mariah.

Mariah debated if it would be better to walk back to the wagon. Since her feet already pinched in her boots, she decided that riding, even with him, was preferable.

He offered her a boost, and she flung her leg over the back of the horse. Until that moment, she hadn't realized she was still sore and stretched from the previous day's ride. "Move up," Thorne ordered. In what seemed no effort at all, he leaped into the saddle behind her. He circled her waist with his hands and gripped the reins. Then he snatched up the reins of the packhorse, and started their descent down the mountain.

The horse rocked and swayed, and, with every step, Mariah's bottom settled closer between Thorne's thighs. As often as she tried to shift forward, the horse's gait forced her back into the intimacy of his body. His arms brushed her breasts and his breath warmed her neck. She wished the ride would end; she wanted to be held in his arms forever. She cursed herself for being a fool. Nothing fazed the stoic mountain man.

Thorne shifted back as far as possible on the saddle. Little good it did. Mariah's bottom remained pressed into his crotch like glue. Riding double with her had been a tactical mistake. With his body pressed intimately against hers, his head was filled with memories of the passion they'd shared. Although he'd never admit it, that night had been the most delightful of his life. When he returned to his cold, lonely mountain, he would remember her always.

Mariah hadn't spoken a word since they'd mounted the horse. No doubt she was still angry with him, and he couldn't blame her. He'd hurt her badly, but it couldn't be helped. There was no future for them, and it was best she understood from the start. Mariah was a woman worthy to be loved, to be cherished. The man who married her would be one very fortunate man. He'd barely tapped her passion, had gotten a tiny glimpse of the fire that smoldered in her Irish blood. At the thought of her with another man, a rope tightened around his chest. Quickly, he stamped down his rising desire.

He wouldn't have been surprised if she'd have whipped out her pistol and put a slug clean through his stony heart. Only needing his help with the gold kept her from trying.

Again trying to put a little space between them, he gripped the reins between his fingers. All that did was bring his arms closer to her breasts, full, soft, inviting. Sweat beaded on his upper lip. If this ride didn't end soon, he would go crazy with lust.

Lost in his struggle with his own body, he was surprised when they reached the grove where he'd left the wagon and team. Relief blanketed him. His torturous ride had ended. He reined in the horse and started to slip from the back when a noise in the bushes stopped him. Before he could reach for his rifle, a pistol shot whizzed across the horse's head. He leaned over Mariah to protect her.

"Mighty kind of you to deliver the gold to us." The voice was too familiar for comfort. "Saved us a lot of trouble."

Two men stepped from their hiding place—the outlaws he'd left tied up and horseless. Thorne cursed himself a thousand ways. He'd been careless and had walked right into a trap.

The second man, the one called Nick, spoke up. "You and the lady did a fine job. Get down, and be careful about it. Don't try anything, or the lady gets a bullet. Course, we won't kill her outright. We's got other plans for her."

Thorne gritted his teeth. Mariah shivered in his arms. "Don't worry, Irish, I'll take care of you." He slid from the horse, and dropped the reins of the packhorse. "We weren't expecting company," he said. Careful to lift his hands in surrender. One false move and this pair wouldn't hesitate to kill Mariah.

"Don't you try nothing. We'll shoot you dead right where you're standing." He grabbed the halter and glared up at Mariah. "I'll take that gun, little lady. We'll see how you like being thrust up like a calf for branding."

Mariah glanced at Thorne. He nodded, hoping she wouldn't try anything foolish. From her perch high in the saddle, she passed the gun to the outlaw. Thorne reached for her waist. Nick stuck his gun in Thorne's ribs. "What ya think ya doing?"

"I'm helping her down. She hurt her ankle, and she can't walk. I'm just going to set her on the wagon bed."

He shot a hard glance at Mariah warning her to go along with his ploy. If nothing else, he might buy them time to come up with a plan to save their hides.

On cue, she let out a loud moan. "Be careful, I think it might be broken."

He swung her into his arms and headed for the wagon. Her face was blanched, and she appeared to be in pain. Once she was seated, he turned to their captors. "How did you get here? It's a long way to walk."

Nick let out a long, ugly laugh. "This here fellow came along. We told him we was waylaid by outlaws. A'course we killed him and took his horse and gun. Took a bit of work to follow you, though."

Fury surged through Thorne. He should have killed them when he had the chance. Another man was dead because he couldn't commit murder. This pair deserved to die like the rats they were.

"Why don't we jest shoot him now, and take the lady with us," the shorter man said. "We can maybe sell her in Mexico." He tugged the hat from Mariah's head, and grabbed a handful of black hair. "After we have our fill of her."

Mariah remained unmoving under the man's abuse. Her blue eyes shot daggers. He twisted her face to his. Thorne curled his hands into fists. He saw the Irish temper simmer, and he prayed she wouldn't do anything foolish. Without warning, she reached out and socked the man square in the jaw. He staggered back, and Thorne took one step toward them. The gun in his back stopped him. He growled deep in his throat.

"Ya shouldn't of did that, lady." He lifted his hand to slap her when an arrow whizzed through the air and landed in his forearm. The man yelled and dropped his gun to grip the arrow that pierced his arm.

Everything happened at once. Mariah leaped from the wagon and grabbed the gun. Thorne rammed his elbow into the other man's ribs and fell on the man. They struggled for the gun, rolling on the ground in a fight for life and death. Thoughts of their plans for Mariah fueled his anger. For all he knew, they were surrounded by a band of Apaches, but all that mattered was getting rid of the vermin that had dared threaten his woman.

Thorne wrestled the gun from Nick's hand and tossed it aside. They continued to roll in the dirt, exchanging blows. The outlaw twisted free, and pulled a knife from his boot—the same boots Thorne had taken from him days ago. They circled each other. The outlaw struck out and slashed at Thorne.

From the corner of his eye, he spotted Mariah with the gun on the other man, who was grabbing his arrow in his arm and screaming bloody murder. His opponent lunged toward Thorne.

Another arrow slashed through the air and landed in the outlaw's shoulder. He screamed and dropped the knife. Quickly, Thorne scooped up the gun and knife and faced his savior. Or his next opponent.

"Man help man." A youthful male voice came from the trees. Tongo. Never had Thorne been happier to see anybody.

Still cautious, he studied the young Indian. "Are you alone?"

He nodded. "People grateful for Thorne's help. Now we even."

"What ya doing with that wild Injun? He done shot me. I'm bleeding to death." Nick sank to the ground and groaned in pain.

Thorne ignored the painful cry and turned to Mariah. "You okay?" he asked, relieved to see her in charge of the other outlaw.

"Certainly, thanks to Tongo."

He turned to the young Indian. "Don't think I'm not grateful, but what are you doing here?"

"I bring meat to tribe. Shaman hear of man called Thorne. Say Thorne good man. Help Indian. He send medicine bag to Thorne. I follow, see bad men ambush Thorne and his woman." He shoved the leather pouch into Thorne's hand. "Shaman say Thorne face much danger. Wear bag to keep away evil spirits."

Thorne draped the leather thong over his head, then he grabbed the young man's hand and cupped his shoulder in a show of brotherhood. "You are fine man, Tongo. If you or your people need help, go to Los Amigos and see Father Callahan. Tell him Thorne sent you. He will give you help."

The Indian lad shook his head. "Not go to village."

The vehement reply came as no surprise. "Then come to me, on my mountain." Thorne hunkered down and drew directions in the dirt. "You will be safe there. The mountain belongs to me. Soldiers will not bother you."

"Indian believe no man own land. Belongs to all. White man steal."

He couldn't deny the truth of it. "True." Thorne continued

his makeshift map. "Come to me if you need help. If I am not there, take what you want. The cellar house is full of meat, and the cabin has supplies. I ask only that no harm come to my people."

"Shaman right. Thorne good man."

"Thorne is a grateful man. You saved my life and my woman's."

The outlaws began to groan louder. "Is you gonna yak all day with that savage? We need help. Them arrows might be poison. We could die."

Mariah approached, still keeping the gun on the outlaw. "Do you think we should give them the same wherefore they planned for us?"

Thorne shrugged. "I'm thinking about letting Tongo take them back to his village and let his tribe administer justice."

Nick turned even whiter. Blood oozed from his shoulder and stained his shirt. "Not that. We deserve a fair trial. We need a doctor."

"Considering what you'd planned for my woman, I should just let you stay here and let the coyotes finish you off."

"We never meant her no harm. We was just gonna have a little sport with her. Ain't that what you been doing? And her a nun."

Mariah jabbed the gun into the man's ribs. "I ought to finish you off right now, you pile of dung." She let out a string of Irish curses. When she caught Thorne's knowing glance, she flushed. "They deserve it."

"It ain't right. You can't do that to us." The man with the arrow in his forearm sank to the ground.

Thorne's sense of right won out. "We'll take you to Fort Union and turn you over to the Army. The commander can decide your punishment."

"Whatever he decides, it will be too good for them," Mariah said.

"Tongo—" Thorne glanced around and found the young Indian gone. Moments later, the sound of hoofbeats rang into the distance. Their savior had disappeared as quickly as he'd come.

Mariah's gaze followed his. "Do you think he'll allow you to help him?"

"I doubt it. The debt has been paid, and unless he's desperate, he won't seek help from a white man." Thorne fingered the leather bag at his neck. "I'll wear it always, Tongo," he whispered. He turned to the outlaws. "Let's get these two fixed up, and head for Fort Union."

"Then home to the children and Sung Lo," Mariah said.

He ignored her and reached into his supplies for bandages and salve. First chance he got, she was headed east. Alone.

Chapter 11

Thorne both anticipated and dreaded the moment when they would reach Fort Union. It had taken a full day and a half before he spotted the military installation that rose out of the green prairie.

The pair of outlaws were worse traveling companions than a pack of wild pigs. They snorted and complained every mile of the way. To be on the safe side, Thorne had kept them thrust up and only let them move about one at a time, while Mariah kept a pistol on the other.

A vise twisted in his chest as he viewed the fort near the base of a mesa. Fort Union was one of the largest military outposts in the Southwest. Built to protect settlers and travelers on the Santa Fe Trail, the sprawling buildings served as a major military supply station. Blue-uniformed soldiers and men and women in civilian clothing seemed to be everywhere.

He had no great love for the Army, with good reason. If his real identity were revealed, there was no telling what would happen to him. And in course, the children and Sung Lo would be abandoned. He couldn't even imagine what it would mean to Mariah and to his grandmother.

As they neared the outpost, the outlaws began to whisper among themselves. He knew they were up to no good. No telling what the murdering, lying duo would attempt once they reached this outpost of civilization. Thorne was sorely tempted to grab one of the horses and hightail it back to his mountain and let Mariah handle the stolen gold. He wouldn't do that. A woman alone was too vulnerable among a fort full of lonely soldiers.

Strengthening his resolve, Thorne drove the wagon directly past the storehouses, barracks, corrals alive with horses and cattle, and the parade grounds where a sergeant was drilling his men. Mariah squeezed his hand as if offering her support. He nodded, and kept his gaze straight ahead.

Thorne tugged the team to a halt at a large adobe building with "Headquarters" painted in a sign over the door. It was now or never. Over the years, he'd studiously avoided any contact with the military. Now he was thrust in the middle of hundreds of uniformed officers and enlisted men.

"Sergeant!" he called out to the man standing guard at the door. "Can you get a detail to guard my wagon and my prisoners while my lady and I speak to the commander?"

The man stared at Thorne as if to question why this civilian was giving him orders. "What's so valuable in your wagon?"

"That's something I have to take up with your commanding officer. Is he in his office?"

At that moment, a young lieutenant, who appeared fresh out of West Point, stepped into the blaring sunlight. "Is there a problem, Sergeant?" he asked.

The older military man snapped to attention. "This man wants to see General Edwards, sir. And he wants me to guard his wagon."

At the name, Thorne's blood ran cold. He prayed this wasn't the same Edwards he'd encountered during the war and that the man would not in any way recognize Thorne. The years of living in the mountains had hardened him, and the beard and mustache hid his features. Besides, he supposed the military thought him killed by Rebels when he'd escaped.

The lieutenant approached the wagon, his gaze locked on Mariah. A surge of jealousy whipped through Thorne. He draped a protective arm across her shoulder. Thankfully, she didn't resist. "I have prisoners, and something to discuss with the commander. May I see him?"

He continued to stare at Mariah. Though travel weary the woman's beauty shone through the dirt and grime of the road. "Good day, ma'am. Lieutenant Prescott at your service."

"My name's Thorne, and the lady is Miss Mariah O'Reilly."

"My pleasure, ma'am." The young officer bowed at the waist as if he were greeting her at a soirée.

"We wants to see the general!" Nick called from the bed of the wagon. "This man kidnapped us and stole our horses."

As if noticing the pair for the first time, the young officer glanced at the bed of the wagon.

"If I kidnapped them, would I deliver them to the fort? Please, may I see your commander?" Thorne asked, impatient at the delay. The sooner he delivered the gold, the sooner he could get back to his mountain. And the sooner Mariah would be on her way—a very rich woman. A myriad of emotions surged through him at the idea of her leaving. Not the least of all was regret. Regret for what he was missing, regret for what they could have had, regret that he would live out his life alone.

By that time, several off-duty soldiers began to gather around the wagon, eager for some sort of excitement in their boring existence.

"He's lying," the other outlaw protested. "He's in cohoots with the Injuns."

Thorne shot an angry glance at the outlaws. It would do no good to argue with the men. He would let the commander weigh their stories and make the decision.

"Sergeant!" Prescott called. "Please tell the general he has visitors."

"Yes, sir." With a reluctant salute, the sergeant retreated behind the closed door.

Thorne jumped down from his perch. By the time he circled the wagon, Prescott had offered a hand to Mariah.

She smiled brightly at the young man. "Thank you, sir. It's a pleasure to meet a gentleman." She took his offered hand. "Would you be so kind as to have somebody guard the wagon?" Lowering her voice, she moved closer to his ear. "I don't want to lose my valuables."

Growling under his breath, Thorne grabbed each of the outlaws by the backs of their shirts and hauled them to the ground. They squealed and squawked like stuck pigs.

By the time they reached the doorway, the sergeant had returned. "General Edwards is busy. He said to state your business."

Thorne was sick to death of the military and he'd only been here ten minutes. "My business is with the general," he ground between his teeth.

Mariah stepped up before he lost his temper and did something rash. "Lieutenant Prescott, would you please intercede with the general for us? I'm mighty weary, and I desire a place to rest."

The young man nodded. "I'm his aide, ma'am. I'll see what I can do."

Thorne glared at Mariah. She flashed a smug smile. "If we don't get to see the general, can we keep it all for ourselves?"

The outlaws in his hands squirmed and twisted to get away. "No."

Seconds later, Prescott reappeared. "The general said you can have five minutes of his time."

He led the way into the cool interior of the adobe building. The first office was sparsely furnished with a desk and several tables piled with ledgers and maps. Prescott opened the next door, and gestured them in. The outlaws began to balk. Thorne ignored their protests, and shoved them through the doorway.

"General Edwards," Prescott announced, "Mr. Thorne and Miss O'Reilly. I don't know who these other gentlemen are."

"Dismissed," the general said, distracted.

A stone dropped to Thorne's stomach as he viewed the tall officer who stood when they entered. Captain Edwards had been the judge at his court-martial. Though older and noticeably thicker in the chest and waist, the man hadn't changed much over the past ten years. His mustache and hair showed touches of gray, but his brown eyes held the same sharp intensity as when he'd sentenced Michael Harrison to the firing squad.

General Edwards gestured them to chairs facing his wide oak desk. Behind the desk hung portraits of Abraham Lincoln and General Grant.

He eyed Thorne as if struggling to recognize him. "Thorne? Have we met before?" Edwards asked.

"No."

The general shrugged. "State your business, please. I have a very busy schedule."

"Ten years ago, these two, with help from some friends, robbed a wagon containing a gold shipment. Recently, Miss O'Reilly came into possession of a map. She recovered the gold. It's in our wagon."

With every word, the general's eyes grew wider. At the last words, he leaped to his feet. "What did you say? You have a fortune in stolen Army gold outside in a wagon?"

"Oh, don't worry, General," Mariah piped in brightly. "Your men are guarding it for us."

"They's lying!" Nick shouted. "We found the gold, and they stole it from us."

Edwards ignored the outburst. "This I must see for myself." He hurried around his desk and headed for the door. Thorne followed, and gestured for Mariah to keep her pistol on the pair of outlaws.

Outside, Edwards went directly to the wagon bed. Thorne threw aside the blanket and shoved the box toward the general.

"Sergeant Marcus, have your men carry this into my office," Edwards ordered.

"Gold." The word buzzed through the crowd that had gathered around the wagon. The sergeant and another soldier lifted the heavy box and carried it to the general's desk. Both men hovered nearby as Thorne brushed off the lid and showed the identification number stenciled on the lid. Carefully, he opened the box.

"You can check the numbers on the box, General, and I'm certain you'll be able to verify that this is the gold that was stolen in the robbery ten years ago. As far as I know, it's all here."

The man lifted one of the gold bars and weighed it in his hand. "Gold. The Army gave up searching for this years ago. How did you find this?"

Thorne glanced at Mariah. "Miss O'Reilly found it. Before he was killed, one of the bandits gave her part of a map. These gentlemen," he gestured to the thrust-up outlaws, "gave her the rest."

"Ain't true. She stole it from us."

The gold still in his hand, Edwards looked at the pair. "And if she stole it, why did she return it to me? She could have kept it all for herself."

"That would be terribly dishonest, General. I'll be satisfied with the reward." She gave him a mournful look. "There is a reward, isn't there, for the return of this valuable shipment?"

"I'm sure there is. In cases like this, the reward is usually ten percent of the value." He returned the gold to the box. "You'll be a wealthy woman, Miss O'Reilly."

She gave the man a honeyed smile and affected brogue. "I don't want the reward for myself, mind you, but for my parents and family, and that's the truth."

"This is the most amazing thing that's happened to me in the six months I've been at Fort Union." He signaled the sergeant. "Take these men to the stockade. We'll get their statements later." Turning back to Mariah and Thorne, he shook his head in puzzlement. "I'd like to hear the rest of your story. You'll stay for dinner. I'm certain my wife would like to meet Miss O'Reilly, and Father Callahan is here to minister to my men."

"Father Callahan?" Thorne asked.

"Yes, do you know him?"

"Very well."

"Good. The priest can let me know if you're telling the truth. Meanwhile, I'll see that the gold is secured."

Thorne closed the lid on the box. "First, General, I'd like a receipt for the gold. And when you send to Washington for the reward, have it put into an account in a Philadelphia bank in Miss Mariah Rose O'Reilly's name."

Mariah sensed Thorne's reluctance as they entered the commander's dining room that evening. Thanks to Mrs. Edwards's generosity, Mariah wore a clean blouse and simple calico skirt. The woman had sent her Mexican maid to help Mariah with her bath and grooming. She felt almost human with her skin fragrant with rose water, and her hair brushed and shiny.

Thorne's concession to dinner was a bath and the clean shirt he'd brought from home. Even with the proximity of a barber, his hair remained long and his beard every bit as shaggy, but at least it was clean and combed.

Since the moment General Edwards had mentioned the dinner invitation, they hadn't had a moment alone. She spotted the apprehension in his eyes when she'd accepted the invitation. Did he think she was so stupid that she would say or do something to reveal his identity? That was their secret. And she was wily enough not to reveal anything.

Thorne offered his arm as they met outside the commander's quarters. His gaze warmed when he saw her, then turned icy as he led her into the dining room.

General Edwards was waiting with his wife, a woman at least ten years his junior. Blonde, with warm brown eyes, she

smiled when she saw Mariah. "Miss O'Reilly, I'm so eager
to meet you. My husband tells me that you've made an extraordinary discovery. You've located a stolen gold cache? I must
hear all about it."

The lady's gracious hospitality immediately put Mariah at
ease. Thorne released his hold on her arm, and gave Edwards
a cursory greeting. A black-robed priest put down his wineglass
and stuck out his hand to Thorne.

"Good to see you, old friend," the priest said with a lilt of
Irish in his voice.

"Father." Thorne accepted his hand and shook it vigorously.

"General Edwards said you're quite a hero."

He glanced at Mariah. "Actually, Miss O'Reilly located the
gold. I was just her guide."

Mrs. Edwards gestured to the table set with china and crystal.
"Let's sit down and eat. We want to hear the entire story."

Mariah was seated between Edwards and Lieutenant Prescott.
Thorne and Father Callahan sat across from her.

In as few words as possible, Thorne told how Mariah had
been on a stagecoach waylaid by bandits and how the pair was
now in the stockade. He neglected the part of her disguise as
a nun, and her reason for being in New Mexico. He knew the
priest would never offer forgiveness for such a vile offense.

Between courses, the general questioned Thorne, while his
wife seemed fascinated with Mariah's part in the adventure.
From time to time, Edwards sent Thorne a questioning glance.
Did the man recognize him? She prayed not. No telling what
might happen to him if the Army got hold of him.

Dessert consisted of cheese and the fresh fruit—apples,
plums, and pears that grew in the valley of the Mora River.
The wine was delicious. When she returned to Philadelphia,
she would give up beer in favor of wine, like elegant people
drank.

Mrs. Edwards smiled at Thorne over her glass. "Mr. Thorne,
are you from Virginia, by any chance?"

Only Mariah caught the tightening around his eyes. "No, ma'am. Why do you ask?"

"My wife makes a game out of studying speech patterns and guessing people's origins. She's usually quite good at it. Exactly where do you hail from?" the general asked.

"I've traveled quite a bit. I may have picked up some of the drawl during my journeys."

Mariah jumped in to divert the conversation from Thorne. "We often do the same with the Irish in Philadelphia," she said. "It's also sort of a game to guess from what part of Ireland one hails." She'd dropped into the brogue of her parents. "Those from the north speak quite differently from those in the south. For sure, the speech of Belfast is vastly different from Dublin. And that's the truth."

Father Callahan laughed. "Aye, lass. I gather you were born in America, but your parents came from County Cork."

She laughed. "And you, Father, hail from Blarney. And, of course, you have the gift."

"That I have, lass, that I have." The priest's dark-green eyes turned serious. "It seems you're a fine Irish girl. Are you Catholic?"

"Why, yes, sir. I attended St. Bridgit's in Philadelphia. Though I was the terror of Sister Mary Louise."

"And I gather you live with your parents. That you're an unmarried woman?"

Under his stern gaze, she shifted on the chair. "Yes, sir. With my parents and brothers and sisters."

The priest slammed his hands on the table and rose from the chair. His wineglass tumbled, dripping the remains of red wine on the linen cloth. "You, a fine Irish lass spending days and nights in the wilderness with a man. Without a chaperone." He made the sign of the cross. " 'Tis a disgrace to God and to your parents." Pointing a finger toward Thorne, he hardened his voice. "And you, Thorne, to compromise the reputation of a lovely young woman like Miss O'Reilly."

Mariah's face heated. "But it's all right, Father," she said, struggling to defuse the explosive situation. "It was my decision."

Thorne stood and faced the priest. "No need to worry, *Padre*. We're to be married when we reach Philadelphia."

If she hadn't been seated, Mariah would have dropped straight to the floor. He'd made up the story to protect her reputation.

Mrs. Edwards stood and lifted her wineglass. "How lovely. Why don't we just have the wedding here now? We can protect Miss O'Reilly's reputation, and have an excuse for a party." She flashed a winning smile at her husband. "Isn't that a wonderful idea, dear? You can issue a special license, and Father Callahan can perform the ceremony. You and I can stand up as witnesses. We'll have a grand time."

The general shifted his gaze from Thorne to Mariah. Her heart sank like a stone to her stomach. She opened her mouth to protest, when her words were cut off by the commanding voice of the officer. "We'll use the chapel. Father, lead the way."

As Thorne clutched her elbow, Mariah tried to hold back. "This is crazy. I can't marry you."

"We don't have much choice," Thorne whispered. "Go along for now. Smile and act happy. We'll figure out something later."

It was the only way out. If he protested too loudly, Edwards was sure to become suspicious, and the sooner he and Mariah got away from the fort, the safer he would feel. Under the man's relentless stare, he could almost feel the noose tighten around his neck.

Mrs. Edwards seemed to be having a grand time, as she invited every man, woman, and child between her quarters and the chapel to witness the nuptials. Father Callahan walked beside Thorne as if he were afraid the reluctant groom would balk. More than likely it was the bride who would split and run.

At the wide double doors that led into the adobe chapel,

Mrs. Edwards tugged Mariah out of his grip. "You go in, Mr. Thorne, while I help Miss O'Reilly get ready."

Surrounded by half a brigade of armed soldiers, what choice did he have? Thorne strolled down the aisle to the altar, struggling to control his emotions. This wasn't fair to Mariah. She was only going along with the scheme to save his hide. She sure deserved better than a fugitive mountain man as a husband. With the money from the reward, she would have her choice of suitors. Men with potential, men who could give her the big house she wanted. Men without a price on their heads.

He swallowed down his trepidation. He studiously avoided Edwards's stare for fear the man would recognize him. The general stood at his side, while the priest waited before the altar.

Lit by candles on the altar and along the walls, the chapel had a warm, peaceful glow. He shifted from one moccasined foot to the other. Even facing the firing squad, he hadn't felt this degree of agitation.

Mrs. Edwards entered and took her place beside her husband. The pews were half filled, mostly with curiosity seekers looking for a bit of excitement.

When Mariah stepped into the candlelit aisle, he thought his heart would stop beating. In spite of her simple blouse and skirt, she was every inch a bride with a white lace veil draped over her dark hair. Bathed in candlelight, she was a vision of loveliness. Slowly, she walked down the aisle accompanied not by music but by the hum of whispers in the audience.

She deserved better, and he vowed to make it up to her. As she stood at his side before the Father Callahan, his friend, and before God, he felt like the biggest hypocrite in the world. Marrying under false pretenses had to be a sin, or a reason for an annulment . . . That was it. Upon returning to Philadelphia, she could get an annulment.

What a way to begin a marriage—planning its demise.

Father Callahan began the wedding ceremony by instructing him to take Mariah's hand. Her small fingers trembled in his large, rough palm. He tightened his grip in an effort to reassure her. As the priest recited the marriage vows, Thorne studied every word. Before God and man, he was taking a wife and promising to be faithful all the days of his life.

When they came to the part for him to repeat the vows, Father Callahan looked at him expectantly. "I don't know your given name," the priest whispered.

Thorne faltered for a moment. "Just Thorne," he said.

Not to be put off, the priest pressed the subject. "Your given name."

Mariah leaned forward. "He hates it, Father. Please don't make him say it."

He shot her a look of gratitude. With a shrug, the priest continued the ceremony. Their vows were repeated, the blessing pronounced, the prayer said, and Thorne found himself locked in the bonds of matrimony with a beautiful woman.

Somehow, it didn't seem quite as bad as he'd expected.

Chapter 12

Everything had happened so fast. Mariah's head was spinning by the time she and Thorne entered the guest quarters where they would spend the night.

Together.

Following the ceremony, they'd been treated to more wine and refreshments by the general and his wife. She wasn't accustomed to anything more than an occasional mug of beer, and she wasn't sure how much wine she'd consumed over the evening.

The room was neatly furnished with a large bed covered with a colorful woven blanket, a bureau, a small rectangular table, and two chairs. After all, she reminded herself, this was a military outpost in the middle of New Mexico Territory not the luxurious La Pierre House in Philadelphia.

Somehow she'd managed to keep up her part of the act, pretending undying love for her bridegroom. To her surprise, it wasn't as difficult a task as she'd expected. Mariah rather liked being the center of attention, of having the toasts made to her. She enjoyed the good wishes for a long, happy marriage. Only *she* knew that marriage wouldn't last any longer than it took for the ink to dry on the special license General Edwards had issued.

A twinge of pain twisted her heart. She couldn't deny that she had feelings for the impossible mountain man she had tied her life to. However, he'd made it clear he didn't give a fig for her.

She glanced at him as he released her arm and moved to look out the window. Now that they were alone, he couldn't bear the sight of her. The very idea that he'd rejected her love, and now planned further rejection, fueled her resolve to break through the barrier he'd erected around his heart. Then she'd give him a taste of his own medicine.

Mariah had consumed enough wine to release her inhibitions. She stood in front of the mirror over the bureau and fingered the white lace veil. Her blue eyes sparkled in the candlelight, from the wine, and from planned mischief.

"I look quite lovely, if I must say so myself."

The thought spoken aloud brought Thorne's gaze to hers. He let the curtains fall, closing off the thin beam of moonlight. "You are a beautiful woman, Irish." On a long sigh, he sank into one of the straight-backed chairs. "Thank you for helping me out of a jam."

She released the pins that held the veil, and carefully laid the lace on the bureau. "I gather you've met General Edwards in the past."

"He was a captain during the war. He's the man who sentenced me to the firing squad."

Her blood chilled at how close to hell he'd come that day. "I didn't know. We'll have to leave before he recognizes you or becomes suspicious."

He nodded, his gaze still on her. "I spoke to Father Callahan about the gold. Since everybody in the fort has heard about it by now, you're going to become a local celebrity. We should get away before some Santa Fe newspaper gets wind of it and wants to interview us."

She pulled the pins from her hair and let the thick black tresses tumble down her back. "What about my reward?"

"I believe Edwards is an honest enough man not to try to cheat you out of your reward. I've asked the *padre* to keep an eye on him, just in case the money isn't waiting for you when you return to Philadelphia."

With long, slow strokes, she worked her brush through her tumble of curls. "Don't you mean when *we* return home?"

"I can't go back, don't you understand?" His mouth narrowed into a tight slash under his mustache.

Tossing her hair over her shoulder, she met his cold stare. Slowly, she released the top button of her blouse. Her fingers trembled as she loosened one after the other, exposing the thin chemise she wore to her new husband. "Then how are you going to explain my leaving so soon after our marriage?"

He tugged on his beard, a sign he was thinking over the situation. "I'd planned to have Edwards give you an escort to the nearest railroad depot in Colorado. But that would only draw his suspicions. I have to return to the mountain for Sung Lo and the children. I don't like to leave them alone for too long."

With the front of the blouse open, she tugged it from her skirt. "I'll go back with you. After all, I promised the children."

"You can't."

"Do you plan to leave me here?" She shrugged the blouse from her shoulders and draped it across a chair.

"I sure as hell wish I could. But I'll make arrangements for you to return east as soon as we reach the mountain." In spite of his harsh words, his heated gaze touched her bare shoulders and the tips of her breasts tightened against the chemise.

Married a few short hours, and already he wanted to get rid of her. Her feminine pride injured, she would just see how easily he could reject her. She released the button of her skirt and let it drop to the floor with her petticoat. Clad only in her chemise and pantalets, she took one step toward him. She swayed, her head spinning. Reaching out for something solid to support her, she gripped Thorne's wide shoulder. "Too much wine, I suppose."

He scooped her up in his arms and deposited her into the center of the bed. "You're a little drunk. You'll feel better in the morning."

The room had stopped spinning, and she felt light as a feather. "I feel wonderful." She snuggled on the bed. "A feather mattress and clean sheets. Come lie down with me."

Even in her suddenly drowsy state, she saw the heat in his gaze—the same fire that had blazed like a bonfire the night they'd made love. She smiled. He wanted her. As hard as he was trying to deny it, he wanted her. Tingles shot through her. She wanted him even more. Mariah opened her arms.

"That isn't such a good idea." He retreated a step toward the chair.

"Why? We're married. And I'm sure the general expects us to sleep together." She yawned, and her words slowed. "What if somebody finds out you didn't . . . that we didn't . . ." Trying to seduce him became too much of a bother. She closed her eyes, and gave in to much needed sleep.

Thorne stared down at the woman slumbering peacefully. His wife. His woman. She was beautiful and appealing. Her full white breasts spilled over the top of her chemise, the tips dark and puckered against the thin material. Her long, shapely legs tempted him beyond measure. Never would he forget the way she'd wrapped her legs around him and given herself to him. He had every right to join her and relieve the hunger that had never quite been quenched. But to do so would ruin the next step in his plan.

He shook out the blanket, and spread it across her body. Unable to stop himself, he brushed a stray curl from her cheek. Soft as a butterfly's wings, her skin invited a kiss. For a brief second, he entertained the thought of kissing her, of holding her, of making love with her. His body burned, and his spirit yearned for her touch. His soul ached for her.

Stepping away, he cursed himself for his weakness. For her

sake, he had to remain strong. Again he moved to the window. This was his first visit to a military installation since his desertion. Over the years, he'd steered clear of anybody in a blue uniform. The danger was too great. It still was.

Armed sentries marched back and forth guarding the post from Indians and outlaw bands. Off-duty men gathered in groups, playing cards, sharing tales of battle or loneliness for home. A few staggered in from an evening at Loma Parda, a rowdy village of bars and prostitutes. In such a large fort he expected the amount of nighttime activity. He stepped back into the shadows as a guard passed near the window. Quickly, he extinguished the candles. Mariah was right. It wouldn't do to let anybody suspect he was anything but an amorous bridegroom on his wedding night.

Returning to the chair, he removed his moccasins and shirt. In just his breeches, he stretched out on the edge of the bed, careful not to disturb his sleeping wife. In spite of the soft bed and inviting companion, Thorne braced himself for the most miserable night in his life.

A bugle-blaring reveille jerked Thorne awake the next morning. For a brief moment, he was back in the Army, roused to face the firing squad. Perspiration wreathed his forehead. He wiped away the dampness with his forearm, grateful that the weight holding him down wasn't shackles, but a warm, soft woman.

His gaze shifted from the streak of sunlight peeking through the curtains to his woman. Awareness hit him smack in the gut. His wife, Mariah, lay curled into his side, her hand resting intimately across his stomach. His reaction to her touch was immediate and expected.

Sometime during the night she'd thrown off the blanket and sought his body for warmth. Her breasts pressed against his chest, the tips hard and eager. He swallowed to gain just a modicum of control. She shifted and cuddled closer into his arm that pillowed her head. Her hand dropped an inch lower on his abdomen, a hairbreadth from his aroused member.

Mustering every bit of self-discipline, he remained statue still. He was in heaven, and in a hell of his own making. He wanted her so badly, he throbbed with the need. When he was certain he couldn't take another second of the torture, a light knock sounded at the door.

Both thankful and angry at the intrusion, he slid off the bed. "Who is it?" he called out.

A soft feminine giggle came from the other side of the heavy wooden door. "It is Juanita. *Señora* Edwards send breakfast. She say you stay as long as you wish."

He slid back the bolt and took a linen-covered tray from the girl. "Where is the general?"

"There was trouble last night. *El general* has gone to Loma Parda."

"*Gracias.* And give our thanks to Mrs. Edwards for her kindness."

The girl smiled, and bustled away. With the guest quarters set apart from the other buildings, they were afforded a bit of privacy. He closed the door and set the bolt. When he set the tray on the table, he encountered Mariah's questioning gaze.

"Breakfast," he offered as way of explanation.

She stretched her arms over her head, her body lithe and sleek as a wildcat's. His gaze dropped to the edge of the chemise, certain her breasts would spill out from the top. He buried his nails into his palms to keep from capturing the fullness in his hands. On a groan, he tore his gaze away from the temptation lying on the bed and plucked the napkin from the tray.

"Isn't that nice? Warm bread, hot coffee, fruit, jelly, butter. Pour me a cup of coffee, won't you, Mountain Man?" Mariah's sleep-dusted voice came from over his shoulder. Her arm brushed his as she snatched a ripe peach from the platter. She sank her teeth into the fruit. A trickle of juice drizzled down her chin. "Umm," she moaned, her eyes alight with sensual pleasure. A slender finger caught the drop and she licked it off with her tongue.

Thorne wondered how much torture a man could endure before he went totally mad. Standing so close, he felt the warmth of her body. She hadn't bothered with a single stitch of decent outer clothing. The chemise strap slithered off one shoulder, and it was only sheer luck that kept the top from sagging to her waist.

His control about to snap, Throne grabbed his shirt from the floor and shoved his arms into the sleeves. He didn't bother with the buttons. "Woman, don't you have an ounce of decency? Parading around like that in front of a man?"

She dropped the half-eaten peach on the tray and spun to face him. Her blue eyes blazed with fire. She set her fists on her hips, straining her bosom against the thin fabric. "In a small chamber with four sisters, there was little room for modesty. And in case you've already forgotten, you *are* my husband."

As if he could forget the events of the past evening. "Not for long. As soon as you get back to Philadelphia, I want you to apply to the Church for an annulment. It would save the disgrace of a divorce, and permit you to marry in the church when you find the rich man who'll give you a big house and that one child. Thank God we didn't consummate the marriage."

Crimson crept up her neck to her cheeks. "Have you forgotten what happened in the canyon? I can only assume that was a 'consummation.' "

He shoved his feet into his moccasins. "Since we weren't married, it's only a technicality. Go to confession if you have to, do penance, then get the annulment." Frustrated, his voice turned to a husky grunt.

"Where are you going?" she asked as he darted for the door.

"To see about the horses and fresh supplies. I'll meet with Father Callahan and see that he protects your interests. Get dressed while I'm gone."

"Won't the general get suspicious if you leave your bride so early?"

Avoiding looking at her, he reached for the latch on the door. If he didn't get away immediately, he wouldn't be able to leave at all. Then where would the annulment be? "He's gone to the village about five miles from here. We'll be gone long before he returns."

"And if I refuse to leave?"

"I'll hog-tie you and toss you into the back of the wagon— unmentionables and all. The men should get a real wallop out of that."

"You . . ." She picked up a china cup.

He managed to reach the other side of the door before the china shattered against the wood. A string of Irish curses followed.

Thorne took a deep breath of cool dry air and pasted on the grin of a well-satisfied male. An impossible task considering the fire in his blood, and the ache in his loins.

The camp was alive with activity. On the parade grounds a sergeant was drilling his troops. Merchants from the various shops were preparing to open for business. Women carried baskets for their purchases. Activity would slow by afternoon when the sun burned at its brightest. He avoided the officers gathered near headquarters, and headed toward the chapel.

Stepping into the darkened interior, he paused to gather a bit of peace. So far, he'd told nothing but lies to the good priest, who'd become friend and mentor. The first was his name, his identity. The latest was his marriage to Mariah.

The priest was saying Mass, his voice a litany of Latin phrases. The small congregation listened with rapt attention. He slunk into the shadows, feeling he had no right to enter the holy place. But he had to speak to Father Callahan before he returned to the mountain. Besides, he owed the priest a donation for performing the wedding ceremony, and doing him a favor in his absence.

Soon the Mass ended, and the people began to file out.

Thorne waited until the priest shed his vestments, then he shifted into the light to greet his friend.

"Father." He moved toward the small, rustic altar. "May I have a moment?"

A surprised look passed over the priest's face. "Thorne, I didn't expect to see you at Mass so early."

"I have to get back to the mountain, *Padre*, to the children and Sung Lo."

He nodded in understanding. "I suppose that I can quit looking for families to adopt the children, now that you're a married man. Surely a fine Irish colleen like Mariah will agree to keep the youngsters."

Reluctant to add another lie to his growing list of offenses, he shrugged off the subject. "She is a good woman. That's why I want to ask you another favor." Reaching into his pocket, he pulled out a number of gold coins.

"You don't have to pay for favors, Thorne. We've been friends for years. I will accept the donation in the name of the Lord." The priest shoved the coins into the pocket of his robe. "Now, what can I do for you?"

Thorne dropped to the first pew of the church. Though small, and crudely built, the chapel held a peace he'd never felt in a big church or cathedral. Of course, a lot of his contentment came from the serene man who personified God himself. "It's about the gold. I would like you to keep an eye on Edwards, to make sure he'll do the right thing by Mariah. She deserves the reward, and her family needs it."

"Edwards has only been here for six months, but he seems like a good man. He questioned me about you. I told him that you've been a friend, and contributor to the mission in Los Amigos. I think he believes your story about the outlaws, and he's already dispatched a message to Washington about the recovery of the gold."

"Now it's up to Washington to pay the reward."

"Just to keep the politicians honest, I've sent a message to an old friend asking his help in expediting the reward."

Thorne met the priest's gaze and noted a sly twinkle in his eye. "And who might this friend be?"

"Just a soldier I helped during the war—U. S. Grant is his name."

He should have known Father Callahan wouldn't let him down. "It's good to have connections. Thanks, *Padre*."

For a long moment Father Callahan eyed him, as if he didn't quite know how to proceed. He'd never seen the outspoken priest at a loss for words. After a long sigh, the cleric clamped a hand on Thorne's shoulder. "My son, I know something else is troubling you. The confessional is open, and anything you say will be held in strictest confidence."

Thorne shivered at the knowing gleam in the man's eyes. How safe would his secret be if he spoke it aloud? "There's nothing bothering me, except that I've gained a wife unexpectedly."

"Thorne, I've known you for nigh on to six years, ever since I opened the mission at Los Amigos. During that time, I've been aware that you've been keeping a secret, but it wasn't my business to pry. Whatever it is, your wife deserves to know the truth about you, and your identity."

He swallowed the rock that had suddenly lodged in his throat. "My identity? You know who I am?"

"Not exactly. But not long ago, a stranger came to the village looking for a man. He showed a small photograph. The image looked familiar, but I merely brushed off his questions. He had an accident, and I helped him arrange transportation back East—to Philadelphia. That's quite a coincidence, isn't it. I believe his name was O'Reilly, the same as your bride's."

Caught, Thorne couldn't continue with the lie, not in church, not to his friend. "Her brother."

"And the nun everybody was searching for?"

"Mariah, disguised in a habit."

"I thought as much. Take a word of advice. No matter how fast or how far you run, sooner or later somebody will catch you. Mariah did, others will, too."

"I'll remember your advice." He offered his hand. "I'd best get back to Mariah, before somebody starts looking for me now."

The priest pumped his hand vigorously. "Give my wishes to your lovely wife. You're a lucky man, Thorne, having a beautiful, young, Irish woman. She'll give you lots of fine children." Releasing his fingers, the priest made the sign of the cross. "*Vaya con Dios, mi amigo.*"

Thorne nodded. "*Hasta la vista, Padre.*"

He stepped into the bright sunlight, his mind in turmoil. The priest's last words rang in his head like the church bells, "Fine children." His footsteps slowed. His blood turned to ice. What if there already was a child? What if his carelessness had fathered a baby? How could he send Mariah away if there was any possibility of a child? There would be no annulment then.

Nor would he want one.

Chapter 13

Fuming from her encounter with Thorne, the stubborn mountain man who was now her husband, Mariah plopped down on the bed and ate as much of the breakfast as she could hold. The fruit she couldn't eat she wrapped in a napkin and added it to her meager belongings. Let Thorne fend for himself. Or let him go hungry.

Her gaze fell on the folded scrap of lace she'd worn the night before. It was a sad reminder of her folly—hers and Thorne's for letting themselves be roped into a marriage neither wanted. She didn't want a husband, and he didn't want a wife. Yet, in the eyes of God and man they were legally united in holy wedlock—till death do them part.

She fingered the fine filigree, and held it up to her face. A lovely bride she'd made, in her travel-worn clothes and borrowed veil. Her heart tightened, and a knot leaped into her throat. For a while, she'd imagined herself falling in love with that reclusive hermit. Imagine Mariah Rose O'Reilly living on a mountain in the middle of the wilderness. Sure, and it would never happen. And that was the truth.

First thing when she returned home, she would contact Father

Morgan at the church and file for her annulment. Then she would show Thorne that she didn't need him at all. Not at all.

The squeak of hinges pulled her out of her reverie. Frowning as was his custom, Thorne blocked the doorway. His body shut out the early-morning sunshine. She dropped the veil and spun to face him.

"Are you ready?" he asked, his voice as chilled as his gaze.

Two could play this game. "No. I thought I'd visit with Mrs. Edwards for a while. Thank her for her kindness, and for letting me borrow this." Carefully, she folded the lace into a small square.

"Leave a note. I want to get home."

"That would be terribly rude. She and her husband have been quite good to us." The mention of the general brought the expected glare from Thorne.

"The wagon and horses are outside. We have fresh supplies and water. I want to leave now." He braced his feet as if ready for a fight.

"Don't you think you should close that door before everybody in Fort Union hears our lovers' spat."

He turned, as if surprised he'd neglected that tiny detail. "I'm sorry, *dear*," he said in an exaggerated tone as he closed the door behind him. "If you aren't in that wagon by the time I count to ten, I'll toss you in bodily."

"Won't that just make everybody wonder? Especially that nice Lieutenant Prescott." He took one step toward her; his eyes blazed with fire. "Just give me a minute to write a note, and I'll join you. I know you're so eager to get on with our honeymoon." She shot him a haughty glance and sat at the table with paper and pen in hand.

If looks could kill, Mariah would be stone-cold dead. Growling like a wounded bear, Thorne folded his arms across his wide chest and guarded the doorway. He scanned the room, his gaze landing on the now-empty tray. She grinned. "I assumed you didn't want breakfast, so I ate it all."

His expression didn't change. "I'll eat some fruit on the road. I bought peaches and apples for the children."

Her note of thanks finished, she folded it and scrawled Mrs. Edwards's name on the envelope. "Shall I give this to the lieutenant, or deliver it in person?"

He snatched it from her fingers, and pulled open the door. With an angry gesture, he picked up her bag and waved her outside. Taking her time, she shoved her straw hat over her hair and tugged on her gloves. The tight set of his shoulders and the thin slash of his lips signaled impatience barely held in check. Let him stew in his own juices, she thought. It served him right for the way he'd rejected her.

After tossing the bag into the rear of the wagon with an assortment of baskets and boxes, he gave her a hand up into the wagon. "If it doesn't break your face, you had better at least attempt a smile," she whispered. "Prescott will wonder why you're so angry with your lovely new bride." She lifted a hand and waved to the young officer. "Captain!" she called. "Oh, I'm sorry, *Lieutenant*." Thorne remained on the ground at her side, his face set in a stony grin. He looked for all the world like a man carved from marble. She plucked the note from his fingers. "We must be on our way. Would you be so kind to deliver our thanks to General and Mrs. Edwards?"

"I'd be happy to, Mrs. Thorne. Last night surely was exciting. Your finding the gold, and then a wedding. Everybody's talking about you." He glanced at Thorne as if he'd just noticed his presence. "You, too, Mr. Thorne."

Only Mariah noted the flare of his nostrils, and the forced smile on his face. "Thanks. My bride and I are eager to reach Santa Fe. I promised her a real honeymoon."

She refrained from socking him in the jaw. Honeymoon? The man would just as soon sleep with a polecat as with her. "We're planning to stay in the finest hotel and eat in the elegant dining room there." She fluttered her eyelashes at Thorne, as Jenny did with her beaux. "Not all our meals, of course."

The young officer blushed at her implied meaning. "Have

a good journey,'' he said. With a snappy salute, he continued toward the headquarters, her note in his hand.

"He certainly is handsome,'' she mused as Thorne climbed up beside her.

"He's a boy.''

"He's close to my age.'' She turned and glanced over her shoulder at the young man. As if he sensed her scrutiny, he glanced back at her. Thorne snapped the lines, and the horses took off at a jerk. Mariah wrenched sideways into Thorne's shoulder. She grabbed his arm to keep from tumbling to the ground. His arm was hard and unyielding under her touch. Like the man himself.

Some devilment goaded her on. "I understand he's from a fine family in New York. He'll make some lucky girl a good husband.''

Thorne didn't blink an eye or move a muscle. She snuggled closer to his side, making sure her breast pressed against his arm. "He's the kind of man I'll look for as a lover. After I'm wealthy, of course. And after I get the annulment.''

By then they were nearing the edge of the large military encampment. A troop of soldiers, the Stars and Stripes flying in front of them rode in the opposite entrance. "Why, I believe that's General Edwards returning. I wonder what he's going to think when he finds we're gone.''

He shook the reins, forcing the horses into a run. "Nothing. Father Callahan will explain that we were eager to get on with our honeymoon.''

"Humph!'' She shoved away from him, putting as much space as possible between them. The man was clearly made of thorns. He prickled her every which way. "More likely you're eager to get rid of me, so you can hide further back in that miserable mountain of yours.''

"Exactly. As soon as I check on the children and Sung Lo, I'll see you to the nearest railroad and send you on your way.''

"Have you considered returning with me?''

"I can't.''

It was a never-ending argument, so she decided to drop it for now. But he wasn't getting off so easily. No, sir. Mrs. Thornton was depending on her. She'd given her word, and she intended to see the man return to his grandmother, come hell or high water.

Once they were away from the fort, Thorne slowed the team. It did no good to take out his frustration on innocent horses. The poor dumb animals weren't at fault for the mess he'd gotten into. Somehow he had to find a way to broach the subject of the possibility of a child. Surely she must have at least considered the chance they'd taken.

He followed the Mora River, avoiding the small villages along the route. Soon the valley gave way to foothills, and, by nightfall, they had entered the mountains. He and Mariah had spoken little, no more than necessary when they'd stopped to rest the horses and snack on the fruit. With the approach of autumn, the days grew shorter, and the evenings cooler. In the higher altitudes, the leaves were turning, the aspens taking on a yellow hue. In Pennsylvania, it would be another month before the colors changed. In Virginia, even later.

Accustomed to the routine, Mariah stayed out of his way as he set up camp. He'd found a sheltered grove of cottonwoods near a stream, with plenty of dry wood and water. With the fire blazing, and the fish he'd caught frying in the pan, he realized he hadn't seen her for quite some time. His stomach knotted. Hadn't she learned a lesson about wandering away from camp?

He stood and grabbed his rifle. Listening for any sign of her whereabouts, the only sound was an occasional whinny of the horses and the wind whistling through the trees. "Mariah!" he called. No answer.

Cautiously, he approached the stream. Surely she hadn't tried to bathe in the chilled water. Guided by the bright moon, he again called her name. His voice was lost in the gurgling water dancing over the rocks. Panic twisted a knife in his chest. Where could the blasted woman have gone?

The moon and stars gave enough light to follow her trail. Crushed grass, broken twigs, and an occasional footprint led him in what appeared to be a circle. Through the trees, he caught the glow of his campfire. A figure was crouched over the frying pan. He darted through the trees, his finger on the rifle trigger.

He stopped short when she lifted her gaze to his. "Letting our supper burn while you traipse off into the woods?" Mariah asked.

His breath coming in hard gasps, more from fright than exertion, he glared at her. "Where the hell have you been?"

Seemingly untouched by his anger, she ladled the fish onto two tin plates. "Nowhere. I washed up in the stream, then found my way back to camp." She stuck a forkful of fresh trout into her mouth. "Mmm, delicious. You're quite a good cook. Although they could use a little more salt."

"Why didn't you answer when I called?" He fisted his hands to keep from shaking her.

Lifting wide, innocent eyes, she said, "I didn't hear you."

On a deep growl, he sank to the ground near her. Her act didn't fool him one bit. She'd been leading him on a merry chase, ignoring him, wanting to have her own way.

"You sound like an old bear coming out of hibernation when you growl like that."

"I am an old bear and I want to hibernate."

"So, when I leave, you'll sneak back into the canyons of the mountains and nobody will ever find you."

"That's right." In truth, it was all he'd ever wanted, yet for some odd reason, the idea of being completely alone didn't quite hold the same appeal it once had.

"What about those ointments and remedies you've been working on? Will you keep your discoveries to yourself? Won't you share your findings with the world?"

She'd hit a sore spot. His work was too important not to share. "I'll think of a way to get them into the right hands."

"I'll be glad to help."

"I don't need help."

She licked her fingers and dumped her dish into a bucket of water. "I'll wash these, if you give me permission to go down by the stream."

He suppressed the next growl that threatened to spew from his throat. "I'll take care of it. You stay close to the fire. Next time I'll just let whatever animal is lurking in the darkness have you."

With a bubble of laughter, she stood and stretched. Her breasts pressed against her blouse, and her arms reached up as if searching for the moon. "I'm a might too tough for a rabbit or squirrel. And I'm not fool enough to go wandering alone without my gun."

Picking up the frying pan, he dunked it in the pail with the dirty dishes. He felt like dunking his head under the cold water. "Irish, you'll be the death of me yet," he muttered, making his way through the bushes to the stream.

"Don't be long, darling," she called after him. "We're still on our honeymoon, remember?"

Honeymoon. He reached the bubbling water, and resisted jumping in headfirst. How could he forget when all he could think about was her soft, smooth flesh pressed to his? Of the feel of her silky hair on his chest. Of burying himself in her sweetness until nothing else mattered but the two of them— not yesterday or tomorrow, just now. Instead, he splashed his face until the heat dissipated from his flesh. The sooner he sent her packing back to Philadelphia, the sooner he would be able to breathe normally again.

When he returned to the campsite, he was surprised that she was seated demurely beside the fire. Her bedroll lay on the ground on the opposite side of the fire from his. Hairbrush in hand, she tugged it through her tangle of long, raven hair. He couldn't help following every movement. The gesture was so feminine, his heart beat double time and his pulse raced. He hadn't been away from women so long that he didn't recognize pure old-fashioned temptation when it slapped him in the face. The ploy wasn't going to work. As bewitching as she looked with the moonlight spilling on her face, he steeled himself not to fall victim to her charms.

He gathered up a pile of dry leaves and pine needles and shook out his blanket, leaving room for Mariah.

"How long will it take to get home?" Her voice blended with the song of the wind and the water.

"Tomorrow evening, if we get an early enough start." Stretching out on his blanket, he continued to stare at her. She tossed her hair over her shoulder and twisted it in a long, single braid. "Come, get some sleep. Tomorrow will be a hard day." He patted the pile of leaves beside his bedroll.

She picked up her blanket and shook it out. "I'll sleep over here. I'd rather take my chances with a rattler than a cantankerous old bear."

Mariah awoke the next morning feeling as if she were the bear that hadn't gotten its full winter's sleep. In spite of her bravado, she'd slept little, listening to every insect, animal, and wind whisper in the night. The moment Thorne pulled that battered old hat over his eyes, he'd dropped off to sleep, his snores keeping time with the rumble of the water over the stones. She kept her gun clutched in her fingers, and imagined all sorts of dangers lurking in the darkness. In spite of her fear, she refused to move into the shadow of Thorne's protection.

He seemed rested and full of energy as he hitched up the wagon and cleared the campsite. No doubt the fact Mariah would soon be out of his life for good was the reason for his good humor.

She forced a smile she didn't feel, and boarded the wagon. The going was rougher in the higher altitudes. By midday, they'd dropped into a narrow valley and through the pass between mountains. Thorne informed her they were now on his land, part of the hundred thousand acres he owned. That meant they were nearer his mountain, the place he called home.

Mariah blithely informed him that when she got home, she hoped she never saw mountains again. And the closest she wanted to get to horses were the ones pulling carriages or streetcars.

The sun had dropped low behind the hills, and the sky was streaked with the rainbow glow of twilight when they reached the barn where Thorne stabled his animals. For the past hours, he'd appeared deep in thought, and from time to time he'd shot a glance at her. More than once, she felt as if he were about to speak but changed his mind.

For a long moment, he remained still, his elbows braced on his knees, the lines tight in his hands. He turned to her, a bit of tenderness in his gaze. His look took her back for a moment, it was so unlike him. It was the way he'd looked at her when they'd made love. Mariah bit her lip to push away the memories of that precious night that meant nothing to him.

"Irish," he said. "I want to talk to you about something."

"I'm listening."

"It's about—" Before he finished his sentence, a child's shouts rent the air.

Juan and Running Deer darted through the bushes into the clearing. "Thorne! Sissy!" the little girl cried. "You come back." Neither child hesitated. They jumped aboard the wagon, and flung their arms around Thorne and Mariah's necks.

Mariah returned the hug and kissed both youngsters. "I promised, didn't I?" She shot a glance at Thorne. What was he about to say when they were interrupted?

"We miss you and Thorne, too."

Thorne pulled both children onto his lap. "Where's Sung Lo?"

"He watch cabin with his big knife." Running Deer tugged on Thorne's beard. "You bring us something?"

Mariah laughed. Children were the same the world over. "Did you behave while we were gone?" she asked.

"We very good. Clean out garden for Sung Lo. Catch rabbits. Say prayers." The last was for Mariah, who'd encouraged them to pray.

"Then I suppose I'll find something in the back of the wagon for you." He reached behind him and pulled out a paper-wrapped package Mariah hadn't noticed before. "Running Deer, you carry this, and Juan can carry that basket of ripe peaches. The kind that run juice down your pretty chin."

The little girl giggled. Mariah had never seen Thorne so playful with the pair. With the package tight in her arms, Running Deer allowed Thorne to set her on the ground. He jumped down after her and helped the little boy with his basket of fruit. Then he turned to Mariah.

As her feet touched the ground, she looked up into his eyes. "What were you about to tell me?"

He shook his head and stepped away from her. "It can wait."

She shrugged, aware it would do no good to press. Thorne would tell her in his own good time. He probably only wanted to remind her of his plans for her trip home.

Stepping away, she retrieved her bag and some of the newly purchased supplies from the rear of the wagon. Mariah followed the children up the narrow path, leaving Thorne to feed and stable the horses.

Running Deer chatted constantly, sharing her every thought with Mariah. She'd clearly missed Mariah and Thorne, and was delighted to see them. The ever-silent little boy toted the basket of fruit, but his eyes spoke more eloquently than words. He loved her and he wished she could stay with them always.

She shifted her burden in her arms. Was she reading Juan's emotions, or her own? What would happen to these precious children and the wonderful old Chinese when she left? Her heart ached at the thought of never seeing them again. How could Thorne be so heartless to send them away? After the lovemaking they'd shared, how could he send Mariah away?

Easily. The man had no heart.

Sung Lo greeted her with a wide smile and deep bow from the waist. Unable to quench her delight at seeing the old man, she dropped her bundles and gave him a big hug—much as she would give her father. His face pinked and he mumbled something in Chinese.

He gestured her inside. "Good see Sissy. Eat. Chop, chop."

His broken English brought a smile. He'd set the table for five and a pot was bubbling on the fire. She hadn't smelled something so delicious since she'd left home.

"Thorne bring presents." Running Deer set her package on the table. "And peaches," she added.

Juan rubbed his stomach while eyeing the ripe, pink fruit. Maybe Thorne had a tiny piece of a heart, after all, to think about the children while he'd been in such a precarious situation at the fort.

Sung Lo relieved Mariah of her burden, new rainbow-colored blankets for their beds. Four. None for Mariah.

Wife or not, there was no place in his life for Mariah.

Running Deer's squeal brought her out of her thoughts. "Thorne, can we open present?" The little girl flung her arms around the big man's legs as he entered the cabin.

Thorne looked into pleading dark eyes. A tiny smile tugged at lips nearly hidden by his beard. "Yep." He dropped the load of supplies he'd brought from the fort. With one arm, he lifted the little girl to his shoulder. She giggled and tugged on his hair. He settled on the bench with the little girl on one leg and Juan on the other. Sung Lo hovered nearby. Thorne picked up the paper package. "Let's see what's in here."

Not wanting to intrude, Mariah moved to the bed and reached for her valise. "I think I'd like to clean up before dinner."

"Don't you want to see what I've brought?" Thorne asked, slanting a glance over his shoulder.

"I suppose." She sank on the cot and watched from across the room.

Thorne slit the string with his knife and unfolded the brown paper. He handed a tissue-wrapped package to Running Deer.

The little girl tore the paper, and stared wide-eyed at a beautiful doll. "A baby," she cried, flinging her arms around Thorne's neck. "Thank you. I show Sissy." Hugging the doll to her chest, she raced into Mariah's open arms. "I call her Rosie. She look like Sissy."

Tears misted Mariah's eyes. The doll had black yarn for hair, and wore a skirt of multi-colored tiers. It was a beautifully handmade doll, one any child would love. She oohed and ahhed and declared that the doll was as beautiful as Running Deer.

Her gaze shifted to Thorne, and to Juan, waiting patiently on his lap. "What's this?" He handed a smaller package to the little boy. Unlike the girl, Juan carefully removed the tissue and smoothed it out with his fingers.

At first Mariah didn't see what held the child's intense stare. Thorne lifted the object and placed it in the boy's mouth. "Blow into it, Juan. It's a whistle. You'll be able to sing with the birds."

The boy blew gently, making a weak squeak. Fascinated, he took a deep breath, and the shrill noise rent the air. Sung Lo covered his ears and muttered in Chinese. On Juan's next try, the noise turned into a melody. Thorne had given the boy a voice.

He raced to show Mariah, and she didn't try to stem her tears. Maybe the stoic mountain man had a bit of a heart after all.

Next, he handed a tooled leather sheath and knife to Sung Lo. "For my friend," he said, emotion making his voice husky. Again, she wondered where the old man would go when Thorne hid deeper into the mountain. The children might find families, but the old man had nowhere to go.

She wiped her eyes, and looked up to find Thorne gazing down at her. He hunkered down in front of her. "I didn't forget you, Irish."

"I didn't expect anything. You've done enough for me."

He'd risked his life and freedom so she could get the government's reward for her family.

"Take it." He pressed a small package into her fingers. His touch shot flutters up her arm, clear to her heart. As if scorched by her hand, he stood and turned away. "Let's eat."

The children deserted Mariah and ran to the table. Running Deer clutched her doll in her arms, and Juan made squeaky noises with his whistle. Sung Lo had threaded the sheath onto his belt, and he proudly displayed the knife.

Mariah weighed the heavy object in her hand. "It doesn't feel like a rattlesnake," she said in an effort to lighten her mood.

"Don't be so sure." Thorne glanced over his shoulder.

Slowly, she removed the tissue to reveal a beautiful silver bracelet. Two inches wide, the silver cuff was engraved with twining roses and set with small turquoise stones—the exact color of her eyes.

Her breath caught in her throat. A stunning piece of jewelry was the last thing she had expected from Thorne. As beautiful as the bracelet was, it was a poor substitute for his love. She cuffed it on her arm. If this was all he would ever give her, she would wear it always as a reminder of the time they'd shared.

Their eyes met and held. "Thank you, Mountain Man," she said. "It's beautiful."

As if pleased with her reaction, he smiled. "Come and eat."

Take advantage of this offer to enjoy Zebra's newest line of historical romance novels....Splendor Romances (formerly Lovegrams Historical Romances)- Take our introductory shipment of 4 romance novels -Absolutely Free! (a $19.96 value)

Now you'll be able to savor today's best romance novels without even leaving your home with our convenient and inexpensive home subscription service. Here's what you get for joining:

- 4 BRAND NEW bestselling Splendor Romances delivered to your doorstep every month
- 20% off every title (or almost $4.00 off) with your home subscription
- Shipping and handling is just $1.50.
- A FREE monthly newsletter, *Zebra/Pinnacle Romance News* filled with author interviews, member benefits, book previews and more!
- No risks or obligations...you're free to cancel whenever you wish...no questions asked

To get started with your own home subscription, simply complete and return the card provided. You'll receive your FREE introductory shipment of 4 Splendor Romances and then you'll begin to receive monthly shipments of new Zebra Splendor titles. Each shipment will be yours to examine for 10 days and then if you decide to keep the books, you'll pay the preferred home subscriber's price of just $4.00 per title. That's $16 for all 4 books with $1.50 added for shipping and handling. And if you want us to stop sending books, just say the word...it's that simple.

4 Free BOOKS are waiting for you!
Just mail in the certificate below!

If the certificate is missing below, write to: Splendor Romances, Zebra Home Subscription Service, Inc., P.O. Box 5214, Clifton, New Jersey 07015-5214

FREE BOOK CERTIFICATE

Yes! Please send me 4 Splendor Romances (formerly Zebra Lovegram Historical Romances), ABSOLUTELY FREE! After my introductory shipment, I will be able to preview 4 new Splendor Romances each month FREE for 10 days. Then if I decide to keep them, I will pay the money-saving preferred publisher's price of just $4.00 each... a total of $16.00. That's 20% off the regular publisher's price and I pay just $1.50 for shipping and handling. I may return any shipment within 10 days and owe nothing, and I may cancel my subscription at any time. The 4 FREE books will be mine to keep in any case.

Name _____

Address _____ Apt. _____

City _____ State _____ Zip _____

Telephone ( ) _____

Signature _____ SP1198
(If under 18, parent or guardian must sign.)

Terms and prices subject to change. Orders subject to acceptance by Zebra Home Subscription Service, Inc. . Zebra Home Subscription Service, Inc. reserves the right to reject or cancel any subscription.

Chapter 14

He had to talk to her. Thorne tossed a towel over his shoulder and made his way toward the stream. He'd watched Mariah with the children. She truly cared for them. Father Callahan was right, she would make a good mother.

The knots in his stomach tightened. The pains had worsened since the idea of a baby had hit him. It could possibly be weeks before she would know if he'd fathered a child. By then she would be home with her family in Philadelphia—facing her ordeal alone.

Without the support of the father.

Without his ever being sure.

As ten years ago, he found himself with few choices.

It was nearly dark when he shoved aside the bushes that guarded the hot springs. Mariah had disappeared soon after they'd eaten. He knew she'd headed for the stream and a full bath. Surely she was done by now, and he would have the privacy of the spring to relax and sort out his options.

He stopped dead. A pile of female garments were spread over the grass. Mariah was still in the pool.

Not daring to venture closer, he closed his eyes and pictured her as she'd looked under the waterfall in the canyon. Moonlight glistened on the water, and her body shone like porcelain. Desire shot through him at the memory of their lovemaking.

He battled the need to go to her, and quench his fire in her sweet, silky body. Reason ordered him to retreat while he had the chance. Either bathe in the fire of lust, or chill in the icy loneliness of perdition.

Mariah offered warmth and affection, the closest he'd come to love since he'd chosen his country over Suzanna. Without Mariah, he had nothing but the hell he'd created out of fear.

He ached for one last time with her. One time to store away enough warmth to last a cold, lonely lifetime.

Reason told him that one more time would ruin her chance for an annulment. He backed away, regret weighted like iron shackles on his legs.

The thicket of bushes separating them, he paused to take a long gulp of the cooling mountain air. If he had any sense at all, he would race down stream and immerse himself in the chill water. Yet, he remained anchored by his own needs. As he forced one foot in front of the other, a startled noise from the pool stopped him.

At first, he didn't hear anything but the buzz of night insects and the gurgle of the bubbling spring. Then it came again, a human voice. A distressed female sound. "Oh, no!" she cried.

Mariah. In trouble.

Instincts overrode common sense. He darted through the bushes into the clearing where she'd left her clothes. She was there, in the pool. Her head and shoulders dropped below the water.

Afraid she was drowning, he tossed aside his towel and jumped in with her. The shallow water to his chest, he braced his feet on the rocky bottom. He grabbed her arms and hauled her up into his chest.

"Irish, are you okay?"

She shook her head and shoved against his chest. "What are you doing? Let me go."

Again she dropped under the water, her hands brushing along his legs. Confused, he again tugged her to the surface. "Woman, are you trying to drown yourself."

"No, you idiot. Get out of my way."

He tightened his grip. "What are you doing?"

Water dripped from her face and off her chin. He hair clung to her creamy shoulders. "My bracelet. I lost my bracelet."

"Your bracelet? Are you trying to kill yourself over a trinket?"

"No. I want to find it. Help me."

This time when she ducked into the pool, he went with her. Thank goodness the gathering dusk obscured her body from his view. Feeling was another matter altogether. As he brushed his fingers along the rocky bottom, he encountered her warm foot and the soft flesh of her legs. She kicked out at him, and broke the surface for air. He came up at the same time. His hands brushed her from her naked hip to bare breast. The fire in his blood burst into an inferno. Quickly he dropped back into the pool and sifted his fingers through the stones that lined the pool. As he was nearly out of breath, he touched something different. He looped his fingers into the cuff and carried it to the surface.

"I've found it," he managed to say, gasping for breath.

She turned to face him, and snatched it from his fingers. "Thank you. I was afraid I'd lost it for good."

He gripped her shoulders and forced her to face him. "Why did you bother? I would have bought you another one."

In the growing darkness, he saw the softness in her gaze. She slipped the cuff onto her wrist. "But this is the one you bought when we married."

Carrying her hand to his face, he kissed her wrist above the silver bracelet. "Does it mean that much to you?"

"It's a reminder of you and the children."

"How will you remember me, Irish?" Unable to stop himself, he ran a row of kisses up her arm, his teeth nibbling gently on the warm, wet flesh.

She shivered. "As the gruff mountain man who takes in strays and gives them love and care."

"Is that all?" By then, he'd given up all hope of reason. He needed her to once again feel like a whole man—to fill the shell that had merely existed before she fell into his arms. He pulled her hard against his chest, the tips of her breasts burning into his flesh through his shirt. His hands brushed along her spine until he cupped her bottom and showed her the full power of his passion.

Her fingers twisted in the hair at his nape; her lips found the sensitive spot at his throat. "As a wonderful, strong man who—" She shivered. "Make love to me, please."

Even as his mind sent out warnings, he refused to listen. He scooped Mariah up in his arms and climbed over the rocky ledge. She clung to his shoulders, her lips and teeth working magic on his flesh. Gently, he laid her on the grass and covered her with a large towel. He tore off his wet clothes and joined her on the ground.

His lips and hands discovered and explored her hidden desires. She responded to his touch with the joy and passion of a wanton. Her body blended with his in harmony as perfect as a symphony. With every kiss he gave, she returned twofold. Thorne gave his all. Mariah held nothing back. When they joined bodies, it was the glorious merging of souls and spirits. He had never felt so fulfilled or complete as a man. This beautiful woman had given him back his soul, his purpose for living.

As he gathered her to his chest in the afterglow of love, he dreaded the moment when he would have to let her go. Too many obstacles stood between them. Barriers beyond their own making, circumstances that even now could be at work to tear them apart.

He shivered, more from his own devastating thoughts than from the chill of the mountain night.

Mariah stirred in his arms. "Isn't it a glorious night?" she whispered, her voice husky with passion.

His gaze never left her face. "The most beautiful I've ever seen."

She smiled; her fingers brushed his lips. "I wonder if I would like your making love to me without your beard."

Regret washed over him. This was their last time together. A folly on his part that could ruin all her plans for the future. "Irish, there's something we have to discuss."

"You sound so serious. Do you bewail what was so wonderful between us?" She leaned on her elbow, and stared at him.

His heart urged him to total honesty. "No. I can't regret what happened, but sometimes in our folly, there are consequences. What if you have a child?"

She sat up and hugged the towel to her breasts. "A child?" Her voice faltered. "I hadn't thought about that."

"I can't let you go without knowing for sure one way or the other."

"It's impossible. I can't have a child."

Confused, he sat up and studied her in the dim moonlight. "You mean you can't conceive?"

"I mean that it would be my problem, and I'll deal with it."

"How?"

Tugging the towel around her body, she stood and snatched up her clothes. "You've made me a wealthy woman. I can support myself and my family. I won't ask for your help." Her tone turned icy.

Heedless of his nudity, he stood and faced her. "Dammit all, Irish. I'd want to help."

"How, Thorne? You won't leave your mountain, and I have to get back to my family. You were right. There's no future for us. As soon as I get home, I'll apply for that annulment."

"You can't if you're pregnant."

Her eyes shot daggers. "Those things can be worked out with the Church. I'm not so naive to believe that a little money passed to the right hands won't work miracles. I won't ask you or your rich family for anything. I'll gladly raise my child alone.'' Clad in nothing but his bracelet, she stomped away from him.

In that instant, he made the only decision possible. The one that had been hovering at the edges of his mind for days. ''You won't have to. I'm going back with you.''

His words stopped Mariah in midstride. She spun to face him across the grassy bank. His magnificent body gleamed in the moonlight. The leather medicine bag rested in the center of his chest. Wide shoulders stiff, his hands braced on his bare hips. ''You're going back to Philadelphia with me?'' Surely she'd misunderstood.

''You were right. I've been running away too long. My grandmother needs me, and I want to see her again before it's too late.'' Emotion washed across his face. Turmoil was written in his gaze.

''What about the Army?''

''I'll have to take my chances. They may offer leniency since I helped you return that gold.'' He grabbed his trousers and pulled them on his legs. ''It's only a matter of time before somebody else finds me. I want to see that the children are protected and provided for before that happens.''

Her heart sank at the thought of the chances he was willing to take for those he loved. If only he loved her just a little. ''Sure, and your grandmother will help you. My family will, too.''

''We'll tell the others in the morning. We can be on our way in a day or two.''

''And in a few weeks we'll be home.''

''*You'll* be home, Irish. I don't have a home, or a country.''

''Thorne . . .'' She took one step toward him. He halted her with a hand. Her heart went out to the man. He was so alone and forlorn.

''It's getting cold. Go to the cabin. I'll be back by daybreak.''

She nodded, aware there was little she could do for him. Not that he wanted her help. However, she would do everything within her power to help the children and, of course, Sung Lo.

* * *

Thorne watched the sunrise from high on the mountain. The sun eased its way over the hills from the east as if reluctant to show its full glory. The sky turned from gray to pink, as the golden globe make a decision to burst upon the land. How many more sunrises would he see? A man on borrowed time, he gave thanks daily for each and every one.

As much as he loved the mountain, the time had come to leave. He had run as far as he could go. When he'd arrived here, he'd come with nothing but the clothes on his back, a horse, and rifle. Leaving, he would take what had become his family—and a wife.

Shirtless and barefoot, he lifted his hands, welcoming another day. The warmth from the sun barely chased away the night's chill. Through the long night, his thoughts had kept him ignorant of the cold. Mentally, he'd made the plans for the journey. The hardest part would be informing the children.

This was best for them. They needed a home, education. And Juan should see a doctor. Even now, Edwards could have remembered him and was sending a troop of soldiers to arrest him. This way, he could surrender on his own terms. It would give him time to see his grandmother, and make a will to provide for the children and Sung Lo. He would name Mariah the executrix, and, of course, he would take care of her and their child.

His heart twisted at the thought of never seeing his son or daughter, or not watching Running Deer grow into a beautiful woman and Juan into a fine man. Or being with Mariah. He quenched any feelings he had for her. It wouldn't do him or her any good to admit how much he cared.

Thorne wasn't a man given to prayer, he wasn't sure he believed in a God like Father Callahan, or even like Mariah. Yet, he couldn't help but whisper a supplication to whatever Almighty was out there to give him strength and courage. To protect his family in his absence.

Slowly, he turned, and started down the nearly invisible path to the cabin. On the way, he stopped and retrieved his shirt and moccasins from near the pool. From the spot where he'd made love to Mariah the night before. It had been foolishness on his part, but he'd needed her as surely as a garden needs water.

Mariah was waiting outside when he approached the clearing. She was wearing a simple calico dress, and her long hair was blowing in the morning breeze like the wings of a raven. Emotion caught in his throat. If only things were different. If only they had a chance of a future together. If only he didn't care.

"Have you changed your mind?" she asked.

"No. I gave you my word. I must tell the children."

"They're eating." She led the way into the cabin.

Both children gave him wide grins when he entered. Running Deer clutched her doll to her chest, and Juan wore his whistle on a ribbon around his neck. He picked it up and played a tune for him. Thorne forced a smile he didn't feel.

"Sung Lo, will you please sit down. I have to speak to all of you." He took his seat at the head of the table, and waited for the old man to find his place.

"Thorne eat." Sung Lo shoved a bowl in front of him. As usual, it was one of his concoctions, but beside his bowl was a golden, fluffy biscuit.

He took a bite, just to satisfy the old man. "You know that Sissy Rosie came from far away to see where we live." He cleared his throat before he could continue. At his side, Mariah squeezed his hand in encouragement. "Now we have to go with her to see where she lives. We'll go on a long journey. First we take the wagon, then a stagecoach, then the train. Then we'll be in Philadelphia."

The children tilted their heads in confusion. "What train?" the little girl asked in her innocence.

"It's a great iron horse that pulls wagons with many people

inside,'' Mariah informed them. "It's so much fun. You'll get to see all kinds of wonderful things.''

"Sung Lo see iron horse. No like. Stay here.'' The Chinese folded his thin arms over his chest.

Thorne was afraid of this kind of reaction. "You have to leave. It's too dangerous for you alone. You can go to San Francisco where there are many Chinese.''

The old man looked at the children. "Do children go with Sissy?''

He slanted a glance at Mariah, silently asking for help.

"Yes, we'll all be together,'' she said.

"Then Sung Lo go with Sissy, too.''

Running Deer tugged on his shirt. "What 'Delphia?''

"Philadelphia, that's where Sissy lives.''

"We live with Sissy?''

"Of course,'' Mariah said. "I have brothers and sisters, and I know they'll love you lots and lots.''

"Then we go to 'Delphia. Juan go. Sung Lo go.'' Warm brown eyes met his. "Can Rosie go?'' She displayed her doll.

"Rosie, and anything else you want to bring. I want you to gather your clothes, and let Sissy help you pack.'' He studied the old man, his face a wreath of frowns. "You, too, Sung Lo. Pack your knives, we may need them on the road.''

Mariah released his hand and he felt the loss. "I'd best get started. When do you want to leave?''

"As soon as we pack and secure the cabin. I'll leave the stores here in case Tongo or his people decide to take up my offer. I won't be needing them where I'm going.''

"You don't think you'll be back, do you?''

"Irish, I doubt I'll be alive in another couple of months.'' He stood and started for the door. She caught his arm and jerked him to a stop.

"Don't say that. Anything can happen. Have faith.''

"I'll remember those words when I'm facing a firing squad.''

He pulled out of her grip. "Start packing. I want to leave this mountain today."

Thorne's rush to leave caught Mariah off guard. She'd expected him to procrastinate and stall as long as possible. His love for his mountain was evident. He probably felt it was best just to up and go before he changed his mind.

By afternoon, they'd loaded their few personal belongings into the bed of the wagon. Along with his clothes, Thorne carefully packed the herbs, roots, and concoctions he'd prepared, along with his ledgers and notes. Sung Lo brought along his cooking pots and cleaver, plus supplies to prepare their meals on the road. He huddled in the rear with the children, as if afraid of what lay ahead. Mariah, too, was a little afraid for all of them. She was going home. They were going to totally foreign territory. Running Deer hugged her doll, and Juan played a jaunty tune on his whistle. Mariah fingered her bracelet, and vowed to never take it off. Thorne touched the medicine bag as if asking for protection.

As they left the mountain, Thorne turned the wagon toward the northeast. Seated beside him, it took only a few minutes for Mariah to wonder about their destination. "Is this the way to Los Amigos?" she asked.

"No. I decided we should board the stagecoach at Cimarron instead." He held up his hand to stop her from asking more questions. "It'll be safer."

"Oh." She nodded in understanding. If the soldiers came looking for them, their first stop would be Los Amigos. Heading north to Cimarron would buy Thorne a bit of time.

The journey was rough, the road little more than a cow path through the foothills. They stopped often to give the children a chance to stretch and eat. The basket of peaches was nearly gone by the time they found a small stream beside which to camp. Sung Lo prepared the evening meal, and did a much better job than she'd had when she and Thorne did the cooking.

Mariah and Thorne remained awake after the others had fallen asleep. All day, she'd wanted a moment alone with him. Now that the time had come, she had nothing to say.

"Well, Irish," he said, tossing a log on the fire. "Looks like you're going to complete your mission. You're a pretty good bounty hunter. I'm going willingly."

"You can still change your mind," she said.

"No. The next one who comes looking for me might be after a reward, and take me dead or alive. At least you wanted me alive."

Her heart sank. She hadn't told him about the reward from his grandmother for his safe return. She felt like Judas, selling him out for thirty pieces of silver. How would he feel if he knew? Not that it mattered what he thought. He'd made it clear that once she got the annulment, they need never see each other again. Unless there was a child from her indecent behavior. As much as she loved Thorne, she didn't want him tied to her because of a baby. If he didn't want her for herself, he couldn't have her at all.

"You wouldn't be much good to your grandmother dead."

He circled the fire and sat beside her on a fallen log. "Irish, I want you to do a favor for me." He pressed a folded sheet of paper into her hand. "This is my last will and testament. If anything happens to me, take it to my grandmother. She'll see that it's legally executed."

"Nothing's going to happen to you. You're too tough."

"You never know. Put it into one of those secret pockets you have in that skirt." He pulled a leather bag from his shirt and handed it to her. "Take this. There's enough gold for you to get back to Philadelphia, and take care of the children until my will is executed."

She weighed the heavy bag in her hand. The coins inside clinked loudly in the quiet night. "I don't need this. Nothing's going to happen to you."

He closed his hand over hers. His touch was warm and sure.

"Take it. Use it to buy some traveling clothes for you and the children. Regardless, it's yours."

"You've done enough for me by letting me have the reward. I don't want your gold."

"If I'm arrested, the Army would take it from me. They won't bother you, and you'll need it to get home."

"You sound as if you expect the soldiers to come looking for you."

"I just want to be careful. Edwards is no fool. Sooner or later he'll remember who I am."

"I hope not. The children and Sung Lo need you." *I need you.*

He brushed a finger over the silver bracelet. "I'm trusting you to take care of them, Irish."

"I will," Mariah whispered. "I promise."

Chapter 15

Late the next afternoon, they rode into Cimarron. Set among shady cottonwood trees and fragrant pines, the town served as a major stop on the Santa Fe Trail. Mariah recalled the rough and rowdy town from her journey a few weeks earlier. In her disguise as a nun, she'd been relatively safe from the dangerous men that crowded the town.

As they traversed the dusty main street, Thorne pointed out the three-story adobe mansion that Lucien Maxwell had built from which to rule his nearby million-acre empire. She stared at the mansion that covered a full city block. She'd seen palatial homes in the East, but this one rivaled even those.

Bars and saloons burst with music and noise, and the merchants seemed to be doing a landslide business. Horses and wagons lined the street, while plainly clothed women carrying baskets on their arms visited on the boardwalk. Fancy ladies wearing little more than chemises and corsets advertised their wares on the balcony above several saloons. Occasionally, a cowboy staggered from a bar and tipped his hat, losing his balance with the gesture.

Throne stiffened when they passed a group of blue-uniformed

soldiers near the blacksmith's shop. Mariah squeezed his arm to reassure him that they were safe. They'd agreed that she would register at the hotel as Sister Rose Smith in order not to tempt fate any more than necessary. Meanwhile, he and Sung Lo would check the stagecoach office and sell the team and wagon.

Nobody paid heed to still another family entering the town. Not even the soldiers lifted their heads. When the wagon stopped, Mariah adjusted the black veil over her head and pasted on her most devout expression. Thorne helped her and the children to the ground and handed her their bags.

He hunkered down to eye level with the youngsters. "Listen to Sissy, and do as she says. I'll be back in a little bit."

Both nodded, their eyes fearful at the strange sights surrounding them. Small hands clutched Mariah's black skirt. "We'll be fine. Go see about passage on that stagecoach," she said.

Thorne nodded. "Thanks, Irish. Meet me in the back alley in about an hour. I'm not sure I want to use the front entrance."

"Yes, sir. In an hour."

Mariah lowered her gaze in an effort to appear demure, and approached the front entrance to the St. James Hotel. The building was much larger and elaborate than she'd have imagined for a small town. On her previous pass through, she'd had only hours before her stagecoach left, so she'd had no time to enjoy the accommodations. This time she would take advantage of every amenity offered.

Dragging the children at her side, she entered the lobby. Men in suits and rough clothing gathered on the high-backed velvet couches and chairs, reading newspapers or holding conversations. Deep-brown bureaus lined the walls. She stepped lightly on the long carpet runner to the desk.

She waited impatiently as the gentleman in front of her signed the guest book. His clothes were dusty from the road, as were hers. He was about her age, soft-spoken and polite. He asked for his usual room at the end of the hall on the first floor and paid the clerk. After taking the key, he turned and tipped his hat to Mariah. Cold hard eyes sent shivers up her spine. She'd seen that face before, though at the moment she couldn't remember where. She dismissed the unlikely possibility and faced the desk clerk.

The middle-aged man slicked his hand through his hair and smiled at Mariah. "May I help you, *señora*," he asked.

"It is *Sister*," she remarked, in her best Sister Mary Louise voice, with a touch of the brogue. "Sister Rose Smith."

"Smith?"

"Is there something with being a Smith?"

"No, ma'am." He snickered. "We just get a lot of Smiths here."

" 'Tis a fine and honorable name."

The man wiped a sneer from his thin lips. "Sorry, Sister. What can I do for you?" He shoved his spectacles further up his long, hook nose. His gaze met hers over the gold rims. His black suit had seen better days, as had his dingy white shirt.

"I would like two rooms, please."

"Two?"

Exasperated at the man's crude behavior, she dropped the demure act and gave her best imitation of every stern nun she'd ever encountered. "One for me and one for the children. Connecting, if you please. I prefer the first floor, and near the rear door." At his quizzical look, she went on to explain, "I have a fear of fire, you see, so I try to position myself as near as possible to the exit. And besides, we don't want the children disturbing the other guests."

He looked over the desk as if spying the children for the first time. "They yours?"

She slapped her gloved hand onto the counter, wishing she had a ruler to swat his knuckles. "Of course not."

"We don't allow Indians."

Biting back an angry retort, she fixed him with a glare that would freeze hot water. "Sir, I am on a mission of mercy. I'm taking these unfortunate orphans to their new homes as part of my missionary work. Do you think we should sleep in the streets with the riffraff?''

"Ah, no. You're a Catholic nun?''

"I'm a novice. I have yet to take my final vows.'' She glanced at the guest book. "We're quite fatigued. I would appreciate lodgings for tonight.''

Jerked out of his curiosity, the man passed the pen to her. She signed her alias under the name of R. H. Howard in the guest book. The clerk named the sum, which she found extravagant, but rather then elicit further attention, she dug into her pocket and pulled out the silver coins. No use showing gold. Even women weren't safe from robbers.

The clerk snapped his fingers, and a smooth-faced youth raced to the desk. Taking her bags, he guided her to the rooms near the end of the hall. As she approached her door, Mr. Howard exited the room across from hers. For a brief instant, their eyes met and held. Recognition nagged at the edges of her mind. Jerking the brim of his hat low on his forehead, he slipped out the rear door. She gave the young man a small coin, and accepted the keys to both rooms.

Closing the door behind him, she leaned against the wall and took a deep breath. So far, so good. If Edwards had sent his men looking for her and Thorne, they would never suspect a nun with two children. She looked down into the frightened faces of the youngsters. Tears hovered at the corners of their eyes.

"Isn't this a fine room,'' she said in an effort to reassure them. "Look, a real bed to sleep in.''

Neither child moved. Running Deer hugged her doll tighter, and Juan clutched his whistle. She knelt beside them. "It's all right to be afraid. This is new to you. But Thorne, Sung Lo, and Sissy are here to take care of you. We're all going to a new home.''

Tiny tears streamed down the little girl's cheeks. "Like old home. Want go back.''

Mariah pulled both children into her embrace. "Honey, we

can't. Not right now. Be a brave girl and boy. We're going to have fun. Thorne promised to get you a treat if you're real good.''

"We be good," she said, wiping her face with her sleeve. Juan nodded, and played a tune on his whistle.

Picking up both children, she staggered under their weight to the bed. "Let's see how a real bed feels." She fell across the bed, and sank into the feather mattress. "Isn't this grand?"

They bounced and grinned. "Soft. Good."

"You can lie there while I wash up a bit," she said. Throwing off the veil, she loosened the buttons of her blouse and wiped her dusty face with a damp washcloth. It was the best she could do for now. Tonight, she would order a tub and hot water for a full bath. First, she would see about a good hot dinner.

She turned to the children, watching her from the center of the bed. "I'm going to get us something to eat. Be very quiet while I'm gone."

Picking up the veil, she again draped it across her hair. She couldn't wait to reach Pueblo where she could shed the disguise. First thing, she would find a dressmaker and buy a proper traveling suit. And decent clothes for the children. She wanted them looking their best when they reached Philadelphia.

It took only a few minutes to order from the dining room. The waiter looked at her strangely when she listed all the food she wanted, enough to feed a half dozen men. She shot him a stern look and remarked she was very hungry. A nice tip changed his attitude. After that it was "Yes, ma'am, I'll deliver it in a half hour."

Next, she had to locate Thorne. It had been at least an hour since she'd left him and Sung Lo. She opened the door to her room and saw that the children had fallen asleep. Quietly, she continued down the hall to the rear exit. The alley was steeped in shadows in the growing twilight. Thorne had promised to meet her here. She bit her lip, hoping nothing had happened to him.

"Irish." The husky voice came from behind her. Spinning around, she struggled to see past the barrels of trash and garbage.

"Th—" She stopped short of calling his name. Instead, she opted for their alias. "Smith?"

Two figures stepped into the last remains of daylight—one tall and broad-shouldered, the other smaller than she. At first glance she didn't recognize him. She jerked back a step. When she'd last seen him, Thorne was wearing buckskins and shaggy hair and beard. This man was neatly attired in canvas trousers, plaid shirt, leather vest, and shiny boots. To top it off, under a new tan hat, his hair was short and his cheeks smooth.

Her hand flew to her throat. He was incredibly handsome.

"It's me, Irish. Thanks to Sung Lo's ministrations, I look almost human."

The Chinese man grinned from ear to ear. "Sung Lo make Thorne pretty."

She struggled to quiet the pounding of her heart. She'd figured he was a nice-looking man under all that hair, but he far surpassed her expectations. The old photograph of the young man didn't do the mature man justice.

"You surprised me, is all."

"Did you have any trouble?"

"No, did you?"

He looked around to make sure they were alone. "I sold the horses and wagon and bought the clothes. I booked us on the stagecoach. It leaves at daybreak."

"Good. I got rooms and ordered dinner. Wait here until it's delivered, then I'll come for you."

"It might be best if we stayed away. No use raising suspicions."

"I'll be careful. I requested rooms near the door. You can slip in and without anybody being the wiser."

"Irish, you're a wonder." His gaze darted to the side. "Somebody's coming." In a flash, he and Sung Lo were gone, disappearing into the shadows.

She dug her hand into the pocket where she kept the revolver.

A man materialized from the alley—Mr. Howard, who had the room across the hall from hers. Taking a deep breath, she remarked, "Lovely night, isn't it? I came out for a breath of this fresh air."

He tipped his hat. "You'd best be careful out here alone, ma'am. No telling what kind of varmint you might run into."

She gripped the handle of the gun. "I've got protection, sir."

"Protection?" He shot her a quizzical glance.

"The Lord and his angels. They're my protection." *Not to mention a loaded six-gun.* She preceded him into the hallway. "Good night, sir."

Behind her closed door, she relaxed. Minutes later, the waiter delivered a tray filled with a variety of the dishes she'd ordered. He set the dinner on the table, and departed with another generous tip.

With the children still asleep, she slipped discreetly into the hallway and out the rear door. "Smith!" she called.

"Irish!" Thorne answered.

"All's clear." She hurried back into the hallway and waited as Thorne and Sung Lo made their way into her room.

Once they were safely inside, she twisted the key in the lock. "I got connecting rooms. You can enter yours through here."

Thorne studied the open door to the next room. "Irish, you thought of everything."

She removed the veil and ran her fingers through her hair. "I try. Sit down and eat while it's hot."

The children stirred on the bed. They stared at Thorne as if they had no idea who the stranger was. "It's me," he said in his deep, gruff voice. "And Sung Lo."

Together the youngsters leaped from the bed into his arms. "We 'fraid you go, leave us."

He brushed his hands up and down their backs. "If I have to leave, you'll have Sissy and Sung Lo. Promise you'll be good for them?"

"Not go," Running Deer implored, her young face shiny with love.

Without answering, he rose, carrying both children in his arms. At the small table, he sat with a child on each leg. "Let's see what treats Sissy got for us."

Mariah didn't think she could love a man any more then she loved this rough mountain man who showed such gentleness and kindness to two little orphans. Her heart did a flip-flop, and she resisted the urge to stroke her fingers along his smooth jaw. Too bad he didn't have even a tiny place in his heart for her.

Within an hour, they'd devoured the food, and finished a bottle of fine French wine. Even Sung Lo indulged in the beef steak, potatoes, and roast chicken. However, he refused the wine.

All the while they were eating, she kept trying to remember where she'd seen that Mr. Howard. "Thorne, did you notice that man in the alley?"

"The one who warned you about being out there alone?"

"Yes. Did he look familiar to you? I think I've seen him somewhere before."

He took one last sip of the wine and returned the glass to the table. "Irish, I've been up on that mountain for a mighty long time. I avoid strangers, and try not to make eye contact so they won't notice me."

"Well, I've seen him."

"Maybe you've seen a picture of somebody that resembles him."

She jumped up and nearly upset the table. "That's it. I saw his picture. On a wanted poster."

"A wanted poster?" He stared at her as if she'd gone stark raving mad.

"Yes. My brother collects the posters, hoping to capture a criminal and get the reward. Pinkerton's men locate photographs, or have artists make sketches of outlaws. Francis is friends with the local Pinkerton operatives, so he gets the latest posters. We both study their faces."

"You recognized that man."

Pointing to the hall door, she said, "Yes. That Mr. Howard is really Jesse James."

He shook his head in disbelief. "Didn't the James brothers ride with Quantrill? And the Youngers?"

"Yes. They've robbed a number of banks. I'll bet there's a big reward for his capture, dead or alive."

"What would he be doing here?"

"I don't know. It's as good a place as any to hide from the law." She cringed, aware that she and Thorne were doing the exact thing.

He caught her hand and tugged her back to her chair. "Listen, Irish, you're like a dog with a bone. You don't let go until you pick it clean. This time you have to let it go. James is a dangerous man. I heard he kills because he likes killing. Forget him. Let somebody else get the reward."

She knew he was right. "Just wait until I tell Francis I came face-to-face with Jesse James. That the infamous outlaw slept in the room right across the hall from me. Won't he be thrilled?"

"We don't want to bring any unnecessary attention to ourselves. And dealing with James would do just that. We'll take that stagecoach tomorrow morning and get away from here."

On a long sigh, she returned to her chair. "I know you're right. Nuns simply don't go around capturing notorious outlaws." Disappointed, she spread her hands. "But wouldn't it be a grand story?"

"Irish . . ."

"I'll let it go. The reward from the gold is enough. We'd better get to bed. The children are exhausted. You, Sung Lo, and Juan can take that room. Running Deer and I will stay here."

He stood and stretched. "Thanks for everything."

"Don't thank me, Mountain Man. If it wasn't for me, you wouldn't be in danger."

"You were right about being found. Just like you spotted James, sooner or later somebody would have found me. I'm grateful my grandmother hired you instead of a Pinkerton man.''

''So am I.'' Even without the promised bonus, she wouldn't change a thing. Meeting him—loving him—was worth more than all the treasure in the world. Too bad he didn't feel the same about her.

At the connecting door, he glanced over his wide shoulder. ''Not to mention you're a heck of a lot prettier.''

''Thanks, I didn't think you noticed.''

''Irish, even a blind man would notice. Without seeing, he would know you're something special.''

Her skin heated at his unaccustomed compliments. Before she could think of an appropriate response, he was in the next room. The emotional wall between them was as real as the one made of wood and wallpaper.

Thorne wasn't sure of the time when the noise from the other room woke him. First the door hinges squeaked, then soft voices, and the sound of something dragging across the floor.

He bolted upright in the bed, careful not to wake Sung Lo or Juan, who slept between them. Throwing his legs over the side, he reached for his pistol. Surely Mariah had enough sense not to leave the room in the dead of night. His heart fell to his stomach. A man she thought to be Jesse James slept in the room across the hall. Knowing her foolhardy ways, anything was possible with the woman. There was no telling what a killer like James would do.

Wearing only his trousers, he slid along the wall to the door. He'd left it ajar, but somehow it was now shut tighter than a miser's purse strings. He twisted the knob, and inched the door open. Fearful for what he would find in her room, he held his breath and peeked inside.

A kerosene lamp burned on the table beside the bed. A small body lay snuggled under the covers. Running Deer. But where was Mariah? Had she gone and left the child alone? Or had something happened to her? Not wanting to frighten the girl, he slid into the shadows along the wall.

A soft moan came from the far corner. Mariah's voice—the same low purr of pleasure as when they'd made love. His heart nearly stopped beating. Outraged, he wanted to know, to see what she was doing, who she was with, but he was afraid. Afraid of his own reaction, of what he would do if she were with another man. Afraid of the urge to kill that had been absent during the war. Disgust burned in his gut.

"You can quit skulking in the shadows and come scrub my back," she whispered. He stopped cold, too shocked to move. "Don't wake Running Deer. I had a hard time getting her to sleep."

The plop of water splashing on the floor shook him out of his daze. His eyes adjusted to the dim light. He spotted the slipper tub, and the back of the woman glaring at him over her bare shoulder.

"You're taking a bath?" he spit out around the stone in his throat.

"What else would I be doing in this tub? It's certainly too small for anything else. Are you planning to shoot me?"

Aware of the gun in his hand, he shoved it into the waist of his trousers. "No. I thought, I wondered . . ." How was he going to admit that he'd been a complete fool? That he'd been so frightened for her, he'd completely lost track of reason. "I heard a noise."

"And you thought I'd gone and left that child alone?"

"Yes," he muttered, too embarrassed to admit the truth of what he'd thought.

"Do you take me for a fool?"

"No. I was worried about you. There is a notorious outlaw across the hall."

She was little more than a shadow in the tiny streak of lamplight. Her hair was piled on top of her head, and her shoulders gleamed like the finest porcelain. From past intimacies, he knew her body as well as his own. He was inches away from her naked flesh, warm and smooth as silk. His body reacted with a force that left his knees weak.

He took one step toward her. All he had to do was reach out and he would touch that creamy flesh. He stretched out a hand.

"Sissy?" The weak whimper came from the bed. Running Deer sat up, and rubbed her eyes.

"I'm right here, honey," Mariah said, her voice soft with affection. "Go back to sleep. I'll be to bed in a minute."

"You woke her up. Get out of here," Mariah whispered.

Thorne slipped into the shadows. "Sorry."

"Why Thorne here?" the little girl asked.

"I came to tell you goodnight," he replied. Stepping close to the bed, he adjusted the cover over her small body.

She wrapped her hand around his fingers. "Thorne, will I like 'Delphia?"

His heart ached for the child. "Of course you will. And everybody in Philadelphia will like you."

"Will you be 'Delphia?"

He couldn't answer the child truthfully; he had no idea of what the future held for him. "I'll be with you." Water splashed behind him as Mariah stepped from the tub. He didn't dare glance at her. "Go to sleep. We have a busy day tomorrow." He kissed the top of the child's head, and patted her hand.

Quietly, he returned to his own bed knowing full well he wouldn't get a wink of sleep. Visions of a black-haired beauty danced in his head. Pictures of a perfect female body rising from the tub haunted his dreams. Drops of water kissed where he longed to run his tongue and lips. A towel wrapped the form he wanted to cover with his own body. Erotic images clouded any chance of sleep.

Thorne was still wide awake when the first glimmer of dawn sneaked into the crack between the window curtains.

He hurriedly dressed and roused Sung Lo and Juan. Knocking

softly on the adjoining door, he was surprised when Mariah pulled it open. She was fully clothed in her black skirt and blouse, the veil draping her shoulders like a shawl.

"Did you sleep well?" she asked.

"Like a contented baby," he lied. "And you?"

"I always sleep well after a relaxing bath."

Longings stirred him. Needs that would go forever unfulfilled. Acting on his needs would only cheat Mariah out of the annulment and her chance for a normal life. "Sung Lo and I will slip out the rear door. We'll meet you at the stage depot. It's two doors down."

"I saved some of the bread and jelly from dinner. Come in and grab a bite before you go."

"I'll take it with me. We don't want anybody to catch me here with you. Nuns don't usually have gentlemen callers early in the morning." He wrapped half a dozen slices of bread in a linen napkin.

"Since when are you a gentleman?"

Her stern expression brought an unbidden grin. "I'm not. But Sung Lo is."

"Correct. I'll feed the children, and we'll be along shortly." Moving to the hallway door, she slipped it open a crack. "The coast is clear."

He signaled to Sung Lo, who bowed to Mariah and waved to the children. The old man made it to the rear door, and held it open. Unable to resist the woman who'd given him too many sleepless nights, he planted a quick kiss on her lips. "Thanks, Irish."

She covered her lips with her fingers. "Be careful, Mountain Man."

With a nod, he followed the old Chinese into the pale morning light.

Chapter 16

The crowded stagecoach offered little comfort on the fifty-mile journey to Raton Pass, their destination before dark. Squeezed between an overweight widow and the children, Mariah refused to give up her seat at the rear. For safety and their protection Thorne opted to ride on the top. Sung Lo followed suit.

Between whizzing, coughing, and sounding as if she were about to throw up, the widow kept up a running narrative about her family. Mariah didn't care that her daughter-in-law was a terrible cook, or that her grandchildren were the most intelligent and beautiful in the world.

Three men were relegated to the rear facing seat. They politely introduced themselves, and struggled for their own comfort. Mr. Roy, a tall, thin, forty-something man worked for the railroad and was headed for Pueblo. A shorter, rough-looking man called himself Mr. Jones, but he gave neither his destination nor his business. The third man, Mr. Wallace, was younger, not much older than Mariah. He flashed her a flirtatious smile, until he noticed her habit and assumed she was a nun. After that, he politely avoided her gaze.

Mariah repeated her story about being on a mission of mercy, escorting the orphaned children to their new homes.

Both children were extremely quiet, clearly frightened from being uprooted from their home. Mariah tried to make the journey as pleasant as possible under the difficult circumstances. She, as well as they, would have been much happier if Thorne and Sung Lo had been inside with them. As dusty and windblown as she was, she could only imagine how uncomfortable it was on the top of the coach.

The sun had dropped deep into the valley when they reached the high road across the rugged Raton Pass. Dug and graded by "Uncle" Dick Wootton, the man maintained a heavy chain across his toll road. The driver stopped, paid the toll, and drove into a corral for another change of horses and driver.

Taking advantage of the chance to stretch, Mariah and the children walked away from the other passengers. From the top of the pass, she had a fantastic view of Colorado to the north, and over the plains, mesas and mountains of New Mexico to the south.

A long shadow appeared next to hers. Without turning, she knew Thorne had followed her. He didn't touch her, or speak— he simply gazed into the distant.

"You're going to miss it, aren't you?" she asked, her voice soft.

"Those mountains have been good to me. I'm going back a richer and smarter man." Mariah noted the longing in his voice. "Better still, I'm returning a whole man. I'm ready to face the consequences of my actions."

She clutched the hands of the children to keep from reaching for him. More than anything, she wanted to hold him and assure him he was doing the right thing. "It's going to work out."

He hunkered down in front of the children. "Didn't I promise you a treat if you were real good for Sissy?" Both youngsters nodded. "I forgot to give it to you this morning." Thorne reached into his shirt pocket and pulled out two peppermint sticks and gave one to each child. They threw their arms around his neck. "Now remember, you're to do everything Sissy tells you, and, Running Deer, I want you to be very quiet. As quiet as Juan."

The little girl nodded, and clutched the candy in her fingers. "I be quiet."

"They've both been so good, you'll have to buy them a whole box of goodies when we reach Pueblo."

For the first time that day, Thorne smiled. "I'll buy them a bushel." He stood, and glanced toward the road where the stagecoach was being fitted with a fresh team. "By the way, I forgot to give Sissy hers." Reaching into his pocket, he pulled out another stick of candy.

Mariah returned his smile. "Thank you, sir."

"Sister, it looks like we'll soon be on our way," he said in a loud voice. "Hope you're having a pleasant journey." He tipped his hat and sauntered toward the road where Sung Lo waited.

It was nearly dark when the driver ordered everybody back into the coach and announced they would have breakfast in Trinidad, Colorado Territory. As she lifted her foot to enter the coach, Thorne offered a hand up. "Don't worry, Irish," he said for her ears only. "We'll make it home."

"I hope." She flashed him a tiny smile.

The widow, Mrs. Hoover, stared at Thorne. "That certainly is a handsome man, don't you think, Sister?" she asked.

Mariah snuggled the children close to her so they could get a bit of sleep. "I didn't notice."

"You seemed to be having quite a conversation while we were waiting for the driver to hitch up the team."

"He was speaking to the children, not to me." Another lie added to the wagonload dragging behind her. A woman would have to be blind not to notice his good looks. Maybe he'd made a mistake by shaving and cutting his hair. He was bound to draw attention—if only from the women. That ugly monster called jealousy twisted its tail around her heart. The silver bracelet weighed heavy on her wrist. It was a constant reminder of their marriage, a marriage Thorne couldn't wait to end.

She shoved aside her pain at the thought of an annulment. He wanted it, and she wasn't fool enough to want a man who didn't want her.

The horses took off with a jerk, throwing Mrs. Hoover against her, and the three men facing her nearly landed in her lap. They mumbled apologies while struggling to remain in their seats.

Mariah closed her eyes, and tried to sleep. With an arm around each child, she pulled their heads to her lap. Within minutes, the exhausted youngsters were breathing deeply and evenly—the sleep of children and the innocent, her mother always said.

Night riding was considerably slower along the narrow path that served as a road. It had been scary during the daylight. She couldn't figure how the driver kept the vehicle and horses from tumbling over the mountain in the dark.

In the gray predawn, the driver pulled into a small corral and informed the passengers they'd reached Trinidad. Mariah shook her head to clear away the cobwebs. She surprised herself to realize that she'd actually fallen asleep. By the time she came fully awake and alerted the children, the men had exited the stagecoach, and Thorne was waiting at the open door to help her down.

She opened her mouth to greet him, when Mrs. Hoover took his offered hand, and mumbled something she couldn't quite hear.

"May I give you a hand with those youngsters, Sister?" he asked.

Grateful for his offer, Mariah gave him a sleepy smile. "Thank you, sir, that's very kind of you."

Rubbing the sleep from her eyes, Running Deer flung herself into his arms. "Thorne, I miss you."

Mariah glanced around, but realized that the others had

entered the small adobe building that served as way station and restaurant.

"I'm right on top of your head." He pointed to the roof.

The little girl giggled as he set her on the ground. Juan came more slowly, his hand clutched Thorne's shirt as if he didn't want to let go. After turning over the children to Sung Lo, Thorne reached out for Mariah. His fingers closed around her hand. Her heart beat faster, as it did whenever he came near. Thank goodness they were alone, with nobody to see the color that surfaced to her face.

"How are you doing?" He helped her to the ground and held her hand a few seconds longer than necessary—but not nearly long enough to satisfy her lonely heart.

"My body is crushed, my legs stiff, and my hearing is impaired from the noise Mrs. Hoover blasted into my ears. Other than that, I'm fine." Realizing she'd spent a better night then he, she repented of her complaints. "I'm sorry. It had to be cold and dusty on the roof."

"We survived. Want to change places?"

"No thanks." She shook out her skirts and adjusted the veil on her head. "I can't wait to reach Pueblo and change into decent clothes."

He fell into step beside her. "Irish, I'm afraid you may have to keep up the charade a little longer. At least until Denver. It wouldn't do for any of our fellow passengers to get suspicious if you suddenly turn into a beautiful, fashionable young woman."

She couldn't prevent the frown on her face. "I suspected the same thing. But you just wait until I reach Denver. My pocketbook will be a lot lighter after I finish shopping."

With a soft chuckle, he held open the door to the cabin. "Irish, I'll spring for a whole new wardrobe for you if we make it out of this mess."

Before she stepped into the light, she gave him a saucy grin. "You'll be sorry you offered."

The smell of grease and coffee permeated the small eating room. The children and Sung Lo waited at the long table, and

the others were too busy with their own meals to pay her and
Thorne much mind. Just to keep up appearances, she nodded
to him and stepped away. ''Thank your man for looking after
the children,'' she said, as if addressing a stranger.

''He likes children. It was his pleasure.'' He tipped his hat
and moved to the far end of the table. ''Have a good day,
Sister.''

''Sissy,'' Running Deer called to Mariah.

Afraid the child would give them away, Mariah touched a
finger to her lips to silence the girl. ''Did you pray?'' she asked.
''Let's be quiet and hurry and eat. We don't have time to dilly
dally.''

A squat Mexican man and younger woman served bowls of
what looked like some kind of cornmeal mush. The coffee
was hot and strong, and the tortillas warm. Mariah's stomach
growled with hunger. While urging the children to eat, she
cleaned her own bowl. They wouldn't eat again until they
reached Greenhorn, about fifty miles north.

After tending to their needs, it was time to climb back into
the stagecoach for the next leg of the journey. By then, the sun
had barely broken the horizon, and the sky was a pale gray-
pink. Mariah returned to her seat, and snuggled the children
next to her.

The road skirted the foothills into the Purgatoire Valley.
She stared out the windows at Fisher's Peak looming in the
foreground. To the west, the snow-covered peaks of the Culebra
Range rose in purple-and-silver splendor. For the first time,
she had a smidgen of regret at leaving. She knew how much
Thorne loved these mountains, and she wondered if they'd
somehow gotten under her skin. Shoving away the preposterous
thought, she set her mind on home, her family, and Mrs. Thornton's reaction when she saw her beloved Michael.

Most of all, she wondered about the children. How would
they adapt to their new home? How would they be received
by Thorne's family? She made up her her mind that if they

were anything but welcoming, the children and Sung Lo would become part of the rowdy O'Reilly clan.

She and Thorne didn't have a moment to speak at the midday stop at Greenhorn. The driver announced they were behind schedule, and to hurry with their meal. He wanted to reach Pueblo later that night.

It was dark, the stagecoach uncomfortable, and the children restless when they finally reached their destination. Mariah hurried the children to the hotel and registered for a room. As before, she asked for a room on the first floor near the door. Although the clerk gave her a questioning stare, he granted her wishes. She casually repeated her room number so Thorne would know her whereabouts. To her dismay, Mrs. Hoover was given the room next to hers.

The woman stopped her at the door and invited Mariah to dine with her. Mariah used the fatigued children as an excuse and said she was going to order food sent to her room. She'd had all she could stand of the woman for the past two days.

Once in her room, she removed the veil and the many pins that stabbed her scalp. She combed out the braid and rubbed her head.

"We hungry," Running Deer said from her perch on the high bed.

Mariah smiled at the children. "I'll go order some food for us." She draped the veil over her loose hair and started for the door.

Before she had a chance to reach the knob, a fist pounded on the door. She opened it and spied a slender young man, his arms laden with a heavy tray. "*Hermana*, dinner."

Her mouth gaped at the assortment of food piled on the tray. "I didn't order anything."

He set it down on a table, and bowed elegantly. "*El hombre.* He say bring to *Hermana* Rosie."

"*Gracias*," she said. She reached into her pocket and pulled out a copper coin.

The young man backed away shaking his head. "No, *seño-*

rita, el señor give *mucho dinero.* Antonio bring bath and hot water when *señorita* ready.''

"Thank you.'' Thorne had thought of everything. She watched the young man saunter down the hall and wondered which room was Thorne's. She didn't have long to wonder. The door next to hers crept open. Expecting to see Mrs. Hoover's rotund figure, she was surprised when Thorne and Sung Lo slipped into the hallway. He glanced each way, before gesturing her aside and entering her room.

"What are you doing there?'' she asked. "That's Mrs. Hoover's room.''

Thorne shut the door and twisted the lock. "Not anymore. After I told her the story of how a widow was murdered in that very bed by outlaws, she begged me to switch with her. She is now safely on the second floor where she won't see or hear you.'' He grinned, proud of his ingenuity.

Mariah laughed. "You're incredible.''

"Thank you, Irish. I try.''

By then, the children had spotted him, and raced into his embrace. "Thorne, we be very quiet. Sissy say we good,'' Running Deer informed him.

He gathered the youngsters into his arms, enjoying the warmth of their small bodies. They depended on him; how long would he be able to take care of them? Worse, how long would he be with Mariah? Why did he have to come close to losing the people he cared for before realizing how much they meant to him?

"Then I suppose I owe you another treat.'' He reached into his pocket and pulled out two more peppermint sticks. "Save them for after you eat your dinner.''

"Got one for Sissy?''

Lifting his gaze, he met Mariah's soft blue eyes. He had a lot more he wanted to give her. But with his uncertain future, he would keep those wants hidden in his heart. "Of course.'' He pulled another candy stick from his pocket and pressed it into her hand. Her touch ignited fires in his blood that he'd struggled for days to quench. Snatching back his fingers, he gently stroked Juan's hair, wishing it were Mariah's.

"Thank you," she whispered, hugging the treat to her chest as if it were something precious. The bracelet on her wrist caught the candlelight. True to her word, she wore it always. The thought warmed his heart. "The children are starved. Let's eat."

After the meal was completed, Thorne got up to leave. Every moment with Mariah was pure physical torture—and exquisite bliss. He wasn't sure what had happened to him in the past weeks. She'd gotten under his skin, make him feel alive, and showed him everything he'd missed since the start of the war.

"Do you have to go?" she asked, her hand brushing his.

The children and Sung Lo looked up expectantly. "Yes. I want to check on railroad travel, and get off a telegram to reserve first-class tickets on one of the Pullman cars. We'll all be more comfortable than in coach."

"Will you send a telegram to my brother and parents, letting them know when we'll arrive home?"

He nodded. His grandmother deserved to know about his return. "Write it out, and I'll send it."

She sat at the small desk and wrote out a brief message to her brother. "You may read it, if you like."

Taking the note, he read the few words. "*Eureka. Inform Mrs. T. Coming home. Tell Ma and Da I'm fine. All my love, Rosie.*" He folded the note and shoved it into his pocket. "We can send our schedule when we reach Chicago. By then, we'll know the time of arrival."

"Good. Thanks for ordering a bath. We need it."

He opened the door a crack and checked the hallway. It was empty, so he signaled Sung Lo to leave. With a brief wave, he closed the door and gave Mariah her privacy. The old Chinese went directly to their room, while Thorne continued to the front desk. He found Antonio, the young man who'd delivered the meal and informed him to deliver the tub and water to Sister Rose.

Avoiding the men lounging in the lobby, he continued to the door. It took only minutes to reach the depot of the Denver and Rio Grande Railroad. The narrow gauge line had reached Pueblo the past year, making travel much easier and faster. He booked passage in the coach, and arranged for passage from Denver on the Kansas Pacific. They would go through Kansas City, where they would change trains to Chicago. He booked first class in Pullman cars all the way through to Philadelphia. Since they would have a day's layover in Denver, he arranged for rooms at the American House. With Mariah's telegram on its way, he headed back to the hotel.

All the while, his mind was on Mariah. Only occasionally did he think of her as his wife. His soon to be former wife. Often he thought about the passion they'd shared. His mind drifted to how she'd looked a few nights before in the small tub. Desire surged through him at the reminder that she was even at that moment soaking naked in the warm water. As expected, his body reacted in kind.

Taking the back alley, he entered the small courtyard at the rear of the hotel. Only a few lamps burned behind the curtains of the rooms. Most of the guests were asleep for the night, as he should be. The bathwater he'd ordered would be ice cold. So much the better. He sank to a low bench and dropped his hands between his spread knees.

He heard the squeak of the door, and, out of habit, he lunged to his feet and slunk into the shadows. There was still a chance that Edwards was looking for him. A woman slipped through the doorway, her slender body silhouetted by the dim lamps. Long black hair curled over her shoulders, tumbling almost to the waist of her severe black skirt. His heart nearly stopped beating.

She lifted her hands over her head and took a deep breath. She breathed a sigh, as if relieved to be outdoors in the fresh air. Her blouse strained across her bosom, and the moonlight caught the silver bracelet at her wrist. Mariah, alone in the darkness.

It was as if his very dreams had materialized out of the night. He held his breath. No good would come of going to her, touching her, holding her. Loving her. The very idea of loving her shocked him clear to his soul. There was no place in his life for love. Even if he had a future, which he doubted, he'd long ago vowed to never let that emotion rule his life. Once was enough.

She moved closer, and hugged her arms around her waist as if to ward off the chill of the night. Her gaze searched the darkness. He eased deeper into the shadows.

Stepping closer to the tree that hid him, she whispered, "Mountain Man, I know you're here. Please don't hide from me."

Torn with indecision, he held his breath. The fragrance of rose water wafted from her hair. Surrender came easy. "Don't you know it's dangerous for a woman to wander alone in the darkness?"

At the sound of his voice, she turned. "I'm not alone. Sung Lo told me you hadn't returned. I figured you were out here enjoying this glorious night."

Millions of stars glittered in the dark sky, lending their glory to the mortals on earth. It truly was a night of beauty, a night for lovers. He steeled his heart against his desires. Catching Mariah by the shoulders, he turned her back toward the hotel's rear door. "Get inside," he whispered between his teeth.

Ignoring his warning, she spun in his arms. Her hands rested lightly on his chest. His heart pounded against her fingertips. "I have you to protect me."

Thorne gave up trying to be a gentleman. "Who's going to protect you from me?"

Her fingers walked up his chest and circled his neck. "Since when do I need protecting?"

His hands slipped around her waist to her back. Her hair tickled his arms like strands of silk. "You're playing with fire, Irish."

Jean Wilson

She reached on tiptoe, her lips brushing his. "I'm already ablaze."

He bent his head, his mouth ready to claim what was rightfully his.

"Sister Rose, is that you?" The female voice was followed by a series of coughs and wheezes.

Mariah let out a fitful moan, and buried her face in his shirt. "Get rid of her," she whispered.

"Ma'am?" He glared at the widowed Mrs. Hoover, who stood just outside the rear door in the dim lamplight. "Is something wrong?" he asked in a voice as hard as flint.

Holding a kerosene lamp, the woman inched closer. "I just came out for a breath of fresh air. Is that woman Sister Rose?" Her voice demanded an answer.

He mumbled a few Spanish expletives, hoping the woman didn't understand the language. "Madam, this woman is clearly not a nun." He cradled Mariah in his arms to hide her face.

"She certainly looks like the sister."

"You're mistaken. I paid a silver dollar for her services." Even in the darkness, he spotted the high color on Mrs. Hoover's plump cheeks. A bit of deviltry leaped up in him. "Ma'am, did you know there are dangerous men in Pueblo? Two miners were fighting over a woman over at the saloon. No woman is safe out here alone. You wouldn't want to be mistaken for a *puta*, would you?" Leaving her with the threat of being mistaken for a prostitute hanging in the air, he slid into the shadows of the night, taking Mariah with him.

"A dollar." Mariah jabbed her elbow into his ribs. "I'm worth at least five."

He laughed. "You didn't want that old busybody accusing Sister Rose of consorting with a man, did you?"

"She would drop dead right on the spot."

The door to the hotel closed with a bang. Again, Thorne turned Mariah to the path that led to the door. "We shouldn't be seen together. Who knows what other passengers could be lurking in the darkness?"

On a sigh, she nodded her agreement. "I only wanted to know when our train leaves tomorrow. I'd like to pick up some new things for the children."

"Noon, or thereabout. I'll meet you at the depot. It's too dangerous for us to be seen together." And it was too dangerous to his peace of mind to even be near her.

She turned and lifted her face. "Can't you at least give me a goodnight kiss?"

Unable to resist her innocent plea, he planted a chaste kiss on her cheek. "Good night, Irish." He shoved her toward the door, and slid back into the shadows.

How he managed to stay away from her was beyond him. He watched as she moved slowly to the doorway, glancing over her shoulder from time to time. As she opened the door, she blew him a kiss and disappeared into the safety of the hotel.

By counting the windows, he knew which room was hers. He continued to watch as she turned down the lamp, her body silhouetted on the curtains. The trip to Philadelphia was going to be a long, tiresome, and agonizing journey.

Chapter 17

The black locomotive hissed, puffed, shrieked, and spewed cinders everywhere. It squealed to a stop at the depot like a huge dragon blowing smoke from its nostrils. The noise frightened the children, who'd never seen such a monster in their young lives. They cowered behind Mariah's black skirt, tears streaming down their blanched faces.

Mariah stooped to their level and tried to reassure them there was no danger. Riding on the train would be a wonderful experience. Running Deer's only intelligible words were, "Want Thorne."

Mrs. Hoover clucked her tongue, drawing Mariah's attention. She'd hoped to escape the woman. "What's wrong, Sister?" she asked, her voice full of censure. "Are they backward?"

Biting back an angry retort, she kept her gaze on the children. "No, ma'am. This is all new to them, and they don't know how to react. I'll have them calmed down in a minute." The whistle blew, and the conductor sang out for the passengers to embark. "You'd better get aboard if you want a good seat," she warned.

With a loud humph, Mrs. Hoover swung her wide skirt

and hustled toward the boarding platform. Left alone with the children, Mariah hugged them tightly to reassure them that everything was all right.

"Need some help, Sister?" came the husky voice from over her shoulder.

She turned to find Thorne and Sung Lo at her side. The old man flashed a wide grin and reached for Juan. The boy went immediately into his arms. Running Deer threw herself into Thorne's embrace. He lifted the child to his shoulder and wiped her face with his handkerchief.

"Thank you, sir," Mariah said, in case anybody was listening. "They're frightened by the train."

"It like dragon in Thorne's book," Running Deer said between sniffles.

"This dragon won't hurt you," he said in a soft, gentle voice.

Mariah's heart tripped at the kindness and concern he showed the children. She dropped her voice to a whisper. "Is it safe for you to be with us?"

"Doesn't matter. They need me. I'm merely helping a lady in distress. Nobody will think anything of it. Let's get on board."

Bags in hand, Mariah led the way to the platform. As she'd expected, Mrs. Hoover frowned when she saw Thorne and Sung Lo escorting her aboard. They settled in a seat on the opposite end of the coach from the inquisitive widow.

"Thank you, sirs," Mariah said, loudly, adding a bit of the brogue. "The good Lord will surely bless you for coming to the aid of these poor helpless children."

Thorne nodded, barely suppressing a grin. "Our pleasure, Sister. If you need help in Denver, we'll be at your disposal."

"I'm sure that won't be necessary."

When Sung Lo started to mumble something, and take the seat beside them, Thorne grabbed his arm and led him further to the rear. Both children knelt on the seat, and waved to the men. After the first chug-chug and clattering wheels, they settled down and pressed their faces to the window. Mariah momentarily relaxed, though she wished Thorne and Sung Lo sat closer.

Through the window, she watched the passing scenery, aware that every mile that clicked by brought them closer to home, and the uncertainty of Thorne's situation. Her heart ached for him. He was a man who valued his freedom—his ability to roam freely through the countryside.

During his stay in the mountains, he'd collected plants and roots, and experimented with herbal remedies and medicines. He'd learned secrets Indians seldom shared with white men. Maybe he could be on the verge of an important medical discovery. Mariah considered the possibility.

She agonized that she and her selfish plot to earn his grandmother's bonus, as well as the reward for the gold, might have taken from him what he held dear. She gripped the crucifix that was part of her attire. Her prayers were for his safety, for his freedom, and for his chance for a full and happy life. Even if it meant a life without her.

An hour later, they stopped again, this time at Fountain, one of the oldest settlements in central Colorado. Mariah glanced back at Thorne. His long legs stuck out into the aisle and his new gray hat covered his face. She suspected that he was wide awake, alert for every movement going on around him. Several men were playing cards on a makeshift table between the seats, while others were reading or sleeping. A young couple, clearly newlyweds, sat across from her. So intent on each other, they noticed neither the scenery nor the other passengers.

A rope twisted around her chest. How she wished Thorne would look at her like that, hold her hand, and plan a life together. They'd been married less than a week, and their few intimacies had been purely sexual. He'd never spoken one word of love, or commitment, or caring. She'd opened her heart to a man who had no place in his life for her.

The train took off with a loud blast of the whistle and spray of cinders. Jerked out of her reverie, she began to make her

own plans for the future. First off, she would apply for the
annulment. Then she would buy a big house, fancy clothes,
and seek out a place in society. She would go to operas, to
concerts, and let Philadelphia know that Mariah Rose O'Reilly
had arrived.

As hard as she tried to concentrate on her own life, she
worried what the future held for Thorne. When his identity as
Michael Harrison became public, would he be arrested, sent to
jail, or worse? She clutched the rosary and prayed that Mrs.
Thornton, with all her money and influence, would be able to
attain a pardon for her beloved grandson.

Later that afternoon, the conductor called for Colorado
Springs. The newly established resort town sat near the base
of Pike's Peak, with access to the mineral waters at Manitou
Springs. Mariah hustled the children to the platform. They had
about a half hour while the train took on water and fuel to grab
a bite to eat. She followed the other passengers to a small cafe
about a hundred yards from the depot.

After placing a hurried order for beef stew and milk, she
studied the poster on the wall extolling the virtues of the mineral
baths. She frowned at the reminder of the bubbling pool on
Thorne's mountain. The place where they'd last made love. A
place she would never see again. As she was certain they would
never make love again.

Even as she tried to put Thorne out of her mind, she caught
a glimpse of him from the corner of her eye. He and Sung Lo
sat at a table in the corner, his back to the wall. The children
waved to him, and he gave them the merest nod.

Running Deer clutched her sleeve. "Thorne like us no
more?"

The girl's distressed expression upset Mariah. She wrapped
an arm around the child and whispered, "He loves you, darling.
This is just a game we're playing. He and Sung Lo wish you
to stay with Sissy Rosie. We'll all be together again soon."

She brushed a kiss across the girl's cheek. "Here comes our food. Doesn't it look good?"

Juan frowned, but he shoved his spoon into the bowl. Mariah easily read his eyes. "Not as good as Sung Lo's, I suppose," she remarked. Both youngsters grinned.

After her first bite, she had to agree. However, the apple pie was much better, though not as good as her mother's. Her heartbeat sped up at the thought of her parents and home. In spite of her great adventure, she'd missed her family. But wouldn't they be thrilled at the results of her success?

The whistle from the train signaled an imminent departure. Mariah paid their bill and gathered the children. She hurried them to the depot, and boarded the train. Thorne and Sung Lo followed at their heels. Once in the coach, Mariah settled back into the same seat they'd previously occupied. As the whistle again shrieked, a shadow fell over her. Expecting to see Thorne, she was disappointed to view the rather rotund figure of Mrs. Hoover. She'd avoided the widow at the cafe, preferring not to deal with the woman's nosiness.

"Sister, do you mind if I sit here by you?" The widow settled in the seat on the other side of the aisle. "That cigar smoke chokes me up." To prove her point, she let out a long stream of coughs and sneezes.

Mariah glanced over her shoulder at Thorne and caught the hint of a smirk on his face. He clearly enjoyed her discomfort at having to deal with the prying woman. She was sorely tempted to turn the inquisitive Mrs. Hoover over to the man she thought was so handsome. That was an interesting thought, but however much he might have earned it, nobody deserved that degree of torture. The train pulled out of the station with a jolt. The children tumbled into their seats, by now beginning to enjoy the ride.

Mostly, she ignored the woman, making only noncommittal grunts and nods. One question caught her off guard. The woman focused her attention on Running Deer and Juan.

"Sister, exactly where are you taking these children? I mean who would want to adopt them? An Indian, and what's the boy, a half-breed?'' She looked down her nose at the youngsters, who hadn't taken their eyes from the window.

Her attitude infuriated Mariah. She knew there was prejudice against Indians and Mexicans. Even young children had to face ignorance and bigotry. If she had her way, they would never know of such censure.

Mariah locked gazes with the woman. ''Mrs. Hoover, I'm sure you're aware that I'm on a mission for the Church. These children are under my care and my protection. Any plans we have for them are of the strictest confidence. I cannot, nor will I, reveal where they are going. I can assure you, that they are aware they will be treated with kindness and love, and I will see that they have a wonderful life.''

Unable to bear the condescending attitude for another second, she said, ''If you will excuse me, I would like to stretch my legs and get a breath of fresh air.''

''Humph! Well, I never,'' Mrs. Hoover grumbled, and turned toward the window.

Mariah whispered for the children to stay put, that she would return in a few minutes. She strutted past Thorne, who again appeared to be asleep. At the rear of the car, she opened the door and stepped onto the platform between cars. The wind whipped at her skirts, and pulled at the veil on her head. At least it cooled her temper. She gripped the rail for balance. Rolling hills and gulches covered with heavy stands of pine passed by. As they approached a mass of curiously eroded sandstone, a hand settled on her shoulder. She jumped, startled by the unexpected touch.

''It's called Elephant Rock.''

Clutching her hands to her chest, she spun around and scowled. ''You scared the life out of me.''

''Sorry, Irish. I wanted to make sure you weren't planning to jump.''

''After enduring that woman for an hour, I'm sorely tempted.''

He laughed, the sound carried away by the wind. Elbows on the rail, side by side they watched the scenery whiz by.

She liked being with him, enjoyed his descriptions of the passing countryside. It was growing dark as they approached the high outcrop of salmon-colored stone that resembled a medieval castle. "Castle Rock," he said. "Our last stop before Denver."

"I can't wait to get out of this awful habit." She shook her finger in his face. "And don't tell me I have to keep wearing it. I'll strangle you with this veil."

He caught her finger and brought it to his lips. "No, Irish, you'll be able to don the most fashionable attire you can find. You want to look like the wealthy woman you are when you step off that train in Philadelphia." His lips brushed the tip of her finger, then he turned her wrist and planted a kiss on her palm.

Shivers raced through her. Every time she thought she would be able to live without him, survive without his love, he did something endearing and turned her heart upside-down. Before she could respond, the door slid open and Sung Lo appeared in the dim light.

"Children look for Sissy. Big lady look for Sissy. Sissy come." He gestured to the shiny young faces peeking around his legs.

"We hungry," Running Deer announced.

"Go back to your seats," Thorne said. As the train skid to a stop, he leaped onto the depot platform.

Hurriedly, Mariah returned to her seat, taking the children with her. "We'll get supper when we reach Denver. It won't be long."

Mrs. Hoover slanted a haughty glance at Mariah. "You and that man were out there for a mighty long time," she said. "And alone."

Mariah had taken all she could from the woman. "Madam, I don't know what you think that gentleman and I were doing on the platform of a moving train, but I can assure you, nothing improper happened." She settled in her seat and gathered the children to her. "There wasn't enough room."

The woman's face turned red and puffed out like a frog. She stuttered a few times, then turned her back on Mariah. "I should report you to the nunnery. You bring disgrace on your order."

"I rather believe you're right. I'm not sure I'm cut out for this kind of life."

Her temper seething, Mariah picked up her bags, and retreated to the rear of the coach. Without a word, she plopped down beside Sung Lo, taking the seat Thorne had vacated. The children were delighted and hugged the old Chinese.

Moments later, the whistle signaled their departure, and the conductor called, "All aboard." So far, Thorne hadn't returned, and they were about to leave. She rose to go and look for him, when the first clack of the wheels started up the tracks. Falling back to the seat, she pressed her face to the window to block out the inside lights. Where was he? The train picked up speed. Her heart sank. Had he run away to avoid facing his past? Did he expect her to return to Philadelphia without him?

Well, she wasn't going to go without him. She reached for the emergency cord, just as the door burst open. Windblown and heaving for breath, Thorne slammed through the opening. He carried a straw hamper on his arm, and his hat in his hand.

"You didn't have to leave without me," he muttered. His eyes widened when he spotted Mariah in his seat. "Sister, what . . . ?" He cut off his question. "Oh, I suppose you couldn't take any more disapproval."

"Exactly. Where have you been? I thought you'd missed the train."

He took the empty seat across the aisle. Juan climbed on his lap. "I went to get something to eat." He reached into the basket and pulled out a shiny red apple. "Here you go, son. Just for you." The boy grinned from ear to ear.

"What got Running Deer?" The little girl stuck her head into the basket.

"Bread, cheese, some peach jam, and more apples." He

met Mariah's surprised stare. "I brought enough for you, too, Sister."

"You nearly missed the train to get something to eat?"

He grinned, and cut off a chunk of cheese with his knife. "I figured these younguns were hungry."

She spoke for his ears only. "You had me worried to death."

"Now, Irish, you didn't think I would go back on my word, did you?" He shoved the chunk of cheese into her mouth.

Ashamed of her lack of trust, she frowned. "Good. I'm hungrier than I'd thought."

"Don't look now, but that widow woman is about to bust her corset. What did you tell her?"

"Only that we didn't have enough room on that platform to do anything disgraceful. Or immoral."

He choked on a bite of cheese. "No wonder her face is redder than this apple. Do you think I should offer to share our supper with her?"

"Forget it." Mariah broke off a piece of bread. "She can afford to skip a few meals."

Sung Lo laughed, a tittering sound that made the children giggle. "Lady no like Sissy?"

"Sissy no like lady," she said.

For the next few minutes they ate in silence. When she glanced to the front of the car, several other passengers were staring at them. Mariah checked her veil to make sure horns hadn't sprouted from her head. Satisfied that they were just busybodies incited by the angry widow, she returned to her tasty supper. Thorne had risked missing the train for the children. For a man who considered himself a recluse, who wanted to be left alone, he'd shown nothing but kindness to the little ones. No wonder she loved him.

Not that it did any good. She'd promised to keep their marriage secret, and as soon as she reached Philadelphia, she would seek the annulment he desired.

With the children fed, and satisfied, they napped, Running Deer in Thorne's big arms, and Juan with Sung Lo. Mariah wished it were she in Thorne's embrace, having him hold her like the newly wed young man a few seats in front of her was holding his bride.

The conductor entered the door and make a great show of pulling out his gold pocket watch. He informed the passengers that they would arrive in Denver in about a half hour. As if this were her signal to cause more trouble, Mrs. Hoover approached, followed by two other women Mariah hadn't even met. Their husbands cowered behind them.

Mrs. Hoover placed her hands on her ample hips. "Tell me, Sister, exactly what order are you with? Are they housed in Denver?"

Totally annoyed and on the verge of letting her Irish temper flare, Mariah stood and looked down on her accusers, women several inches shorter than she. She slipped into the brogue of her teacher at the convent school. "Madams, I do not know what you're accusing me of. If you wish to speak to the mother superior of the nunnery, I'll be happy to introduce you when we reach St. Louis. Until then, I would solicit your prayers for a safe journey for myself and these children."

Not to be outdone, the widow glared right back. "I'm sure she would like to know how cozy you've become with these two men. Why, I wouldn't be surprised at what you have planned for these unfortunate children."

Behind her, she felt the tension radiate from Thorne like the hot rays of the sun. Her own anger was about to erupt in something quite unladylike, and definitely not meek. But then, the nuns she knew from home showed temper from time to time.

"Do not concern yourself with their safety, as if you care. As for these men, they've offered help that the women have withheld. And as I told you before, I will probably leave the order when I return to the convent." She shot a glance over her shoulder at Thorne. His mouth was set in a hard line, and she doubted he could hold his temper much longer. Only holding the sleeping girl kept him from leaping up, of that she was certain.

"And when you contact Sister Mary Louise at St. Bridgit's, be sure you get my name right. It's novice Rose Smith. That's S-M-I-T-H."

The woman let out a loud snort, turned on her heel, and led her small entourage back to their seats. Mariah watched their progress, catching a furtive glance from the conspirators. The husbands hurried their wives along, clearly uncomfortable by the exchange. She was sure the trouble-making widow had incited the others, who now wanted nothing more to do with the situation.

Although the exchange had attracted the attention of their fellow passengers, only a few were bold enough to show that they'd noticed. Mr. Jones, who had ridden on the stagecoach from Cimarron, winked and grinned. He hadn't spoken much during their ride, so she was rather surprised at his reaction. For a woman who hadn't wanted to bring attention to herself, she'd caught the focus of the entire train car. Thankfully, there were no soldiers aboard.

Her gaze again strayed to the mysterious Mr. Jones. It suddenly dawned on her that the man had the makings of a lawman. Or a Pinkerton man.

Mariah dropped to her seat. How could she not have noticed? He had all the marks—the steely eyes that didn't miss anything, the gun that hung from the hand-tooled holster, and the way he'd studied every passenger before taking his seat. And his name. She'd chosen Smith, he'd chosen Jones. Operatives seldom used their real names while on an assignment. She certainly hadn't.

The conductor approached and spoke quietly to Mr. Jones. The man nodded, and followed the conductor to the rear car.

Thorne had studied every movement, although he appeared uninterested in his surroundings. She leaned to him and whispered, "That man, I believe he's some sort of operative."

"Wells Fargo," he answered just as quietly.

"How do you know?"

"The stagecoach driver told me."

"He isn't suspicious, is he?"

He shifted the child in his arms. "No. But wouldn't he be surprised to learn that you're his kind? And that you encountered Jesse James in Cimarron?"

She sat back, proud that her disguise had worked. If she could fool another detective, she was well on her way to a successful career at the agency, and the partnership she'd earned.

Chapter 18

A discreet knock on the door of Mariah's hotel room woke her the following morning. She stretched and yawned. Upon arriving in Denver late the previous night, they had gone directly to the American House Hotel. Thorne had booked two suites, one for Mariah and Running Deer, and the other for the males. The little girl lay snuggled into Mariah's side, lost in much-needed sleep.

Since she'd chosen to travel west with the minimum of baggage, she was forced to sleep in her chemise and pantalets. Aware of her lack of decent apparel, she hesitated in opening the door that led from the bedroom to the sitting room.

"Who is it?" she called, glancing around for something with which to cover her unmentionables.

"Your breakfast, ma'am" came a youthful male voice. "I'll set it up here for you."

"Breakfast?" She swiped a stray lock of long hair from her eyes. Fatigued after the long day's travel, she hadn't bothered with her usual braid. "I didn't order breakfast." Sitting on the edge of the soft mattress, she tugged the silk counterpane from the bed and wrapped it around her shoulders.

As she staggered into the sitting room, the door clicked shut, and she was alone. A large tray waited on a small dining table. Hugging the silk spread to her chest, she lifted the linen cloth and inspected the assortment of foods laid out. A folded piece of white paper stuck out from among a crystal vase of fresh flowers.

"Irish, enjoy your breakfast. Our eastbound train leaves at ten tomorrow morning. I'll be busy today, and I'm taking Juan and Sung Lo with me. See how much of my gold you and Running Deer can spend." It was signed with a large "T."

A wide smile curved her lips. Her heart fluttered. Thorne must care a little to think of her breakfast, and invite her to go shopping at his expense. Sometimes the man was so kind and giving, gentle and loving. At other times he was as cross as a hungry old bear. She didn't know whether to kiss him or kick him.

She moved to the window and pulled aside the plush curtain. If he loved her as she loved him, she would fight at his side for his freedom. And she would make the marriage as real as her parents'. Regardless of his feelings for her, she vowed to do everything within her power to see that he was vindicated of his so-called crimes.

The wrap dropped from her shoulders. Outside the sun was shining, and glinted like silver off the Rockies in the distance. From her third-floor window, she spotted Cherry Creek, which had flooded a few years earlier and nearly washed the town away. Thorne had been more than generous in the selection of their hotel. She dug her toes into the thick carpet and returned to a silk brocade chair.

In spite of her state of dishabille, she felt elegant and pampered in the luxurious surroundings. Oh, wouldn't Jenny swoon in a room like this? When Mariah received the full reward for locating that Union gold, she would decorate a room for her sister with nothing but silk and velvet.

She settled back with a cup of coffee in her hand, the cup one of fine china. They would eat from nothing but the finest china money could buy. Of course, her mother would say she was wasteful, but after years of struggle to raise her family, Mary Kathleen and Sean O'Reilly deserved a bit of luxury in their lives. She might even hire a maid.

Mariah settled her feet on the small, elegant settee. A room like this one would be just grand. Of course, all the rooms in Mrs. Thornton's Society Hill mansion resembled this one. Thorne's grandmother owned the largest shipyard on the Delaware River. He had grown up in this kind of luxury, while she knew little more than a two-story brownstone with three small bedrooms, a parlor and kitchen. No wonder he didn't want to stay married to the daughter of Irish immigrants. Not that it mattered to her. She didn't want to be tied to a dominating male like him anyway.

Determined not to feel sorry for herself, Mariah devoured eggs, steak, fresh fruit, and coffee with rich cream. By the time she'd finished and dressed in a calico skirt and blue shirtwaist, Running Deer had awakened. After she fed and dressed the girl in her usual canvas britches and shirt, she led the way to the shopping district on Sixteenth Street.

She easily found a dressmaker willing to accommodate a customer with gold coins. The dressmaker agreed to sell her the velvet-trimmed blue traveling suit and print afternoon gown that had been ordered for the wife of a gold miner who went broke overnight. With slight alterations, both frocks fit Mariah as if they'd been made for her. After a stop at the milliners', an emporium, and other shops along the way, her arms were loaded by the time she returned to the hotel. Of course, she used her own money, the generous expense fee from Mrs. Thornton.

She'd purchased several dresses and a pair of shoes for Running Deer, along with new trousers and shirts for Juan. She wanted them to make a fine impression on Thorne's grandmother when they reached Philadelphia. Included in her purchases were gifts for her entire family—Mexican silver hair combs for the girls, Indian arrowheads for the twins, Bowie

knives for Francis and Kevin. She even got knives for Danny
Malloy and her brother-in-law, Jamie. She found a beautiful
gold watch for Sean, and a gold locket for her mother.

Upon her return to the hotel, she ordered a bath for herself
and the nearly exhausted child. On her one night in Denver,
Mariah had no intention of hiding in her room. The glittering
dining room was too inviting, and the aromas wafting through
the lobby made her stomach growl. The dressmaker had delivered the gown and suit, and both awaited her in her suite.

After her bath, Mariah twisted her long hair into an elegant
chignon, leaving a few curls touching her cheeks and neck.
Then she donned the lovely day dress and the new shoes she'd
found at the cobblers. Her mother would be shocked at the
deep, ruffled neckline that bared more bosom than anything
she'd ever worn. Obviously the French dressmaker didn't quite
understand her instructions. She grinned. Wouldn't this just
knock that staid mountain man clear off his feet?

She hadn't seen him since the past night when they'd checked
into the hotel. From time to time, she heard doors slam, and
voices from the adjoining suite, the one he shared with Sung
Lo and Juan. She was tempted to knock on his door and give
him a gander at her elegant looks. She frowned. If he wanted
to be with her, he would have invited her to dinner. Clearly,
he was happy without her. And, after the annulment, she would
be perfectly happy without him.

She dressed Running Deer in a new dress of pink gingham
with a white eyelet apron. At first, the girl balked at wearing
something other than her trousers, but when Mariah remarked
how pretty she looked, the child allowed her to tie matching
ribbons on her braids. Satisfied with their appearance, Mariah
opened the door and stepped into the hallway. She bit her lip
in concentration. Perhaps Juan or Sung Lo would like to join
her for dinner in the dining room. Besides, she wanted to check
on the little boy.

She knocked on the door, and twisted the bracelet on her

arm. Sung Lo answered and bowed low, as if he didn't recognize her. "Hello, ma'am," he said.

Over his shoulder, she caught a glimpse of Thorne. He wore a neat pair of wool trousers, a stiff white shirt, string tie, and black leather vest. His gaze raked her from head to toe, his gray eyes warming when his glance lingered momentarily on the deep scoop of the neckline. His smile turned her legs to mush.

Running Deer dashed past the Chinese and raced into Thorne's arms. He lifted her high in the air. "Sissy say must wear dress," she said.

He smiled at the child. "It's a very pretty dress. You and Sissy are both very beautiful ladies."

Mariah stepped into the room. The compliment flowed over her like warm honey. "We're going to dinner in the dining room. Would you care to join us?" She reached for Juan, who was wearing spanking-new pants and shirt. "Looks like I'm not the only one who went shopping."

The boy looked up to Thorne for his answer. "I was about to order our dinner, but eating in the dining room will be a treat for the youngsters."

He picked up his new gray hat and gestured to the door. "Shall we give Denver a treat?"

Sung Lo backed away. "Stay here. No like eat room."

Thorne nodded his assent. "I'll have a meal delivered. You rest. We've had a busy day."

Hand in hand, the children raced to the winding staircase. Thorne offered his arm, and Mariah placed her gloved hand on forearm. "I suppose you've made quite a dent in that bag of gold," he said.

"Actually, I did not open the bag. It's safely hidden in my room. The gold and my gun didn't quite fit with my new gown." She tried to pull away, but he pressed his other hand over hers. "I used my own funds—the money your grandmother gave me for expenses."

"I told you the gold was yours to use as you see fit. I want to pay for anything you bought for the children."

"It wasn't much. Your grandmother was quite generous."

"Yes, I'm sure she was."

They reached the lobby and turned toward the dining room. Several men stopped and tipped their hats to Mariah. She forced herself not to blush when their gazes lingered at her exposed bosom. Thorne growled deep in his throat, and tightened his grip on her arm. She smiled inwardly. He was jealous. Her heart warmed at the thought that he cared at least that much.

"You're growling like an old bear again," she whispered as they waited to be escorted to a table.

"Be thankful I don't carry you back upstairs and—"

Before he finished his threat, the headwaiter approached and showed them to their table. Her imagination ran wild wondering what he would do if he carried her back to her room. Fire ignited in her blood. Except for the children with them, she would have dared him to try.

The food was delicious, the wine rich, and the light conversation warming. Besides shopping for new clothes, Thorne revealed that he'd gone to the bank. After buying the mountain and acreage, he'd had quite a bit of money left over from the sale of his gold mine. He'd arranged to transfer the money to a bank in Philadelphia. He was even richer than she'd thought.

Halfway through the dinner, both children nodded, their eyes closing. "I suppose I'd better take them back upstairs," Mariah offered.

Thorne stood, and signaled her to remain seated. "You stay here and wait for dessert. I'll take them up and be right back." He leaned closer and whispered, "The way you're dressed, I'm crazy to leave you here alone. If anybody bothers you, just shoot them."

She laughed. "Good night, darlings," she said. The youngsters hugged her, then raced to keep up with Thorne's long stride.

Mariah relaxed and sipped her wine. The dining room was

truly elegant with red carpet, embroidered table covers, and linen napkins. The china, crystal, and silver sparkled in the candlelight. She wished she could dine like this every day of her life. At each table gentlemen in suits and ladies in evening apparel enjoyed the excellent cuisine and expensive wine. Many wore diamonds and gold. Mariah's only jewelry was the silver bracelet Thorne had given her. And as lovely as her new gown was, it didn't compare to the silk and satin of the other women. She twisted the bracelet, the only reminder of her marriage to the man she loved.

She felt movement at her shoulder. Expecting to see Thorne, she was surprised to see a strange man smiling down at her. "What's a beautiful woman like you doing in a place like this alone?" he asked. His nearly black eyes sparkled, and a dimple pierced his chin. The man was very handsome in a black suit and brocade vest. A gold chain dangled across his waist.

As he lowered himself into the chair Thorne had vacated, a large hand snatched the back of his collar. "She isn't alone. She's my wife."

The stranger jerked to his feet and backed away. Thorne's rigid stare would stop a clock at twenty paces. "Sorry, I thought she was alone."

"I left her for a minute to take our children upstairs." He sank into the chair. "Get lost."

The man turned on his heel and strutted away. The encounter left several other diners staring at them. Appalled, Mariah glared at Thorne. "What happened to your southern manners?"

"I lost them during the war, along with everything else," he rasped deep in his throat. The pain was unmistakable.

"It wasn't necessary to be so rude. He didn't mean any harm."

"How do you know? He could be a gambler, or even a molester."

Knowing he could be right, she changed the subject. "What did you mean calling me your wife?"

He took a sip of wine. "You are my wife. Remember Fort Union?"

With a low growl of her own, she slapped her napkin onto the table. "A temporary lack of judgment on my part. As soon as I reach Philadelphia, I fully intend to remedy that mistake."

"Meanwhile, I'll protect what's mine and see that you return to your parents safely."

"You're impossible." She stood and stalked out of the dining room.

Thorne followed at her heels. Head high, shoulders back, her bosom swelled above the low neckline of the gown. Another growl threatened to rumble from his chest. He'd never thought himself a jealous man, yet when he spied the stranger making overt advances toward her, something inside him snapped. He should have tossed the fellow out on his dandy behind.

With every step she took, her hips swayed, sweeping her skirt across the floor. It didn't take much soul-searching to realize what his problem was. Plain and simple, he wanted her. He had ever since he'd learned she wasn't a nun. Even before then, if he were brutally honest with himself. The few times they'd been together didn't nearly make up for the desire that burned in his gut.

Hands gripping her skirt, she began to walk up the stairs. With his longer legs, he could have caught up with her in a few strides. But watching her brought a modicum of pleasure to his tortured body. At the landing on the second floor, she stopped and propped her hands on her hips. Her blue eyes shot icicles at him.

He stopped in his tracks and faced her. "What's got you so head up, Irish? I thought you liked me taking care of you."

She heaved a long sigh. "I don't need protecting. You should know that by now. And I don't appreciate your reminding me of our marriage when you've made it clear you want it ended."

Thorne was torn. Yes, he wanted the annulment. No, he wanted to stay married to Mariah. He couldn't have it both ways. "If I knew what my future held, things might be different."

''Might? No, Mountain Man, you don't want a wife, and if you did, it wouldn't be me.''

As she turned to continue up the staircase, he caught her arm and spun her around. ''Why wouldn't it be you?'' Another couple descending the staircase stopped to stare. He hadn't meant to cause a scene. ''Irish, can't we discuss this in private?''

''There's nothing to discuss.''

Biting his tongue to keep back another growl, he followed her to her room. She slipped the key into the lock and shoved open the door. When he started to follow her, she stopped him with a hand to his chest. ''This is as far as you go.''

He glanced over her shoulder at the empty sitting room. Beyond the next door was a large, inviting bed. One he wanted to share with his wife. ''I left the children asleep in my suite with Sung Lo. Running Deer will spend the night on the settee.''

''Is that your way of saying you want to spend the night with me?'' Her voice dropped to a painful whisper.

''Yes.''

Mariah stood her ground, her blue eyes blazed with fire. ''Don't you recall reminding me that if we sleep together, we'll jeopardize our chance for an annulment?''

His own words came back to haunt him. ''Do you want an annulment?''

''It doesn't matter what I want. You were right. We don't want to take a chance on having a child together.''

''I'll take that chance.'' And make the marriage as real in fact as it was on paper.

''I won't be your wife in the Colorado and then be tossed aside when we reach Pennsylvania. You made it clear the first time we made love that you wouldn't offer marriage. You only married me to save your own hide.''

''And your reputation.''

She laughed, a sound full of scorn. ''My reputation was ruined when I left home unescorted, and spent days, weeks, with a man outside the bonds of matrimony. Didn't Father Callahan tell us as much?''

"Irish, let's go inside and talk. We don't want the entire hotel to know our business."

"My name is Mariah. I don't need reminders that I'm nothing but an Irish tart to a man like Michael Thornton Harrison. Your kind doesn't object to a little romp with a woman like me. They always refuse marriage, or in your case, demand an annulment."

He caught her arm as she attempted to slip into the room. "I never said or thought any such thing. I certainly wouldn't hold that against anybody. If I knew I had a future, things could be different."

"I don't want the great and aristocratic Michael Thornton Harrison to be stuck with a poor Irish woman. What would your family think? Or your rich friends on Society Hill?" She shook off his hand, and rubbed her arm as if to wipe off his touch.

"I don't give a darn about what anybody says about me. You should know by now that your background doesn't mean a thing to me. My revered grandmother was an Irish immigrant. And aren't you about to become a very wealthy woman?"

"A wealthy, independent woman. Without a husband to tell me what to do with my money." She shoved against his chest. "Good night, Mountain Man." She closed the door and turned the key in the lock.

"Damn." He slammed his fist into his palm. Just when he was ready to acknowledge the stubborn woman as his wife, she completely shut him out.

To be perfectly honest with himself, he couldn't blame her. He'd been the one to initiate the marriage, and he'd been the one to offer an annulment. No, he'd insisted on an annulment. Now he was left high and dry while the woman he loved slept in a soft feather bed alone.

Loved? The word tore through his chest with the force of a mini ball. He didn't love Mariah; he couldn't love any woman. The only woman he'd ever loved had rejected him at the start of the war. Suzanna had been unable to understand his need to support the Union. She turned to his brother for comfort, and had married Gabriel.

Thoughts of all he'd lost during the war flooded back. Upon his return to Philadelphia, he stood to lose his freedom, and possibly his life. Unless he had something to offer Mariah, the annulment was the only way out for them. It wouldn't be fair for her to be labeled as the wife of a traitor. And sleeping with her would only increase the chances of creating a child. He would never want any child of his to know his father had been accused of cowardice in face of battle.

He turned toward his own room. As much as he ached for his Mariah, leaving her alone was his only choice.

Mariah listened until his footsteps faded and the door to the next suite opened and closed. Only then did she let the tears fall. Alone in the privacy of her room, she could finally admit how badly she was hurting.

It would have been so easy to give in, to invite Thorne into her room, to spend the night in his strong arms. To feel his warm lips on hers, to have his hands caress her body until she forgot even her name. She'd never imagined she could desire a man the way she wanted Thorne. This had to be love. Her love for him overrode common sense. Unless he showed in some small way that he truly cared for her, she would sleep alone. His reasons for ending the marriage made perfect sense—to him. To her, they were just his way of saying he didn't want a wife. As his wife, she would fight heaven and hell to gain his freedom. And with her tenacity, she wouldn't stop until he was free and pardoned of any supposed crimes.

Even though he'd spent the last years in the mountains of New Mexico, he was still Michael Thornton Harrison, son of an aristocratic Virginia planter, and grandson of Philadelphia's elite. The mountain man she'd fallen in love with was slowly disappearing. By the time they reached home, she doubted she would even recognize the man.

Heedless of her new gown, she threw herself across the bed and gave in to self-doubt and self-pity. Tomorrow, she would have to face him with a haughty smile. Tonight, she wished she had her mother's breast to cry on.

Mariah placed her hands on her stomach. What if a child were already growing in her body? With all her heart, she wished they'd made a baby together. Then, she hoped they hadn't. True, he would want to remain her husband if a child were on the way, but Mariah didn't want him that way. Unless he wanted her for herself, she didn't want him at all.

She blew her nose, and dried her tears. Mariah Rose O'Reilly was soon to be a wealthy woman. She didn't need a gruff mountain man or social dandy. She would do just grand on her own.

And that was the truth.

Chapter 19

The next morning, Mariah adjusted her new hat at a jaunty angle, pulling the sheer veil over her eyes. She hoped the thin silk would hide the dark circles around her eyes—the result of another sleepless night. Thankfully, Running Deer had spent the night in the other suite, allowing Mariah time to wallow in her misery.

Certain she looked elegant and stylish, she knocked on the door of the men's suite, and waited for Thorne to answer. The royal-blue suit with ivory blouse had been worth the extra money it cost to have it altered in time for the trip. She certainly hoped that stubborn mountain man appreciated her appearance.

After a moment, Sung Lo peeked around a slit in the doorway. "It's just me, Sung Lo."

The old man bowed at the waist and gestured her into the room. She glanced around the room for Thorne. The two children sat on the settee. The stoic mountain man was nowhere to be seen. She gritted her teeth. There was no use his hiding in the bedroom. Sooner or later he would have to face her.

"Come along, darling." Mariah touched Running Deer's hand. "You have to get into your new dress."

In an unusual show of rebellion, the little girl folded her arms across her chest and refused to move. "No like dress. Want pants like Juan."

Mariah sat beside the children and brushed a hand over the girl's mussed pigtails. "Boys wear pants, girls wear dresses. You'll look ever so pretty."

For the first time, the child refused to obey Mariah. "No want to look pretty."

Letting out a long sigh, Mariah began to release the girl's untidy braids. "Thorne wants you to look pretty."

A single tear rolled down her dusky cheek. "Thorne not here. He gone."

"Gone?" Mariah's heart skipped a beat. She looked at the old Chinese. Had he left her to tend the children with his help? "Where?" She asked anxiously.

Sung Lo shrugged his narrow shoulders. "Thorne leave early. Say give to Sissy." He handed her an envelope.

Hands trembling, she tore open the flap. The word "gone" echoed in her ears. He'd promised to make to the return trip and she hadn't thought him a man to go back on his word. She pulled out four first-class tickets for seats on a Pullman Hotel car on the Kansas Pacific Railroad. Four. Not five.

"Where did Thorne go?" she asked, almost afraid to find out.

"He say go early. Meet Sissy on train."

Her heart slowed to normal. He simply didn't want to face her this morning. Did he, too, have a sleepless night, or had he found solace elsewhere? She choked back the swell of fury. The man did more to provoke her than anybody she'd ever met. Even her encounter with the despicable Willard Shepherd years ago hadn't evoked the amount of irritation as this man who called himself Thorne. He was named right. He prickled her every which way. Well, he couldn't avoid her forever.

She returned her attention to the rebellious child, and struggled to keep her tone even and soothing. "You can wear the pants under the dress. But if we don't hurry, we won't have time to stop at that candy store before we go to the depot.''

At the reminder of a special treat, the little girl wiped her face with the back of her hand. ''Can Juan have candy, too?''

She combed her fingers through the child's long, thick hair. ''We'll all have candy. Even Sung Lo.'' She winked at the old man, who granted her a wide grin. ''Finish packing while I get this pretty girl ready.'' Turning to Juan, she brushed a hand over his head. ''You look mighty handsome today.''

Throwing himself into her arms, Juan gave her a hard hug. Then he picked up the whistle from around his neck and played a short, mournful tune. His music spoke louder than words. She fully understood their anxiety. They were headed for a strange place with strange people. In their place, Mariah would be terrified. Yet, these young children had borne more tragedy and sorrow than most adults experience in a lifetime. Her heart cried out for them, and she vowed to make their lives as happy as humanly possible.

Within a few minutes, they were on their way to the dining room for breakfast. The train was scheduled to leave at ten o'clock, which gave them ample time to stop at the confectionery on the way to the depot. The children ate heartily, but Sung Lo wrapped most of his meal into a napkin and stashed it in the pockets of his black tunic. Mariah tried to explain they would have places to stop and eat on the way, but he shook his head and gathered all the leftover rolls from the table. When Mariah tried to pay the bill, the waiter informed her that ''Mr. Smith'' had already taken care of everything.

At the desk, she learned that ''Mr. Smith'' had hired a carriage to take her to the depot. A young boy carried their bags, and soon Mariah, Sung Lo, and the children were on their way to the railroad station.

The train began to board shortly after her arrival. A tall conductor, as slim as a skeleton, escorted them to their assigned seats. The cushioned seats on the sleeper were wide and luxurious, far different from the coach seats on their last train, and from the ones Mariah had endured in the coach going west a few weeks earlier. Thorne had arranged the finest accommodations available on the Kansas Pacific line.

After she'd settled the youngsters in their seats, she glanced around for Thorne. Even as the conductor announced their departure from Denver, he still hadn't shown his face. Sung Lo clung to the upholstered handles of the seat, and closed his eyes as the train let out a shrill whistle and began its slow chugging away from the station. The youngsters pressed their faces to the window. Running Deer clutched her doll and Juan wrapped his fingers around his whistle. In the facing seat, Mariah rubbed her bracelet as if it were a magic lamp and she could make a wish.

The train picked up speed, and soon they were roaring over the Colorado plains. Mariah settled back, not knowing for sure if Thorne had boarded or not. She alternated between anger and anxiety at the cavalier way he'd treated her and the children.

Had he changed his mind—or was he simply avoiding another confrontation? With every click of the wheels, with each sway of the train, her anger grew. She glanced at the children who so depended on him. He wasn't a man to go back on his word, nor was he the type to neglect the children. She'd bet half her reward money that he was hiding away on the train to avoid her.

She dug her nails into her palms, the new gloves taking unneeded abuse. Above all else, Mariah hated being ignored.

After about an hour, and still the reclusive Thorne hadn't shown his face, she determined to find him and give him what-for. Her fingers itched to wrap around the man's neck and shake some sense into him. She whispered to Sung Lo to watch the children, and she headed toward the rear of the passenger car. As she reached for the door that led to the adjoining car, a hand on her arm stopped her.

"Ma'am, you can't go out there." The dark-skinned porter in sparkling white uniform doffed his cap.

"Why not?" she asked.

"That's the gentlemen's club car. No ladies allowed."

"I am looking for someone, and I wondered if he's in there."

"If you mean Mr. Smith, he's there all right. The gentleman asked me to keep an eye on you and his children."

She planted her hands on her hips. No use taking out her anger on the poor helpless porter. "Oh, he did, did he? Will you kindly inform Mr. Smith that Mrs. Smith would like to see him?"

"Yes, ma'am, I'll do that. Will you please return to your seat?"

Mariah stomped back up the aisle and dropped into the plush seat. At least he'd made it aboard, she thought. But he couldn't avoid her forever.

Several boring hours later, the train slowed and came to a screeching stop. The conductor informed the passengers that they had twenty minutes to eat while the train took on fuel and water. Hurriedly, Mariah gathered the children and headed with the crowd to the exit. Sung Lo chose to remain on board and eat what he'd brought from the hotel.

The instant she stepped to the platform, a strong hand clutched her elbow. "This way, Irish. I'll see that you get your meal and have time to eat it."

She shook off Thorne's hand as if she hadn't heard or seen him. After the way he'd treated her, she wanted no favors from him. She and the children could fend for themselves.

Thorne fell into step at her side, acting for all the world like a devoted escort. Once inside the small clapboard building that served as dining room and kitchen, he guided them to a table. "Wait here. I'll get your food."

"I can get our meal," she grated between her teeth.

He locked gazes with her. "Irish, don't be stubborn. I've already bribed the conductor to see that we're served immediately. He's talking with the proprietor now."

Mariah understood from her past experience on the train how

hard it was to get service and still have time to eat. While the other passengers pushed and shoved for a place at a table or the long counter, their food was placed in front of them. If it weren't for Thorne's high-handed manner, she would have appreciated the special attention.

Thorne took a chair between the two children. "Are you being good for Sissy?" he asked.

"They're very well behaved." She cut into the overcooked piece of meat she assumed was beef. "How are you enjoying the trip?" she asked, her voice as frosty as a winter's morning.

He shrugged. "The club car is smoky, but I've already won a hundred dollars at poker. Could prove to be a prosperous trip."

Running Deer leaned her head against Thorne's arm. "Thorne no like us?"

Leaning over, he kissed the top of the child's head. "I like you all, sweetheart."

The little girl shoved away her half-eaten meat and potatoes. "Why you not sit with us?"

That was exactly what Mariah wanted to know. She looked at him expectedly. Did he understand that by avoiding her, he was hurting the children? She shot an angry glance at him.

"Do you want me to sit with you?" His warm gray eyes met her angry blue ones.

"I want. Juan want. Sung Lo want." The girl lifted her imploring gaze to Mariah. "Sissy want."

A smile threatened at the corners of Thorne's mouth. "Does Sissy want?" he asked in that deep, gravelly voice that vibrated clear to the center of her heart.

"I really don't care, one way or the other. So far, we've managed perfectly fine on our own."

His gaze bore into hers, catching the lie her eyes couldn't hide. "I'll sit with you."

"If it isn't too much trouble."

"No trouble at all." He cut into his meat, and shoved a large chunk into his mouth. After he devoured the entire meal, he pushed the plate aside with a grunt. "I've eaten rattlesnake better than that."

Mariah shoved the poorly cooked food around with her fork. "Maybe that's what this is."

He laughed. "No, Irish. Rattlesnake is much more tender." Pushing back his chair, he stood. "Take the children on board when the conductor calls. I have an errand to run."

"Try not to miss the train. You had the children and Sung Lo worried sick in Colorado Springs." She refused to admit how worried she'd been.

"I promise I'll make it in time." He lowered his voice to a whisper. "Hell, I bribed that conductor enough. He'd better not leave without me."

"I wondered why he was so attentive to my needs. For a time, I thought it was my looks."

He skimmed the backs of his fingers along her cheek. "Irish, I also tipped the porter to keep the men away from you."

Her skin tingled from his gentle touch and her heartbeat fluttered. That made her as angry with herself as she was with him. "Be off with you. And if you miss the train, I'll not worry or fret."

On his way through the doorway, he paused to speak to the conductor, who nodded and glanced at his large watch. She tried to eat, but the bland food stuck in her throat. She couldn't wait to get home to her mother's cooking. Or Sung Lo's, for that matter. Once in Philadelphia, she might open a Chinese restaurant for him. Wouldn't that be a fine investment for her newfound riches?

This time, Thorne didn't miss the train. The conductor called his last "All aboard" and banged a loud gong. He easily located Mariah, Sung Lo, and the children. With a wide grin, Thorne nudged her aside.

"Make room, Irish. I've a treat for you."

She shifted to make room. Her eyes shot daggers at him. He

hoped the treat he'd found would make up for his lack of attention that morning. It had taken from the time they'd boarded until the meal break to get his emotions under control. After another sleepless night, he'd been unwilling to face Mariah and his own confusion. When he'd seen her struggling with the children, he knew he'd wronged her. And hurt the innocent in his inability to deal with his feelings. For the remainder of the trip, he would play the dutiful escort, and enjoy what little freedom that might remain for him.

"What this time?" she asked. "More apples?"

"Better."

The two dark heads of the children leaned over her, eager to find what treat he'd brought for them. When he unwrapped a towel, the aroma of freshly baked pie rose with the steam.

"Pie? An apple pie?"

"Peach."

"Where in the world did you get it? There's no bakery in that tiny spot on the rails."

Handing each of them a spoon, he grinned with self-satisfaction. "Oh, I only brought four," he said, his gaze locked on Mariah's pink lips. "Looks like we'll have to share." He dug in his spoon, took a bite, held it out to Mariah.

She opened her mouth, and closed her lips over the offered treat. A tiny moan came from her throat. "Don't tell me you stole this off some woman's windowsill."

"In a way. I smelled something baking when I entered the cafe. I'd hoped it was being served to us. When it wasn't, I simply followed my nose, and bought it from a lady who was more than willing to part with it."

She laughed. "For an exorbitant price, I'd imagine."

He cut off her words with another spoonful of pie. Feeding her, sharing the same spoon, was an intimate activity shared by lovers. Her pink tongue snaked out and swiped across her lips. He hurriedly shoved the spoon into his mouth to bite back the urge to replace the spoon with his kiss. The desire that had burst into full bloom the minute he'd seen her threatened to double him over. He regretted that they were in view of half a car full of people. Most of all, he regretted leaving her the past night.

The five of them continued until the pie tin was empty, licked clean. Mariah wiped the children's faces, and they returned to their places at the window sharing the facing seat with Sung Lo.

Thorne reached over and swiped his index finger across her lips. "You forgot to wipe your own mouth." He carried his finger to his mouth, and licked off the tiny crumb. He refused to think about his uncertain future. He had this trip, these few days of freedom to be with the ones he cared for. After that, he would deal with whatever fate had in store for him.

They were well into Kansas when the porter assisted the passengers into making up their beds. Mariah had spent the day beside Thorne, his arm drifting across her shoulder as he napped. His kindness and consideration had confused her. After he'd so generously brought the pie, then proceeded to hand feed her, her anger had dissipated like the vapor on a mirror. How could she be mad at a man who did something so endearing?

After tending her personal needs in the curtained ladies' wash area at the rear of the car, Mariah returned to the alcove to sleep. The Pullman car was quite ingenious: seats reclined into beds, and a bunk dropped from the ceiling. Assisted by the porter, she climbed a small ladder to the upper berth beside Running Deer. Sung Lo and Juan shared the lower.

Sitting cross-legged on the narrow bed, she struggled out of her suit and into a new white nightdress. She wondered where Thorne had disappeared to. He'd left when the porter had come to set up the beds. As she stretched out on the narrow bed, the curtain parted.

"Make room, Irish."

She hugged the covers to her chest. "Thorne, what are you

doing here?'' she whispered. The lamps in the coach had been dimmed, and the sounds of snoring blended with the clatter of the train.

He heaved himself up to the edge of the bed and kicked off his boots. ''I'd like to get some sleep.''

''Then go to your own bed.''

''That fool of a conductor wanted me to share an upper with a man who weighed at least three hundred pounds. That berth would crash right down to the bunk beneath us.'' He elbowed her over. ''If I have to share, I'd rather it be with you.''

''Didn't you bribe him enough?''

''The coach is full, and we're expected to sleep two to a bunk.''

''Running Deer and I already make two. You can't sleep here, and that's the truth.''

Ignoring her protests, he stretched out his full length and snuggled into her side. ''She doesn't take up any space at all. Irish, it's perfectly legal since we're married.'' His lips nuzzled her ear. ''Besides, we can't do anything in these cramped quarters and with Running Deer with us.''

''You only remember we're married when it's for your convenience.''

''Like now. Good night, Irish.''

He curled up to her back, spoon fashion with his hand draped across her waist. His breathing turned deep and even, but Mariah spent the better part of the night keeping his hand from straying to the intimate parts of her body. By the pressure of his body against her, it was clear how much he desired her.

Truth be told, she wanted him every bit as much. However, with him, it was temporary; Mariah wanted Thorne for a lifetime. All or nothing. He couldn't have her, then toss her aside when they reached Philadelphia. Unless he wanted the marriage to last, there was no consummating it. Not again. She certainly didn't want to jeopardize the annulment.

The clatter of the wheels and the swaying of the train finally lulled Thorne into a deep sleep. It hadn't been easy pretending

sleep with the soft body nestled under his arm. He bit his lip
to keep from laughing every time his hand shifted an inch and
she tossed it back at him. He awoke briefly when the train
stopped at some town along the route, but he ignored the loud
whistle and snuggled into the warmth beside him.

Footsteps on the solid wooden floor awoke him before dawn.
He tried to move, but found a slender leg wrapped around his
thighs, and an arm anchored to his chest. Mariah had turned
in her sleep shifting her nightdress high on her waist. His heart
nearly stopped beating. Needs he couldn't hide burst into full-
blown desire.

Unable to resist the temptation lying in his arms, he planted
tiny kisses across her cheek. She shifted slightly, pressing her
unbound breasts to his chest. The soft moan from her parted
lips invited further exploration. He dipped his tongue into her
ear, and she squirmed closer. His arousal pressed into the soft
confines between her legs.

Hunger battled with common sense. Desire warred with
integrity. If they were alone, he would simply roll her over and
claim her fully as his wife. Although that was impossible under
the circumstances, it wouldn't hurt to kiss her, to feel her soft
body, to enjoy the sweet fragrance of her long, unbound hair.
To torment his body beyond endurance.

With one finger, he brushed the hair from her face. He had
to stop before things got even more heated and he wouldn't be
able to stop himself. Her eyelids fluttered open. A smile curved
her mouth. Her gaze met his.

"Morning, Irish," he whispered. Beyond the curtain separating them from the narrow aisle, people were stirring, speaking
in hushed whispers, their words drowning in the loud clatter
of the train.

"Morning," she returned. As sleep disappeared, and awareness grew, her mouth formed an O. "What are you doing?"

"Not nearly what I'd like." He lowered his voice to a whisper. "We'll have to wait until we get to a nice hotel to make
love."

''Not on your life, Mountain Man.''

Placing both palms against his chest, she gave him a hard shove. Her strength caught him by surprise. He tumbled from the bunk, through the curtains, and landed smack on his backside in the middle of the passageway. A woman gasped, and a man chuckled. The conductor towered over him, his face in a perpetual frown in the glow of the lantern on his arm.

''I suppose it's time to rise,'' he said, pulling what little dignity remained over him. Standing, he picked up his boots, and stuck his head back into the opening of the curtain. ''I'll get you for that, Irish.'' Then he winked and left her alone to dress.

Mariah fumed all the way to Kansas City and beyond. Even the elegant meal in the hotel restaurant didn't improve her humor. Imagine Thorne's nerve. When it suited his pleasure, he acknowledged their marriage. Other times, he argued for an annulment. There would be no pleasure for him from Mariah O'Reilly, and that was the truth.

Late that night, they boarded the train for Chicago. Again, he'd booked first-class passage on a Pullman Hotel car. This time, Mariah set out to foil any plans Thorne had of sharing her berth.

As the train pulled out of the depot, the porter came through and helped make up the beds. Thorne hoisted Running Deer into the upper berth, and grinned at Mariah.

She returned his smile. ''How about giving me a hand up?'' she asked.

''Up?'' He eyed her suspiciously. ''I paid extra for a lower for us alone.''

''I'm going to share the bunk with Running Deer again.'' She tickled the child under the chin. ''Won't that be just grand?''

The child wrapped her arms around Mariah's neck. ''Running Deer want sleep with Sissy.''

A defeated look on his face, Thorne placed his hands on her

waist and lifted her up to the bunk. His hands rested on her waist for a minute longer than necessary. He stroked her back gently, reminding her of the intimacies they'd shared. Her body heated at his touch. She slapped his hands aside and pulled her legs up to sit Indian-style, which was all the room allowed in the cramped bunk.

From his place on the floor, Juan gazed at Thorne with wide, imploring eyes. He tooted a few poignant notes on his whistle.

She stuck her head from between the curtains. "I promised you would sleep with Juan tonight." The boy gazed at Thorne, his eyes shiny with unshed tears. How lonely and alone the child must feel, she thought. His every emotion was mirrored in those deep-midnight eyes. "He's so looking forward to being with you," she said.

Thorne hunkered down at eye level with the child. "Of course you can bunk with me, son. I might even tell you a story or two." He looked up at Mariah with a familiar smug grin. "Can you top that?"

"I'll sing to Running Deer." With a curt nod, she yanked the curtains closed.

All around them people were climbing into uppers, and snuggling down into their bunks. The man in the next berth fell asleep and was snoring by the time Mariah struggled out of her now-wrinkled blue suit and slipped into her nightdress. Running Deer slept in her slip, her new dress a rumpled mess.

Mariah cuddled the child into her chest, and hummed an Irish lullaby. The girl fell into a deep sleep. Mariah heard every noise and sound—the clattering of the train, the whispered conversations, loud snores, and Thorne's husky voice speaking softly to the boy. His deep, resonant sounds pierced her heart, making her regret her decision to avoid him.

The lights dimmed, and it seemed everybody was sleeping when something pinched her toe. Thinking it was the man in the next berth being very rude, she kicked, then pulled her knees up to her chest. A hand brushed her ankle and tickled the sole of her foot. Shocked at such indecent behavior from a stranger, she opened her mouth to call the porter, when she saw that the hand came from the berth below hers.

Thorne. She caught his fingers and twisted with all her might. He pulled back the offending hand, and almost immediately, his head popped up under the curtain.

"Are you trying to break my fingers?"

"You deserve to be shot for accosting a woman like that."

Even in the darkness, she spotted the grimace on his face. "You aren't a woman, you're my wife."

"Not for long. I'm counting the days until I can file for that annulment."

With a roar like a wounded bear, he dropped to his own bunk. "That's two I owe you, Irish."

"Keep counting, Mountain Man. The tally will get a lot higher by the time we reach Philadelphia."

She dropped off to sleep, satisfied to finally get the upper hand on her sometimes husband.

Chicago was a wonder. Even late at night, the depot was as busy as noonday. It had been years since Thorne had been to a city, but he'd kept up with the news through week-, and even month-old newspapers. A couple of years earlier, nearly the entire town had been destroyed by fire, he knew. Thanks to a remarkable building project, more and more buildings were going up every day. And each day another railroad laid tracks into the growing city.

Since their train to Philadelphia didn't leave until noon the next day, he'd telegraphed ahead for suites at the Palmer House. Upon their arrival, he learned that only one suite was available. Mariah eyed him suspiciously, but graciously conceded.

"We'll have to make do, Irish," he said. "I'm not about to traipse all over Chicago looking for rooms."

Head held high, she allowed the porter to show them to their rooms. Once inside, she escorted the youngsters through the sitting room to the bedroom. There, she turned and glared at him. "The children and I will share the bed," she announced as if she were Queen Victoria herself. "I'm sorry, Sung Lo, but I hope you'll be comfortable on the settee."

The old man bowed, his face lined with fatigue. "Sung Lo like settee."

Thorne set his hands on his hips. "What about me?"

"You can sleep in the lobby, for all I care." With that, she slammed the inner door. Before he could reach her, she set the lock.

Not to be outdone, he faced the closed door and called, "Irish, I'll find a woman willing to share her bed."

The door jerked open, and she stood glaring at him. "Be my guest." She pressed a ten-dollar gold piece into his palm. "Enjoy yourself."

As she stepped back, he jammed the door with his foot. For once, he was grateful he was wearing boots instead of the moccasins packed in his valise. He flipped the coin and caught it in his fingers. "This should buy a nice, obliging woman."

Her eyes flashed daggers. "That's a fine way to talk in front of these children."

"You brought up the subject."

She lowered her voice. "Do what you want. Go where you please. Sleep wherever you desire."

He stroked the coin along her cheek. "I desire to sleep with my wife."

"Not tonight, Mountain Man. Never."

"Never is a mighty long time." He dropped the coin down the open neckline of her blouse. Her eyes grew wide. "Payment in advance." Turning on his heel, he strolled toward the door that led to the hallway. At his back, the door slammed so hard, the pictures on the wall tilted.

"Sissy mad at Thorne," Sung Lo said, a wry smile on his wrinkled face.

"She'll get over it. Keep watch, old friend. I'll be back after a while."

After being hemmed up in a train and in hotel rooms for

nearly a week, he needed to get out and think. Fog had rolled in off Lake Michigan, giving the gas lamps a strange yellow glow. He walked toward the waterfront. In less than two days, they would arrive in Philadelphia. Thorne had no inkling of what awaited him upon his return. Unless his grandmother was successful in gaining him a pardon, this was one of his last nights as a free man.

He was sorely tempted to board one of the steamers docked at the wharves and get lost where he would never be found. As he paused to watch deckhands loading on cargo, he knew he would do no such thing. He'd promised Mariah he would return to his grandmother. And he owed her his word if nothing else. Under the circumstances, he couldn't be the husband she deserved, but he wasn't going to leave her to face the consequences of his actions. Besides, the children and Sung Lo were his responsibility, not hers. Even if he was arrested, he could still make provisions for their care.

Knowing Mariah's determination, she would probably hunt him down and drag him back.

No, whatever awaited him in Philadelphia, he would face it and take his punishment like a man.

Chapter 20

Mariah glanced at the empty seat across from hers. Thorne had spent the better part of the day there, slouched down, with his hat over his face. They'd boarded the Pennsylvania Railroad at noon and were chugging toward Philadelphia at over twenty-five miles an hour. The closer they got to Philadelphia, the more solemn he became.

After the first meal stop, he'd excused himself to the club car that was for men only. Mariah couldn't blame him for wanting to be alone. She understood his concern. She also realized that she'd been selfish and uncaring. He was possibly facing prison, or worse, when they returned home. Her heart went out to him.

That night, the porter made up the bunks, and Mariah tucked Running Deer and Juan into the upper. Sung Lo snuggled into the lower across the aisle, and Mariah sat on the edge of her berth, contemplating her next move. After tonight, the chances of her being alone with Thorne were slim. She'd thought all day about the way she'd rejected his advances. With so little time in their future, she wanted, she needed, to be with him as long as he was free. Even if they couldn't make love, she could hold him and let him know she cared.

Mariah struggled into her nightdress and pulled the covers to her chin. The lamps had been trimmed, and the passengers snug in their berths. It seemed like hours since she'd pulled the curtain closed. Waiting for Thorne to come to bed, she felt her eyes grow heavy. She tried to stay awake, but was losing the battle with fatigue.

The train had just pulled out of a tiny station when she heard footsteps coming toward her. A hand slid the curtain open, and the bunk sank when the large figure sat on the edge. One boot, then the other dropped to the wooden floor. She opened her eyes, and recognized Thorne silhouetted in the dim light. Pressing as close to the window as possible, she waited until he stretched out. His clothes reeked of stale cigar smoke. She sneezed.

Thorne jerked upright, hitting his head on the upper berth. "What the hell . . ."

Mariah covered his mouth with her hand. "It's just me. Don't wake up the entire train."

Rubbing his head, he dropped back to the bed. "Irish, what are you doing here? Where's Juan?"

"With Running Deer."

"Where am I supposed to sleep?"

"Here. I want you to spend the night with me."

"With you? Here?"

Again, she covered his mouth with her hand. "I know we can't, well, you know. But I want to lie beside you, and hold you in my arms."

He let out a long, deep growl, much like a wounded bear. "Are you determined to drive me crazy, Irish?"

"I hope not. We may only have a short while together, let's not fight."

"I never wanted to fight with you. Let's get some sleep."

She sneezed, once, twice, three times. "Can you take off those smelly clothes? The cigar smoke is making me sneeze."

On a soft chuckle, he propped on an elbow. "Are you sure

you want a half-naked man lying next to you? I might not be able to control myself.''

''Well, you'll have to. We don't want the entire train spying on us.''

''Right.'' He tugged off his shirt and trousers and shoved them off. She turned to face him, her breasts pressing against his bare chest. ''What changed your mind?'' he asked.

Her fingers brushed his day's growth of whiskers. His skin felt wonderfully abrasive against her fingertips. ''I realized—''

''Be quiet over there or I'll call the conductor.'' The harshly whispered female admonishment came from the other side of the thin curtain. ''Some people want to sleep.''

''Oh, leave them alone'' came another voice, this one male. ''I reckon they're married.''

Mariah bit her lip to keep from laughing. So much for privacy. She snuggled her head against Thorne's shoulder. His arms circled her waist. He kissed her gently on the lips, then nestled his face in her hair. ''Thanks, Irish.''

''Is that all the kiss I get for being so generous?'' she whispered. ''I kind of like you without the beard.''

''You're playing with fire.''

She offered her mouth, pressing her lips to his. He accepted the gift. His mouth covered hers in a kiss that was warm and giving, gentle and passionate. Her tongue tangled with his, and she tasted the sting of whiskey. Brushing her fingers across his jaw, she sighed with happiness. Just for this moment, he was hers. If possible, she would have given herself freely and willingly to the man she loved. Thoughts of the annulment, and the future, flew from her mind. She had this moment with Thorne, and she relished every stroke of his tongue, every brush of his fingertips on her flesh.

The kiss ended, and he nestled her closer to the intimacies of his body. ''I wish we were still back on the mountain,'' he said, his lips nestled in her hair.

A woman coughed, a man wheezed, and footsteps sounded inches from their heads. Mariah covered her laughter by burying her face in his shoulder. "So much for privacy. Good night, Mountain Man."

"Sleep well, Irish."

Contentment covered Mariah like a soft summer breeze from the meadow. She closed her eyes, thankful for the time she'd had with this man. With his problems hanging over his head, he might not be able to give his heart, but being with him was enough for her. If he had to go to prison, she would have the memory of loving him to warm her lonely heart.

The night passed quickly, Mariah snug and content in Thorne's embrace. He held her as gently as he would hold a child. Sometime before dawn she fell into a deep, comfortable sleep. The sound of Running Deer's voice awoke her. Others in the car were already moving about, talking and making their way to the small washrooms at either end of the car.

She rolled over, and reached for Thorne, to awaken him. Her hand touched the curtains, and the empty sheet. Disappointed, she sat up and answered the child's call.

"I'm down here, sweetheart," she said. "Hop down."

The little girl swung down and knelt beside Mariah. "Thorne say let Sissy sleep."

"I'm awake now. Is Juan still sleeping?"

She shook her head, the disheveled braids dancing around her shoulders. "He go with Thorne and Sung Lo. Say bring back food for Sissy."

Mariah pulled up the shade and glanced out the window. They'd arrived at another station, and were near the siding. Hurriedly, she tugged the shade down, and struggled into her clothes. She swapped the wrinkled suit for a simple skirt and white shirtwaist. After dressing the child, she twisted her hair into a bun, and took her place in line at the ladies' washroom. By the time she finished, the bunks had been transformed into comfortable facing seats with a table between.

The whistle blew, and she looked out the window for Thorne and company. He waved to her, and picked up Juan to hurry along before the train took off without them.

Sung Lo placed a basket on the table and settled down across from Mariah. "Good food," he said.

Thorne handed Juan across, and sat beside Mariah. She smiled her thanks for his thoughtfulness. Not only had he let her sleep, he'd bucked the crowd to provide her breakfast.

"Thank you." She picked up a buttered biscuit and spread it with jelly and offered it to the little girl. Both children ate with appreciation, picking at the crumbs and licking their fingers.

"Good," Running Deer said. Juan played a cheerful tune on his whistle. "Do they have jelly in 'Delphia?"

"My mum is the best cook in 'Delphia. She'll fix you pies, and cakes, and cookies. Yum-yum," Mariah said to pacify the child.

Both youngsters rubbed their stomachs. Even Sung Lo laughed at their antics.

In spite of his cheerful smile and light banter, she knew Thorne was troubled. When they pulled into Pittsburgh, she almost expected him to balk and run. Instead, he remained on the train at her side. Every seat in the car was filled with passengers headed to Harrisburg or Philadelphia. The conductor announced they would reach the end of the line late that night.

Thorne leaned closer. "I have to talk to you, Irish. Let's go out on the platform where we can be alone."

The children were dozing, and Thorne signaled Sung Lo to keep watch over them. The old man nodded, and placed his hand on the hilt of the knife at his waist.

His fierce expression was almost laughable. Although he wasn't nearly as tall as Mariah, the Chinese man took his responsibilities seriously. He would guard the children with his life.

At the end of the car, Thorne shoved open the heavy door and escorted Mariah onto the narrow platform between train cars. The wind whipped her head, pulling loose the pins and long tendrils of hair. The Pennsylvania countryside passed by, the sun gleaming on the farms and hillsides.

"I'd never thought I'd see Pennsylvania again," Thorne said, his voice deep and wounded.

Mariah's heart twisted. If she hadn't bull-dogged him, he would even now be safe on his mountain in New Mexico. She swallowed the lump in her throat. "Are you sorry you've come back?"

He backed her against the side of the doorway and faced her. "No. It was time. I'm ready to accept my fate. I could have died on that mountain, and my grandmother never would have known. Now I'll get to see her, and make my farewells."

She caught his leather vest in her fingers. "Don't talk like that."

"I have to be realistic." He covered her hands with his. "That's why I have to talk to you. Do you have my will?"

"Yes, and the gold."

"Good. You can keep the gold, and I want to make sure you see that the children are cared for. If necessary, find good parents for both of them."

"I won't do that. They belong with you. You're the only parent they've known."

"Irish, let's not argue about that again. There's something else I ask of you." He took a deep breath before continuing. "My valise is filled with the papers and notes about my experiments. I've been working on a number of new medicines, and I want you to make sure they get to the right people. In my will is the name of my mentor from medical college. If he's still living, give the entire package to him. He'll be able to put it where it will do the most good. If not, you can contact the head of the Pennsylvania University. He'll decide how to use the information."

"No, Thorne, you deserve the credit for your work. You should give it to them yourself."

His deep chuckle was without humor. "That's hardly possible if I'm in prison."

Tears pooled in her eyes. "You'll get your pardon. Have faith."

"I lost my faith in northern Virginia ten years ago." With one long finger, he brushed away the tear. "Don't cry for me, Irish. I'm not worth it."

He was worth the world to Mariah, but he would never know how she felt. "I'm not crying. It's the wind."

Wrapping an arm around her shoulder, he pulled open the door leading back to the passenger car. "Let me get you out of this wind. Your hair is a mess."

"Then I had better repair it before I scare the children." She slipped out of his arms and stepped behind the curtain that partitioned the ladies' wash area. Only then, did she let the tears flow. If anything happened to Thorne it would be her fault. Hers alone for her selfishness in bringing him back to Philadelphia. All she'd thought about was the bonus for his return. She'd given little consideration to his needs, or the children and the old man who depended on him.

She splayed a hand across her stomach. Even now, she could be carrying his baby—a child who deserved to know his father. He was a father who deserved to know his child. A man who deserved a lot better than the hand fate had dealt him.

Thorne fought a losing battle to keep his spirits from sagging. He knew that his grandmother was waiting for him in Philadelphia. Who else would be there? By now, General Edwards could have figured out his identify, and sent word out for his arrest. Or, by contacting the President for a pardon, his grandmother could have put the wheels into motion for his arrest.

For the remainder of the journey, Mariah didn't leave his side. She held his hand, and more than a few times apologized for doing her job. It didn't matter that she was the one to locate him. Sooner or later, somebody would have recognized him. At least he'd had these ten years of freedom to work on his experiments. He didn't regret a moment of his life. The children and Sung Lo had blessed his life with happiness, and Mariah

. . . Mariah was a woman who'd fallen into his lap and changed him forever. She was a summer breeze that had refreshed his life.

It was late by the time the train pulled into the Market Street station of the Pennsylvania Railroad. The children were half asleep, but Sung Lo sat on the edge of his seat. Only Mariah knew what awaited her when she exited the train. She couldn't contain her excitement, and had spent the last hours relating stories of her large and loving family.

Thorne often wondered what it would be like to have a family like hers. His mother had died when he was an infant, and when his father remarried, Gabriel had been the apple of his eye. Mostly, Thorne had spent his youth in military schools or with his grandmother. Now, he was facing her again. Mariah was right. For his own peace of mind, he had to see her before it was too late. And she deserved to see him.

With his father gone, she was all he had left. As for Gabe, there was no love lost there. His brother's hatred had nearly cost Thorne his life; it had cost him his freedom. To him, New Mexico had been a very large prison. Now he didn't know if he had traded one prison for another.

The passengers began to disembark as soon as the conductor let down the steps to the wooden platform. As they gathered up their few bags and valises, the children began to stir.

"We're home," he said, picking up Juan in his arms. The boy rested his head on Thorne's shoulder and clung to his shirt. Mariah caught Running Deer's hand, while Sung Lo carried the bags with the children's meager belongings.

"Come along. I want you to meet the entire O'Reilly family." Mariah led the way to the doorway.

Thorne followed more slowly. The instant Mariah stepped foot on the platform, she was surrounded with what looked like the entire Philadelphia police force and as many women and children.

An older man in a dark-blue uniform grabbed her in a bear hug. Running Deer clung to her skirt, the child's face pale and

damp with tears. Thorne started to reach for the little girl when
Mariah passed her valise to a young boy and lifted the child
in her arms. Running Deer buried her face in Mariah's shoulder.
A beautiful woman who couldn't be much older than Thorne,
shoved the man aside and planted kisses on Mariah's cheeks.
Then she stepped back, and every man, woman, and child came
up and kissed Mariah.

Though they were all talking at once, she raised her hands
to silence the noisy throng. "Everybody, I want you to meet
my friends. This beautiful girl is Running Deer." She pulled
Thorne to her side. "This is Thorne and Juan. And this handsome gentleman is Sung Lo. Just wait until you taste his
cooking."

One by one, the men introduced themselves—her father,
Sean, her brothers, Kevin, Andrew and Joseph, and several
police officers whose names flew past his head. The girls held
back, and hid their giggles behind their hands. Mariah pointed
out Maggie, Jenny, Maureen, Annie, with her baby and husband, Jamie. As he was trading pleasantries with her mother,
a dark-haired officer greeted Mariah, planting a too-familiar
kiss on her mouth.

Thorne clutched Juan tighter in his arms, and resisted the
urge to tear the man away from his wife. From the corner of
his eye, he saw her pull away from the man, and shift Running
Deer to her other arm. Her father reached for the child and
gave her a warm smile. The usually shy girl eagerly went into
Sean O'Reilly's arms.

With everybody talking at once, Thorne looked over their
heads for his grandmother. He scanned the crowded terminal,
but she was nowhere to be found.

Mariah, too, was looking for somebody. Another suitor? he
wondered, his stomach clenching into a knot.

"Da, where's Francis?" she asked.

Her father pulled her to Thorne's side. "He's outside with
Mrs. Thornton. They're waiting in her carriage." His blue eyes
twinkled as he told Thorne, "I met the lady. Your grandmother

is quite a fine woman. I hope you make her proud,'' he said, more of a warning than a statement.

Thorne nodded. Leaving Mariah to trail behind with her family, he worked his way through the crowd toward the exit. The terminal was larger, and busier than when he'd left Philadelphia to join the Army all those years ago. A lifetime ago. He'd been a young man of twenty-one when war broke out. At twenty-four he'd become a fugitive. At thirty-three, the prodigal son was returning home.

The terminal was ablaze with gas lamps and chandeliers. As he stepped out into the cool Pennsylvania night, he was amazed at the brightness of the lights and the number of carriages and cabs awaiting passengers. Several horse-drawn streetcars waited for fares.

Even from the distance he recognized his grandmother dressed in a wine-colored gown and a cape. Her gray hair was covered with a small hat of feathers and flowers. As he moved closer, he noticed how small and frail she appeared. Yet, her gray eyes were steely with determination. A young man stood beside her, his red hair rumpled by the breeze. Mariah's brother, Francis, he wagered.

He hastened his pace, eager to greet the one person who had always stood by him, who believed in him. Another figure appeared out of the shadows. His blood ran cold. He nearly tripped over his own feet.

An Army officer in full uniform studied him. A sword hung at one side and a pistol at the other. He slapped an envelope against his gloved palm.

The order for Thorne's arrest. Of that he was certain.

Chapter 21

"Michael . . ." Mrs. Thornton opened her arms and stepped toward him.

Ignoring the hammering in his chest, he raced toward his grandmother. It had been so long—too long. Until that moment he hadn't admitted how much he'd missed her, how much he loved her. That he needed to come home.

At his side, Sung Lo took Juan from his arms, freeing him to embrace the woman. He wrapped his arms around her frail shoulders and kissed each cheek. Her skin was soft and pale. Although she was close to seventy, few wrinkles marred her face. Fine lines crinkled at the corners of her eyes, the exact color of his. Tears rolled down her cheeks.

"My darling Michael. I can't tell you how long I've waited and prayed for this moment." She moved an arm's length from him. "Let me look at you." Her gloved hand stroked the day's growth of whiskers on his jaw. "You're more handsome than ever. Are you taller, or have I shrunk?"

He laughed, unable to hide his happiness. "I've grown older and grayer. You're as beautiful as I remember."

Her gaze shifted to Mariah at his side. "Miss O'Reilly, thank you. Your brother said you could do it. You've brought my grandson home to me.''

For how long? he wondered. Hurriedly, he introduced Sung Lo and the children to his grandmother. A smile covered her look of surprise. ''I have a surprise for you, too. This is Colonel Masters, from President Grant's office.''

Lieutenant Michael Thornton Harrison stood at attention and faced his destiny. The serious expression on the officer's face didn't help his frazzled nerves. His grandmother looped her arm in his.

Colonel Masters cleared his throat, and opened the envelope in his hands. Behind him, the O'Reilly clan had quieted, as if waiting for something to happen. He glanced over his grandmother's head and caught Mariah's gaze. Silently, she offered support, and for a moment he thought he saw love in her eyes.

The officer read from an official-looking document. Words and military jargon buzzed in his ears. Listening to the officer's solemn voice drone on, he waited for the words that would seal his fate—the order for his arrest. But the document was a decree from President U. S. Grant. A stone dropped to his stomach. Something was strange. Unless he was hearing things, he was being exonerated. President Grant had granted the pardon.

The President of the United States of America had used the power of his office to grant Lieutenant Michael Thornton Harrison a full and unconditional pardon!

When the officer finished reading the proclamation, he handed the paper to Thorne. ''You're a free man, Harrison.'' From the look on the man's face, it was clear he didn't agree with the President on this matter. As an officer, he was obligated to obey the orders of his Commander-in-chief.

Unable to believe the unexpected turn of events, he stared at the outstretched envelope. He tucked the pardon into his pocket and locked glances with Mariah. Her beautiful face glowed with happiness.

By finding him and forcing him to return home, she'd given back his life. Along the way, though, she'd stolen his heart.

Mariah threw her arms around his neck and planted a loud kiss on his mouth. "You're free. I told you to have faith."

"I should have known my grandmother could do anything she set her mind to." He only wondered how much in campaign contributions it had cost. "She's much like you, Irish. You wouldn't give up until you brought me home, and she wouldn't give up until I was a free man."

Her family closed in on them, shaking hands and offering congratulations. Running Deer stretched out her arms for him. He took the frightened child into his arms. In the confusion he'd forgotten about the children and their needs. Both were exhausted and should get to bed. Sung Lo, too, looked about to fall over from fatigue. Mariah looked happy enough to dance the night away with her family and friends.

Mrs. Thornton tugged at his arm. "Let's go home, dear. Mrs. Murphy has prepared a supper of all your favorites."

He smiled down at his grandmother. "I've got to get these children to bed. I hope Murph won't mind making up three more rooms." How easily he'd fallen into the old habit of using the butler's nickname.

She smiled. "He and the Missus will be delighted to have somebody to brighten up that old house. We walk around as if we're in a mausoleum." She glanced around at the confused crowd. "It looks as if the O'Reilly clan is already celebrating."

He spotted Mariah surrounded by her friends, the dark-haired policeman's arm draped over her shoulder. If his grandmother hadn't looped her arm in his, Thorne would have reminded his wife that until they got the annulment, they were still married. And that he wanted her to come home with him. Instead, he guided his grandmother toward her waiting carriage.

"Is Sissy coming with us to 'Delphia?" Running Deer asked, her gaze on the boisterous Irish clan.

Mariah met the child's glance. She disengaged herself from

her family and gently brushed a hand across the girl's head. "Go with Thorne, darling, I'll see you tomorrow."

The child buried her face in his neck. "Want Sissy."

So did Thorne. He wished he could take her home with him and announce to the world that she was his wife. However, now that she was home and with her beaux, she'd already forgotten about him. "Sissy will come see you tomorrow."

"I promise. Be good for Thorne, and I'll bring you something special when I come."

"We good," she said in a small, weary voice.

"Take care of them, Mountain Man, or you'll answer to all the O'Reillys."

"Trust me, Irish. Now that I'm free, they'll always have a home with me."

He climbed into the carriage with his grandmother, and caught a glimpse of the O'Reilly entourage climbing aboard a large Black Maria. It was probably the first time the passengers in the prisoners' wagon were singing and happy to be aboard.

While Thorne and his wealthy grandmother entered the elegant carriage pulled by a team of matching grays, Sean O'Reilly loaded his family and friends into the ugly black wagon borrowed from the precinct.

The contrast and differences between the families was so huge, Mariah's heart sank. A barrier, as real as the stone fence that surrounded Thornton House, stood between her and the man she loved. There was no way she could breach that wall. She watched the carriage pull away, taking her heart with it. Like a caterpillar changed into a butterfly, the gruff recluse she'd loved as Thorne had suddenly been transformed into the privileged and elegant Michael Thornton Harrison.

"Why are you looking so sad, Rosie?" Jenny asked. Her beautiful younger sister looped her arm in Mariah's. "You're a rich and famous woman."

Closeted inside the wagon used to carry prisoners, Mariah choked back tears. "That I am, Jenny. And that's the truth."

Her niece, Molly, leaped from Annie's lap into Mariah's. "You missed Aunt Rosie, sweetheart? You're going to love Running Deer and Juan." She nuzzled the year-old child's belly.

"Are they real Indians?" Joseph asked, nudging his twin aside to sit beside Mariah.

"Running Deer is Cheyenne. Juan is Mexican."

"Wow," Andrew exclaimed. "And that was a real Chinaman?"

"Quit bothering Rosie," her mother admonished the twins. "She'll tell us all about her adventures when we get home." She reached across and clasped Mariah's hand in hers. "Thank God you're home safe. I said more rosaries for you than all my other children combined."

With a soft chuckle, Mariah squeezed her mother's hand. "Why, Ma, I was as safe as Molly in Annie's arms."

"What's all this about your finding stolen gold? A reporter from the *Public Ledger* came looking for you. He said you're going to get a big reward." Francis tugged Andrew away from Mariah.

"It was really Thorne, I mean Mr. Harrison, who led me to the gold. But he wanted me to have the reward." A band tightened around her chest at the memory of their lovemaking after locating the gold. Involuntarily, she touched her stomach, and wondered if they really had made a child.

"He surely doesn't need it. His grandmother has bushels of money," twelve-year-old Maureen added.

"So does he." Mariah remembered the sack of gold in her valise. "He owns a gold mine."

"Rich and handsome. Rosie, you should have snagged him for yourself." Jenny tossed her fiery hair over her shoulder. Little did she know that was exactly what Mariah had done— married the man who wanted only an annulment from her.

Not to be ignored, Joseph tugged on Mariah's sleeve. "Did you see any wild Indians?"

Thankful for the change of subject, she turned to her youngest brother. "I captured a wild Indian, and two outlaws. I even came face-to-face with Jesse James."

"She hasn't even been to Ireland, but I swear Rosie kissed the Blarney Stone," Annie said.

"It's the truth, every word. Ask T—Mr. Harrison."

By the time they reached the brownstone on Lehigh Street, Mariah's head was spinning. She'd missed her boisterous family, but she also missed the peace and quiet of Thorne's mountain. She would forever think of that isolated spot as his retreat. Michael Harrison was civilized Philadelphia, Thorne was wild New Mexico. While Mariah was alone with her memories.

By the next afternoon, Mariah had told her story at least a hundred times. Her adventures amazed even Francis and Danny Malloy, himself a police officer. The twins were impressed that she'd captured an Indian, Francis was dumbfounded that she'd actually faced Jesse James, while Danny accused her of taking unnecessary risks.

Of course she'd left out a few pertinent facts, like making love and marrying Thorne. She promised herself to contact Father Morgan as soon as possible about an annulment.

Word had spread that she was to receive a substantial reward for the return of the gold. Many of her friends and neighbors said she should have kept all the gold for herself. The Irish had a natural dislike and suspicion for the government, left over from their suppression in the old country.

She reminded her father to start looking for a larger house for the family. As soon as her reward reached the bank, they would move into a better neighborhood and finer home. And her mother would have the grandest new stove money could buy.

Needing some time for herself, Mariah dressed in the lovely

emerald-green suit she'd bought before her journey west. She felt sophisticated and elegant in it. A pretty hat perched atop her head, she boarded the streetcar and headed toward Society Hill. She'd promised to visit the children, and no matter what her feelings toward Thorne—no, he was now Michael—she wanted to make sure they were safe and well cared for.

The ride on the crowded horse-drawn streetcar did little to clear her thoughts. For weeks, all she'd thought about was returning home to the conveniences, the stores, the bustling city. Now that she'd returned, her thoughts kept drifting back to that wild mountain, the high meadows filled with wildflowers, and the hot spring where she'd last made love with Thorne. Before she was aware of her surroundings, she'd reached the front door of Thornton House, the three-story mansion on Walnut Street, across from Rittenhouse Square.

Butterflies danced a jig in her stomach as she approached the marble-columned portico. The spacious mansion was Michael's domain, far removed from the crowded rented brownstone Mariah O'Reilly called home. Several times, before leaving for New Mexico, she'd visited Mrs. Thornton, but never had she been as nervous or anxious as now. Somewhere in this huge mansion Michael had spent the night, sleeping alone in a massive bed. While his wife shared a room with her three sisters.

Pulling her dignity around her like a warm cloak, she boldly climbed the four granite steps to the narrow porch. She lifted the brass knocker and let it fall with a loud bang. Seconds later, the old butler she knew as Murphy opened the door.

The tiniest hint of a smile softened the old man's weathered face. "Come in, Miss O'Reilly. The mistress is in the library."

Mariah started to tell him that she'd come to see the children, not Mrs. Thornton. However, it would be extremely rude not to speak to the lady of the house.

At the door to the library, the butler gestured to Mariah. "Madam . . . Miss O'Reilly."

Mrs. Thornton looked up from the papers on her desk. A wide smile transformed her face into that of a very happy

woman. She looked like an entirely different woman from the
one who'd hired Mariah and Francis months ago. "Come in,
my dear, and have a seat. I believe we have business to con-
duct." Her gaze shifted to the servant. "Murphy, will you serve
tea and cakes?"

With a nod, the servant slipped quietly from the room, closing
the door behind him.

Mariah had almost forgotten about her business with the
woman, and about the promised bonus. That was one secret
she'd kept from Michael.

The woman stood and grasped both Mariah's hands in hers.
Her grip was surprisingly strong for a woman of her age. "I
can't express how much I appreciate all you've done for me.
Having my Michael back is a miracle. He told me of some of
your adventures. How you fell from a tree and tumbled down
a mountain. You are truly an amazing woman."

Mariah returned the woman's smile. She understood from
whom Michael had gotten his kindness and generosity. "Thank
you, ma'am. I was doing my job."

"And a fine job you did. A man couldn't have done any
better. I've always espoused the causes of women. Why, I've
managed my husband's business enterprises since his death
thirty years ago. And I've increased his fortune a hundredfold."

A fortune her grandson would inherit, no doubt. Another
barrier between them that Mariah could never overcome. Not
needing another reminder of the position and wealth that
Michael had been born into, she changed the subject. "How
are the children? And Sung Lo?" She perched on the edge of
a large, brown leather wing chair.

On a long sigh, the older woman returned to her chair behind
the desk. She moved slowly, aided by a gold-topped cane.
"They'll have to make a lot of adjustments. Michael is with
them now. Neither child would go to bed until he allowed them
to sleep in his room. They kept asking for somebody called
Sissy."

"That's me. Did Th—Michael tell you that I was disguised

as a nun for my safety? I told the children I was Sister Rose, and they began to call me Sissy.'' Behind her, the door softly opened and the butler set a tea service on the corner of the desk. He left as quietly as a mouse.

"He did mention how ingeniuous you were. And persuasive.'' She reached into her desk and pulled out an envelope. "I promised a generous bonus if you were able to convince Michael to return. Now that he's safely in my home, I intend to keep my word. Here is my bank draft made out to you.''

Mariah hesitated. She deserved the bonus, she'd worked for it, yet somehow it seemed dirty to take it. Like the bounty on an outlaw's head. Or like Judas taking the thirty pieces of silver.

"How generous is the bonus?'' The familiar gruff voice came from the doorway.

Her heart sank. She met Michael's stony glare. In a few long strides, he reached the desk and propped a hip against the corner. He crossed his legs at the ankle and folded his arms across his wide chest. The accusation in his eyes chilled her to the bone.

Her voice failed her. Today he wore gray wool trousers and an elegant linen shirt open at the neck. The leather thong circled his strong neck, and the medicine bag rested in the center of his muscular chest. He'd never looked more handsome, or less approachable.

His grandmother set the envelope on the desk. "I promised Miss O'Reilly and her brother a five-thousand-dollar bonus upon your return. I always keep my word.''

Michael snatched up the envelope. "Very generous. Looks like I was worth even more than Jesse James.''

He was worth more than the world to her, but he would never believe it. "Jesse James nearly fell into my lap. I had to work to bring you back.''

His gray eyes turned to cold, hard steel. The question behind his glare made her shiver. Was making love part of her plan to get him back so she could earn the bonus? She bit her lip to keep her answer in her heart.

"Then you've certainly earned every silver dollar, and a few gold ones to boot." With an extravagant gesture, he handed her the offending envelope.

"Now that our business is settled, Michael, take a chair and join us in a spot of tea." Mrs. Thornton filled three hand-painted china cups from the silver service. Michael slid from the desk to a wing chair matching the one in which Mariah sat.

Mariah tried to swallow around the lump that had jumped from her heart to her throat. She should have explained about the bonus, but she knew he wouldn't understand. A man of wealth and circumstances wouldn't appreciate how hard Irish immigrants like her parents had to work to support their families. When she'd agreed to take the assignment, it was strictly for mercenary reasons. Now that she'd found him, and fallen in love, money was the least of her concerns.

As she lifted the cup to her lips, the door to the library burst open. A frantic, white-faced woman appeared in the entrance with the butler at her heels. Her black gown and white apron were pressed and immaculate, but her gray hair stuck out in disarray from under her wildly askew mobcap.

"Mr. Michael!" the woman shrieked. "You've got to do something about that Chinaman. He's threatening all the kitchen help with a huge cleaver and a knife."

Michael leaped to his feet. "I warned Sung Lo to stay away from the kitchen." At the door, he paused. "I'll take care of him."

Shocked, Mariah stared at the pale-faced housekeeper. Mrs. Thornton had risen, and was trying to placate the woman. "It's all right, Mrs. Murphy. He won't hurt anybody."

"Mum, he was waving that knife around like a madman. The girls hid in the pantry to get away from him."

"I'll see if I can help." Mariah couldn't imagine the gentle little Chinese threatening anybody. She raced behind Michael, who turned at the end of the hallway. When they reached the kitchen, Sung Lo was alone, chanting something in Chinese while chopping up vegetables on a large cutting board.

"Sissy. Thorne. Come. Sung Lo fix eat." Grinning, he waved the cleaver in their direction.

Michael shrugged. "I'll explain things to him, while you try to placate the staff."

"Where is the staff?" She studied the kitchen, with the overturned chairs and pots boiling on the stove, unattended.

"Try the pantry."

Mariah tugged on the knob, calling softly to the frightened maids cowering behind the closed door. A white-faced young girl peered through the opening. "Is he gone?"

"He won't hurt you. Come out." When the girl shook her head and started to shut the door again, Mariah jerked it open. "Don't be afraid. He won't hurt you. Now, come out this instant!" she ordered.

Two maids recoiled behind her back, moaning and grunting something about a foreign devil. She led them to the work table, where Michael waited with Sung Lo.

"There's nothing to be afraid of," he said, his voice soft and placating. "Sung Lo just wanted to help prepare the meal. He's an excellent cook."

Mrs. Murphy, the housekeeper and cook, appeared behind Mrs. Thornton's back. "This is my kitchen, and I don't need any help from a foreigner."

Mariah wanted to laugh. With the woman's brogue, she was as much a "foreigner" as Sung Lo. However, the Irish considered themselves more American than the Indians or other nationalities.

Michael looked to Mariah for help. "Can't you explain?"

She was as much at a loss as he. "Did you try introducing them properly?" At the shake of his head, Mariah decided that was the first step. "Mrs. Murphy, this gentleman is Sung Lo. He's been preparing Mr. Michael's meals for quite some time. You'll find he's an excellent chef, and with a little help from you and the girls, he'll be a great asset in your kitchen."

The woman ventured a step closer. "He won't chop our heads off?"

"No, he's very civilized. He merely wanted to prepare a meal for himself and the children," Michael added. "I'm sure you can share the kitchen, and learn from one another."

Mrs. Thornton set a hand on her housekeeper's arm. "Dear Mrs. Murphy, you've been with me so many years, and you work entirely too hard. Won't it be nice to have some additional help?"

The housekeeper swiped a hand down her pristine white apron. "If it pleases Mr. Michael, I'll make the best of the situation. But I can't have him threatening my girls."

"I'll talk to him, and explain that you're in charge," Michael said. "Why don't you and the girls have some tea, and let Sung Lo prepare a meal? When he's done, you can get back to your own preparations for dinner."

That seemed to satisfy the harried housekeeper, but the maids continued to back away from Sung Lo, who was happily mixing his concoction on the stove. Michael spoke a few soft words to the man, who nodded vigorously.

Following behind his grandmother, Michael took Mariah's arm. "Thanks for helping out."

His touch sent quivers of excitement through Mariah. "Think nothing of it. If he doesn't work out, I'll take him home with me. My mother could use some kitchen help."

"He'll never leave the children."

"By the way, where are they? I promised to stop by and see how they're surviving in this big house."

"This mausoleum, you mean."

She tugged out of his grip. Taking a spin around the wide hallway, she waved her arms. Her heels tapped on the shiny marble tile floor. "Oh, I don't know. This is a fine and elegant home. It suits your position in society."

"What position? It's only by my grandmother's influence and money that I'm not in prison right now."

"Ah, Michael Harrison, but you're not. You'll take your place in society as a wealthy eligible bachelor."

He lowered his voice for her ears only. "I'm not a bachelor, I'm already married."

His declaration brought a thrill to her heart. Did he mean he wanted to stay with her? His next words dashed all hope.

"At least until we can get the annulment."

She hardened her heart against the pain that nearly doubled her over. "I'll see my priest this evening. You certainly don't want to remain tied to a bounty-hunting Irish woman."

"Hadn't you better wait to make sure . . ." He dropped his gaze to her stomach.

Gritting her teeth, she revealed the truth she'd faced that morning. "I'm sure. There is no child."

An emotion crossed his face. Relief or disappointment? Whatever it was, the fragile tie between them was broken. All that remained was to obtain a piece of paper from the Church releasing them from their vows.

"At least you got what you went after."

"I completed my assignment."

"And got the money." His voice returned to the cold, hard tone that chilled her bones.

"I should have explained, but I'm sure you wouldn't have understood."

"Maybe. I saw how excited you were over the gold. I should have known you wouldn't have traipsed across half the country for nothing."

A knife twisted in her heart. If there had ever been a chance for him to love her, it had crumbled the minute he'd found out about the bonus. Eager to get from under his unrelenting disapproval, she resisted the temptation to run from the house. "Where are the children? I'd like to see them before I go."

He raked a hand through his hair. "They've been asking for you since last night. I like to never got them to sleep." He guided her toward the wide, curving stairway.

"I understand they slept with you."

"We set up a cot for Running Deer, and Juan shared my bed. Even Sung Lo refused to go to his own room. He dragged in his mattress and slept on the floor."

"They're used to having you with them, like in the cabin."

At the landing, he paused. An Oriental carpet, its colors dulled with age, lined the long hallway. "This certainly isn't my cabin. There are enough bedrooms in this place for the entire O'Reilly clan and all their friends and suitors."

If she didn't know better, she'd have suspected a note of jealousy in his voice. But all it was only another form or reproach. "I'm not so sure. Jenny has quite a number of beaux."

"How about you, Irish? That one fellow seemed to be awful familiar with you last night. If I were your father, I'd have taken him to task."

He was jealous. That warmed her heart. "If my father knew about you, he'd have you horsewhipped."

"We're married."

"Temporarily."

With that all too familiar growl, he led her down the hallway. Mariah smiled to herself. He might be wearing fine linen, but inside he was still as touchy as an ornery old bear.

Chapter 22

Sean O'Reilly had delivered the invitation in person. The brawny police officer had insisted that Michael attend the party to celebrate his daughter's homecoming.

In spite of the citified clothes, he still had trouble thinking of himself as Michael. For too many years he'd gone by Thorne. But he'd left Thorne on that isolated mountain and brought Michael home.

The O'Reillys had a lot to celebrate. Not only had his daughter been successful in her quest, she'd returned a wealthy woman. Since she gave the credit to Michael, Sean insisted that he celebrate with them. Of course, he was to bring the children and the Chinaman.

After his initial anger at learning she'd brought him home for a bonus from his grandmother, his temper soothed. It was only right that she get paid for her mission. He had to admit she'd done what few men could have accomplished. His grandmother had wanted him back, and Mariah had succeeded in reuniting him with his only family. And in returning, he'd gained his freedom. Michael Harrison was no longer a fugitive. He was now free to continue his medical experiments and

develop cures from his herbs and roots. Five thousand dollars
was little enough for getting his life back.

When the carriage entered their block on Lehigh Street,
Michael had no problem picking out the O'Reilly house. It was
the one with the crowd on the stoop that spilled into the street.
The doors and windows were open to let out the laughter and
music. He was certain that Mariah was smack in the middle
of the revelry. For the young policeman's sake, he hoped that
Malloy wasn't romancing her.

The driver stopped the carriage, and Michael helped the
children to the ground. They were still frightened, and continued
to sleep in his room. Yesterday's visit from ''Sissy'' calmed
them, but they'd spent the entire day at the window looking
for her. Sung Lo refused to leave the house, choosing to remain
in the kitchen with the still-frightened maids.

Jenny O'Reilly spotted him first, and dragged him into the
middle of the melee. The small parlor was crowded from wall
to wall, as was the kitchen. Mariah was perched on a high
stool, retelling the story of capturing a wild Indian brave. She
wore the gown she'd bought in Denver, the one that exposed
entirely too much of her bosom. How had her father let her
out in public like that? Michael was tempted to remove his
jacket and drape it over her shoulders. Instead, he gritted his
teeth and smiled.

When she spotted him, she lifted her mug of beer and called
his name. ''Mr. Harrison. Let's give a toast to Mountain Man.
I couldn't have done it alone.''

Somebody shoved a mug of beer into his hand. From the
slur in her voice, Mariah was already on her way to getting
drunk. She hopped down and gathered the children up in her
arms. ''I'm glad you came. I want you to meet everybody.''

The youngest girl, Maureen, took the children under her
wing and introduced them to the other youngsters in the family
and in the neighborhood. The house was filled with laughter
and song. Somewhere a fiddle played, and, in the street, men
and women were dancing a jig.

Mariah set her hands on her hips and glared at him. "What brings you here? I assumed you would be at the opera or a concert."

"You assumed wrong. Your father invited me."

"Well, did he now? He should have known you wouldn't fit in with these poor Irish working people."

As she spun away from him, he pulled her closer with an arm around her waist. "I think I fit perfectly with one Irish lass." He lowered his voice and nipped her ear. His gaze dropped to her bosom. "In bed."

Color surfaced to her cheeks. "We never had a bed."

"My regret."

She stalked away, and reached for another mug of beer. Malloy was immediately at her side. Michael started for the man, when he was cut off by four very pretty young women. They wanted to know if Mariah had really encountered Jesse James and a band of outlaws. For the next few hours, he repeated the story, always making sure that Mariah was the true heroine. Like her, he drank beer and flirted. When the fiddler struck up a jig, he danced with Mrs. O'Reilly. Even his grandmother's staid driver climbed down from the coach seat and joined the festivities.

As the fiddler played a slower tune, he noticed Juan listening with rapt attention. Everybody hushed when the boy picked up his whistle and began to play. His tune blended with the fiddle, and even the old musician grinned in appreciation.

Mariah sidled up to him. "Listen. It's beautiful."

Emotion swelled in his chest. He draped his arm across her shoulder and she slid hers around his waist. "It's his voice, he's singing." Being with her, touching her, getting to know her family gave him a sense of belonging he'd lost long ago.

When the song ended, applause broke out into a loud roar. The child ran to him and hugged his legs. He reached down and picked up the boy. "That was great, Juan. The music was beautiful."

"We're so proud of you," Mariah said, her eyes brimming with tears.

Running Deer raced to them. "Juan make music. Mo say he got . . ." She looked up to Maureen.

"Talent," the young girl finished for her. "Can Running Deer spend the night with us?"

The children had captured the hearts of the O'Reilly clan. Michael wondered what it took to win Mariah's heart. Whatever it was, Danny Malloy, who had kissed her at the train station, had the upper hand.

"Let her stay, Mountain Man, Juan, too. The twins are having a fine time with him. I'll take them home tomorrow."

By then, the musician had packed up his fiddle, and the crowd was dispersing. He took it as a hint to leave.

"I'd best get back to my grandmother. I'll send the carriage for the children tomorrow." She swayed slightly, and he caught her before she fell. "Too much beer, Irish."

She grinned at him. "Are you saying I'm tipsy?"

"I'm saying you might need help climbing the stairs."

Immediately, the dark-haired police officer was at her side. "I'll give you a hand, Rosie." He tugged at her arm.

"I don't need your help, Danny." She jerked away from the man.

Michael wrapped a possessive arm around Mariah's waist. "You heard the lady."

Malloy thrust his face into Michael's. "I don't know what went on in that wild country between you and Rosie, but you got no rights to her here in Philadelphia." He shoved against Michael's chest with his hand.

Though several years younger, the man was equally matched in size and weight to Michael. "It's none of your business what went on between us." He stood his ground, refusing to budge.

"You don't belong here. Get in your fancy carriage and go back to your rich grandmother. Rosie belongs to me."

Mariah grabbed the policeman's arm. "Danny, I don't belong to anybody. Go home. You're drunk."

"I'm not going to let this rich man take advantage of you. I've seen his kind before. They think money can buy anything."

By then, a crowd had gathered. Sean O'Reilly shoved into the center of the confrontation. "Danny, Mr. Harrison is our guest. Keep a civil tongue in your head."

"Sean, you don't know what happened when he was alone with Rosie. He could have compromised her virtue." Malloy pulled back his fist and swung.

Michael blocked the punch, and shot back with a hard fist to the other man's jaw. The younger man staggered back, and came back with a growl. He jammed his head into Michael's stomach and both men landed in the trash in the cobblestone street. A gunshot jerked them apart. He looked up to find Mariah standing over them with a smoking gun in her hand.

"Now, I know there's nothing an Irishman likes better than a good drink and a good fight, but not here. Not now. Michael, get in that fancy carriage and go home." She glared at Malloy. "Danny, you didn't know, but Michael's part Irish. He can give as well as take. Apologize."

Malloy wiped the blood from his lip and broke into a smile. "Only an Irishman can punch like that." He stuck out a hand. "We'll have to try again when Rosie's not around."

Michael accepted the offered gesture. "You name the time and place."

"As soon as my jaw heals."

"I'm looking forward to it. Can I offer you a ride home in my fancy carriage?"

The younger man looked to Mariah, who continued to wave the gun at them. "Be a bit safer than staying here. I don't trust a woman with a gun."

He grinned at her. "Neither do I."

With an angry grunt, she shoved the gun into her father's holster. "Men. I hope you beat each other to a bloody pulp.

And don't come crying to me for help. I'll be with a fine, courteous gentleman at the theater. And that's the truth."

Malloy at his side, Michael watched Mariah stagger up the steps and into the house. "I think I could use another drink."

"Sean, got any more beer?" Malloy called.

"Be off the pair of you, before I throw you into the pokey. The party's over. I'm going to bed."

"We can get a drink at Clancy's Pub. Are you man enough to join me?" Malloy asked as he climbed up to the driver's seat.

Michael peeked inside and found the driver asleep. He joined the policeman up top. "If you're man enough to drive this carriage, I'm man enough to let you."

With a deep chuckle, Malloy released the brake and snapped the reins. "I wonder if the pair of us are half the man Rosie is."

"I've wondered the same myself."

Mariah had about given up hope that Michael would return for the children when the elegant coach stopped at the doorstoop. Not that she minded having the children with her. The twins had shown Juan a grand time, and Running Deer was the darling of the neighborhood. None of the Irish in the neighborhood had ever met a real Indian. In her own way, she hated to see them return to the mansion on Society Hill.

As long as Michael made his home with his grandmother, that was where they would live. All except Mariah. She belonged in North Philadelphia with the other Irish like herself and Danny. She'd been totally shocked when the men rode off together. Her father reported that the pair had gone to Clancy's and had spent the better part of the night swapping tall tales and toasts.

Mariah didn't like a bit of it. She knew the girls who hung around the pub looking for a man to buy them a drink or two. And there was no telling what they would do for a man with a few pieces of gold in his pocket. She hoped both of the idiots were sick in their beds from a night of foolishness.

As the driver pulled on the brake, Michael jumped down from the high seat beside the driver. She smiled as she opened the door and stepped out onto the stoop. He was pale around the mouth, and his bloodshot eyes were dark rimmed. Served him right, she thought.

"Looks like you're none the worse for wear," she said as he approached with a jaunty air looking more handsome than ever. Somehow in the past days, he'd come up with several smart, fashionable suits and crisp shirts. Out of place, though, was the hat he'd bought in Cimarron. She hated to think of the condition of that gray pinstripe he'd worn when he'd tumbled into the gutter with Danny during their brief fight. And to think, they were fighting over her.

He grinned. "You should have seen me a few hours ago. I had a devil of a time getting Malloy to leave the pub at dawn. There's no mistaking—Irish can drink Virginians under the table any day."

She laughed at his bout of honesty. "Don't challenge my father. You'll lose all of that gold in your mine." With her arms spread, she gestured to the open doorway. "Speaking of which, I have the gold and your belongings ready with the children."

At the open door, he paused and brushed a gentle finger along her cheek. "Keep the gold, Irish. I don't need it."

Her heart tumbled at his touch. "No, it belongs to you. As soon as the reward comes from the government, I'll have all the money I need."

"I'll send along a telegram and learn what's delaying it. Or I'll get my grandmother on the case. She seems to have an inside track with the President."

She caught his fingers in hers. "I never told you how glad I was when she showed up with the pardon. I didn't want to admit how nervous I was."

"I didn't want to admit I was about to bolt and run when I saw that Army officer waiting for me."

"I'm glad you didn't. You've got your life back."

"Thanks to you."

"As you know I was well paid."

"Irish, you earned every cent."

The patter of running footsteps pulled them apart. Juan and Running Deer leaped into his arms. "Thorne, you come."

"Did you have a good time?"

They both nodded. "Have fun with Mo, and Joe, and Andy." The little girl smiled. "And Sissy, too."

Mariah tugged on the girl's long braids. "Maureen had the best time. She found one of her old dresses for this pretty little girl, and my mother gave Juan something the twins have outgrown."

"I suppose I haven't thought much about their clothes. Do you think you could get a few things for them?"

More than anything she wanted to help him, to do the everyday things a wife does. He didn't want her for a wife. And she didn't have the heart to refuse. "I'll see what I can do. I have to go into the agency tomorrow. Now that I've solved the Michael Harrison case, I'm ready to take on a new challenge."

"New challenge? Don't tell me you're headed out on another bounty hunt. Your next fugitive might not be as cooperative."

"Not just yet. I need time to recuperate. Besides, I got rid of my nun's habit in Denver. I don't want to look at that thing again."

"Rosie, why are you letting Mr. Harrison stand in the doorway. Invite him in." Kathleen wiped her hands on her white apron as she entered the parlor. She grinned at the man holding the children. "How did you like our little *celi* last night? It was nearly as grand as an Irish wake."

Michael winked at her. "I had a fine time, and I have a headache to prove it."

"Come into my kitchen. I have an old Gaelic remedy that

will cure it once and for all.'' At the kitchen door, she glanced over her shoulder. ''Or make you wish you'd died last night.''

Laughing, he followed at her heels. ''Come along, Irish. I'm always interested in new cures.''

With a shrug, Mariah joined them in the kitchen. He set both children on chairs and waited until her mother mixed her special elixir. ''It never fails to cure my da,'' she said.

Kathleen handed him a glass with bubbles foaming over the rim. ''But I must warn you, the drink sometimes makes a man amorous.'' She grinned, a hint of pink at her cheeks.

''Ma, is that where my eight siblings came from?'' Mariah asked, feigning shock.

She laughed. ''Your da likes a drink now and then.''

Michael swallowed down the mixture. ''I am feeling better. Do you mind if I borrow your daughter for a while?'' he asked, his teeth bared like a wolf after a rabbit.

''Annie is spoken for. Jenny, Maggie, and Maureen are too young. That leaves Rosie. And she's already told me and her da that she's a grown woman and she'll choose her own man.''

A blush raced up her face. ''Will you quit talking about me as if I'm not here? Now that I'm a wealthy woman, I may never marry.'' Mariah snatched a cookie from the tray on the table. She broke it and shared it with the youngsters.

Her gaze locked with Michael's. His glance reminded her that she'd already married. So far, she'd neglected to see about an annulment. Tomorrow, she promised herself. She'd start anew with her life as a wealthy woman.

''Now that I'm feeling better, I'd best get these youngsters home.'' He stood and reached for their hands.

''Will Sissy go with us?'' the little girl asked.

Mariah knelt beside the child. ''No, honey. I have to stay here. You go with Thorne. He'll take care of you like always.''

Frowning, the children obeyed, their dark eyes sad and damp. She handed Michael the gold, and the envelope containing his will. Once inside the carriage, they waved until they were out of sight. Mariah turned back to the house and found her mother watching her.

"Poor Rosie. You love him, don't you?"

"Me? Love that stubborn mountain man?" She sighed. "Is it so obvious?"

Kathleen draped an arm across her daughter's shoulder. "A mother always knows. Though I'm certain he doesn't even suspect. I loved your father for months before he took notice of me. And the funny part was that he loved me, and he didn't even know."

Mariah hugged her mother. She had no idea that Michael had had ample opportunity to express his feelings. But the cold fact was that he didn't love her at all. "It's different with me and Michael."

"Rosie, I think he cares a lot. But from what you've told about his background, he's afraid to love. Give him time. He'll come around."

"I hope so, Ma, I truly hope so."

Michael hailed a cab at the shipyard, and ordered the driver back to the house on Society Hill. He was at his wit's end.

Over the past weeks, he'd tried every ruse he could devise, and then some to make the children happy. He'd purchased clothes and toys, books and games, even a pair of ponies for Running Deer and Juan. He simply wasn't cut out to be a parent to two youngsters, or guardian to an old man. Juan and Running Deer refused to leave their rooms unless they were firmly attached to his hand. They hated their clothes and wore their old things. Sung Lo was no better. The old Chinese continued to interfere in the kitchen, usually frightening the maids, and sending Mrs. Murphy scurrying to his grandmother for help.

Worse, every waking hour they asked for Sissy Rosie.

With every mention of her name, Michael's heart took another plunge toward his feet. Truth be told, he missed her more than the children did.

He'd stayed busy trying to get her out of his mind. His old professor from medical college was teaching at the university, and showed great interest in his medicines and cures. He allowed Michael use of the laboratory to continue his experiments. At his grandmother's insistence, he spent part of each day studying her business enterprises. Naturally, she wanted him to take over for her.

In going over the books, he'd learned that for the past ten years, his grandmother had spent a fortune on Rosehaven. Gabriel and Suzanna lived on the plantation, but seemed to be doing little to make it self-supporting. They spent their time traveling England and the Continent. His brother and sister-in-law were due back any day from their latest sojourn abroad.

He dreaded the thought of seeing them again. For all their sakes, he hoped that when their ship docked, they would travel directly to Virginia.

Of course, his grandmother was paying their bills as they came to her accountant. Michael had never revealed that Gabriel was the reason for his court-martial, or that he'd tried to kill Michael in battle. All she knew was that he'd refused to kill a Rebel soldier. Nobody but Mariah knew that his own brother was that man.

As the cab crossed Front Street, he realized they couldn't keep on going as they had. He needed help, and there was only one way to get it. He stuck his head out the window and told the driver to head north to Lehigh Street.

If that stubborn Irish woman refused to help, he had little choice but to move his household in with Sean O'Reilly's family.

Mariah answered the door on the first knock. She jumped back in surprise when she recognized him. Her hair was tied up in a scarf, and her face and apron were smudged with dust. He fully expected her to slam the door in his face.

Instead, she stood her ground. Planting her fists on her hips, she glared at him as if he were the landlord come to evict her family. "As I live and breathe, if it isn't Mr. Michael Thornton Harrison. To what do we owe the honor?"

Since she visited the children while he was working, he hadn't seen her since the day after the *celi*. He didn't at all understand the way his pulse quickened when he locked gazes with her. He propped a shoulder against the doorjamb. "I need to talk to you."

She glanced back into the parlor, crowded with boxes and crates. "I'm busy. We bought a house and we're moving today."

"You're moving and you weren't going to tell me?"

"I didn't think you were interested in what I do, or where I go."

"What about the children?" He caught her arm and tugged her onto the stoop. Two women on the next stoop halted their conversation and stared at him.

"They know we're moving. I promised to bring them to visit as soon as we get settled." She lowered her voice. "If you came to inquire about the annulment, I'll take care of that, too, when I have the time."

His voice dropped to a growl. "I don't care about the annulment. I care about the children. They're miserable. They hardly leave their rooms. Running Deer plays with her doll, and Juan makes tunes on his whistle. They won't wear the new clothes you sent, and at night I hear them crying."

Her eyes softened, and she bit her lip. "What can I do?"

"Irish, I want you to come live with me."

"Live with you?"

"You're still my wife, and I need you." Pink crept up her cheeks. He recognized the signs of her Irish temper being fueled. "Don't get a bee in your bonnet. I want you to help with the children and Sung Lo. Stay with us until they get adjusted to their new home."

She folded her arms across her chest. "What is it you want, Michael? A governess? A nanny? Or a wife?"

He fisted his hands to keep from either shaking her or kissing her—he couldn't decide which. "A friend. You'll have your own room, and free hand with the children. Hell, I'll pay you anything you say."

Tilting her nose in the air, she studied him through lowered lids. "I'm an independently wealthy woman since the reward came through. I don't need your largess. I'll do it to help them adjust to their new lives. Tell them I'll be there tomorrow."

"No, Irish. Now. I have a cab waiting."

She looked down at her dusty gown and apron. "I'm hardly dressed for Society Hill."

A smile crept over his lips. "Woman, you look a heck of a lot better than when we were searching for the gold. You don't even have to pack. I'll buy you a whole new wardrobe."

Turning on her heel, she retorted sharply as she returned to the house, "You already have."

Chapter 23

"Sissy." Running Deer and Juan darted down the stairs and into Mariah's arms.

She stooped to their level to greet them. Tears filled her eyes. They were so lonely and so needful of love and attention. "I'm so glad to see you," she said in a shaky voice. Although she hated to leave her family in the middle of their big move, nothing was more important than seeing to the welfare of these orphans.

"We miss you. Sung Lo think Sissy no like us."

Behind the children, the old Chinese descended the stairs at a slower pace. A wide smile slashed his mouth. "Of course I like you. I love you. Didn't I tell you that a few days ago when we went on a picnic?"

They nestled their young faces in her neck. "We no like 'Delphia."

She glanced up at Michael hovering over them. Pain glinted in his eyes. He'd done his best, but they needed more than he and his elderly grandmother could offer. "I'll show you how to like Philadelphia. And you've already made friends. Joe and

Andy and Mo ask about you every day. They want you to visit them soon.''

The little girl's dark eyes pleaded with Michael. ''Can we see friends?''

He hunkered down beside them. ''One day, real soon, we'll all go for a picnic in Fairmount Park. You can ride your pony, and teach the others to ride. Sissy will be here every day to help you.''

Juan whistled a happy tune and Running Deer clapped her hands. ''We like 'Delphia with Sissy.''

Smiling, Mariah stood and greeted Sung Lo. ''What's this I hear about you chasing the girls with your cleaver? That's no way to win a lady's heart.''

The old man's grin widened. ''No chase. Cook good food. Sissy eat with Sung Lo?''

''Certainly. We'll visit some of the other Chinese in Philadelphia. Would you like that?''

''Like much.''

Michael gestured to the stairway. ''Let's get these bags up to your room. Then you can eat, play, or whatever you wish to do.''

He led the way to a room near the end of the hallway, pointing out the children's rooms and opening the door next to theirs. Her room was elegantly furnished with a large four-poster bed and matching mahogany armoire and dressing table. Ivory brocade drapes covered the long windows. The room was exactly what she'd dreamed for her own. It was larger than the three rooms where her entire family of eleven slept, and even larger than her room in the new house.

''I hope it's satisfactory,'' Michael said as he set her bag on the bed. ''Mrs. Murphy will prepare another chamber if this one isn't to your liking.''

Putting on an air of sophistication, she nodded her approval. ''It will do.''

The children jumped on the bed. ''We sleep here,'' Running

Deer said. "Thorne, Sissy, Juan, Running Deer, and even Sung Lo."

Michael flopped down beside them. "I think you're right. There's room for all. Come on, Irish, join us."

Mariah stood her ground. When she next slept with Michael, it was going to be the two of them alone. And only if he loved her. "Off with all of you. Give me a moment to catch my breath. A poor Irish girl isn't used to these grand surroundings."

"I thought you were an independently wealthy woman," he said, coming to his feet.

"I am. Only I'm just getting used to it."

"We'll give you a minute, then come down to the kitchen. I'm certain Sung Lo has frightened the life out of the staff while preparing something special for you."

He shooed the children out of the room, and hesitated at the door for a second. "Thanks, Irish." As he walked down the hallway, she heard his soft voice. "Welcome home."

"How did you enjoy the meeting of the Literary Guild, my dear?" Mrs. Thornton passed a cup of tea to Mariah.

She accepted the tea, and tried to find a diplomatic way to tell her hostess that she'd been bored out of her mind. However, she smiled and said, "It was interesting."

Mrs. Thornton laughed. "That bunch of snobbish old biddies can hardly be called interesting. What did you really think?"

"I was bored silly. I'd have much rather discussed Mark Twain than John Burroughs." She glanced out the long window of the morning room that overlooked the elaborate gardens. Maureen and the twins had come to spend the day with Running Deer and Juan. From time to time, she caught a glimpse of the children darting in and out among the hedges and flower beds.

"To be honest, so would I. However, they were quite taken with you."

"I rather think they were shocked by me—a poor Irish woman suddenly thrust into the limelight." Mariah felt like a novelty among the socialites. She'd repeated the story of her adventures so many times, she could recite it in her sleep. To keep things interesting, the two bandits had become a half dozen, and her lone Indian youth had become three chiefs. It was all she could do to keep from laughing aloud at the "oohs and ahhs" of her audience. "I'm not part of their social circle," she said on a sigh.

"You soon will be. The young men are standing in line to escort you to various social events. Mrs. Willingspoon's nephew, George, has asked to escort you to the Pennsylvania Academy of Fine Arts to view an exhibit by James McNeill Whistler. His 'Arrangement in Grey and Black' has caused quite a sensation."

Mariah sipped her tea, trying to think of a gracious way out of the engagement. In the two weeks since she'd moved into the Thornton mansion, Mrs. Thornton had taken Mariah under her wing. She was determined to introduce her into her society if it killed both of them. Several of her friends' sons and nephews had already called on Mariah and asked to escort her to various functions. None of the young men interested her in the least. Compared to Michael, they were dull as dishwater. "Really, Mrs. Thornton, that was too kind of you. However, I did promise Michael to look after the children."

"You'll only be gone a few hours. They'll be fine as long as Michael is home."

She set her cup down. She'd seen little of Michael in the past weeks. He spent his days either at the university medical school using their laboratories to develop his medicines or at the shipyard. In the evening, he often worked with his grand-mother on her records and investments.

In spite of his busy schedule, it seemed that every time she went to a concert, to tea, or simply to a small gathering, Michael was there. Sometimes he was alone, but, more often, he escorted a beautiful woman.

On her excursion to the Walnut Street Theater for a performance of Edwin Booth in Shakespeare's *Hamlet,* she'd spotted

Michael across the way with a lovely blonde woman on his arm. Michael nodded, then turned his attention to his lady. It took all her self-control not to snatch her arm from Michael's. He was Mariah's husband, at least for the time being. She vowed to see a priest the very next day about the annulment. Unfortunately, she'd been too busy to carry out her threat.

As she struggled for a way to get out of another dreadful evening, a commotion from the hallway caught her attention. At first she thought it was the children, but they were outdoors with her sister and brothers. She glanced at Mrs. Thornton, who seemed as puzzled as Mariah. A man's loud voice, the bang of an object hitting the floor, and the tapping of heels on the marble floor brought her to her feet. The butler entered the doorway. He opened his mouth to speak, but was brushed aside by a man and a woman.

"No need to announce us, Murphy," the man drawled. Dressed in an expensive suit with a diamond stickpin in his striped cravat, the tall, handsome man went directly to Mrs. Thornton and placed a quick kiss on her cheek.

A beautiful woman followed suit. Her silk faille gown rustled as she swept into the room like Queen Victoria herself. Diamonds dripped from her ears and glittered from her fingers. Without being told, Mariah identified the couple. Her stomach tied in knots at coming face-to-face with Michael's brother and his wife.

"Gabriel, Suzanna, I expected you weeks ago." The older woman offered her cheek to the newcomers.

Suzanna Harrison laughed, a deep throaty sound. "We were delayed in Paris. We were invited to so many parties, we simply couldn't pull ourselves away and return to that dreary plantation."

Gabriel shot a stern glance at his wife. "Dearest, Rosehaven is our home. A few more horses like the one we bought in Ireland, and we'll have the finest racing stable in the state."

Noticing Mariah for the first time, Gabriel granted her a quick appraisal. As if pleased with what he saw, he flashed a charming smile and bowed elegantly from the waist. His brown eyes glittered with interest. "I don't believe I've met this charming creature."

"This is Miss Mariah O'Reilly," Mrs. Thornton said. "Mariah, Gabriel and Suzanna Harrison."

Mariah nodded to the newcomers. Gabriel Harrison tilted an eyebrow, and his gaze lingered longer on her body than she thought proper. She wished she had a large horse blanket to cover her blue afternoon gown.

His wife sank into a chair and poured two cups of tea. "Murphy!" she called. The butler appeared as if he'd been hovering in the hallway. "Bring some brandy, please. I need a little fortification after that dreadful ocean voyage."

"Isn't it a little early in the day, my dear?" her husband questioned.

She tossed a long blond curl over her shoulder. "I'm simply exhausted. You understand, don't you, Grandma-ma?" Her sweet feminine drawl would entice the birds out of the trees.

Mariah settled back in her chair to observe the pair. So this was the woman Michael had almost married, the only woman he'd ever loved. The woman who'd betrayed him and married his brother.

Suzanna was quite beautiful, but icy selfishness glittered behind her long eyelashes darkened with cosmetics. Her cheeks were painted with rouge, and a hint of color brushed her lips. Although Mariah had confidence in her own looks, she couldn't compete with the woman's full-blown beauty.

The couple bantered back and forth for several minutes about their journey. Except for his height, Gabriel bore little resemblance to Michael. His chestnut-colored hair was neatly cut, and his mustache trimmed. His shoulders weren't nearly as wide, and his smile appeared forced. Mariah couldn't forget that he was the man who'd tried to kill Michael, his own brother. Her dislike for the couple was immediate and strong.

She shivered, wondering how Michael would react to their unexpected arrival. Her heart twisted. She should warn him before he returned to the house. As she rose to excuse herself, she recognized the footsteps in the hallway. She met Michael in the doorway.

Clutching his arm, she attempted to steer him from entering. "What's wrong, Irish? You look as if you've seen a ghost."

"Michael, don't—"

Her warning was cut off by Mrs. Thornton's voice. "Michael, darling, come in. I have a surprise for you."

Mariah clinging to his arm, Michael stepped through the doorway. He stopped cold, jolted as if he'd been kicked in the gut.

He thought he'd been prepared for the moment he would have to confront his brother and Suzanna. They'd been expected for weeks. However, coming face-to-face with the pair knocked the props clear from under him. Michael felt open and vulnerable.

Suzanna gasped, her eyes wide with shock, and Gabriel sprung from his chair. "Oh, my God," he muttered, his face a mask of disbelief. "Michael."

"Gabriel and Suzanna have just returned from their trip to Europe," his grandmother remarked. "I haven't had time to tell them about your arrival back home." His grandmother stretched out a hand to him. "Isn't this a wonderful reunion?"

Michael growled deep in his throat. "Wonderful." Thousands of emotions hit him at once. Hatred for the brother who'd tried to kill him. Anger for the ten years he'd lost because of his actions. Pain for what his grandmother had suffered in thinking him dead.

Mariah clutched his arm, warning him not to do anything rash, like tossing his brother and sister-in-law out on their rears. The only thing stopping him was not wanting to upset Mrs. Thornton. She smiled as if unaware of the tension that permeated the small room like thick smoke from a bonfire. He fisted his hands, wanting nothing more than to repay his brother for all Michael had lost.

Suzanna recovered her composure first. She offered a hand.

"Michael, as I live and breathe. We haven't heard from you since that dreadful war ended. Gabe and I were afraid you'd been lost to us forever." Her words and manner were as phony as fool's gold.

Gabriel, his face pasty white, leaped from his chair. His movement toppled a bottle of brandy from the table. It hit the floor with a thud, pouring the amber liquid on the Oriental rug. "I heard you were captured."

Thanks to you, he thought. "I escaped the firing squad."

He ignored Suzanna's offered hand. He'd rather grab a rattlesnake than the hand of a faithless woman. To think he'd once loved her with all the passion in his young heart. He'd often wondered what would have happened if there had been no war, if they'd married. A shiver raced over him. Their union would never have succeeded. From the first, she'd been against his desire to attend medical college. Doctors were usually poor, while Suzanna loved the affluent and decadent plantation life to which she'd been born.

"Where have you been all this time?" Gabriel asked, ignoring the liquor that had splashed on his expensive trousers—clothes his grandmother had paid for. Behind the hatred in his brother's eyes, Michael spotted something else. Fear. The arrogant man cowered in the face of meeting his nemesis.

"West. Colorado, New Mexico." He leaned over and retrieved the nearly empty bottle and returned it to the tea table.

"Michael, do have a seat and join us in a spot of tea. Now that the whole family is here, I've just come up with a wonderful idea. I'm going to throw a ball to celebrate Michael's return, and to introduce Miss O'Reilly into society. You will help me with the plans, won't you, Suzanna?" His grandmother filled another cup for Michael.

"I'd be delighted." She slid a glance toward Mariah and studied her like a fighter weighing a competitor's strengths and weaknesses. "Exactly who is this charming Miss O'Reilly?" He had to give the woman credit. She'd recovered from her initial shock of seeing Michael as if he'd only been gone a few hours rather than ten years.

Michael urged Mariah to a small settee and took the seat beside her. For a second he was tempted to reveal the truth, that she was his wife. Instead, he kept up the same pretense. "She's the investigator who located me in New Mexico, and convinced me to return home."

"Mariah is quite the heroine," his grandmother added. "She'll have to tell you how she captured outlaws and Indians, and recovered a cache of stolen gold bars. She's had some amazing adventures."

At the mention of gold, Gabriel's mouth gaped. "Gold?"

"Oh, yes. I got a huge reward." Mariah patted Michael's hand. "Michael didn't want any of the reward, he already has a gold mine of his own. But I'm sure Mr. and Mrs. Harrison aren't interested in my little story."

"But we are, my dear," Suzanna said in the syrupy voice he'd once found mesmerizing that now grated on his nerves. "Some other time, though. I'm exhausted from that long ocean voyage. I'd like to go up to my room and rest. Does Mrs. Murphy have it ready for me."

His grandmother's face pinked. "I'm sorry, Suzanna. I didn't know exactly when you were going to return. I've given that room to Mariah. And Gabriel, Michael is in your room."

"And the other rooms in the east wing are also occupied," Michael said, his words clipped and raw. "Mrs. Murphy can make up rooms in the west wing."

Suzanna leaped to her feet, her once-suppressed temper exploding. More than once, Michael had felt the lash of her tongue. The last time was when she'd called him a traitor and flung his engagement ring back in his face. Her mouth thinned into a hard line. "I have no intention of moving into those other rooms. I had that one decorated to my taste. Have the housekeeper make up the rooms and move this little Irish tart into them."

Mariah and Michael sprung up as one. He clutched Mariah's

arm to keep her from slapping Suzanna across her overly madeup face. "We'll stay where we are. If the west wing isn't good enough for you, go to La Pierre or the Lafayette Hotel." He glared at his brother's wife with so much anger, it was a wonder she didn't keel over from the impact.

"Michael, it's all right. I don't mind moving," Mariah offered, struggling unsuccessfully to free herself of his hold.

He narrowed his gaze on Mariah. "You'll stay next to me and the children."

"Children?" Gabriel shot to his feet. "You're married?"

Michael locked gazes with his brother. He bit his lip to keep Mariah's secret. "They're orphans I've taken in." He stepped through the doorway where the butler was waiting. "Murph, ask the Missus to prepare rooms in the west wing for Mr. and Mrs. Harrison."

"Yes, sir." The old man scurried away as if the beasts of Hades were on his tail.

"Grandma-ma," Suzanna whined. "Can't you do something? This is your home."

The older woman gestured to her grandson with her teacup. "Now is as good a time as any to make a confession." Her gray eyes glinted with a bit of mischief. "Please sit down." She shot a commanding glance that would do Queen Victoria proud. When they'd once again settled into their seats, she continued. "I've been in contact with my attorney. When I thought my Michael was lost, I had planned to leave my estate to Gabriel. Now that I have Michael back—"

Gabriel broke off her words. "You changed your will after all we've done for you?"

She lifted her hands in supplication. "Dears, don't be upset. I've arranged a generous allowance for you. Of course, by now you should have your stables operating with all those horses I've bought. Rosehaven can stand on its own. You don't need my largess."

"Did you know all this?" Mariah whispered to Michael.

"No. I don't need her money."

"Back to Michael. Instead of leaving him my estate after my death, I've turned all my assets over to him for his use and administration. Michael now owns Thornton Hall, the shipyard, my stock, and most of my money. I've kept a small portion for my living expenses, plus setting up a trust for my faithful servants. By rights, Michael could toss us all out on our rears."

No one in the small parlor was more shocked than Michael. He watched the color drain from his brother's face. Gabe had paled when Michael, alive and kicking, entered the room. At the latest announcement, he'd turned ghostly. Suzanna was livid. Whereas Gabe blanched, her face crept from pink, to red, to purple clear up to the roots of her elaborate coiffeur. To think, he'd almost married the faithless woman!

They had expected to inherit since Michael was supposedly dead. Thanks to Mariah's tenacity he'd fooled them all. Only, he didn't need or want his grandmother's fortune. Once they were alone, he would suggest a donation to the university or a grant to the hospital for research. Until then, he would simply go along with his grandmother's wishes, and let Gabriel and Suzanna stew over the situation.

He steepled his fingers in front of his mouth to hide a sadistic grin. He'd known his grandmother had been supporting the couple, as well as financing the plantation and their many trips abroad. He'd been surprised that she'd obviously seen through their money-grubbing schemes and was cutting off their water.

"Thank you, Grandmother," he said, when he finally recovered enough to speak. "I'll do my best to make you proud."

She heaved a sigh. "Now that our business is over, let's get back to the plans for the ball. All the best of society will attend, as well as the governor, the senators, and mayor." With a smile, she turned to Mariah. "We'll invite your family and friends, Mariah. It wouldn't be proper to leave them out of the festivities."

"You'll have common Irish in your home?" Suzanna narrowed an icy glaze at Mariah. Her pale-blue eyes turned to shards of ice.

"*My* home," Michael reminded them all. "I've grown fond of the O'Reilly clan. They're all welcome at Thornton Hall." Especially one member of the Irish family. "A ball sounds like a fine idea."

Suzanna leaped to her feet. "I'll go see if my room is ready. I have a splitting headache. Send the upstairs maid to assist me."

Although she addressed her orders to his grandmother, Michael answered. "The maids have their own duties. You'll either have to hire your own servant, or let your husband help you."

In a flurry of silk and lace, Suzanna stormed from the room, Gabriel hot on her heels. As he left the room, his voice echoed down the hallway. "Murphy, bring me a bottle of whiskey."

Mariah retreated to the garden with the children immediately after breakfast the next morning. The past evening had been so filled with tension, she'd gone to bed with a headache. Neither Gabriel nor Suzanna appeared for dinner, having requested trays sent to their rooms. Michael spoke little, clearly shocked at the sudden turn of events.

Since early morning, Michael had been closeted in the library with his grandmother, probably making plans on how to spend his fortune. Her heart sank. Although she called herself an independently wealthy woman, her small fortune wasn't a drop in the bucket compared to what Michael possessed. She had to remember that all through history, money married money. And men never married out of their class. So far, he hadn't asked about the annulment, but it was only a matter of time before he would want to marry a suitable woman. One from the upper crust with a huge dowry and all the proper social graces. Probably the woman he'd squired to the play, or like the one he'd nearly married.

She sat on a stone bench near the fountain in the middle of the garden. Beyond the tall brick walls, carriages and people milled on the busy avenue. Rittenhouse Square was directly across the street from the mansion.

Sung Lo appeared from the shadows and took a seat beside her. He offered a small cookie, like the ones he often baked for the children. "Thank you," she muttered.

Clad in a black tunic and loose trousers, he studied the children at play. "Why Sissy sad?"

She never could fool the old man. Sometimes she thought he was some kind of mystical Oriental mind-reader. "I'm not sad, I'm just planning another outing. We have to take Juan to a doctor and Running Deer to my mother's. Would you like to go to Arch Street and visit Mr. Mei-Hsian Lou at his Chinese restaurant?"

A wide grin slashed across his face. "Like Chinaman. Speak Cantonese."

"Good. We'll meet you there for lunch."

For long moments, they sat in companionable silence. The children were playing hide-and-seek. Since it was a school day, Maureen and the twins had gone home. From time to time, Mariah heard Running Deer's shrieks, and the sound of Juan's whistle. She'd approached Michael about schooling for the children, but he thought they needed more time to adjust. They still didn't like their new clothes, and more often than not went barefoot or wore moccasins. Mariah had started teaching them to read and write. Both children were bright, and, although Juan didn't speak, Mariah knew he understood and was reading silently.

"Get out of my way, you little savage." Suzanna's angry retort drew Mariah to her feet. Suzanna appeared from behind a row of hedges, dragging Juan by the arm.

Running Deer raced into Mariah's arms. The girl's face was white with fear. "Sissy, lady got Juan."

"Do these heathens belong to you?" She thrust the helpless boy toward Mariah. Tears poured down his face.

Fury welled up in her. She hugged the child close to her body. "They're Michael's foster children."

Dressed in white lawn with tiny embroidered flowers, Suzanna looked as lovely as a fresh spring day. But her countenance was far from lovely. Anger twisted her mouth, and her eyes shot hatred at Mariah. "And what are you? The traitor's whore?"

Her Irish temper a hairbreadth from exploding, she curled her nails into her palms to keep from slapping the smug expression from the woman's face. "What did you call me?"

"Michael is nothing but a traitor. He turned his back on his own family for the Yankees. And you're nothing but an Irish strumpet."

That did it. Nobody insulted an O'Reilly and got away with it. Slowly, she handed Juan to Sung Lo. Then she faced Suzanna boldly. "You shouldn't have said that." Mariah braced both her hands on the woman's chest and shoved. Suzanna stumbled backward. Her legs hit the edge of the fountain, and she teetered off balance for a second.

"Oh, hell," Mariah muttered. "That one was for me. This one is for Michael." With one hand she pushed, and Suzanna landed on her rear in the water. Above her head the fountain spewed in her face.

She gasped and sputtered. Her skirt puddled above her knees, and her hat floated away. Her hair hung limp in her eyes. A goldfish nudged at her legs.

The children covered their mouths to hide their glee. Mariah wasn't nearly so polite. Laughing aloud, she said, "That should cool your temper, and wash out your mouth."

The other woman let out a string of curses that would do an Irish sailor proud. She gathered her sodden skirts and climbed out of the pool. "You bitch, you won't get away with this."

Water dripping from her expensive frock, Suzanna stumbled to the rear door of the house. She looked for all the world like a water-soaked waif.

Mariah gathered the children in her arms. She lifted her gaze to the long windows of the morning room that overlooked the gardens. Michael stood in the window, staring down at the confrontation. How much had he seen? she wondered. With the closed window, she doubted he'd heard the squabble. Was he angry at her?

Actually, she didn't care what he thought about her. She'd done what needed to be done. As she watched, a wide grin curved his mouth, and he clapped his hands in silent applause.

Her spirits soared—he wasn't angry with her. She lifted her skirts and performed a small jig. Then she curtsied and returned to the house to prepare for the appointment Michael had made to have Juan examined by a doctor.

She loved the little boy and girl as if they were her own. The fact that Juan hadn't spoken a word worried Michael and her. Seeing the doctor would put their minds at ease. If there was a reason the child couldn't speak, he could learn to write and use his hands to communicate. And Mariah would be there to teach him, and love him. Even if Michael didn't need her love, the boy did. She would give it willingly and eagerly, do her best to see him happily settled in his new home.

Chapter 24

Michael paced the floor of the doctor's small waiting room. From time to time, he dropped to the chair beside Mariah who stared at the inner door where Juan had disappeared an hour ago. According to the doctors at the university medical college, Dr. Lupen was the best in the field of hearing and speech. He consulted at the Hospital for the Deaf and Dumb, and took patients in his private practice. Since Juan hadn't spoken a word in the time he'd been with Michael, Mariah agreed it was time to have the child checked.

"He'll be okay, Irish." He gripped her hand more for his own support than for hers.

"He'd better be. I don't know why one of us couldn't go in with him. Juan was so frightened when that nurse tugged on his arm. His skin was positively the color of new-fallen snow." She bit her lip and continued to stare at the door.

"Some doctors don't like interference from the patient's family."

She stared at him. In every way but one they were a family. They'd married to protect his freedom, and agreed on an annulment to return hers. She'd made it clear from the beginning that she didn't want the marriage. As far as he knew, she'd already contacted the priest. All that remained was for him to sign the necessary papers.

So far, she'd remained with him for the children's sakes. Seeing her every day and not touching her had turned into a test of his will. A test that became harder with every day that passed.

Every night when he went to bed, he was tempted to open the door that connected their rooms and go to her. He'd chosen that room so she could be near the children, and near him. For all the good it did. If she'd only made half an effort, he would throw the door open and take his rightful place as her husband.

Thanks to his grandmother's interference, she was being courted by any number of wealthy young men, plus a number who hardly had a penny to their names. Like the Irish police officer, Malloy. The Irishman was nice enough, but he wasn't at all the right man for Mariah. Nor were any of the other dandies who'd arrived for tea, or escorted her to one social event or another. It was all he could do to keep up with her.

"Mr. and Mrs. Harrison . . ." The stringent nasal tones of the nurse brought him out of his reverie. They lunged to their feet as one. "The doctor will see you now."

Mariah didn't bother to correct the nurse. In fact, they were Mr. and Mrs. He touched her elbow and guided her into the doctor's office. The man sat behind a large desk, his face bland and without expression. Michael resisted a shiver. The cold, hard look in the man's glacial blue eyes could chill the summer sunshine. He knew little about the doctor. Trained in Vienna, he'd been in the Union for only a few years. But Dr. Lupen came highly recommended.

The moment they stepped across the threshold, Juan raced into Mariah's arms. She picked him up and kissed his cheek. "Are you all right?" she whispered. In answer, the boy buried his face in her neck.

The doctor gestured to the two straight-backed chairs that fronted his desk. If the fee Michael had paid for the consultation was any indication, the man could certainly afford better office furniture. He helped Mariah to the chair, then sat beside her.

Adjusting the monocle on his right eye, the doctor glanced at the papers on his desk. "Mr. Harrison," he began in a voice laced with a thick German accent. "I have examined the boy, and have come to several conclusions." He tugged on the sleeves of a very expensive suit. "I regret to inform you that there is little I can do for the child. Although his hearing seems normal, I can find no reason for his lack of speech. The vocal cords are intact, so I see no physical reason he does not talk."

Michael leaned forward and rested his elbows on his knees. "Then what do you suppose is the problem?"

"Either the boy does not understand the words or his mind is impaired."

"No," Mariah said, her gaze locked on the doctor. "He understands everything that's said. Why he's even learning to read and write."

"He may have learned some, but I'm certain that his problem is mental. Simply put, the boy is an imbecile. In Vienna, I met several doctors who were experimenting with the problems of the mind. You would be better off placing him in the—"

"No! Don't say it." Michael knew what was to come next. Everyone who wasn't in the realm of what society deemed normal was put away. He leaped to his feet. At his side, Mariah turned pale. She hugged the boy tighter. "There's nothing wrong with his mind."

"Mr. Harrison," the doctor continued as if Michael hadn't spoken, "you have asked for my evaluation, and I've given it. I can do no more."

Well, *he* could. Catching Mariah's elbow, he helped her to her feet. "Let's get out of here." He took Juan from her arms. "He may not have a voice, but he has a fine mind. We'll get a teacher who's willing to help. Good day, Doctor."

He all but shoved Mariah through the doorway in his effort to flee the office before he did something rash. On the way out, he brushed past the nurse without so much as an apology or by-your-leave. All he gave her was a deep, rumbling growl. This time, Mariah didn't say a word. Her face was red, and he realized she had as much trouble controlling her temper as he.

On the street, he opened the door of the carriage for Mariah. Once they were settled on the deep leather seats, he let out a string of curses in three languages. "The man is a quack. Regardless of his European education and fine reputation."

"I wanted to punch him right in his long, pointed nose," she said. "Imagine him saying . . . that about our boy. Why, Juan is the smartest, most talented youngster I've ever seen." She tilted his chin with a finger. "We're sorry we took you to that silly old doctor, sweetheart. Play us a tune on your whistle."

The confused child looked up at Mariah. He stuck his whistle into his mouth and played a sad, poignant tune. His song said more than words. The child was lonely and lost, in need of love and affection.

"Juan, would you like to spend the night with Joseph and Andrew? We have to go to my house and pick up Running Deer. You can both stay if you like." Mariah brushed a gentle hand over the boy's head.

The child nodded in the affirmative. He didn't understand the turmoil with the doctor, and he certainly wouldn't understand the tension at Thornton Hall. It would be good for the child to spend some time with the loving O'Reilly family. Too bad Michael and Mariah had to return to the mansion and face his brother and sister-in-law.

"Won't that be just grand?" Michael said. "And that's the truth."

For the first time that afternoon, Mariah smiled. "We can eat at Mei-Hsian Lou's Chinese restaurant. Sung Lo is spending the day with his new friend."

Michael met her gaze over the child's head. "You aren't planning to desert me, are you, Irish? I need you to keep me from knocking my arrogant brother on his . . . Never mind. Just stay close to me."

"Sorry, I've already promised to attend an exhibit with the

nephew of one of your grandmother's friends. Somebody named George.''

"George? I believe the fellow left a message this morning. Seems his aunt had an attack of vapors. He won't be able to escort you. Hope you aren't too disappointed." The lie came quickly. He would send a note to the man using some lame excuse and sign Mariah's name.

She shrugged. "I was rather looking forward to a boring evening with George. Instead, I'll be thrust in the middle of the war and hope for Appomattox.''

"Irish, if this morning was an example, you're able to handle your own against the entire Rebel army.''

"Promise to stay close to me. Next time I might not be able to control my temper.''

He laughed. "I've seen you capture a wild Indian and notorious outlaws. I'd hate to be around if you ever lose your temper.''

"Remember that, Mountain Man.''

"I won't forget.''

The evening proceeded as miserably as Mariah expected. After the delightful dinner at the Chinese restaurant, she was ill prepared for the strain that existed at Thornton Hall. Michael had reverted to the grumpy bear, and his brother wasn't much better.

Suzanna shot daggers at Mariah, but flashed a seductive smile at Michael. Mrs. Thornton carried most of the conversation, with an occasional remark from the others. Mariah almost wished George had kept the appointment. A boring evening with a dull man was preferable to facing bitter enemies across a dining table.

How Michael managed to remain at the table was a testimony to his courage. In his place, she would have tossed the pair out on their bottoms and laughed when they protested. He only kept his composure for his grandmother's sake.

If Mrs. Thornton was aware of the strained atmosphere, she

chose to ignore it. In her dealings with the woman, Mariah had found her shrewd and intelligent. She seemed to have a soft spot for the southerners who'd invaded her home. Or did she? By her confession of the terms of her will, she had thwarted their plans for her money. Michael had everything. She'd as much as told Gabriel and Suzanna they were on their own.

After dinner, Mrs. Thornton urged Mariah to recite the overblown story of how she'd located Michael and brought him home. That alone was worthy of Suzanna's hatred. Michael added a few exaggerated details, making the story nearly unbelievable.

Suzanna hid her distress well, and even offered to take over the plans for the upcoming party. Mariah begged off from helping, using a headache for an excuse. By then, Michael had retired to the library to go over some paperwork from the shipyard.

Thankful to be alone, Mariah wandered into the garden for air. She hugged her shawl to her chest to ward off the chill of the fall night. Without the children or Michael, she felt lost and out of sorts. Sung Lo had gone to his room, and refused to eat at the table with the strangers. He had more sense than the lot of them.

She followed the flagstone walk around the fountain where she'd given Suzanna a dunking that morning. The rosebushes were putting out their last blossoms before winter, and the trees had begun to turn color. The hedges grew high, making a perfect place for the children to play hide-and-seek. She wondered how long Michael would need her. She would need him forever, but she was well aware his need for her was only temporary, until the children adjusted to their new lives.

The tap of footsteps on the walkway brought her head around. A silhouette appeared out of the shadows. Tall and broadshouldered, the man stopped a few steps from her. Her heart skipped a beat. "Michael." She breathed his name like a sigh.

He moved closer, and she realized her mistake. It was

Gabriel, his handsome face barely visible in the dim gas lamp that lighted the street beyond the garden wall.

"Were you expecting my wayward brother, Miss O'Reilly?" he asked, his voice as smooth as sweet butter. He moved closer, and Mariah took a step backward. Her legs encountered the edge of a stone bench.

They were in a secluded section of the garden away from the house, and shadowed by trees. "Yes," she lied. "He's to meet me here."

"Really? I suppose he must have forgotten the appointment." He pressed closer.

Not wanting to show fear or uneasiness, she tilted her head at a haughty angle. "He'll be here."

"I doubt it, my dear. My prodigal brother left the house moments ago with a police officer."

She clutched her shawl. "Police officer? What happened? Where did he go?"

As he stepped closer, she noticed his breath smelled of the alcohol he'd downed most of the evening. "Nothing for you to be concerned about. Just some disturbance on the waterfront near the shipyard. As the owner of the property, my brother was needed to quiet some disgruntled workers. There's been trouble from time to time over wages and hours. But Michael is a fair man, he'll find a way to defuse the situation."

With the bench at her back, Mariah had no place to go except around him. She shifted to her right, and he followed suit, effectively blocking her path. A move to the left, and he was there. It was almost like dancing, but there was no pleasure in the movement.

"You aren't afraid of a harmless southern gentleman, are you, Mariah?" The feral gleam in the man's dark eyes would have frightened a lesser woman. But Mariah wasn't easily intimidated. "Why, you've captured wild Indians and outlaws, and, alas, now I'm afraid you've captured my heart." He reached out a hand to her shoulder. His fingers slid into the hair at her nape. A shiver raced over her. "Cold? I know of

318   *Jean Wilson*

an excellent way to warm a woman." Tugging her closer, he lowered his face to hers. "Are Irish women as passionate as I've heard?" His fingers twisted in her hair, pulling it loose of the pins. "Or should I ask my brother?"

He intended to kiss her or worse. And he expected her to accept it willingly. Of all the gall. Growing up in an Irish neighborhood, Mariah had learned early how to prevent unwanted advances from men. Her father and brothers had taught the girls how to protect themselves. More than one Irish lad had learned a hard lesson from the O'Reilly girls. Leaning into him, as if eager for his attention, she lifted her foot and brought the heel of her shoe down on his instep. He grunted and jerked away. That gave her ample time for the next movement. As if part of a dance routine, she quickly lifted her knee and caught him in the groin. He doubled over in pain, clutching his private parts.

"You'll never find out from me," she said, darting around him and running for all she was worth toward the house. She left him cursing and swearing, and promising revenge on her and his brother.

His threats didn't bother Mariah. She'd faced far worse. For safety's sake, she pulled out the revolver from her valise. A woman couldn't be too careful. Not with predators like Gabriel Harrison on the loose. And she'd thought Philadelphia more civilized than New Mexico.

His footsteps heavy, Michael descended the stairs early the next afternoon. He'd gotten little sleep the past night, but had successfully averted a serious riot at the shipyard. Without question, the men deserved better wages and working conditions. His goal was to negotiate at the bargaining table rather than in the midst of a street confrontation. He'd promised to listen to their grievances and take them under consideration. Thanks to a smart police officer like Sean O'Reilly, they believed him. Sean attested to Michael's sincerity and honesty.

He also hired Francis O'Reilly's Erin Investigators to provide security for the shipyard in case a few hotheads tried to cause trouble. As he entered the foyer, someone knocked on the front door. Since Murphy was nowhere in sight, he turned the knob and pulled the door open. A slim young man stood on the stoop, a small bouquet of nosegays clutched in his fist.

"May I have an audience with Miss O'Reilly, my good man." He pressed a calling card into Michael's hand.

"Mr. George Willingspoon?" Michael stared at the name for a moment before it registered. This was the man who'd wanted to call on Mariah the previous night. The one to whom Michael had sent a message begging off the engagement. "I'm sorry, Miss O'Reilly is indisposed. I'll see that she gets your card." *When hell freezes over,* he told himself. Card and flowers would land in the trash.

A puzzled expression made the man look even younger than he obviously was. He'd clearly been sent by his aunt who'd learned about Mariah's fortune. Nephews were usually penniless creatures living on their family's past fortunes. "I'm sorry to hear that. Perhaps Miss O'Reilly can let me know when we can reschedule our appointment to view the exhibit."

At that inopportune moment, Murphy appeared in the foyer. "Did I hear the gentleman ask for Miss O'Reilly? The lady is in the morning room with Mrs. Thornton."

Caught, Michael gritted his teeth. If the butler had only been less solicitous in his duties. Michael stepped aside and allowed the butler to escort the man into the house. "I suppose she's feeling better," he grunted.

He trailed a few steps behind as the butler led the fellow to the rear of the house. Mariah and his grandmother looked up in surprise as the butler announced the gentleman.

"George," his grandmother said, holding out her hand. "How nice of you to stop by. You've met Miss O'Reilly, of course, and this is my grandson, Michael Harrison."

George bowed to the ladies and stuck out his hand to Michael. After a quick handshake, Michael elbowed the man aside and

settled on the settee with Mariah. George was forced to sit on
a small upholstered chair beside his grandmother.

"I was sorry to hear about your aunt," his grandmother
began. Mariah had shared the story Michael had told to keep
her from going out with the man.

"My aunt?" He looked puzzled. "My aunt is fine. I've come
to pay my respects to you, since Miss O'Reilly said you were
ill."

"My dear George, you must be mistaken. I'm in excellent
health." She shot a confused glance at Mariah. "Never mind.
That's of no concern. These things happen all the time. Would
you like some tea?"

Michael groaned. In every situation, somebody offered tea,
as if a drink of tea would solve the world's problems.

"Thank you very much. That would be quite nice." George
shoved the bouquet of flowers toward Mariah. "These are for
you, Miss O'Reilly. I hope we can make arrangements to view
the exhibit very soon."

She granted the young man a gracious smile. "Thank you,
Mr. Willingspoon, I would very much enjoy an evening out."

Over my dead body, Michael thought. "George, old boy,
will you excuse Miss O'Reilly and myself. We have an errand
to run." He tugged at Mariah's arm, only to have her shake
off his hand.

"Michael, don't be so rude. We have a guest." She lifted
the flowers to her nose and sniffed. Then she flashed the other
man a warm, charming smile.

Michael had ingested all the sugar his body and mind could
stand. "We promised to pick up the children this afternoon."

George puckered his brow. "Children?"

"Yes, Miss O'Reilly's and mine." He clasped her elbow
and all but lifted her to her feet.

"You have children—together?" The young man blanched
and looked Mariah straight in the eye. "I was led to believe
you were unmarried."

Mariah jerked out of his grip. "I am un-unattached. The youngsters are Michael's foster children."

"But they're quite fond of Mariah. They think of her as their mother."

"Michael you've been as cross as a bear for days." Mrs. Thornton waved her hand at him. "Go. Go fetch the children and leave us be."

Entwining his fingers with Mariah's, he tugged her toward the doorway. She held back only long enough to bid farewell. Once out of earshot of the morning room, she refused to go another step.

"What do you think you're doing, Michael Harrison? Dragging me around like a dog on a leash. And what was George talking about? He acted as if I broke the engagement, when you told me he . . ." She planted her hands on her hips and glared daggers at him. "It was a lie. George sent no such message. You did it to keep me home last night."

He shoved his hands in his pockets to restrain from pulling her into his arms. "You're married to me," he blurted without thinking.

"Temporarily, Mountain Man. Only until the annulment comes through."

"And when will that be?"

"Soon. Very soon."

With a loud growl, he tore open the door. "Go back to your dandy. I'm going to fetch the children."

He walked briskly up Walnut Street to work off some of the steam. If the stubborn woman wanted the annulment so badly, then let her have it. He'd be well rid of her once the children adjusted to their new life. And he could just get on with his life without her.

By the time he reached Walnut and Broad, his grandmother's elegant carriage pulled to the side of the street. "Mr. Michael!" the driver called.

A secret smile curved his lips. So Irish had relented and summoned the carriage. He pulled the door open and hopped into the dim interior. Settling on the leather seat beside the woman, he folded his arms across his chest. Heavy perfume filled his nostrils, not at all the light rose scent he'd expected of Mariah. It was too heavy, too overpowering, more like something Suzanna would wear.

Suzanna. He stiffened when he recognized the woman in the expensive silk gown, covered with a heavily embroidered shawl.

"Michael, it's so good to see you." She set her gloved hand on his arm. "I've been wanting a few minutes of your time, but you're always busy with that Irish woman or those br- children."

"What do you want, Suzanna?" He shifted to put a distance between them. Suzanna was as beautiful as ever, but the years had hardened her. She was no longer the young, idealistic girl who'd rejected him when he'd asked her to postpone their wedding for the war. Like many other southerners, she'd been convinced that their glorious cause would end in victory within weeks.

She brushed her fingers along his arm. "Is that any way to talk to me after all we meant to each other? Don't you remember the time we spent together, the picnics, the rides, the parties?"

"It was a long time ago. A lifetime ago. I've forgotten most of it." What he hadn't forgotten was her look when she called him a traitor, or that he hadn't been gone a month when she married his brother.

"I haven't forgotten how we sneaked off alone to that cabin in the woods. How we made love, how you said you loved me." Her voice dripped with honey as she turned and pressed her breast into his arm.

Michael remembered all too well that he hadn't been her first lover, although he let her pretend he was. Still, he'd loved her, and, after all, she wasn't his first, either. "I did love you, Suzanna," he confessed. "It took a long time to get over that fact that you married my brother."

"Michael. I had no choice. I was so alone after you left. My papa would have thrown me out if he'd found out what we'd done. Gabriel offered to marry me." She sniffed, her words broke. "To give your baby his name."

The heat drained from his body. He stared at her as if seeing her for the first time. Her confession struck him like a bayonet to his heart. "A baby? We had a baby? I didn't know. Why didn't you tell me?"

"I wanted to tell you." She wrapped her arms around his neck and buried her face in his coat. "Gabe said you wouldn't care. You turned your back on me and your family when you went off and joined the Yankees. He said he would marry me, so I accepted. What could I do?"

A band tightened around his chest. A child. His child. He hadn't known. He hadn't suspected a thing. At the start of the war, he'd put country first—before his state, his family, and now, he learned, in front of his child. Turning to face her, he gripped her arms and stared at her. "The child? Where is it now?"

She covered her face with her hands and sobbed. "Oh, Michael, it was so terrible. I lost our baby."

Chills raced over him. A sadness, a sense of loss lanced through his heart. He wrapped his arms around her for comfort, for himself and her. "How did it happen?"

"I went riding, and I fell from my horse. When I came to, the doctor told me I'd lost the child." She clung to him, her hands searching his chest under his coat.

"Why didn't anybody tell me?" None of what she said made sense. Suzanna was an excellent horsewoman. They often raced their mounts, and Suzanna would laugh while she awaited him at the finish line. Had she been foolhardy and loss his child to get even with him?

"There was nothing you could do. There was nothing anybody could do. I was devastated for months." Lifting her face, she nestled her lips at his throat.

"I don't understand. Why were you out riding in your condition?"

"You know I rode everywhere. Gabriel dared me. He said I couldn't jump the creek. I tried, and was thrown from my mare. I'm so sorry." Her tears dampened the front of his shirt.

Gabriel. It always came back to his brother. As the second born, Gabe had always been jealous of Michael. Whatever Michael had, Gabriel wanted. Everything from toys, to horses, to lovers. It didn't surprise him when his brother had married his fiancée. Gabriel had wanted Suzanna from the moment Michael had announced the engagement. He hated Michael enough to try to kill him. Had Gabriel wanted Suzanna to lose the child. Another way to take away something that belonged to Michael?

"I love you, Michael. I've always loved you. I'll leave Gabriel if you'll give me another chance."

Another chance? If she'd told him about their child, he would have married her, taken her with him, protected her. A year ago, he might have wanted her. After knowing Mariah, the thought of being with Suzanna repulsed him. "That would be wrong, Suzanna. You married Gabriel. You're his wife."

She cupped his face in her hands. "He doesn't love me. He hasn't made love to me in months. I want you, Michael. I want to try again. To have another child with you."

The very idea of making love to her was disgusting. He tore her hands from his face. "No."

Like a spoiled child who wanted her own way, she crushed her mouth to his, and stroked her tongue across his tight lips. She pressed her full breasts against his chest, and one hand reached for the front of his trousers. Sickened by her behavior, he captured her hands and shoved her away from him.

She fixed him with an icy glare. "It's that Irish tart, isn't it? You'll turn me down for her?"

"Stop, Suzanna. You're making a fool of yourself."

"You owe me, Michael. You owe me for getting me pregnant and then leaving me. After I lost the baby I haven't been able to conceive again."

"I don't owe you or my brother anything. Both of you go

back to Virginia and get on with your lives. I'll see that you get an adequate allowance, but that's all.''

"You bastard." She lifted her hands and scratched his cheek with her long fingernails. The gloves prevented any real damage, but the point was clear. "I'll get even with you, you and your Irish whore. You won't get away with rejecting me a second time."

He stuck his head out the window of the coach. "Stop the carriage, James." Before the vehicle came to a complete stop, he leaped out as if the fires of hell were on his tail.

Indeed they were. The old saying "Hell hath no fury like a woman scorned" raced through his mind. He'd best be on full alert; no telling what a scorned and angry woman would do.

Chapter 25

"Darlings, you'll be the belles of the ball." Mariah watched her sisters curtsy and swirl in front of the mirror in her room at Thornton House.

Kathleen O'Reilly studied her five girls, all resplendent in new silk-and-lace ball gowns. "Isn't this a grand day? I never thought I would live to see my daughters attending a ball on Society Hill." She dabbed her eyes with a linen handkerchief embroidered with her initials.

"Except as maids," Mariah jested.

"It's thanks to Rosie, and, of course Mrs. Thornton." Annie checked the back of her purple gown.

Mariah jumped when Maggie jabbed her head with a hairpin. The weeks had passed in a whirl of dressmakers and seamstresses. To make things easier, Mariah and the children had moved into her parents' home. Mariah was grateful not to have to face Gabriel and Suzanna every day. She'd only returned in time to prepare for the ball.

Her mother had balked at the outrageously expensive gowns Mariah insisted each girl have. She had the money, and she wanted to make her family happy. The men all had expensive new suits, and even the twins wore new outfits—though they weren't allowed in the ballroom. Mariah had invited them to eat with Juan and Running Deer, and watch the festivities from the stairs.

Now the O'Reilly girls, daughters of Irish immigrants, were awaiting their grand entrance into the ballroom.

Maggie patted Mariah's last errant curl in place. "You look like a princess, Rosie."

She surveyed her four sisters and mother. Annie had chosen purple satin, trimmed with rows of ecru lace at the neckline. Jenny's emerald silk exactly matched her eyes, and Maggie wore a gown of white lace over pale blue. At twelve, Maureen would be allowed to stay at the ball until midnight, then she and the twins were to return home. The young girl surely would grow to be the most beautiful of all. Her rose-pink dress was adorned with silk flowers and ribbons.

Mariah stood and stroked her hands down her skirt. She'd fallen in love with the turquoise fabric from the instant the dressmaker had pulled out the sample. The color made her eyes sparkle and her hair gleam with brilliant highlights. More important, it exactly matched the stones in her bracelet. She'd chosen a simple style, with no lace, flowers, or ruffles, all of which were the latest style. Instead, the off-shoulder neckline trimmed with silver beads and tiny pearls scooped low on her bosom. Her only jewelry was the wide cuff bracelet Thorne had given her. Thorne, not Michael, was the man she'd fallen in love with. She missed the gruff mountain man and she didn't know Michael at all.

She tucked her arm in her mother's. It took much persuasion, but they had convinced Kathleen to order the burgundy faille. She'd insisted on a more modest neckline than her daughters. "I hope Papa has his pistol," Mariah said. "He'll need it to protect his beautiful wife." Kathleen giggled like a schoolgirl and led her family to the doorway.

The music drifted up the stairs into the hall. Guests had been arriving for the past half hour. Mrs. Thornton had invited

Philadelphia's elite, including the mayor, two senators, and a variety of political bigwigs. Mariah willed the butterflies in her stomach to settle down to a gentle flutter.

As gracefully as swans gliding on the calm lake, they descended the stairs. Sean, his sons, Annie's husband, and Danny Malloy were waiting in the foyer. Mariah looked over their heads for Michael. She'd seen little of him since she'd moved back to her parents' home. Her days had been occupied with preparations for the ball, working at the agency, and teaching the children to read and write. His time was spent at the shipyard and avoiding his brother. He'd given the agency a lucrative contract to provide security for the shipyard.

She held back, allowing her mother to take her father's arm and the others to pair off. With just her and Jenny waiting for escorts, she stretched out her gloved hand to Danny. The officer offered an arm to each woman, his smile brighter than the hundred candle chandelier hanging from the ceiling.

"You look exceptionally lovely tonight, Irish." Michael stepped from behind a marble pillar and tucked her hand in his arm. "The O'Reilly women will outshine the stars tonight."

"That they will, my friend," Danny said. He gripped Jenny's arm. "Do I get the first dance?" he asked.

Jenny smiled and winked over her shoulder at Mariah.

For her part, Mariah wasn't at all pleased that Michael had surprised her with his presence. "You have the worst habit of sneaking up on me." In spite of her annoyance, she couldn't help but be secretly thrilled that he'd waited for her—that he'd sought her out. In black evening attire, a white shirt, and silk tie, Michael was devastatingly handsome, the epitome of the elegant aristocrat.

"Since we're both the guests of honor, it's only appropriate that we enter together."

"I suppose that was your grandmother's idea."

He covered her hand with his. She wished they weren't each wearing the kidskin gloves. Mariah longed to touch his warm skin, to feel his flesh against hers. "Actually, it was mine."

His words warmed her heart. He'd never been ashamed of her—as a friend. Too bad he didn't want her as a wife. As they neared the archway that led into the large ballroom, he halted for a second.

"Well, Irish, this is what you wanted. Let's show these stuffed shirts what a beautiful Irish woman looks like. After tonight you'll have all of Philadelphia's society at your beck and call."

Her gaze drifted over the glittering ballroom, the men in their evening attire, the ladies in their jewels and silks. Hundreds of candles reflected off the crystal prisms of the chandeliers. Green palms added color to the corners of the room. On a low platform a piano, violin, and viola played softly. Is this really what she wanted? Truth be told, she wished she was back in New Mexico with the mountain man. None of Philadelphia's elite, not even the one on her arm, could compare to Thorne.

"As an independently wealthy woman, I'll have my choice of suitors. Or maybe I'll just reject all of them and remain a spinster."

He chuckled. "You sound like one of those suffragettes who've been stirring up trouble."

"And you sound like my father. He accused me of the same."

Michael pulled her closer to his side than propriety dictated. His arm muscles were solid as stone. "A wise man, Sean O'Reilly."

Far wiser than the one at her side, she thought. She took a deep breath to quell her ravaged nerves, which she suspected were caused more by Michael's warm body than by the strangers in the room. Mrs. Thornton spotted them and rushed toward the entranceway. At her signal, the music stopped.

"Mariah, Michael, what a handsome couple you make!" She clasped Michael's free hand and tugged him into the room. "This must be the happiest evening of my life, except, of course, the day Michael returned to me. Come, I must introduce you to everybody."

For the next half hour, Mrs. Thornton dragged both Mariah

and Michael around the ballroom. She met so many people that by the time the orchestra began to again play, she was dizzy. Politicians, dignitaries, the elite of society—Mrs. Thornton knew them all. Mariah hadn't deluded herself that they would ever be her friends. They might bow and take her hand in the presence of Mrs. Thornton and Michael, but on any given day, she was no more than a common Irish woman to the lot of them.

"Enough introductions, Grandmother," Michael said. "I would like to dance with Mariah." Not waiting for a response, he caught Mariah's hand and whirled her into the middle of the polished wood floor. His fingers rested lightly at her waist, and his hand clasped hers as delicately as holding a fragile teacup. "I've had all I could take of that."

"Thank you. I don't think I could remember another name." She relaxed and allowed herself to be mesmerized by the music and the man.

His fingers slid further along her back, until they rested at her spine. The hand holding hers tugged gently, until her body pressed into his chest much closer than she considered proper. She breathed in the scent of man—of spicy soap and shaving lather. Both were more intoxicating than wine.

From the corner of her eye, she glimpsed her sisters—Annie with her husband, and Jenny and Maggie with young men she didn't recognize. On the sidelines, her father was keeping a watchful eye on his girls. Danny was dancing with a lovely young woman, who was looking at the handsome policeman with adoring eyes.

"It appears your family has captivated all of Philadelphia society," Michael whispered, his breath tickling her ear.

"It seems that way. My sisters are very beautiful."

He twirled, and Mariah felt as if she were flying. "All of Sean's daughters are beautiful, and his wife loveliest of all."

She smiled and her heart took another tumble. "You couldn't have said anything nicer if you'd thought all day."

The music stopped, and he pressed his lips to her ear. "You look exactly like your mother."

Tingles raced over her. There they were, pressed close together, with all of society witnessing. Mariah didn't give a hoot about society. If he'd so much as hinted he wanted to kiss her, she would have caught those full, firm lips with hers, and showed them what-for.

A buzz from the couples remaining on the dance floor jerked her back to reality. Michael stiffened, and pulled away from her. His face turned to stone, his eyes chilled like ice. In the doorway stood Gabriel and Suzanna. They'd paused, allowing the assembly to notice them, like royalty greeting their subjects.

And indeed, no prince or princess ever looked more regal as they swept into the ballroom. From their clothes, to their bearing, to the diamonds and pearls that entwined Suzanna's neck, never had there been a more elegant couple. Yet, Mariah was sadly aware that good looks and fancy clothes did not conceal a black heart.

Michael released Mariah's hand. "Excuse me, Irish. I need a drink." He stalked away and snatched a glass of champagne from a waiter. For a man who seldom drank, he downed two glasses in quick succession.

On the dance floor, Mariah felt alone and adrift—abandoned by the man she loved. A man who didn't give a fig for her feelings.

"Miss O'Reilly?" George Willingspoon bowed and reached out a hand. "May I have this dance?"

Too shaken to respond, she nodded. The gaunt young man danced awkwardly, and it took all her concentration to keep him from stamping on her toes. When the music stopped, another man took his place. His superior dancing skills allowed her to look over his shoulder. Michael was nowhere in sight. Her gaze followed Suzanna's progress around the room. She greeted one dignitary after another, smiling and fluttering her fan. Occasionally she threw her head back and laughed at something said. Her long, slender neck was adorned with so many jewels, it was surprising she didn't tumble over. And her gown. Mariah had never seen so many flounces, tucks, silk roses, and ribbons on one gown in all her life. The fabric was threaded with silver, and the neck was cut so low, she was afraid that at any moment Suzanna's bosom would pop right out of the confines. She smiled at the thought of the woman's total embarrassment.

Her dance partner said something she didn't quite hear, and he smiled down at her. At that moment, she made a conscious decision to ignore the arrogant couple. After all, this was the first ball given in her honor and she'd be darned if she'd let them ruin her special evening.

Mariah danced, she drank champagne, she snacked on cakes and tiny bits of food she couldn't identify, and she laughed at stories that weren't the least bit funny. More than a few men tried to get her to walk out into the garden with them. One glance at her father discouraged any unwanted advances. Her sisters rarely sat down, and she'd never seen them happier. From time to time she'd glimpsed Michael on the dance floor with one beautiful woman after another. Yet, he never approached her again.

At midnight she bid goodnight to her parents, the twins, and Maureen. Francis and Kevin would escort Jenny and Maggie home later. By then her face ached from smiling, and her toes were crimped from the new shoes. Needing a break from the festivities, she decided to take a few minutes to check on the children. She'd seen them earlier safely ensconced on the stairs where they could watch and not be seen.

She sneaked up the back stairs to the second floor. Since she'd arrived at the mansion, Juan and Running Deer had left Michael's room, but they were still too frightened to sleep alone. The pair shared a room, each having a small bed of their own. She found them in their room with Sung Lo in the rocking chair.

"They not sleep until Sissy and Thorne come," the old man said.

''He's busy with his guests. I'll tuck the children into their beds.''

The Chinese studied her with eyes full of knowledge and understanding. ''Sissy love Thorne.''

Sitting on the edge of Running Deer's narrow bed, she fingered the bracelet on her wrist. ''Yes. But he doesn't love me. We're from different worlds.''

''World the same when you love. If you want Thorne to love you, tell him, let him know. He need Sissy. He need love.'' With his words ringing in her ears, he bowed and retreated to his own chamber.

The children clung to her for a long moment. She sang their favorite Irish ditty, and waited until their eyes closed in sleep. For a long moment, she stared at the slumbering children. They needed love as much as she. At that moment she came to a decision, one that would affect all their lives.

Michael watched the O'Reilly clan leave. Mariah and her sisters were in so much demand, that he hadn't tried to get near Mariah after the first dance. He'd avoided her for one reason only. Holding her reminded him of how much he'd missed being with her and making love to her. He ached every time she came near. It had taken all his willpower not to sweep her up in his arms and carry her off to his room. It wouldn't bother him a bit to have the guests enjoying the ball downstairs while he took pleasure in his wife upstairs. When he searched her out, Murphy reported that he'd seen her going up the rear stairs. As he started to follow, Gabriel slipped out of the shadows and ascended the same staircase.

Mariah and his brother? To be betrayed once was a shame, to let it happen twice was a tragedy. His temper flared like wildfire out of control. The woman was still his wife, and, by damn, it was time she acted the part.

Taking the stairs two at a time, he raced into the long hallway. He started for her room, when he heard her voice, soft and seductive. Fury threatened to choke him. It was the same throaty tone as when they'd made love in the canyon, and on his mountain. The sound came from a door opened a crack. Unable to control his temper, he kicked the door open. It banged against the wall. Only when a small squeal shot through his dazed brain did he realize it was the children's room, and Mariah was holding Running Deer to her chest.

She jerked her gaze to him. "Michael, what's wrong?"

His breath coming in short gasps, he felt like a balloon popped with a pin. He shook his head to clear away the fog from too much champagne and anger. "Nothing. I thought I heard a noise in here." Struggling to turn his frown into a smile, he moved toward the children. At the narrow bed he bent over and tucked a blanket around the little girl. Then he turned and did the same for Juan.

Mariah trimmed the lamp and waited for him in the hallway. He felt like an utter fool. When he'd thought her betraying him with his brother, she was tending the children who were his responsibility. Knowing she disliked his brother and sister-in-law nearly as much as he, he should be ashamed of his lack of trust.

Before he had a chance to explain or apologize, she folded her arms across her chest. The movement did little to extinguish the fire burning in his blood. Her breasts thrust in alabaster mounds above the too-low neckline of the blue dress. How Sean ever let her out of her room like that was beyond him.

"Michael, I want to talk to you."

He lifted his gaze from the temptation of her body and met her eyes. In the dim hallway, her eyes were dark and mysterious. Her mouth was pulled in a straight line. "I'm listening."

"I came to a decision tonight."

She paused, and he wondered if he wanted to hear her declaration. Had she decided to marry one of the dandies who'd monopolized her time?

"I want to adopt the children. They need a mother, stability in their lives. I can give it to them. My parents and siblings love them, and they can be part of our family.''

His heart plunged to his feet. Not only was she throwing him over, she wanted to take the children he loved away from him. ''They need a father, too.''

''I'll marry if necessary. I hope you'll agree. As far as I know, you have no legal authority over them.''

''Legal authority?'' Her words torched his temper like a match to kindling. ''I found them half dead, and raised them as my own. I'll never give them up. You can just marry a rich man and have your own.''

''Michael, you're being unreasonable. Think about the children.''

He stalked away before he did something rash. He was torn between hauling her off to his room and loving her, or shaking some sense into her pretty head. ''Never. I'll never give them up.''

Leaving her staring after him, he stalked down the front stairway and went into the library. He needed a drink, and he needed it now. What hurt was that she was right. The youngsters needed a home, with two loving parents. He'd hoped to learn of her feelings for him, then they could make plans to adopt the children—together. Only she wanted to leave him out of her plans, and out of her life. That would never do.

Mariah had no idea why Michael so objected to her offer. True, he loved the children, but so did she. If he'd only have reasoned out the situation, he would understand it was best for them.

If he really wanted the children, why couldn't he want her also? All she wanted was one word, one hint that he cared for her, and she would forget about the annulment and join him in his bed forever. Her heart breaking, she realized she'd outstayed her welcome. It was time for Cinderella to return to her own world before it was too late. The prince didn't want her, and it was well past midnight.

On leaden feet, she headed down the rear stairs into the kitchen. Once there, she could ask Murphy to locate her brother, or Danny, and they would escort her home. The two maids in the kitchen glanced at Mariah and continued with their chores. When a waiter entered with an empty tray, she asked him to fetch Murphy. The kitchen was stifling, and Mariah stepped outdoors to wait. The service entrance was a few feet from the rear door, and a small herb garden grew along the path. She pressed her back against the stone wall of the house and tried to sort out her disturbing thoughts.

Around the corner of the house, gas lamps and candles lit the gardens, but this part of the yard was dark and rather foreboding. The iron gate creaked, and footsteps thudded on the brick walkway. In the shelter of the doorway, she watched the silhouettes of two men hesitate near a large oak.

"I don't like this a bit," one of the pair whispered in a harsh voice.

"We're getting paid cash money to get him. All we have to do is wait for the signal," the taller of the two answered.

Mariah's breath caught. The man pulled out a large pistol, and checked the chamber. "What if we miss? There's coppers here, you know."

"We'll be gone right back through that gate before any of them gets near us. We're to wait over here, until the right time. Come on." They shifted positions and moved toward the garden.

She bit her lip to keep from crying out. *Get somebody— wait for the signal—a gun?* Could the strangers be hired assassins after one of the guests? Mrs. Thornton had invited any number of distinguished persons, politicians, wealthy men and women. Or were they thieves, willing to kill for the jewels dripping like water from the guests?

Mariah realized she couldn't stop these men alone. She needed to find Michael and let him handle the situation. He would know what to do without alarming the guests. He could enlist Danny and Francis to help.

With no sound at all, she slid back into the kitchen. Murphy was waiting for her at the long work table. "Miss O'Reilly, you wish to see me?" he asked.

Chilled to the bone by what she'd heard, she raced to the man. "Where's Michael. I need to see him immediately."

"Mr. Michael?" He thought for a minute. "The last time I saw of him, he was on the terrace with Mrs. Harrison—Mrs. Suzanna Harrison."

Suzanna? Why would he go into the terrace with his brother's wife—the woman he claimed to dislike so intensely? Unless it was only a ruse, claiming to hate her when he still loved her. Mariah shook off the disparaging thoughts and hurried to the door. No matter how jealous she might be, or how angry she felt at being duped, she had to tell Michael about what she'd overheard.

She entered the ballroom, and slipped behind a wall of potted palms. On the way she saw neither of her brothers, and Danny was nowhere to be found. She had to locate Michael. She reached the wide doors that led to the terrace and the gardens beyond. The orchestra was still playing, and the floor was still crowded with dancers.

He's out here, she thought. Past the fountain, two figures slipped into the hedges. There was no mistaking Michael's tall, broad-shouldered silhouette, or Suzanna's throaty laughter.

Mariah snagged her silk gown on a rosebush and heard the fabric rip. None of that mattered when a life hung in the balance. She turned away from the main path and took the diagonal walk that intercepted with the one on which Michael had disappeared.

Her dancing pumps slipped on the damp, mossy bricks, slowing her progress. As she rounded a corner, she skid to a stop.

Michael was kissing Suzanna.

She stuck her fist into her mouth to keep from crying out. The kiss ended abruptly, and Michael shoved the woman away from him. "You owe me!" Suzanna cried. "You won't get away this time." She raised a hand and shouted, "Now!"

From the corner of her eye, Mariah caught the glint of light flashing off metal. Two shadows rose from behind a low hedge. In a split second, she realized that Michael was the intended target for the assassins.

"Michael!" she screamed, racing toward him. She threw her body against his. The instant she touched his chest, gunfire erupted around them.

One, two, three loud explosions.

Pain knifed through her arm.

A woman screamed. "Kill them, you bastards! Don't let them get away!"

Chapter 26

He heard Mariah's voice the instant before she tackled him to the ground and the gunfire blasted over his head. He rolled her over on the grass and dragged her behind a stone bench. Somebody was trying to kill them. Who and why he didn't know. All he knew was that he had to protect her at any cost.

Several more shots, and Suzanna's shrill voice. "You fools, you missed!"

A man yelled, "Let's get out before the coppers come."

"Don't go until you finish the job," the woman shouted.

"Hell, we ain't got paid enough to get hung for murder."

"Michael," Mariah whispered. "Are you hurt?"

He covered her lips with his, both to silence her and because he couldn't help himself. "Hush. I think they're gone, but I don't want to take any chances."

Footsteps rang on the brick path. Another voice, one that sounded much like his brother's. "Did they get him?"

"I don't know."

More footsteps, and shouts. "What happened? We heard gunshots." Mariah's brother. And Officer Malloy.

"It was awful," Suzanna cried. "Somebody tried to shoot Michael."

"Over here!" he called out. "Catch them before they get away."

Malloy raced toward the service gate near the kitchen, while Francis hurried to Michael, still on the ground beside Mariah.

She'd saved his life. Somehow she was there when he needed her, and she'd shoved him out of the path of a bullet. "Irish." He kissed her eyes, her cheeks, damp with salty tears, and her mouth. "Are you all right? Did you get hurt in the fall?"

She groaned. "My arm. I think I hurt it."

Carefully, he scooped her up and set her on the bench that had protected them both. Blood dripped down her arm. Fury exploded in him with the violence of a tornado. The woman he loved had taken the bullet meant for him. And he did love Mariah. Totally and unconditionally. She was his wife and he intended to keep her forever.

"Rosie," her brother said. "You're hurt."

"I'll be okay." She flinched when Michael brushed a gentle finger along the wound.

The bullet grazed her upper arm, leaving an ugly tear in her perfect flesh. Michael had never been angrier or felt more helpless. He should be out searching for the men who'd done this. He glanced around. A crowd had begun to gather. Mariah groaned in pain. His place was at her side, easing her pain, and tending the injury.

"Is Dr. Stephens still here?" He scooped Mariah up in his arms. "Tell him to meet us in the library."

"Michael, put me down. It's my arm, not my legs."

"Be quiet, Irish. I'm taking care of you now."

By that time the ballroom had emptied into the garden. Mariah's sisters made a path for him through the sea of guests. His grandmother stopped him at the door.

"Michael, what happened? They said somebody was shot." Her gaze dropped to the woman in his arms. "Oh, Mariah. Who would want to shoot her?"

"I'll explain later. Right now, we've got to dress the wound and stop the bleeding." At the library door, he yelled for the butler. "Murphy, get some boiling water and lots of clean towels. Then go to my room and fetch that box of remedies on the bureau."

Behind his back, he heard his grandmother make his apologies to the guest. "There's been an accident. Thank you for coming, but the party is over."

Mariah's sisters crowded into the room with him. The younger girls were crying, and Annie hovered over them. "Who would want to hurt our Rosie?" they asked.

A rope tightened around Michael's chest. The bullet wasn't meant for Mariah, but for him. He was certain the entire affair was instigated by his brother and sister-in-law. Mariah was pale, and in spite of her bravado, pain glinted in her eyes. If he could get his hands on any of them, he would strangle them with his bare hands.

He laid her gently on a long, leather davenport. "You'll be good as new, Irish," he promised.

"Did they catch them?"

"Malloy and your brothers went after them." Tearing off his bloodstained gloves, he dropped them to the floor. "Bring me scissors," he ordered. Jenny pressed the instrument into his hands.

"What are you doing?" Mariah tried to sit up. He pushed her gently to her back.

"I've got to cut away the sleeve and gloves."

She slapped his fingers away with her good hand. "Oh, no you won't. This dress cost too much to let you destroy it." She groaned, and fell back against the pillows.

"I'll buy you a dozen like it. Just lie still so we can stop the bleeding."

Dr. Stephens, who'd been his grandmother's physician for years, appeared at his side. The gentleman looked at Mariah for a moment, then opened his black case. He'd treated soldiers during the war, and, even now, gunshot wounds weren't unusual in his practice.

He dabbed the wound with clean gauze, and Mariah grunted in pain. "Clear everybody out of the room," he ordered. "I can't work with an audience."

"She's our sister, we want to stay," one of the girls declared.

His grandmother caught their arms and ushered them into the hallway. "Let Michael and the doctor tend to your sister. She couldn't be in better hands."

Murphy appeared with the water and towels, then he rushed off again. Michael washed his hands, and assisted the physician in cleaning the injury. *It was his fault.* The words echoed in his heart. His fault she'd been hurt while saving his life. "I'll have to stitch it," the doctor said. "It's going to hurt, miss. Do you want some anesthetic?"

She shook her head; her hair tumbled from its elaborate coiffure. "Hold my hand, Mountain Man."

He entwined her fingers in his with a silent promise to never let her go. Annulment or not, he intended to remain married to this woman if he had to cart her off over his shoulder. He kissed her forehead. "I'll be here for you, my Mariah."

Tears poured from her eyes as the doctor worked. She let out small cries of pain, each a knife to his heart. Michael had tended the wounded during the war, but this was the first time he'd had to sit by and watch someone he loved suffer.

As he stared into her tear-reddened eyes, he would have gladly given his life for hers. He loved her—this brave Irish rose who'd given him back his soul. And had stolen his heart.

As the doctor worked, Michael spoke gently in an effort to take her mind off her pain. "Thank you, sweetheart. You saved my life."

A hint of a smile was cut off by a grimace of pain. "Are you worth saving?"

"I'm not so sure I am. What were you doing there in the garden?" Curiosity was eating away at him. How had she arrived at the exact moment to save his life?

"I overheard some men talking, saying they were going to shoot somebody. I went looking for you." She groaned aloud, and his heart shattered. "You were kissing her."

"She was kissing me. I didn't want any part of her."

"What did she mean you owed her something? Do you still love her?" She squeezed her eyes shut against the pain.

He tightened his grip on her fingers. "I don't love her. I'll explain everything when you're feeling better."

"They wanted to kill you."

"They would have succeeded if you hadn't been so foolhardy and brave." Again he kissed her forehead, now damp with perspiration. "Hush, love, let the doctor finish."

Michael insisted the doctor use his special ointment on the injury. Mariah groaned. "Not that awful smelly stuff again."

He ignored her protests, and although the doctor looked skeptical, he dabbed the salve on the wound. When the injury was bandaged, the doctor poured a bit of laudanum into a glass. "This will help her sleep. She'll feel much better in the morning."

But would he? Michael wondered. "I'll take her upstairs." Holding her close to his chest, he carried her from the room. Her family swarmed around him like ants to a grain of sugar. "How is she? Will she live? Should we fetch Mama?"

"She'll be fine," Dr. Stephens said over his shoulder. "Let her get some rest."

The entire entourage followed up the curved staircase and into his bedroom. He laid her gently on his huge bed—the one they would share for the rest of their lives. By then, the drug was taking effect, and her eyes had slipped closed.

Her sisters darted to her side. "I'll fetch a nightdress," one girl said.

Annie shot him an embarrassed glance. "Mr. Harrison, would you mind leaving while we change Rosie's gown?"

His protest at leaving was cut off by his grandmother. "Leave them tend their sister," she said, her tone stern. In the dim light, he noted the lines around her eyes. The night she'd planned as a celebration had turned to tragedy.

He nodded and slipped from the room. Francis was waiting in the hallway. "Did you find them?" he asked.

The other man shook his head. "Danny and Kevin searched the grounds, the carriage house, and the stables. The service gate was open, and we suppose they got away through there." He shook his head and scuffed his feet like a schoolboy who'd failed his assignment. "Sorry. Do you have any idea why they were aiming at you or Mrs. Harrison? Who hired them?"

"No," he lied. Michael was certain Gabriel and Suzanna were behind this. From their few fragmented words in the garden, it was clear they wanted rid of him. With Michael out of the way, they stood to inherit a fortune from his grandmother. This wasn't Francis's concern. Michael would handle them himself—as soon as he was sure Mariah was all right.

"Mrs. Suzanna Harrison was with you when the incident occurred, wasn't she?" he asked.

"Yes. We were in the garden." It all came together in his mind. Suzanna had begged him to go into the garden. She'd worked on his guilt at her losing their child. When he'd protested, she'd kissed him. A Judas kiss, to point him out to the killers. Disgust twisted like a worm in his stomach.

"I tried to interview her, but her husband said she was too upset to talk. They're locked in their rooms."

"I'll speak to them in the morning. Tonight, I want to make sure Mariah is all right." He glared at the closed door behind him. "Set some men at the front and back entrances. Make sure nobody gets in or out."

"Danny and Kevin are taking care of that. I'll get more men if we need them."

He clasped the younger man on the shoulder. "You're a good man, Francis. And a damned fine detective."

"Not half as good as Rosie. Did she tell you what happened?"

Michael related the story Mariah had told him. The younger

man swore under his breath at his sister's impulsive behavior. "She should have found me."

"You know your sister. She'd have captured Jesse James single-handedly if I hadn't stopped her."

He grinned slightly. "That's our Rosie."

"I'm going to spend the night with her. See that your sisters get some rest."

His grandmother touched his arm. "They can stay in Mariah's room. I'll send a maid to help them."

On a long sigh, Michael returned to his chamber. It took a bit of persuasion to convince her sisters to leave, but once they were assured she would rest better alone, they left.

He trimmed the lamp and stared down at her lovely face, peaceful in slumber. Her arm lay under her breasts, the sleeve of the nightdress cut away at the shoulder. Black hair spread across the pillow like the midnight sky. How had he ever been so stupid as to demand an annulment when she'd long ago captured his heart? Only he had been too stubborn to admit that he needed her in his life.

Sitting on the edge of the bed, he tugged off his shoes. His coat, waistcoat, and tie had long ago been discarded. Her ball gown draped over a chair, and her ruined gloves stretched across the bureau.

Her eyes fluttered open. "Mountain Man," she whispered. "Lie down with me."

Pain lurched through his chest. He wanted nothing more than to hold her for the rest of their lives. "I'll be here, Irish. I'll never leave you." Stretching out beside her on top of the covers, he clasped her fingers. His bracelet was still on her wrist, as it had remained since he'd given it to her that day on the mountain. It he had half the sense God gave a donkey, he'd have added a proper wedding ring to her finger.

The sounds in the house diminished. Voices faded, and the household settled down after a night few would forget. At about dawn, he thought he heard the clopping of hooves on

the driveway. Probably the arrival of more of Francis's operatives, he thought.

A light knock sounded on the door, and impatient footsteps
thudded in the hallway. By the gruff voice, he knew Mr. O'Reilly had arrived. Without giving him the opportunity to rise,
the door burst open, and still more O'Reillys gathered around
his bed. He sat up and faced a very irate Irish police officer.

"Harrison, what's the meaning of this? Francis tells us our
Rosie was shot trying to protect you."

Kathleen glared at her husband. "Hold your voice down,
Sean. Rosie is still sleeping."

"How can anybody sleep with Da around? I swear you would
wake the dead." Mariah struggled to a sitting position, blinking
the sleep from her eyes. She'd thought she'd only dreamed of
Michael at her side, holding her hand during the night, kissing
her gently on the forehead. Confessing his love, asking for a
real marriage, wanting to make love with her. But it was only
her heart dreaming. Michael didn't want her that way.

"Rosie," her mother said. "How do you feel? Is it very
bad?"

"No, Mama. It's much better. I'll be good as new before
you can say another rosary."

Michael slid from the bed and pulled her father to the other
side of the room. The men seemed to be deeply involved in a
conversation. From time to time, her father uttered an oath.

Tears rolled from Kathleen's eyes. "Here and I thought New
Mexico was dangerous. But you came back just fine, and you
get shot right here in Philadelphia."

Mariah caught Michael's gaze. She hadn't returned just fine.
Only half her heart had come home. The other half had been
broken by a surly mountain man who'd demanded an end to
their marriage.

Within minutes, the room was crowded with well-wishers.
She overheard bits and pieces of the conversation between
Michael and Francis. It seemed that Gabriel and Suzanna had
disappeared some time during the night, most likely returning

to Virginia. Danny had refused to leave, and he, too, slipped into the room. Only his attention was more on Jenny than Mariah. Her sisters had changed from their ball gowns to the frocks they'd arrived in the day before. Mrs. Thornton hovered over her, and the maids set trays of breakfast on a table.

Running Deer and Juan raced into the room in their night-shirts. They threw themselves on the bed and wrapped their arms around Mariah. Michael tried to discourage them, but she shooed him away. This was where she belonged, with her husband and their foster children. If only he loved her as she loved him, they could be a real family like the boisterous O'Reilly clan. Even Sung Lo stood guard over her, his hand on the knife at his waist.

At her side, Michael spoke to his grandmother. "Grand-mother, I've an announcement to make. I've decided to return to New Mexico. I hope you'll understand," he said, taking the older woman's hand. "I miss my mountain, and the work I was doing with the herbal remedies and medicines." He locked gazes with Mariah. She choked back tears. "I'll adopt Running Deer and Juan, and Sung Lo, if he'll agree."

Mariah was surprised nobody heard the shattering of her heart. The pain brought tears to her eyes. The injury to her arm was nothing compared to the agony in her spirit. His plans made perfect sense, except they didn't include her. The man she loved, and the children she held dear would be lost to her forever.

"Good luck, I'm sure you'll all be much happier than in 'Delphia." Her voice was tinny in her ears.

He settled on the edge of the bed at her side and twined his fingers in hers. Lifting their hands, he planted a kiss on her knuckles. "I'm going to need help. Never know when I'll need somebody to push me out of the way of a bullet."

"Michael, what are you saying?" She held her breath, afraid to wish.

"Can I convince you to leave your civilized Philadelphia

and return to the Wild West? I'll build you a house even grander than Maxwell's.''

"Now just a minute, young man. You can't just take my Rosie away like that,'' her father said. Sean sidled up to Michael ready to do battle.

"It's all right, Sean. Mariah and I are married. We were married in New Mexico. Unless she's gotten an annulment, we're very well married.''

Shocked at the turn of events, Mariah had trouble understanding his meaning. "Do you want to take me with you? You don't want the annulment?''

He pressed his lips to her palm. Tingles raced up her arm and settled in the center of her chest. "I never wanted to end our marriage, I only offered the annulment because I thought it was what you wanted.''

Tears flooded her cheeks. "I never wanted it, either. I kept putting off going to the priest.''

"I love you, Irish. I fell in love with you that day you tumbled down that hillside and into my life. Will you have me as your husband, for, say, the next fifty or so years?''

Words lodged in her throat. Michael loved her, he wanted her, and she was too shaken to even speak. The children jumped on the mattress. Running Deer hugged her neck. "We love you, Sissy.''

Juan offered a smile brighter than the sun. "I love you, Sissy,'' he said in a small, weak voice. She had to strain to hear, but he'd spoken for the first time.

The room went silent, all eyes on the child whose voice they never heard. Whatever had stopped his voice had been released by love. "I love you, too, darlings,'' she said, hugging both youngsters to her chest. Juan began to sing, as if the dam that had blocked his voice had burst and he couldn't stop. Her heart overflowed with joy.

"Well, Rosie,'' Jenny asked. "What do you say?''

She tossed a pillow at her sister. "I say you all leave so I can tell my husband how much I love him, and that I want to announce to the whole world that I'm his wife—in every sense of the word.''

Cheers rang in the room. Mrs. Thornton hugged Kathleen, and Sean slapped Michael on the back. "Let's get out and leave them alone," Sean ordered. "But mind you, young man, we'll be right outside listening." The brawny Irishman picked up a child in each arm. "Come with Grandpa." They smiled and kissed his cheek.

Mrs. Thornton hugged Mariah. "I've been praying that Michael would finally realize you're the exact match for him. I couldn't be happier." She shook her finger at her grandson. "Don't forget to write, and invite your old grandmother to that grand house you're going to build."

Michael laughed, a sound that thrilled and delighted Mariah. Within seconds, they were alone.

He settled on the bed at her side. "You love me, Irish? You don't mind returning to the wilds of the West?" He cupped her face with his hands.

She captured his wrists. "After yesterday, I think the West is not nearly as dangerous as Philadelphia."

"With the modern train service, you'll be able to visit your family whenever you please."

Their lips met in a kiss that was gentle and warm, a prelude to a lifetime of happiness. "You just remember, Mountain Man, I only want one child."

He laughed. "Of course, my Mariah, one at a time."

This time his kiss was hard and demanding, drawing from her all the love and desire hidden in her heart. She'd searched for treasure, looked for gold, but she'd found the greatest treasure in Michael's love.

BOOK YOUR PLACE ON OUR WEBSITE AND MAKE THE READING CONNECTION!

We've created a customized website just for our very special readers, where you can get the inside scoop on everything that's going on with Zebra, Pinnacle and Kensington books.

When you come online, you'll have the exciting opportunity to:

- View covers of upcoming books
- Read sample chapters
- Learn about our future publishing schedule (listed by publication month *and author*)
- Find out when your favorite authors will be visiting a city near you
- Search for and order backlist books from our online catalog
- Check out author bios and background information
- Send e-mail to your favorite authors
- Meet the Kensington staff online
- Join us in weekly chats with authors, readers and other guests
- Get writing guidelines
- AND MUCH MORE!

Visit our website at
http://www.zebrabooks.com